Emily Forbes is an award[...] Medical Romance for Mil[...] over twenty-five books an[...] in the Australian Romantic[...] which she won in 2013 for her novel *Sydney Harbour Hospital: Bella's Wishlist*. You can get in touch with Emily at emilyforbes@internode.on.net, or visit her website at emily-forbesauthor.com.

Lifelong romance addict **JC Harroway** took a break from her career as a junior doctor to raise a family and found her calling as a Mills & Boon author instead. She now lives in New Zealand and finds that writing feeds her very real obsession with happy endings and the endorphin rush they create. You can follow her at jcharroway.com, and on Facebook, Twitter and Instagram.

ALI AND THE REBEL DOC

EMILY FORBES

PHOEBE'S BABY BOMBSHELL

JC HARROWAY

MILLS & BOON

First published in Great Britain 2023
by Mills & Boon, an imprint of HarperCollins*Publishers* Ltd,
1 London Bridge Street, London, SE1 9GF

www.harpercollins.co.uk

HarperCollins*Publishers* Macken House, 39/40 Mayor Street Upper, Dublin 1, D01 C9W8, Ireland

Ali and the Rebel Doc © 2023 Harlequin Enterprises ULC

Special thanks and acknowledgement are given to Emily Forbes for her contribution to the A Sydney Central Reunion miniseries.

Phoebe's Baby Bombshell © 2023 Harlequin Enterprises ULC

Special thanks and acknowledgement are given to JC Harroway for her contribution to the A Sydney Central Reunion miniseries.

ISBN: 978-0-263-30611-8

07/23

MIX
Paper | Supporting
responsible forestry
FSC™ C007454

ALI AND THE REBEL DOC

EMILY FORBES

MILLS & BOON

CHAPTER ONE

'IF ONE MORE auntie asks me when I'm going to settle down, I'm going to scream,' Ali said as she walked into her sister-in-law's kitchen. Dee was bent over a kitchen drawer, her back to Ali as she rummaged through the contents, but Ali kept talking. 'You'd think they'd have given up by now. How many different ways can I say I don't want kids?'

Dee straightened up, a triumphant look on her face as she grasped two candles, both shaped as the number one, in her hand. 'But you're so good with them,' she replied with a grin as she pressed the candles into the centres of two separate cakes.

'Because I can hand them back.' Honestly, Ali couldn't imagine anything worse than having to deal with children twenty-four-seven. That was not her idea of fun. She loved her family, which was fortunate because with four siblings, parents, grandmothers and aunts, uncles and cousins, plus nieces and nephews, there was literally no way of escaping them. Life was a constant stream of family gatherings. Which was why she was amazed that the message hadn't got through. She didn't want to have kids. She didn't plan on having kids.

She loved her nieces and nephews, all ten of them—

soon to be eleven—and she loved being Awesome Auntie Li-Li but she didn't want her own children. She never had and she wasn't about to change her mind at this point in her life. When she and Adam had got married, she knew people thought she'd change her tune but that hadn't happened. She also knew people found it hard to reconcile her position with her career as an obstetrician, but she was weary of having to constantly explain her decision. After all, it was her body, her life and her prerogative.

'I hear you,' Dee said with a laugh, 'but I'm not letting you hide in here. Go outside and mingle with my friends.'

'I've delivered most of their babies—I know far more about them than I want to,' Ali said, only half joking. 'I don't need to mingle.'

'Well, in that case, you might as well make yourself useful. Can you take some more plates and forks outside?' Dee passed Ali a stack of bamboo plates. 'I'll bring the cakes out when I find the matches. The sooner we sing "Happy Birthday" the sooner everyone will go home.'

'I thought you liked hosting parties.'

'I do,' Dee said as she let out a big sigh, 'but I'd forgotten that first birthday parties aren't really for the kids but for the adults. I've been going non-stop for two days getting ready, plus today and tomorrow for what? Kai and Leni aren't going to remember this. Remind me not to do this again for the next one.'

'Next one! Are you pregnant?'

'No, I was speaking hypothetically. Perhaps remind me not to get pregnant again as well. Having three kids under three is exhausting.'

'And people wonder why I don't want my own,' Ali

said as she grabbed a handful of forks and headed into the garden.

To her left she spied her twin brother standing with his arms wrapped around his fiancée, looking determined not to let her go again. They looked happy and she was pleased for him, she knew their road to happiness hadn't been easy. *Life* wasn't easy.

Yarran was a single dad, raising his son, Jarrah, on his own since the death of his first wife, and Ali knew that having him finding happiness again at the age of forty had likely reignited the family's idea that it wasn't too late for her to find someone after her marriage break-up.

But, post-divorce, if anyone had asked her the other big question, 'Do you have a man in your life?', she had responded by saying she didn't want one. That she wasn't ready. Adam, her ex-husband, had done a number on her confidence. She had loved the life they'd built together, only to find out it was all a lie, and their break-up had made her wary of relationships. She'd only recently started to, very tentatively, dip her toe in the dating pool again.

She wasn't lonely—but she didn't want to be alone. There was a difference.

Testing the water had meant putting some parameters in place for dating. He would need to be fit, intelligent and older than her, with adult kids or, better yet, no kids. She didn't want to take on anyone else's children, nor did she want to date someone who might eventually want a family. That wasn't something she could offer. At the age of forty, even if she'd wanted kids, which she didn't, as an obstetrician and gynaecologist she knew her chances of conceiving were greatly diminished.

Maybe there was someone out there for her, but if she did happen to meet someone who would make her consider another relationship, she knew it wouldn't ever lead to motherhood. That was not for her.

So, while she was single, she was trying to focus on the positives in her life. Work was her passion. Her focus. Followed by her family. And her close-knit group of friends. She had her career, her health, her family and friends, her own apartment. She had everything she needed.

Except good sex.

That was one thing she'd had with Adam, until he started cheating on her. Her patients had always told her that it wasn't marriage that took the gloss off sex but having kids. That had been another good reason to remain childless, Ali had thought, except now she had neither— she didn't have kids and she wasn't having sex.

Maybe it was time that she did something about that, she mused as Dee brought out the cakes.

Everyone gathered around the table to sing before the twins tried to blow out their candles, eventually needing help from their older sister.

Ali's phone buzzed in her pocket as she handed plates of chocolate cake around. She pulled it out and saw the hospital's number on the screen. As she swiped to answer she was hoping someone needed her. It would give her an excuse to leave and avoid more questions about her personal life.

'Dr Edwards? This is Sylvia, an RN on the general surgery ward. I'm sorry to interrupt your weekend but there's a note here saying to contact you if there are any medical issues regarding Emma Wilson.'

Honestly, why couldn't people just get to the point?

she thought. As Head of Obstetrics and Gynaecology, Ali wasn't familiar with the nursing staff on General but she curbed her impatience. Having her weekend interrupted was par for the course, she was well used to it by now and Sylvia was only doing her job.

'What's happening?' Ali asked. She wouldn't normally have patients on this ward, but Emma was complicated. She'd initially been admitted with injuries sustained in a fire, but she also happened to be thirty-two weeks pregnant and was, therefore, now under Ali's care too.

'Her blood pressure is very high. It's one-sixty over one hundred and five. I've checked it a couple of times just now and it's not changing. This morning it was one-thirty over ninety. I thought you should know.'

As far as Ali was aware Emma hadn't had hypertension during her pregnancy but she wasn't surprised to hear her blood pressure was elevated. Emma had undergone multiple surgeries since being admitted to Sydney Central several weeks ago—undergoing skin grafts and then an emergency appendectomy—but that reading was dangerously high and Ali was concerned.

Gestational hypertension wasn't uncommon, but Ali knew that prior to her accident Emma hadn't had any of the usual risk factors and that set alarm bells ringing. Hypertension could be perilous, especially in pregnancy as it could develop into pre-eclampsia, which could threaten not only Emma's life but the lives of her unborn twins. Ali needed to get to the bottom of this.

'Does she have any other symptoms? Fever? Oedema? Pain?'

'She's afebrile.' That was good, it reduced the likelihood of an infection. 'But she was asking for pain relief, that's when I checked her blood pressure.'

'Where was her pain? Was it a headache? Abdominal pain?'

'Abdominal.'

'Has one of the doctors on duty seen her?'

'It's the weekend so we've only got a registrar. They asked me to call you but I can call Dr Hurst if you prefer?'

Abdominal pain could be attributed to many things, including Emma's previous injuries and surgeries, but Ali's sixth sense was stirring. On numerous occasions she'd sensed things that she couldn't explain—it was something that seemed to run through the women in her family—and over time Ali had learned to trust her instincts. And her instincts were telling her it was related to Emma's pregnancy.

'I'll come in now,' she said. 'If I need to, I can call Dr Hurst once I've seen Emma.' Ivy Hurst was Head of General Surgery and one of Ali's closest friends, she'd definitely consult her if she needed to, but Ali was now Emma's primary medical expert and she wanted to examine Emma. 'Did Emma mention any nausea or visual disturbances?' she queried.

'She didn't mention anything. Would you like me to check?'

'No, that's okay, I'm on my way. Can you do a urinalysis for protein and a blood test to check liver function? And alert the radiology department; ask them to bring a portable ultrasound down for me and find out who the sonographer on duty is in case I need them.'

Ali needed to be at the hospital. She could wait for the test results to come in, but test results could only tell her so much, and seeing Emma in person would give her information that the numbers couldn't. It also gave her a legitimate excuse to say her goodbyes. She loved her family, but she'd had enough questions for one day.

Ali ran through Emma's history in her head while she drove, knowing she'd familiarise herself with her file when she got to the hospital, but mulling over what she remembered to date.

Emma had been brought to the ED at Sydney Central two months ago. She'd been injured in a house fire, sustaining serious burns to her lower limbs, and Ali's twin, Yarran, had been one of the firefighters who had been involved in her rescue. Emma had undergone skin grafts and then battled infections before also undergoing an emergency appendectomy. To complicate matters further, Emma had been twenty-four weeks pregnant at the time of the accident. To say she'd had a traumatic few weeks was something of an understatement.

Emma had come through the surgeries but remained in hospital waiting for the birth of her babies. She didn't need any further complications. But, luckily Emma was a fighter. Ali just hoped she had some reserves left.

Emma was being managed by a team of specialists that had included Ali from day one because of her pregnancy. As the department head, Ali didn't have a patient caseload as such, but she would give advice or lend her expertise as needed. Emma was a patient who warranted close attention for several reasons, including the fact that she was a high-profile patient as well as high risk.

Emma's husband, Aaron Wilson, was a local celebrity, hosting a top-rated reality television show, and the media interest in Emma's case was enormous because of who she was married to. Emma and Aaron were regulars on the red carpet and in the Sydney society pages. Aaron was a quintessential Aussie man who'd done well for himself. He'd started with nothing except a trade as a carpenter before applying for a spot on a home improvement show and eventually, when the network realised how much the viewers loved him, he'd been offered his own show.

Aaron and Emma were a lovely couple but the intense interest from the media had been another reason Ali had wanted to make sure she was the Ob-Gyn looking after Emma. She wanted to make sure she received the best care, but she also wanted to avoid any negative publicity. It was her responsibility to protect the hospital and her department from that. Ali was new in her role as Head of Obstetrics and Gynaecology and she couldn't afford to have any mistakes. There was enough to deal with in this role as a female and she was determined to prove she'd been appointed to the role on her merits.

It was something she was used to as she was always trying to prove herself. Always making sure no one could question her position. As an Indigenous female she often felt, rightly or wrongly, that she had to work doubly hard—even triply hard—to make sure no one could question her appointment to the top job. Throughout her school and university years she'd strived to be the best, craving recognition of her hard work and intelligence and not wanting to give people an opportunity to cut her down or to say she had been given a hand up the ladder because she was female and Indigenous. She wanted to earn her position and she wanted people to *rec-*

ognise that it had been earned. Not given. Not handed to her to meet a quota.

She knew she was doing a good job so far and she had no intention of letting things slip, she thought as she grabbed her stethoscope from her office and headed for the surgical ward.

'Hello, Emma,' Ali greeted her patient. Since Emma's initial admission Ali had only seen her on a handful of occasions for routine pregnancy checks. She had monitored Emma and the babies to ensure they weren't being stressed by Emma's injuries and surgeries. So far, perhaps surprisingly, the babies had been unaffected, but Ali was concerned that might all be about to change.

Today's visit was not routine so she modulated her tone, not wanting to frighten Emma or her husband Aaron, who was sitting beside her. 'How are you doing?'

'I didn't realise they'd called you in on a Sunday, Dr Edwards,' Emma apologised. 'I feel okay, especially compared to what I've been through over the past couple of months. I'm sure this is nothing. Just a blip.'

'How's your pain?'

'Easier.'

Sylvia had accompanied Ali into the room. The blood-pressure cuff was still around Emma's arm and Sylvia inflated it. Ali glanced at the screen, checking the numbers. The reading hadn't changed. It was still higher than Ali would like.

'That's good but now that I'm here there are a few things I want to check, just to be sure.'

She glanced surreptitiously at Emma's fingers, checking for oedema, pleased to note there was no obvious swelling at this stage. She knew there was no point checking Emma's feet as her injuries from the fire would complicate things there.

An ultrasound machine had been wheeled in and left in the corner of the room. Ali pulled the curtain around Emma's bed for additional privacy as she said, 'I'm just going to check the babies.' Ali lifted Emma's pyjama top and squirted gel onto her abdomen ready for the ultrasound. She'd have a quick look and if she saw anything untoward, she'd call a sonographer for a more thorough scan. Blood flow to the babies seemed normal and both babies' heart rates were within a normal range.

'Is everything okay?'

'The babies are fine,' Ali replied. 'Tough, like their mum.'

Emma breathed out a sigh of relief and said to Aaron, 'You can stop squeezing so hard now.'

'Sorry,' Aaron replied, letting go of Emma's hand.

There was a knock on the door and as Sylvia drew back the curtain a second nurse stepped into the room.

'I have the test results,' she said as she handed printouts to Ali.

Ali scanned the list of numbers, absorbing the results. Emma's liver function was within normal limits but there were high levels of protein in Emma's urine, indicating that her kidneys were not working effectively.

'What do they say?' Emma asked.

'Your liver is fine but there are traces of protein in your urine.'

'What does that mean?'

'It means your kidneys are under stress.' It could also be indicative of kidney damage, but Ali hoped that wasn't the case.

'What caused that? What do I do now?'

'There's nothing you can do. You've developed a condition called pre-eclampsia, but it wasn't caused by anything you did,' Ali hurried to reassure her patient. 'It's a complication of pregnancy.'

'Is it related to the fire? To Emma's other injuries?' Aaron asked.

'No.' Ali shook her head. She wasn't a hundred per cent sure that it wasn't related to Emma's recent medical history, but she'd never had a pregnant patient like Emma before, with critical injuries and multiple interventions, so she couldn't rule it out completely. But telling them that wouldn't achieve anything. It didn't really matter how this condition eventuated. What mattered was what happened next.

'There are a few risk factors, most of which don't apply to Emma,' Ali said.

'But there are some that do?' Aaron asked, picking up on what Ali hadn't said.

Ali nodded. 'Yes. We see a higher incidence with first pregnancies and twin or triplet pregnancies but plenty of women have the same risk factors without developing this condition,' she explained, knowing it was crucial to give the right amount of information. Too little would leave them worried. Too much would leave them overwhelmed and anxious. 'Pregnant women with diabetes or who are overweight or used assisted reproductive technologies or have a family history can also be at risk, but Emma doesn't tick those boxes.'

'Does it hurt the babies?'

That was a difficult question to answer. While the babies were in utero they should be fine, but it was almost always impossible to leave them there without risks to both Emma and the babies. 'Not as such,' Ali answered vaguely.

'How do we fix this? What can you give her?' Aaron asked.

'Nothing.' That was the big problem.

'What do you mean nothing? There has to be something you can do?'

Ali knew that some studies suggested that magnesium supplements could help but those same studies also showed that once the urinalysis showed traces of protein it was too late. 'The only cure is to deliver the babies,' Ali told them. Delivering the baby usually dropped the mother's blood pressure pretty quickly.

Aaron and Emma spoke in unison.

'But Emma's only thirty-two weeks.'

'The babies are too small, they can't be born now.'

'I know you're concerned,' Ali replied. Emma was right—the babies would be small, and, because she was carrying twins, they were likely to be smaller than a singleton, but she was wrong to think they couldn't be born now. It wasn't ideal but if Emma's condition worsened the alternative was far worse than premature babies. Both Emma and the babies' lives could be at risk. 'The babies will be small but ninety-five per cent of babies born at thirty-two weeks survive.' In Ali's opinion those odds were good. 'But there is a risk,' she continued, 'a couple actually. The biggest issue for the babies is that their lungs aren't fully developed yet. I can administer corticosteroid injections, which is an anti-inflammatory medicine that helps the babies' lungs to mature. Waiting gives me a chance to do that.'

'You're going to inject the babies?' Aaron asked.

'No, not the babies. I give the injections to Emma but ideally you need two injections, twenty-four hours apart. Which is why I'd prefer to wait if we can.'

'Is it safe to wait?'

'At the moment, yes, but if that changes, I will deliver the babies if it becomes necessary. The other risk is to you, Emma. If your condition worsens it can cause seizures and, in the worst-case scenario, it can be fatal.'

'Emma could die?' Aaron exclaimed.

'That outcome is very rare and usually occurs when the condition hasn't been picked up, but we would be monitoring Emma for any exacerbation of symptoms.'

'So, it's a catch-22? The babies or Emma?'

'No, we're not having to choose. Let me tell you what I recommend. If you agree, I'll organise the first injection for Emma now and hopefully we can delay needing to deliver the babies until you've had both doses. I'll postpone delivering the twins for as long as possible but if we can gain another twenty-four hours that gives them a better chance at having reduced breathing difficulties. You'll be closely monitored and if you develop any additional symptoms, I'll review your situation.'

'What other symptoms are we looking for?' Aaron asked.

'Swelling in Emma's hands, feet or face. Headaches. Visual disturbances.'

'Like what?' Emma asked.

'Black spots. Blurred vision. We'll watch you but you need to report anything unusual, anything you're not sure about, any changes to how you're feeling. I know this sounds scary and it's unexpected and worrying but you're in the best place. We'll keep a close eye on you. Now, would you like me to organise the first injection?'

Emma and Aaron agreed as Ali knew they would.

'You're sure this is the only way?' Aaron asked as he followed Ali out of the room.

'I think this is the best option.' Ali tried to sound calm and in control. She'd made it difficult for them to make any other decision but she was convinced this was the best choice for this situation although the outcome was out of her hands really—all she could do was monitor Emma and hope she had made the right call.

'I feel so useless,' Aaron said. 'It's my job to keep my family safe, to fix things. How did we get here?'

'Aaron, it's *my* job to keep Emma and the babies safe.'

Aaron sighed and Ali stopped walking, wanting to let him finish and then get back to his wife. 'I'm not used to feeling so helpless or inadequate. You know I was a carpenter by trade, back before I got my television gig? Give me some tools and I will fix anything. But I can't fix this. Do you know how useless that makes me feel?'

'Your job is just to support Emma. She is in the best place. I'll take care of her. If I think she's in any danger, I promise I'll intervene, but if I can keep the babies in for just one more day and give the steroids time to work their magic that's one less thing to worry about.' She put one hand on his arm, trying to reassure him, trying to persuade him to return to his wife's bedside. 'I'll be back with the injection.'

Ali sat at her desk and reached for her phone. She'd administered the cortisone injection and spoken to the paediatrician on call. She'd also spoken to Ivy, her good friend and Head of General Surgery, updating her on Emma's condition and checking that Ivy didn't have any other concerns. Ali had wanted a second opinion on the test results and she'd also wanted to ask Ivy how she thought Emma would cope with more abdominal surgery, assuming she'd have to undergo a caesarean section, so soon after her appendectomy. That surgery had been performed through a laparoscope so, in theory, a C-section shouldn't present any problems as long as there was no infection.

Ivy had been more concerned about the need for another anaesthetic so now, on Ivy's recommendation, Ali was making a third phone call, this time to Jake Ryan, the anaesthetist who had looked after Emma during her other surgeries. Ali hadn't met Jake, but Ivy spoke highly of him and so she also wanted to line him up for the procedure if necessary. In her mind there were a lot of benefits to keeping the anaesthetist consistent and she wanted to have all her ducks in a row if Emma needed a third anaesthetic in the space of a few weeks.

It was only when her call went to his voicemail that she remembered it was Sunday. A quick check of the time told her it was after six. Most people, even doctors unless they were on night duty, would have left the hospital.

She left a message asking him to call her mobile when he had a minute before she turned her attention to Emma's file. She updated the notes and then read through the file again, familiarising herself with all the details, wanting to make sure she didn't miss anything. She took her time. She had nowhere else to be.

Ali was in a world of her own, focused on Emma's

history, when a knock on her door startled her out of her headspace.

Her door was ajar and she looked up to find a man in green scrubs standing before her.

A stranger.

A tall, handsome stranger.

'Can I help you?' she asked.

'Dr Edwards?' She saw him double-check the name-plate on her office door. 'I'm Jake Ryan, the anaesthetist.'

You're Jake Ryan?

She almost spoke aloud but held her tongue just in time, realising she'd sound rude, but he wasn't what she'd been expecting, not at all.

She took in his features. He had a symmetrical face, fine boned but with a strong jaw and an aquiline nose. His cheekbones were sharp and well defined, chiselled—she didn't know if that was a thing but it was the only way to describe them. His eyes were dark, his lips full and his dark brown hair was thick, cut shorter on the sides but with length on top. At a guess he looked to be in his mid-thirties, over six feet tall, slim and rangy.

'You left me a message,' he said when she remained mute. She hadn't expected an anaesthetist who looked like a menswear model, nor had she expected him to turn up at her door and his appearance had taken her by surprise, leaving her speechless. 'You wanted to talk to me?' he continued. 'About Emma Wilson?'

CHAPTER TWO

'I DID.' Ali finally found her voice and was relieved she sounded normal. She'd half expected her voice to squeak.

'Is now a good time?' he asked as he looked around her office. 'I can come back.'

She shook her head. 'Now is fine.' He obviously got the impression he was interrupting but that was far from the truth. 'I wasn't expecting you to call past,' she said. 'I thought you'd phone me back.'

He shrugged, drawing her attention to his broad shoulders under the thin cotton of his scrubs. He might be lean and rangy, but he was perfectly proportioned with wide shoulders, narrow hips and long legs.

'I was in the hospital,' he explained. 'I saw you'd called me from your office number so I thought I might as well see if you were still in the building.'

He was still standing in her doorway and she realised she hadn't asked him in.

'Come in,' she invited as she stood up and extended her hand. 'I'm Alinta, but please, call me Ali.'

He crossed the room in a couple of long strides and reached for her hand. 'Nice to meet you,' he said as his fingers closed around hers. His grip was firm but not overpowering, strong but not domineering. A standard handshake, nothing out of the ordinary, but his fingers were warm and her skin sparked under his touch. The little burst of heat left her off balance and she almost reached for her desk with her left hand, looking for some support, looking for something to stabilise her.

His touch had disturbed her, not in a bad way, but it left her disconcerted. She knew some would say her equilibrium had been knocked off-kilter, others would say something about her soul but she felt it even more deeply than that. Her ancestors would say his touch had stirred her spirit.

It wasn't an unpleasant feeling but it was unsettling. Unexpected.

She had a flash of recognition as he continued to hold her hand in his. There was something familiar about him but she couldn't put her finger on it. She knew she hadn't met him before, not in this lifetime, but her sixth sense was tingling.

There was an idea of something more substantial, something important, but she couldn't grab hold of it. It was just a fleeting feeling, dancing around the periphery of her brain, refusing to settle. She wanted the thought to settle but she knew she needed to be calm in order for it to make sense and she was far from calm. She was flustered. It was unlike her, but something about Jake was mixing her up.

'You said you wanted to talk to me about Emma?' he asked as she tried one last time to make sense of what she was feeling. But his voice interrupted the sensations that had been swirling around her and they disappeared as quickly as they had arrived when he let go of her hand. 'Has something happened?'

Jake's questions helped her to get back on track.

She gathered her thoughts. 'You know she's pregnant?' she asked, cringing inwardly at the silly comment. Of course he'd know Emma was pregnant. Perhaps her mind wasn't totally focused.

'Yes, of course. She's expecting twins,' Jake replied as they both sat down.

Ali nodded. 'Unfortunately, she's developed pre-eclampsia. She's at thirty-two weeks' gestation now and I'm preparing for the possibility that I may have to deliver her babies early.'

'How early?'

'I don't know yet. I'm hoping to delay as long as possible. I've given her a dose of corticosteroids and I've got my fingers crossed that things might stabilise but I'm not that hopeful, if I'm honest. It's really wishful thinking on my part rather than a feeling based on anything concrete. If I do have to deliver the twins early, Emma will need a C-section and, given her recent trauma, I'd like the delivery of her babies to be as pleasant an experience as possible so I'm planning on performing the C-section with a spinal block so, all going well, she can hold her babies when they're delivered. I'd like you to be the anaesthetist for the delivery—I think that consistency will simplify things and will help Emma feel secure but I wasn't sure if you had an area of speciality anaesthesiology. I needed to know two things—one, are you happy to work in obstetrics and two, can you do a spinal block for Emma?'

'I can do whatever you need. A spinal block shouldn't be a problem. If it's an emergency—and I imagine it could be depending on what happens—she can have another general. She's had a couple, but she didn't have any problems with the actual anaesthetic and it's a few weeks now since her last surgery.'

'That's good to hear.' Ali smiled, finally able to relax. 'I'm hoping we won't have an emergency situation. Emma has had enough to deal with.'

'I agree. So, I'm happy to help in whatever way you need.' He smiled in return as he stood up. 'You have my number. I'll expect a call.'

Was he flirting with her? Ali couldn't tell. She was out of practice as dates had been few and far between lately and her job wasn't particularly conducive to meeting eligible men. Perhaps he was just being friendly.

She watched him as he turned and walked out of her office. He was long and lean. He looked like an athlete. Maybe a long-distance runner. He moved easily. Smoothly. Sensuously.

Ali was unsettled. She shook her head, trying to clear her mind, trying to focus, but all she could think about were his eyes. There was something in them that connected to something in her. His gaze had been intense, his eyes piercing. It almost felt as if he could see inside her head, could read her thoughts. She really hoped that wasn't true. Because her jumbled, chaotic thoughts about him weren't for public consumption.

Jake stepped into the lift. On autopilot he pushed the button to take him from the fourth floor back to the first and as the doors slid closed his thoughts went to Dr Edwards. Ali.

She looked younger than he'd expected. He'd double-checked her office door when he'd seen her, making sure he was in the right place. But the nameplate had read *Dr*

Alinta Edwards, Head of Obstetrics and Gynaecology.
It had to be her, sitting behind the desk, but she didn't
look much older than some of the resident doctors, far
too young to be the head of a department.

He was relatively new to Sydney Central. Born and
raised in Sydney, he'd studied medicine there but hadn't
come across Ali at university. She must be younger than
he was, early thirties maybe?

He'd been living in Melbourne and had only recently
moved back to Sydney. Roster-wise, he'd got the short
end of the stick, covering emergency surgery with lots
of weekends and after hours, so it was no surprise he
hadn't come across Ali in the hospital either. He'd been
called in for a few emergency deliveries, but those had
all been handled by other obstetricians. He suspected, as
she was Head of Obstetrics and Gynaecology, that Ali's
patient caseload would be light and wouldn't routinely
include emergencies.

Was it wrong to hope she'd need to call him for Emma?

He didn't want Emma to have more emergency surgery
but if it was going to give him a reason to see Ali again
it wasn't all bad. She intrigued him. Young. Attractive.
No wedding ring. She'd had a serious air about her but
when she smiled she was an absolute knockout. With her
black hair, brown skin and dark eyes, the flash of white
teeth in a wide smile had felt like a powerful punch to
the chest, figuratively knocking the air from him.

He hadn't felt such a sudden, unexpected attraction to
a woman in a long time and he was keen to see her again.

He checked his watch. He was running late to meet
friends for dinner but they would be surprised if he was
on time. That was one good thing about his job, no one

expected him to be on time and no one would ask why he was late. They'd assume he'd been held up at work, which was mostly true. They wouldn't assume he'd just met someone who had piqued his interest. Who he was keen to find out more about. Will and Chris would be like dogs with a bone if he let that slip.

He hoped she was single. Though it would be just his luck to find out she was very much part of a couple and chose not to wear a ring. But before he could think about dating, he needed to get himself sorted. First up? Finding somewhere permanent to live because staying in his cousin's spare room was not a long-term option.

He'd keep this encounter to himself for now. His love life had been dissected and commented on enough for two lifetimes. He didn't need anyone else's opinion on what he should be doing. Since his divorce he'd had plenty of well-meaning friends try to set him up. He'd dated but nothing had stuck. He wasn't ready, hadn't been interested. But suddenly he found he was interested. Very interested.

Ali was in her office, having just given Emma her second steroid injection for the babies' lungs, when her phone buzzed.

She read the message.

Coffee? Perc Up—four p.m.?

The message had gone to a group chat, which included Ali and three girlfriends—Ivy, Harper and Phoebe—who had all met at medical school. They had now been friends for over twenty years, but it was only recently that they'd all been in the same city again. And not only were they all in Sydney, they were all working at Sydney Central Hospital as heads of their respective departments. Some days, Ali still found that difficult to comprehend. Not because she doubted her ability—it had been her goal to achieve this career highpoint and she'd worked hard for it—but to be able to realise it, as an Indigenous woman, was something special. Something she was very proud of. And to have four women heading up departments in the same hospital was a thrill, especially given their friendship. It made working together easy and fun. Ivy was Head of General Surgery and Harper the new head of the emergency department but Ali worked most closely with Phoebe, who was Head of Neonatal Surgery.

She needed a coffee and she wanted to catch up on Ivy's news. She 'liked' the message and sorted herself, knowing she had time for a break as she'd be working late anyway. As usual.

Ali deliberately delayed her arrival at the café by a few minutes. Since Harper had returned from the UK their friendship remained a little strained and Ali was still reluctant to be in a situation where she and Harper were alone together. They'd been as close as sisters once upon a time, before Harper had started dating Ali's twin brother, Yarran. Before Harper had broken Yarran's heart when she'd rejected his marriage proposal in favour of a job in London.

She'd left without a word, to either Yarran or Ali, leaving them both in pain, breaking her friendship with Ali at the same time as breaking Yarran's heart. But where Ali felt betrayed, Yarran had been devastated and his heartache hadn't ended there. While he'd eventually got over Harper, married Marnie and had a little boy, he'd then found himself widowed, dealing with his wife's death and becoming a single parent. Ali blamed Harper for that too.

She knew she was being unreasonable but, in her mind, if Harper had accepted Yarran's proposal, if she'd stayed in Sydney, Yarran wouldn't have gone through any of that pain. She knew Yarran would say the pain was worth it though because without those events he wouldn't have his son, Jarrah.

But now Harper had returned from London and she and Yarran had found their way back to each other. They were engaged to be married. Ali wanted to support Yarran's decisions, but she was still trying to sort through her own feelings. She knew Yarran and Harper's relationship was really nothing to do with her, Yarran's happiness should be all that mattered, but she worried. She didn't want to see him hurt again. He was the most important person in Ali's life. Older than him by five minutes, she had always been very protective of him, but he obviously trusted Harper and Ali would have to trust Yarran's judgement. Trust that Harper wouldn't break her twin's heart a second time.

She also hadn't quite forgiven Harper for not saying goodbye to her. She knew she would have to put the past behind her because Harper was, all these years later, going to be part of her family and, for Yarran's sake and the sake of family unity, Ali knew she'd have to find a way of dealing with her own feelings of betrayal.

Ali had to adjust and accept. She'd have to forgive, if not forget. It would be difficult but she'd do her best. For Yarran's sake.

But for now, Ali had decided the best course of action was to avoid being alone with Harper. Until she'd achieved forgiveness and reached acceptance, she was best off avoiding any situation where she might put her foot in her mouth. The last thing she wanted to do was upset Yarran.

Ali was relieved to see that all three women had arrived before her, and Ivy, Harper and Phoebe were sitting on the leather Chesterfield couches by one of the large windows overlooking the street. Perc Up had comfortable seating, natural light, and myriad indoor plants gave the café a relaxing, peaceful vibe, far removed from the harsh artificial lights and noisy, bustling atmosphere of the hospital.

'Hi, have you ordered?' Ali asked as she dropped her handbag onto a couch.

'Harper and I have. Phoebe just sat down,' Ivy replied.

'I'll order for you, Phoebs, your usual?'

Phoebe shook her head. 'Can I have a peppermint tea?'

Ali frowned. 'No coffee?'

'I'm trying to cut down on my caffeine intake. It's getting a bit out of control.'

'You don't want decaf?'

Phoebe pulled a face and Ali laughed. 'Point taken. Peppermint tea coming up.'

'How is Emma today?' Ivy asked when Ali returned from the counter.

'Her blood pressure is still high but she hasn't developed any other concerning symptoms. Not yet anyway.' Ali knocked her knuckles twice on the wooden coffee table.

'Are you talking about Emma Wilson?' Harper asked. 'What's happened?' she added when Ivy nodded.

'She's developed pre-eclampsia,' Ali replied. Most of the hospital staff were aware of Emma's accident. Her story had been reported on in great detail by the media but as Head of the Emergency Department, Harper hadn't treated Emma since she'd first been brought into Sydney Central. 'And I'm hoping to buy her some more time before delivering her babies.'

'How many weeks is she?' Phoebe asked. Ali hoped Emma wouldn't need to consult Phoebe but, seeing as Phoebe was Head of Neonatal Surgery, it wasn't out of the realm of possibility that Emma, and her twins, would cross paths with her too. Especially if the twins were born several weeks early.

'Just at the end of thirty-two weeks. I've given her a second dose of corticosteroids today and now it's just a matter of time. I'm planning to wait as long as possible but, as you all know, there's not much I can do.'

'Did you get hold of Jake Ryan?' Ivy asked.

'I did. He came to my office last night.' She could feel the heat rising in her face as she recalled his chiselled features, easy smile and relaxed manner. Ali was pleased she had a dark complexion that hid her response to the memory.

'What did you think?'

'He seems competent.' Ali tried for a neutral response. Something professional.

'That's one word to describe him,' Ivy said with a smile. 'Tall, dark and handsome would be three others.'

'I hadn't noticed,' Ali replied with a grin.

'Liar.' Ivy laughed.

'Okay, I'll admit he was pretty easy on the eye.' She knew there was no point pretending he wasn't gorgeous. She might be forty years old but that didn't mean she wouldn't notice a good-looking guy and there had never been any topics that were off limits between the four of them. At least not until Harper had broken that trust... but that wasn't Ivy's fault.

'I don't know Jake,' Phoebe said, 'but he might be horrified to hear you girls talking about him like that.'

'He's relatively new,' Ivy replied as the waiter delivered their order. 'I think he's been at the Central for about three months, but don't worry, Phoebs, we're not objectifying him. He's also intelligent and charming and he's got a fabulous bedside manner.'

'He's an anaesthetist,' Harper cut in. 'His patients are asleep. He hardly needs much of a bedside manner for that!'

Ivy laughed. 'Fair call, but my point is he seems to be the whole package, but if you're not interested, Ali, I can introduce him to Phoebe. He's too good to let go.'

'Is he even single?' Ali shouldn't be asking but she had to admit she was curious to know the answer. She'd been curious since last night. 'Given how eligible he sounds, that would be surprising.'

'I haven't asked him directly,' Ivy answered, 'but nursing staff usually have their fingers on the pulse when any hot new colleagues appear and they seem to think he's eligible. I can find out for you. It's time you started dating again, don't you think? I'm not saying it has to be Jake,' she added when Ali stayed silent, 'but you would look good together. He's pretty cute.'

'Have you forgotten you're engaged to Lucas?' Ali

said, trying to divert the focus of the conversation away from her love life, or lack of, and Jake. For some reason it was making her uncomfortable.

'Not at all. But just because I'm getting married doesn't mean I've lost all my senses. My eyes still work. But speaking of Lucas, that's why I wanted to catch up with you all. I wanted to know if you're free on Saturday night,' she said as she looked around the circle. 'Lucas and I were thinking of having drinks to celebrate our engagement. I know it's short notice but I don't want to have drinks without the three of you there. I feel like we haven't seen each other properly for ages.'

'That is short notice,' Harper said. 'What's the hurry?'

'Lucas thinks it would be nice to do something to mark the occasion but it seemed silly to have a big engagement party seeing as we want to get married in a few weeks, so we decided on casual drinks.'

'This Saturday?' Phoebe asked.

Ivy nodded. 'Yes. Are you free? I really want you all to be there.'

Ivy was the most sociable one of the four friends. The one who had always organised the parties. Ali suspected that Ivy used her busyness as a shield. As long as she was in the thick of things, camouflaged by her surroundings, people didn't look too closely at her.

'I'm free,' Harper said, 'and I think Yarran is rostered off but I'll check.'

Phoebe had her phone in her hand. 'My diary is clear,' she said as she looked up from the screen.

Ali didn't need to check her schedule to know the answer. 'I'm free too,' she said, not without a little disappointment. 'My social life is non-existent unless you count our family birthday parties and Sunday barbecues.'

'Maybe you'll meet someone at the party,' Ivy said. 'Lucas has some single friends. I'll make sure they're invited.'

'I hope Lucas's friends are a higher calibre of human than Adam is,' Ali said. Her ex had cheated on her and then left her. She'd thought they'd wanted the same things in life, thought they had the same goals and aspirations, only to find out that he wanted those things but not with her. Her confidence had taken a hiding and her subsequent trust issues meant she'd struggled on the dating scene since her divorce. Harper's betrayal hadn't helped either.

But she was lonely and, if pushed, she'd admit she'd like some company. Yarran had Harper... Ivy had Lucas. Phoebe was the only other member of their little group who was also single. It would be nice to be part of a couple again but she wasn't sure she had the energy for a relationship. Not unless it was easy. And it *should* be easy, shouldn't it? But she knew she wouldn't say no to good sex. And she could have that without a relationship. Maybe the party would be perfect timing.

'I'm sure he can rustle up some decent men,' Ivy was saying. 'One for you, Ali, and one for you, Phoebs.'

'Don't worry about me, I'm not looking for anyone,' Phoebe replied.

'Ooh, did you meet someone at the conference?' Ivy asked.

Phoebe shook her head as she picked up her cup and sipped her tea, successfully avoiding answering Ivy's question. Ali wasn't sure if anyone else noticed, and it could have been coincidental, but she was sure Phoebe had dodged the question on purpose. But it was the sort of tactic Ali had employed herself in the past so, while she filed the thought away and vowed to get to the bottom of it later, she took pity on Phoebe in the short term and changed the subject. 'How was the conference, Phoebs? I don't think I've asked you.'

'It was actually really good. There were some interesting speakers and a few surgeons were trialling some innovative techniques.'

'I see you're following Zac Archer on his social media,' Harper said. 'Did you meet him? He's supposed to be a brilliant surgeon.'

Phoebe nodded. 'I got to watch him perform heart surgery on a newborn. He was incredible.' Phoebe's eyes were shining and, as interesting as surgery could be, Ali found it hard to believe she'd be quite so excited by a surgical procedure.

'So, just some options for Ali, then,' Ivy said, refusing to be deterred from her self-appointed role as matchmaker.

'Please don't make it obvious that I'm a single woman,' Ali said. 'I'm happy on my own.'

'That's what I said and look at me now,' Ivy said as she stretched out her left arm to admire her engagement ring.

'I'm happy for you and Lucas. But, I promise, I'm fine.'

'You said your social calendar is looking bleak.'

'It is. But work's really busy and I don't have the time or the energy to date.'

'Ali, you're forty, not a hundred,' Ivy persisted.

'I've just found the last dates I've gone on to be hard

work. And they shouldn't be. It should be easy. Exciting. Not exasperating or excruciating.'

'Think of dating as a challenge. You've never backed down from a challenge before.'

'I'd rather challenge myself in other ways.'

'And when was the last time you did that?'

She wasn't sure. 'When I accepted the job as Head of Obstetrics and Gynaecology,' she said, unable to think of anything more recent.

'So, months ago. I'll make a deal with you,' Ivy countered. 'I won't set you up with anyone but next time an opportunity presents itself for you to step out of your comfort zone or try something new—be it an invitation to dinner or an activity—you say yes. I don't like to think of you sitting at home alone.'

'Ivy, I'm fine.'

'I know. But there's no harm in having some fun.'

CHAPTER THREE

ALI WALKED INTO the hospital just as the sun was barely over the horizon. She was always there early, wanting to be on hand when the doctors did their rounds, wanting to be present, in case there were issues, but this morning she was earlier than usual. Unable to sleep, she'd woken before sunrise, her mind going over Emma's situation. Feeling uneasy and unable to go back to sleep, she'd gone for a run, showered and when she was still feeling twitchy she decided to listen to her sixth sense and go to work.

She had moved Emma up to the labour ward on the fourth floor and when she exited the lift she bypassed her office and headed towards Emma's room.

'Dr Edwards!' One of the nurses called out to her as she approached the nurses' station. 'Has someone already phoned you?'

Ali could feel goosebumps rising on her forearms, making the fine hair on her arms stand up. 'No. What is it?' she asked, even though she could guess the problem.

'Emma Wilson is complaining of a headache. Pain relief isn't helping and she's just reported that her vision is blurry.'

'What was her blood pressure at the last reading?'

'One-ninety over one hundred and twenty.'

Ali turned on her heel. 'Come with me,' she called back over her shoulder to the nurse, not waiting to make sure her instructions were followed as she hurried to Emma's room.

She slowed down as she approached Emma's door. She didn't want to barge in like a whirlwind and frighten her patient. She needed to keep her as calm as possible.

'Good morning, Emma.'

Emma was lying in bed, eyes closed, her hands clenched into two fists, but she opened her eyes when she heard Ali's voice. Ali could see the pain in her eyes and noticed it took Emma a moment to focus on where she stood. Aware she would appear blurry, she moved closer to the bed.

'Dr Edwards.' Emma's jaw was tight, it was obvious that speaking was painful too, perhaps moving her jaw aggravated her headache.

'I hear you're not feeling so great,' Ali said as she looked at Emma's hands. They were swollen now, her fingers puffy, the skin stretched tight.

Her condition had deteriorated overnight and Ali wondered why no one had alerted her. But regardless of that, she should have come in when she first woke up. She'd known something wasn't right. She just hoped she hadn't left things too late.

There were a couple of things in her favour. Emma was conscious. She hadn't had a seizure. They were small things to be grateful for, but Ali would take anything at this point.

'I'm just going to take your blood pressure,' she said. The cuff was already wrapped around Emma's arm and

Ali hit the button on the machine to inflate it. 'You've got a headache and blurred vision?'

Emma started to nod her head before stopping and choosing to answer verbally instead. 'Yes.' Maybe talking was the lesser of two evils.

'Any other new symptoms? Nausea, difficulty breathing?'

'No.' Emma's voice was just above a whisper.

'I'm just going to listen to your breathing,' Ali said as she placed her stethoscope on Emma's chest while she kept an eye on the blood-pressure reading. She'd already made the decision to take Emma to Theatre when the machine beeped. She checked the reading—one-ninety-five over one hundred and twenty.

'Emma, your condition is deteriorating. I need to deliver the babies.' Ali spoke slowly and softly. She didn't want to alarm Emma—her condition was precarious enough without adding fear into the mix.

'Today? We can't wait?'

Ali shook her head. 'I'm afraid not. Time is critical. Your blood pressure is climbing and headaches and blurred vision can precede a seizure. That's dangerous and it could be fatal. I promised you I'd do what's best for you and your babies. This is best. Waiting could put your life at risk and would likely mean an emergency caesarean. That would mean a general anaesthetic, another one, which I'd rather avoid, but more importantly if we do it now you can have a spinal block, which means you'll be awake when I deliver the babies and you should be able to hold them, all going well. It will be a far more positive experience for you and Aaron, less traumatic, better memories. If we do it now Aaron can be with you. In an emergency situation that would be very unlikely. I'm not going to risk your life or your babies. There will be a team of specialists in Theatre with me. This is the safest option. For all of you.'

'Okay.' Emma was clearly not capable of concentrating or focusing but she acquiesced quickly, another indication she was too sick to argue.

'I'll call Aaron and get him in here as quickly as possible while we get you prepped for Theatre.'

Jake had been called and he was already scrubbing at the sink outside Theatre when Ali walked in. She stood beside him, flicking the tap on and running the water over her hands and forearms.

He turned his head and smiled at her and as their eyes met Ali had a strange sensation of being hot and cold at the same time. She could feel tiny goosebumps on her skin yet she could also feel warmth spreading through her limbs and belly, as if she could feel her blood flowing through her veins.

'We meet again,' he said. 'I was looking forward to seeing you again but also hoping for it not to be here.'

Ali's stomach flip-flopped as he smiled at her. She was surprised again by how attractive she found him. She'd thought she'd committed his face to memory but it turned out she was wrong. He was gorgeous and when he smiled he just looked even more handsome.

'Not ideal, I agree,' she replied before she turned away, not wanting him to see her flustered. She squirted her hands with soap and started rubbing vigorously as Jake continued talking.

'I've spoken to Emma,' he said. 'She's got a canula in

and I've given her something to relax her. I'm hoping that might also help with her headache and the spinal block should drop her BP too.'

Through the window above the sink Ali could see Emma was already in Theatre, her hand clasped tightly in Aaron's. Ali had explained the urgency of the situation to Aaron, explained that he could lose Emma if they waited. He'd been concerned about the babies but she'd reassured him they had an excellent chance of survival. A ninety-five per cent chance according to the statistics.

She didn't want to think about the other five per cent.

Lost in her thoughts, she didn't notice that Jake had finished scrubbing and she was in his way as he turned from the sink to dry his hands. His hip bumped against hers and the brief contact triggered a sense of unsteadiness. She felt unbalanced, unsettled, even though she knew she was stable. She needed to focus. She had a surgery to perform.

She had to concentrate. She took a deep breath as she gathered her thoughts.

'You okay?' Jake asked.

Ali nodded. 'I wish I didn't need to do this but it's the only option.' Using work as an excuse was the safest way to answer. She wasn't about to tell him that she'd be fine if he weren't around upsetting her equilibrium and disturbing her train of thought. Maybe it was a mistake to have asked him to be the anaesthetist.

'We've got this,' he said.

He uttered three simple words that made Ali feel as if she was part of a team. The team she'd told Emma about. Ali would be the surgeon but she wasn't doing this alone.

The team were experienced. She had support. She'd asked Jake for help because Ivy had suggested it. Because Jake was good at his job. That was what Ali needed. What Emma needed.

Jake was a colleague, one of several who would be in Theatre with her. She could handle this. She could put aside her feelings, she was good at that, she could push them aside to deal with later. Much later.

'Ready?'

She looked up and met his gaze and nodded. 'Ready.'

They walked into Theatre together. The last to arrive. The operating room was full—Ali, Jake, Paul Minter, the paediatrician, an obstetrics registrar, Aaron, a nurse and two midwives, one for each baby.

'How are you feeling, Emma?'

'A little sleepy. I will be awake for the delivery, won't I? I don't want to miss this.'

Ali nodded. 'If everything goes to plan, yes, you will.' She wasn't about to make a promise she might not be able to keep but she was determined to give Emma the best experience she could in the circumstances.

'She'll be okay after this?' Aaron asked.

'Emma's blood pressure and all other symptoms should resolve quickly once we deliver your babies,' Ali reassured them.

'Can you turn onto your left side, Emma, and curl your knees up? I'm going to start the spinal block,' Jake said. 'You'll feel a little prick, some pressure, then a cold sensation. The block will numb you from the waist down but it will take a few minutes to have effect.'

'Once you're numb I'll make two horizontal incisions, both about ten centimetres long.' Ali stood in front of

Emma and held up her fingers indicating the distance, talking to her patient, keeping her distracted, as Jake worked behind her. 'One in your abdomen and one in your uterus. We'll set up a screen so that you and Aaron won't see any of that. I'm sure you've seen babies delivered by C-section on television but, in my opinion, parents don't need to see that in real life. We're only creating beautiful memories today.'

Emma was rolled back into a supine position as the nurse and the registrar erected the screen just below Emma's chest, blocking her line of sight.

'Okay, Aaron, your position is up here with me, on this side of the drape where you can continue to hold Emma's hand,' Jake instructed. 'And if you've got Emma's playlist on your phone, I'll get that connected through the speakers for you.'

Aaron would be able to take photos and play the music Emma had chosen in her birthing plan—another bonus of not having to undergo an emergency procedure.

'I love this song,' Jake said as the music started to play. He sang along to the first few lines as everyone laughed, easing the slight tension that always seemed to be present in the moments before a surgery commenced. 'What? Can't you see me in a boy band.'

Actually, it wasn't hard to imagine, Ali thought. He had a good voice. She could picture him twenty years ago, up on a stage, with all the girls, and some men too no doubt, in the front row hanging off his every word and movement. He commanded attention and he'd certainly caught hers with his engaging smile and easy, relaxed manner.

'The performing arts' loss is medicine's gain,' she quipped, keeping the conversation light.

'Just be glad Emma didn't pick opera. That's not my forte.'

Ali picked up a pair of forceps and some gauze and looked at Jake, wanting to know if the anaesthetic would have taken effect. He nodded and Ali dipped the gauze in cold antiseptic solution before wiping it over Emma's skin. She didn't react but Ali double-checked, just in case.

'You can't feel that, Emma?'

'No.'

Ali swapped the forceps for a scalpel. 'You might feel a little bit of pressure with the cuts but no pain. Any discomfort, let me know.'

Ali concentrated, blocking out the sound of the music, as she prepared to start. Fortunately, Jake had stopped singing. His voice was good but she knew it would distract her.

She made a small initial cut, giving Emma a chance to object if she felt any discomfort.

'Do you know if the babies are girls or boys?' Jake was chatting to Emma and Aaron as Ali worked.

'Girls.'

'Have you picked out names?'

'Twin One is Jasmine and Twin Two is Poppy.'

'Have you got that, Dr Edwards? Don't mix them up!' Jake teased.

Ali looked up and met Jake's gaze. She could see the crinkles at the corners of his eyes above his mask and knew he was smiling.

'Got it.' Ali smiled back.

The registrar and the theatre nurse kept the incision clear, mopping up blood and cauterising vessels.

'And that's perfect timing and a perfect baby,' she said as she lifted the first twin out. She held her behind the sheet as the registrar clamped the cord before holding her up for Emma and Aaron to see. 'Mum and Dad, meet Jasmine.'

Jasmine cried on cue. It wasn't a lusty, full-bellied cry but not bad for a premmie baby.

Emma had tears in her eyes but she didn't bother wiping them away. She held her hands out towards Ali, reaching for her daughter.

'We'll quicky get her checked over and cleaned up,' Ali said. 'Then you should be able to hold her.'

'Aaron, did you want to cut the cord?' Ali asked once the cord had stopped pulsating.

'I think I'll stay up this end, thanks.'

The registrar cut the cord and then Ali handed Jasmine to the midwife. 'Now for the next one.'

Ali repeated the procedure to deliver baby Poppy. She lifted Poppy up as the midwife brought Jasmine back and laid her on Emma's chest.

Poppy was noticeably smaller than her sister and her cries were softer, a little mewl like a newborn kitten, but both girls looked perfect. Ali handed Poppy to the second midwife and took a minute to watch Emma and Aaron as they looked in total amazement at their daughter lying on Emma's chest.

'She's so tiny,' Aaron said.

'And so fair. I wasn't expecting that,' Emma said.

'That's not unusual,' Ali told her. Like Ali, Aaron was Indigenous, but it was common for babies with mixed parentage, Caucasian and Aboriginal, to be quite fair skinned at birth. 'She's got her dad's dark eyes and her complexion may change as she gets older. I've seen it in my own nieces and nephews.'

'She's perfect. They both are,' Aaron said as the midwife brought Poppy over and handed her to Aaron. 'Well done us,' he said as he bent down to kiss his wife.

Ali had to agree with him. Jasmine and Poppy were gorgeous babies. Small with perfectly shaped round heads, ten fingers and ten toes, pale eyelashes and dark eyes. After all the tragedy and horror, it was such a beautiful moment to witness—the start of Emma and Aaron's journey as parents, as a family. Ali did love babies— other people's—and she always felt privileged to be part of these moments in people's lives.

She lifted her eyes from the family tableau and once again her gaze met Jake's. As if they were perfectly in sync.

Was he thinking the same as her? About how amazing this was? Or did he know what it was like? She had no idea and, despite what Ivy thought, he could easily be in a relationship. He could have a family. A partner.

She found she really, really wanted him to be single.

He was still watching her and she realised she had been holding his gaze a little too long. She really had to stop doing that! Once again, she had the feeling he could read her thoughts. And she did not want him to know what she was thinking about right now.

She quickly looked away, intent on finding something else to occupy herself with. She busied herself delivering the placentas and checked the dosage of pain relief before it was injected through Emma's drip as one of the midwives took some family snaps with Aaron's phone before she took Jasmine away to do her five-minute Apgar score and measurements.

Emma was completely oblivious to what was happening to her now, she was totally focused on watching the midwife and paediatrician as they checked the babies. Listening as they relayed the measurements.

Ali listened too as she checked the board, making sure all the instruments and supplies were accounted for before she sutured the incisions.

At twenty-eight centimetres and seventeen hundred grams, Jasmine was slightly longer and heavier than Poppy. Poppy's second Apgar scores were also a little lower than Jasmine's. Her colour wasn't quite as good and her cries weren't as strong but her score was reasonable. In addition, her respiration rate was faster than Jasmine's but her oxygen levels were lower. Ali doubted Emma and Aaron would pick up on the difference but she heard the numbers.

'We're going to take the babies to the neonatal intensive care unit,' the paediatrician told Emma.

'Intensive care?'

'It's routine with what we call moderate preterm infants born between thirty-two and thirty-four weeks,' Paul reassured her. 'Poppy's oxygen is a bit low so we're going to supplement that for her.'

'Is she okay?'

'She's fine. We'll keep an eye on her. Once you're cleaned up, we'll get you into a wheelchair and bring you to the NICU.'

Ali tied off the sutures and stuck a dressing over Emma's wound. The edges had come together nicely and

Emma's scar should be quite discreet once the incision healed. She let the registrar attend to Emma's post-surgical care.

'Your vitals are looking better, Emma, and your wound has come together nicely. It could take ninety minutes or so before you get the feeling back below your waist so we'll put a catheter in for you and then get you into a wheelchair so you can visit your daughters.'

Ali waited until Emma was safely transferred into the chair and was heading for the NICU with Aaron before going to change.

'That went well,' Jake said as they stripped off their protective layers.

'It went okay,' Ali said as she threw her gown into the linen skip.

'Surely you can relax now. You delivered two healthy babies.'

She could feel a little frown between her eyebrows and a little niggle of disquiet in her mind.

'What is it?' Jake asked.

'I'm concerned about Poppy's oxygen levels. They're not unusual for a small premmie baby but they're not as good as Jasmine's.'

'Should they be the same?'

'Not necessarily. But I'd prefer it if they were both good. I'm just worried about her lungs. Wondering if the steroids had time to help.'

'You did your best. It's impossible to control everything and it's unrealistic to think you can.'

'I know. Believe me, I know.' Sometimes she felt as if she wasn't in control of anything. But work was her happy place. Where she knew what she was doing. Where she felt as if she was on top of things. As opposed to her personal life. 'Emma has been through so much. I wanted to help her.'

'You did help her.'

'I would have preferred *not* to deliver her babies, though. Not yet anyway.'

'I think we both know it's not a perfect world. Don't beat yourself up about it. Emma is fine. You delivered two healthy babies. Everyone survived. Sometimes that's even better than we can hope for.'

She knew how lucky Emma was to have survived. The twins too. She just hoped they'd keep surviving.

'If you need to download, call me. You have my number,' he said.

Ali nodded. 'Thank you.' Her heart was racing but at least her voice sounded normal.

'You're doing well, Emma,' Ali said as she completed her day one post-surgical check.

She was moving slowly but her wound looked good, she was afebrile and her blood pressure was back to normal.

'How are Jasmine and Poppy? Have you been able to hold them?' Ali asked. She'd walked past the NICU on the way to Emma's room but hadn't gone in. Emma was her patient but the babies were under the care of the paediatrician. They weren't her responsibility even though she didn't always feel that way.

Tears welled in Emma's eyes, catching Ali off guard. Ali expected her to feel a little fragile after all the trauma she'd been through recently but the post-baby blues shouldn't have hit her this quickly. Something else must be happening.

Ali looked at Aaron, hoping for a clue as to what was going on, but he also looked close to tears.

'I've been able to hold Jasmine but Poppy has been having some trouble with her breathing so I've only been able to touch her while she's in her crib. She needs me, I know she does, and it's breaking my heart not to be able to hold them both.'

'What sort of trouble is she having?' Ali's throat felt tight, her mouth dry as her concerns about the babies' lungs rose to the fore again.

'Dr Minter said her breathing rate is still high compared to Jasmine. He thinks she might have something wrong with her heart. He was organising an ultrasound, I've forgotten what it's called, the one that shows the blood flow through the heart?'

'An echocardiogram,' Ali told her just as Paul Minter walked into the room. All eyes turned to him.

He was smiling and Ali relaxed. Whatever it was Paul's expression was telling them he could handle it.

'The results of Poppy's scans are back.' Ali, Emma and Aaron all waited silently for him to continue. 'As I suspect they show an issue with Poppy's heart, *but*,' he stressed, trying to keep everyone calm, 'it can be fixed.'

'What is it? What's wrong with her?' Aaron and Emma spoke in unison.

'She has a ventricular septal defect—big words, I know, but it's what's usually referred to as a hole in the heart.'

'A hole in her heart!' Emma cried.

'It's not uncommon and, as I said, it can be fixed.'

'But I had lots of ultrasounds while I was pregnant. I had one just three days ago. Why didn't this show up on any of those?'

'Depending on the size of the hole it's often not detected until after birth and, with twins, it's more difficult to diagnose in utero as the babies can get in each other's way and obstruct the sound waves. Sometimes these holes will close by themselves if they are small, but Poppy's hole is on the larger side. If her vital signs stay elevated it's an indication that her heart is needing to work harder than it should be. I suspect she will need surgery to repair it.'

'What type of surgery?

'Open-heart surgery.'

'Open-heart surgery!' Emma repeated before turning to Ali. 'You told me the babies would be okay!'

Ali knew she hadn't actually said that. She'd said their chances of survival were very good, she hadn't ever promised that they would be completely fine.

'Emma, Aaron, this is fixable.' Paul got the new parents to return their attention to him, allowing Ali to breathe again. 'We can operate here in the hospital. I'll consult with Dr Mason—she is Head of Neonatal Surgery—and I expect we will get a neonatal cardiac specialist to consult as well.'

'When will this happen?'

'I'll speak to Dr Mason today but I'm hoping we can wait until Poppy is a little stronger. Until she puts on a little bit of weight. She's safe in the NICU at the moment.'

Jake pushed open the door to the hospital's rooftop garden. He often came up here to catch some of Sydney's glorious sunshine. After years of living in Melbourne he was relishing the fact that Sydney often had beautiful, sunny winter days and he preferred to take his breaks outside.

It was rare to find the rooftop empty but there was a cool wind today and so there was only one other person on the roof. He smiled at his good fortune when he realised it was Ali.

He'd been impressed by her professional skills but he couldn't deny he also found her attractive. Lithe, dark, mysterious. Intelligent, beautiful and interesting. She was an intriguing combination.

But he doubted she was single. Women like that didn't tend to be.

He wondered if he should ask Ivy about her. But then he thought of all the reasons why it was best not to. She was out of his league. Head of the department. Since his divorce he was dating, but only casually and he didn't think she was the type of woman to do casual dating. She seemed too in control. He also tried to avoid dating colleagues. He'd seen the mess it had got some of his friends into when their relationships soured, and he was still relatively new at Sydney Central. He just wanted to settle into his job. Find a house. Focus on sorting his life out post-divorce. He had a lot on his plate.

Ali was standing by the edge of the rooftop, running her hand through a cluster of tall, soft grasses, lost in thought staring out across the city. She looked vulnerable, lonely, but he wasn't sure why he got that feeling. She could just be thinking about what to have for lunch.

But as he drew nearer, he could tell she was upset. He

wondered if he should give her some space but what if he could help her?

'Ali? Is everything okay?'

She spun around, her eyes wide. She obviously hadn't heard him approaching. She shook her head and he heard her voice catch in her throat when she spoke. 'I've just found out that one of Emma's daughters, Poppy, has a ventricular septal defect, a hole in her heart. She's going to need surgery.'

He took his phone out of his pocket and looked at the screen.

Ali frowned and said, 'What are you doing?'

'I told you to call me if you needed to download. I'm just seeing if I missed a call from you.'

'I didn't call you.'

'I can see that. Why not?'

'Did you really mean that?'

'Of course. I'm happy to talk. Or to listen. You know this isn't your fault, don't you? Delivering the twins early possibly saved Emma's life and it didn't cause the hole in Poppy's heart. There's nothing you could have done to change this situation.'

'But should I have picked it up earlier?'

'What difference would that have made?'

'It might have given Emma and Aaron time to prepare. It was just such a shock for them.'

Jake didn't know how it worked but he did know that Ali hadn't been Emma's obstetrician initially. 'Was that your job? You weren't Emma's original obstetrician, were you? If no one else picked it up, why is this on you?'

'I feel I let her down.'

'How?' Ali was obviously upset and he wanted to help

her. To cheer her up and reassure her. 'You saved Emma's life. I used to think that was what being a doctor was all about. That's why I wanted to become one. To save lives. Then I realised that doctors do so much more than that. We heal. Create life. Sometimes take one.

'I know most medicos don't think anaesthetists build rapport with our patients in the same way as other doctors do, and that's true for the most part—we breeze in, ask a few questions and then try to keep everyone alive. No relationship but a lot of responsibility. But I've been the anaesthetist for all of Emma's surgeries so I feel like I've got to know her. Or her situation at least. All you can do is your job to the best of your ability. There's a lot of things that can go wrong but things went right yesterday. You did everything right.

'You need to reset yourself,' he continued. 'What do you do when you need to relax? When you want to get away from it all?'

'I run. I read. I catch up with friends and family.' He smiled and she paused. He watched as her eyebrows drew together in a frown. Even when she was glaring at him, she was still stunning. 'What are you smiling at?' she asked.

'Just thinking we have very different ways of resetting,' he said.

'What do you do?'

'I climb things.'

She gave him a half-smile, which was better than a frown. 'What sort of things?'

'Big things.' He was grinning now. 'Rocks, cliffs, waterfalls. Those types of things.'

'That sounds dangerous…' Ali paused '…and not at all relaxing.'

'I didn't say I used it to relax. Just to reset and refocus. You can't think of anything else when you're fifty metres up a cliff face, clinging to a crevice by your fingers and toes. You have to focus. You have to problem-solve. You can't afford to be distracted. Every decision you make, from the route you choose, to where to place your hand, is magnified a hundred times. The smallest mistake, the tiniest hesitation, the littlest lapse of concentration can be disastrous.'

'I guess I can see how clinging to a vertical surface, several metres off the ground, could make you focus.'

'You should try it.'

Ali laughed. Jake was pleased to hear it. 'I think you need to work on your sales pitch if you expect anyone to try it after your description.'

'No, seriously, you should give it a go.'

'Why? Are you trying to kill me?'

'Not at all, but I figured you're the type of person who'd be up for a challenge.'

'Why would you think that?'

'You don't get to be the head of a department, especially at a young age, if you back away from a challenge.'

Ali wondered how old he thought she was, but she wasn't about to ask. He might think fifty was young.

'Here, have a look,' he said as he put his coffee cup down and pulled his phone out of his pocket. He scrolled through his pictures and held the device out to her. He swiped through a few pictures of him in what looked like various life-threatening positions on random cliff faces.

'You're not going to convince me to give it a go with those photos. The whole thing looks terrifying.'

'You wouldn't start with that. There are indoor climbing centres. They're safe, out of the weather, with people to train you. Give me your hands,' he said as he spun back to face her and reached out towards her.

Ali was puzzled but did as he asked. She put her hands in his. They were warm and gentle. He wrapped his fingers around her palms and his touch grounded her. She felt a similar connection when she was barefoot on the land. Grounded, connected to country. Now she was connected to Jake. It was a surprising sensation. A sense that her body already knew him from an earlier time, in an earlier place.

He lifted his hands and extended her arms away from her sides.

'What are you doing?'

'Checking your reach,' he replied. 'It's good.'

'Good for what?'

'Climbing. You're a good build for it. You've got long limbs and a light frame.'

She pulled her hands from his. She felt foolish, standing there holding onto him. 'I've got terrible upper-body strength.'

'You don't pull yourself up with your arms, your legs do the work. You just need a strong grip. There's a good climbing gym not far from here that I use for training. You should try it out.'

'Are you offering to teach me?' As the words left her mouth Ali realised with some mortification that he hadn't meant that at all. She could tell by his expression that hadn't been his intention and her comment had taken him by surprise. 'Sorry, you weren't inviting me to go with you, were you?'

'It's okay, I've been trying to persuade you to give it a go so the least I can do is show you the ropes. I'm going tonight after work. Let me put the address in your phone and if you don't have babies to deliver and can get away you could meet me there,' he said, his words implying, very clearly, that it was up to her whether she went or not. That he wasn't inviting her on a date.

She didn't have plans for tonight and it was unlikely she'd be busy with a patient, but as she unlocked her phone and handed it to him, she thought maybe she could pretend to be held up at work and thereby avoid any awkwardness. But then she thought of Ivy telling her to take some risks, of the girls saying she liked a challenge, of Yarran and Harper finding love again, of Ivy and Lucas's whirlwind romance, and decided maybe it was time she did do something to shake up her life. Perhaps she would try rock climbing. But she didn't necessarily have to go with Jake.

CHAPTER FOUR

HER PLAN HAD been to search the internet for a different gym and to make some other enquiries. But that didn't explain how she found herself at Jake's gym nine hours later.

She'd gone home and grabbed her gym bag and thrown some things into it—with no idea what constituted suitable clothes, she'd assumed running gear would do—even while she had no real intention of climbing. And once she saw the wall she was pretty sure she wouldn't be persuaded to change her mind. Liking a challenge was one thing but this looked as terrifying as she'd imagined. More so.

The climbing walls were high, easily over ten metres and vertical, and the ones that weren't vertical were overhangs. She didn't think she had a fear of heights, she'd been on the hospital roof just today, but now she wasn't so sure.

The walls in the reception area were covered with long lists of rules and she baulked when the guy at the desk handed her a waiver to sign. She was just thinking about walking out when she heard her name.

'Ali. You made it. Are you feeling brave?'

She thought that might possibly be the worst thing he

could have chosen to say. She swallowed, trying to dislodge the lump in her throat. 'I'm having second thoughts, to be honest. I didn't realise the walls would be so high and are those handholds on the ceiling?'

Jake laughed. 'Relax. They're for bouldering. You won't need to tackle those.'

'That's the good news.' She smiled even as she wondered if she was crazy to be here. But the upside of scaling a wall was getting to spend time with Jake and she had to admit she was finding him to be easy company.

But the really good news was that Jake was dressed for climbing. He was wearing shorts and a loose T-shirt, nothing fancy, but enough to reveal that his long legs were lean and muscular and his arms were toned. He looked good. He might be too young for her, definitely not in the demographic she was after, and he might not even be single, but that didn't mean she couldn't admire the view.

'You're here now,' he said. 'You might as well have a go. There are change rooms behind you and I'll meet you in the gym.'

Nothing ventured, nothing gained. He was right. She was here now. She got changed and took a deep breath, steeling herself to enter the gym. She saw Jake halfway across the cavernous space talking to another man.

'Ali, this is my cousin, Will,' he said as she walked up to them. 'Will, this is Ali, one of my colleagues.'

Ali thought Will looked a bit like Jake but when she shook Will's hand she was intrigued to find that, despite the similarity in looks, she didn't get the same sense of knowing Will as she did Jake. There was no sense of connection.

Ali knew this wasn't a date, she knew Jake hadn't

really even meant to invite her, but she was still disappointed to realise she wouldn't have him to herself. 'I'm interrupting,' she said.

'No, not at all,' Will replied.

'Let's get you sorted,' Jake said. 'You picked up some shoes at the desk?'

Ali held up her left hand. 'These things? I don't think I've ever seen shoes quite like these.'

'They help you to grip the handholds.'

'Hang on. I'll be gripping handholds with my feet?'

'It's not as hard as it sounds. Trust me.' Jake winked at her and her belly did a slow roll.

Ali wasn't convinced she should trust him but she was here now and it wasn't in her nature to give up. She sat on the ground to pull the shoes on. 'Okay, what's next?' she said as she stood up.

'You'll need a harness.' Will passed one to Jake and he stepped close, obviously about to attach the harness for her. His proximity made her nervous and she was about to say she could do it when she realised she couldn't. She had no clue where to start.

Jake bent down and spread the harness on the ground. 'Step into it,' he said, before sliding it up her legs after she'd done as he asked. His hands grazed the outside of her bare thighs before he reached the hem of her running shorts. Goosebumps sprang up even though his fingers were warm and her skin felt as if it were on fire. Her knees wobbled and she prayed her legs would support her. She didn't know how she was going to manage to haul herself up a wall—it felt as though all of her strength had deserted her.

He had moved to one side of her now and was talking so she forced herself to concentrate. He'd said rock climbing was all about focus and concentration, so she needed to heed his advice and pay attention.

'Tuck your shorts under the harness,' he told her. 'You don't want it rubbing on your skin.'

Thank God he had left that for her to do, she thought as she pushed the hem of her shorts under the harness straps at the top of her legs. She didn't think she could handle his hands touching the tops of her thighs. Next time she'd wear leggings, not shorts. Although depending on how tonight went there might not be a next time.

She held her breath as he reached his arms around her to clip the harness closed before tightening the straps.

'Last things, carabiners and a chalk bag.' He knelt down and clipped a carabiner onto her harness. 'That's for the safety rope,' he said, before attaching a soft bag filled with chalk dust. 'This helps with your grip if your hands get a bit sweaty. You probably won't need it, but I'll strap it on just in case. Okay, that's it. You're good to go.'

'I feel like a Christmas turkey. Trussed up and about to meet my maker.'

'I've been doing this for years. I won't let anything happen to you,' he said.

And she believed him.

'You're going to show me what to do first, right?' she asked.

Jake nodded. 'I'll send Will up the wall to demonstrate. That way I can talk you through what he's doing. It's not hard, I promise.'

She raised one eyebrow but kept quiet as Will clipped himself onto a rope and handed the end to Jake, who threaded it through his own harness.

'My job is to belay him.'

'To what?'

'Belay. It means I'm managing the rope for the climber. If he falls, I have to apply tension to counteract the fall. It's a safety mechanism. On belay!' he called out.

'Climbing,' Will responded.

'Climb on,' Jake said. He looked briefly at Ali, so she knew he was addressing her, before turning his attention back to his cousin. 'There's a lot of terminology in climbing, a lot of it for safety reasons, but it's not that important in an indoor setting. Outdoor climbing is more difficult because of the conditions. There are more things to watch out for—wind, falling rocks—and it's harder to hear.'

Ali watched in amazement as Will scaled the wall. He didn't race up but moved slowly and smoothly, his movements considered, and she could tell he was thinking about where to place his hands and feet.

'It looks more graceful than I imagined.'

'It's like doing ballet on a wall,' Jake agreed.

It wasn't the first time she'd seen rock climbing, but it was the first time she'd seen it in real life. It was also the first time she could get a real perspective of the height of the wall and the distance between the handholds. 'It also looks much more difficult.'

'Will is taking an intermediate route.' Jake spoke to her without taking his eyes off his cousin.

'That looks hard to me.'

'Don't worry. The routes are colour-coded according to difficulty. You'll start on an easy route. For example, look at the yellow holds on the adjacent wall, see how close together they are, and evenly spaced, almost like a ladder? That's a "very easy" route. The blue handholds on that wall are graded "easy". See how he's keeping his arms straight? Straight arms conserve energy. He's pushing himself up the wall with his legs. Watch how he keeps one hip close to the wall—that works with your centre of gravity, keeps your weight over your feet and brings your shoulder close to the wall, makes it harder to fall off and easier to grip.'

'Can I start on "very easy"?' she asked.

'I thought you liked a challenge,' he said as Will reached the top of the wall and Jake was able to take a moment to look at Ali.

'We'll see,' she replied with a smile. She wanted to appear confident. She wanted to impress Jake. Wanted him to think she was assured and capable. All around her people of all shapes and sizes were scaling the walls. Children, teenagers, people older than her. She'd put aside her reservations, she decided. What was the worst that could happen?

'Ready to lower,' Will called down.

'Lowering.'

Jake let out a short length of rope as Will sat back in his harness and started to walk down the wall.

'Are you ready to give it a go?' Jake asked once Will was back on the ground and had unclipped the rope.

Ali took a deep breath and exhaled slowly before nodding.

'Come over to this wall,' Jake directed. He threaded a rope through her harness as she stood at the base of the wall. 'This type of climb is called top roping, where the rope is attached at the top of the wall and you work with your belayer. That's me.' He grinned. 'Try the blue route. I promise it's not that difficult. The first thing you need to do is take a look at the route, plan your first ten grabs. That way you're less likely to get yourself tied up in knots. We're trying to move smoothly, to conserve energy, so you can make it to the top. You don't want to look like you're playing a game of Twister.'

'Aren't you supposed to be telling me this is easy, not telling me I'm likely to get tied up in knots?'

'You'll be fine. Women generally make good climbers. They use their brains and they seem to be able to do two things at once—climb and think a couple of steps ahead to avoid precarious situations. Men rely more on their brawn. They know that if they get themselves into a tricky spot their strength will usually get them out. Women tend to prefer to avoid getting themselves into those situations in the first place.'

'That sounds sensible.'

'If anything goes wrong, if you get stuck and can't reach a handhold, just let go of the wall.'

'What? You want me to let go of the wall? Are you crazy?'

'I'll be controlling you. I can lower you down. There's nothing to worry about.'

'Hmph.' But she was smiling, she was almost excited now to give it a go.

'On belay!' Jake called out. 'Now you say "climbing", I say "climb on" and off you go.'

Ali stepped closer to the wall but looked over her shoulder at Jake before reaching up for the first handhold.

'Remember straight arms and keep your hip close.'

As she made her way up the first couple of feet she could hear Jake below her, suggesting which handhold to use as he controlled the rope. As she climbed higher, she was conscious of the view he had, looking straight up at her.

But she couldn't think about that. She had to concentrate. If she had to problem-solve, if she had to choose the handholds for herself, she didn't have time to worry about what Jake might be thinking as he looked up at her.

She blocked out Jake's voice and decided to make her own decisions.

She saw a handhold to her right and reached for it before figuring out it was both further than she thought and green. She should be looking for a blue handhold.

Her hip rotated away from the wall and she found herself swinging out into nothing as her right foot slipped. Her centre of gravity shifted and then her left foot slipped.

She was falling!

Her heart was in her mouth but before she could call out, she jerked to a stop.

Jake had stopped her fall. He'd said to trust him, he'd told her he'd keep her safe and he'd kept his word.

He lowered her to the ground. 'Are you okay?' he asked as her feet hit the matting on the floor.

'Yes.' She was breathing heavily and her heart was racing but she was okay. She'd only been a few feet off the ground and the floor was covered in thick foam matting—she doubted she would have done any damage, in any case, even if Jake hadn't been so quick to respond.

'Did you want to try again?' he asked.

'Definitely.' The adrenaline racing through her body made her ready for another challenge and she'd always been competitive. Growing up with a twin brother and a mother who had been a professional athlete, she'd always felt as though she had something to prove. Add being an

Indigenous female into the mix and that only made her more determined to prove something to herself and to Jake. She was not going to give up at the first fall.

She glanced over to her left where several teenagers were scaling an adjacent wall. She wasn't going to let them show her up. She wanted to prove that a forty-year-old woman could do this.

She looked at Jake and waited for his instruction.

'On belay.'

'Climbing.'

She tried again, making sure to use only blue grips this time, and made it to the top of the wall.

'Well done,' Jake called up to her. 'Now you just have to get down.'

She looked back over her shoulder, at Jake. He looked a long way down. Right, she hadn't really thought this through.

'Sit back in the harness,' Jake told her, 'like you're sitting into a chair.'

She was nervous.

'I've got you,' he called up to her. 'You've got to trust me.' Trust was something she had difficulty with, but she realised she would have to do as he said if this wasn't going to go pear-shaped.

'Did I mention I have trust issues?'

'I've caught you once already,' Jake said. 'I'm not going to let anything happen to you. Sit back. Good! Now straighten your legs, keep your feet level with your hips. Remember how Will did it. Bend one knee a little and push off the wall with that foot, take a step down and repeat on the other side. I'll let the rope out, you just walk backwards down the wall.'

Jake talked her back down the wall. By the time her feet hit the ground she was smiling from ear to ear.

'I made it.' She was buzzing. She looked up at the wall. 'I can't believe I just climbed that.'

'You did great. I told you you'd be good at it.' He was grinning too, looking pleased with her effort, and Ali's heart skipped a beat. 'Did you think about work?'

'Are you kidding? Not at all,' she said as Jake began to unclip her harness. The harness dropped to the floor and she bent down to pick it up. 'Thank you, I enjoyed that. I wasn't sure that I would.' She'd surprised herself. She enjoyed the sense of achievement, but it was Jake's company that had made it a far better experience than it might otherwise have been.

'Let me take that,' Will offered, reaching for her harness. 'We're going to grab a quick bite to eat in Chinatown, why don't you join us?' he invited.

'I don't want to intrude,' she replied. She couldn't remember the last time she went out with new people. She spent time with her girlfriends and her family but avoided most other social interactions; her confidence had taken a hit when her marriage ended.

'You're not intruding. My partner Chris is meeting us and it would be nice to have extra company.'

Ali looked at Jake, wondering how he felt about his cousin's invitation. 'You're welcome to join us,' he said.

'Okay, thank you, that sounds good.' She wasn't ready for the night to end just yet. It was the most fun she'd had in a while.

Will and his partner, Chris, were good company. Jake was a little quiet and Ali worried that perhaps she shouldn't have joined them but maybe this was their usual dynamic.

Tall and well-groomed, Chris was certainly outgoing and chatty. He was also very well dressed, albeit with an edgy style, and Ali wasn't surprised to find he worked in theatre, specifically set design.

'Do you work in theatre as well, Will? Is that how you met?'

'We met through mutual friends. I'm an architect.'

'Commercial or residential?'

'Residential. The Sydney market keeps me busy.'

'And do you climb, Chris?' Ali asked, wondering why he hadn't joined them at the gym. She thought perhaps he'd been working.

'Honey, please.' Chris laughed. 'Have you seen the outfits? Those shoes! If I'm going to work up a sweat exercising, I am *not* going to do it in something so unfashionable.'

Ali would normally be offended if someone called her 'honey', but it was obviously just a figure of speech for Chris and delivered so dramatically she couldn't help but smile.

'Not to mention uncomfortable,' Chris continued. 'I prefer to get my exercise on the dance floor or in the bedroom.'

'Chris, that's a little too much information,' Will cautioned but Ali laughed.

'It's been ages since I went dancing.' And ages since her bedroom had seen any activity too, but that would definitely be too much information!

Dancing was an activity that cleared her mind—she hadn't thought of that when Jake had asked her the question. The last time she'd danced had been when she'd cleaned her apartment. She played music to pass the time but now that she lived in an apartment on her own it didn't take long to clean. It was minimalist and she didn't make much mess. She spent most of her time at work or at one of her siblings' houses. Her life wasn't at all exciting.

'You should take Ali dancing, Jake,' Will suggested.

'I don't dance,' he replied.

'I'll be your dance partner,' Chris offered.

'Thank you. I might take you up on that,' Ali said, 'once I recover from tonight's activities. My legs are starting to feel a little stiff.' She stretched her legs under the table, feeling the tightness in her calves. It had been fun, but Jake still seemed a little tense, maybe it was time to call it a night. 'Thanks for inviting me but I think I should head home and get in the shower if I'm going to be able to move tomorrow.'

She'd enjoyed the evening—it had been lovely not to talk about her work, her nieces and nephews, pregnancies, babies and her lack thereof.

'I'll walk you to your car,' Jake offered, leaving Ali slightly disappointed that he didn't try to talk her into staying longer.

'Thank you for tonight,' she said once they were alone. 'I needed that.' She knew Jake hadn't intended to invite her along, and she'd ended up spending the whole evening with him, but she was grateful as she'd enjoyed herself more than she had in a long time.

'Which part?'

'All of it. The climbing. The conversation. The company. A chance to get away from work. It was fun. I enjoyed it.'

'You're welcome any time. You can also go to the gym on your own if you want to. There will always be someone to belay you.'

'I'm not sure if I'll do it again but I appreciate you letting me join you tonight.' She knew there was no point getting caught up with Jake. And there was no point in going climbing again without him.

She had to admit she was attracted to him, and he was her type with one exception—he was too young. Her next partner would be older, past the age of wanting a family. She didn't want to get her heart trampled on again. She didn't want false promises, didn't want to be dumped for someone younger, someone of child-bearing age. The next time she dated someone *she* would be the younger woman.

'This is me.' She had her car keys in her hand and pushed the button on the fob to unlock the door.

Jake opened the driver's door for her and she stopped to thank him again before she got in. They were standing close together, him holding the door, and her pressed against the side of the car. If she wanted to, she could lean forward and kiss his cheek. His mouth.

She wondered what it would be like to kiss him. Maybe they could swap climbing for sex? That was an offer she knew she'd take up. She didn't need to date him for that. Maybe that was an option to consider.

CHAPTER FIVE

ALI HAD JUST left Emma's room after another follow-up check and had bumped into Ivy in the corridor on her way to see Emma. It seemed there were a lot of staff at the Central invested in Emma and her babies. As they chatted outside the NICU Ali saw Jake walking towards them. She could feel a blush staining her cheeks and hoped no one would notice.

'Jake,' Ivy said when she spotted him. 'What are you doing up here?'

'I'm looking for Aaron. Is he up here?'

Ali nodded as she willed her blush to fade. 'He's in with Emma,' she said.

'How is Emma going? And the twins?'

'They're okay,' Ali replied. 'Emma is able to hold Jasmine and also have a little bit of contact with Poppy. She's still on oxygen but stable.'

'I'm glad we bumped into you, Jake,' Ivy said. 'I've been meaning to email you. Lucas and I are having a few people over tomorrow night for drinks to celebrate our engagement. We'd love you to join us if you're free? You're welcome to bring a date too, although there'll be plenty of people you know. Plenty of colleagues. Ali is coming.'

'Are you bringing a date?' He turned back to Ali.

Strangely, she sensed that her answer to his question would determine whether he accepted Ivy's invitation or not.

She was nervous but she couldn't lie. 'No.'

A wide smile broke across Jake's handsome face and Ali felt as though a thousand butterflies had been released inside her belly.

'It sounds fun, thanks, Ivy. This is my first full weekend off since I started here. I'd love to come.'

'Good. All sorted. I'll email you the address.'

'OMG, I can't believe you just did that,' Ali said as Jake headed down the corridor to Emma's room.

'Did what?' Ivy said with an innocent tone, which was contradicted by a cheeky grin.

'You know exactly what. Inviting Jake to your drinks.' Ali knew Ivy had done it on her behalf and although she tried to be affronted, in reality all she felt was excitement tinged with a little nervousness. Had she and Jake just crossed a line? Committed to something unspoken? She felt ridiculous—forty years old and her hormones were running rampant.

Ivy laughed. 'You should be saying thank you. One of us might as well get to enjoy his company. I can tell you like him and you weren't going to invite him.'

'I can find my own dates.'

'I'm not saying you can't, but you said you weren't bringing one tomorrow night. I'm not making you turn up together and what happens next is completely up to you. I'm just putting the pieces in place. So, you're welcome.'

Ali and Phoebe arrived together at Lucas's apartment. Ivy's dress code had said 'Cocktail' and Ali was pleased she had a reason to make an effort. She wouldn't mind a bit of attention and it was nice to be able to swap her scrubs and gym gear for a pretty dress. Who knew who she might meet tonight? She pretended she hadn't chosen her outfit with Jake in mind, but that didn't stop her nerves from kicking in as the lift took her and Phoebe closer to the top floor. Would he already be there?

The lift had mirrored walls and she checked her reflection one final time before reaching her destination. Ivy had discussed in great detail how fancy Lucas's apartment was and Ali suspected the 'little drinks' could be an extravagant affair and had dressed accordingly. She wore a navy trench coat, to combat the winter evening chill, over a gold sequin shift dress that skimmed her slim figure and complemented her skin tone. She'd pulled her dark hair away from her face to show off her gold drop earrings. The only other jewellery she wore was a charm bracelet that had belonged to her gran.

The lift doors opened and Ali and Phoebe found themselves in Lucas's penthouse apartment. The apartment was stunning and Ali squeezed her jaw tight, afraid her mouth was going to gape open in wonder. She looked around, taking it all in—the large marble kitchen island under a statement pendant light, original artworks and the monochromatic colour scheme. Despite the colour scheme the apartment wasn't cold or austere, it felt inviting and comfortable. Soft couches, thick rugs and plenty of lamps were positioned around the room, giving the space an elegant ambiance.

The apartment was expansive and she couldn't help but think her entire apartment would fit into Lucas's kitchen and living area. She had been happy with the purchase of her own two-bedroom apartment, which she'd bought following her divorce. It was newly constructed, the right size for her—she didn't want to rattle around in something when she lived alone—and she'd enjoyed decorating it with new pieces of furniture mixed in with things she'd inherited that held special meaning. It had been a purchase she'd been proud of, one she'd handled on her own from finding the apartment to making the offer, arranging finance and moving in. After her divorce it had felt like a major achievement and she'd felt as if it had been a big step forward into her new life, but it could only be described as modest, especially compared to Lucas's.

Lucas's apartment was beautifully decorated, understated and tasteful and there was no hiding the fact that it must have been expensive. Not just the decor—the view alone was worth millions. Large sliding glass doors on the far side of the room had been opened to allow access to the generous balcony and, framed through the doorway, Ali could see the iconic Sydney view of the Harbour Bridge and the Opera House. It was incredible.

A DJ was set up towards one end of the room where the indoors merged with the outdoors and two bartenders had commandeered the kitchen island and were mixing cocktails and pouring champagne.

She didn't think she and Phoebe were late, although it had taken her longer than usual to get ready, but the apartment was already heaving with people. The majority of guests seemed to be hospital staff, which was not surprising, she thought, as Ivy came to welcome them.

Ali smiled; the party might have been Lucas's idea but Ivy had obviously run with it. She was the most sociable of the four girlfriends and she'd clearly invited everyone she could think of or had bumped into at the hospital. Including Jake.

The moment she thought of him was the moment the crowd shifted, as if sensing where her thoughts were headed. The guests parted, leaving her looking directly at Jake. He was talking to one of their colleagues but his eyes were on Ali.

A member of the wait staff offered to hang her coat up for her, distracting her momentarily, but she kept her eyes on Jake as she slipped it from her shoulders to reveal the gold sequin column dress she wore underneath. She saw Jake smile and hoped he appreciated her outfit, finally admitting to herself that she'd worn it with the hope it would catch his attention. She wanted to make a statement. Wearing scrubs or exercise gear might be practical but she wanted him to see what she could look like with a little bit of effort. She might be forty but she didn't want to be invisible.

He was still smiling as he started to cross the room. He came straight to her, not even pretending to stop and chat to anyone else as he made his way through the crowd. She was flattered. This was what she'd wanted although she hadn't been brave enough to admit it to herself until now.

She waited for him to reach her side, confident that her side was exactly where he was headed. His eyes hadn't left hers. She knew she was his destination.

Jake swiped two glasses of champagne from the tray of a roving wait staff as he passed by, handing one to her when he reached her side. Her pulse leapt as his fingers grazed hers and she was relieved that she didn't slosh champagne out of the glass as her hand trembled.

'Hello,' he greeted her. 'You look amazing.' There was

no hesitation on his part, he obviously had no concerns about what to say and his comment gave her confidence.

She smiled, emboldened by the knowledge that she wasn't invisible. 'Thank you,' she replied as she decided she would be brave tonight. She would take a risk. Take an opportunity to get to know him better if the opportunity was presented to her and, looking at his expression, she suspected she might get that chance. His gaze was dark, intense and direct as he ran his eyes over her and Ali was grateful for the dim lighting as she felt her cheeks darken in response to his observation.

'Girls' night out?' he asked.

'Pardon?'

'I saw you and Phoebe arrive together. You didn't change your mind and bring a date?'

Belatedly she remembered she'd arrived with Phoebe, who was now nowhere to be seen. Both she and Ivy had completely disappeared. When had that happened?

'No date. No partner, no husband and no boyfriend,' she said, wanting to let him know she was single without actually saying the word. She wanted him to know she was available but didn't want to appear desperate. She *wasn't* desperate, she reminded herself. She was just a woman who hadn't had sex in a long time. Perhaps that was all about to change.

She sipped her champagne as she took Jake in. He was dressed all in black—his jeans, collared shirt and jacket were all black. His outfit made him look even taller and leaner than usual. She was wearing heels but he was still a couple of inches taller than her, but not too tall that she couldn't see into his eyes, not too tall that she couldn't watch his perfect lips move as he spoke to her.

He might appreciate her outfit but she also appreciated his. He looked sensational. The other male guests were all in suits and ties and she wondered if he was deliberately not conforming. 'You didn't get the dress code?' She smiled.

'A jacket is as close as I get to cocktail attire,' he said, making it clear he obviously did get the memo but had chosen to ignore it. 'I don't do ties.'

But rather than looking out of place he stood out for all the right reasons. His individual look ticked all of her boxes. 'It's been a while since I've seen anyone dressed all in black—it's a very Melbournian look,' she said. In contrast to the city of Melbourne, Sydney weather, even in winter, was often too warm and sunny to embrace the dark colours of a traditional winter wardrobe. Sydney-siders would wear black but lighten the look with a shirt or scarf, tie or bag in a contrasting colour.

'I've just moved back here from Melbourne,' he said.

'You're from Sydney originally?' she asked as they slowly moved further into the apartment. They were surrounded by other guests now, but none of them were close acquaintances of Ali's and she felt as if she and Jake were existing in their own space.

'Yes. I'm still getting used to being back but it sounds like I need to update my wardrobe.'

'I'm not complaining,' she replied with a smile. He looked hot, there'd be no complaints from her. 'I was born here, I'm a proud Garigal woman,' she said, naming her mob. 'Black is my favourite colour.'

'Clever,' Jake replied with a smile that made Ali's insides melt. 'And I'm glad you approve.'

Oh, she definitely approved.

She was intrigued as to what had brought him back to Sydney but they were interrupted before she could ask the question.

'Hey, sis.'

Ali turned her head to find Yarran and Harper standing beside her. She saw Jake look from her to Yarran and then back as Yarran kissed her cheek.

Harper hugged Ali in greeting and Ali hugged her back, trying to ignore the slight awkwardness she still felt. She hoped that one day she wouldn't tense up remembering how things used to be between them. She hoped one day she wouldn't have these moments of hesitation around Harper.

'Hi, Jake,' Harper said as she released Ali and stepped back, reaching for Yarran's left hand. 'I don't think you've met Yarran. My fiancé and Ali's brother.'

'Your twin brother?' Jake asked Ali.

Ali nodded. Jake had asked about her siblings when they'd had dinner in Chinatown and she was pleased he'd remembered she was a twin.

'Yarran is a firefighter,' Harper continued. 'He's the one who rescued Emma Wilson.'

As Head of the ED Harper also saved lives for a living but Ali was pleased to hear the note of pride in Harper's voice as she introduced Yarran to Jake.

'It wasn't only me,' Yarran commented.

Harper looked at him adoringly, as if he was the ultimate hero, and it made Ali feel better to see how much Harper clearly loved him. 'But you were the one who carried her out of the fire,' Harper said. 'Jake is an anaesthetist at the Central; he's looked after Emma too.'

'Jake Ryan,' Jake said as he shook Yarran's hand. 'It's good to meet you.'

'Jake Ryan? Why is your name familiar?'

'It's a fairly common name.'

'No. I've seen it somewhere recently.' Yarran frowned in concentration.

'Jake is organising the fundraiser at Circular Quay,' Harper said. 'The one your station is taking part in.'

'The abseiling challenge?'

Jake and Harper nodded in unison.

'What fundraiser?' Ali asked. She had no idea what they were talking about.

'It's a charity fundraiser for childhood cancer,' Jake replied.

Ali wondered why she didn't know about it if Yarran and Harper did. Had Harper deliberately not told her? Was she keeping Ali at arm's length, focusing on Yarran? Ali reminded herself that all she wanted for Yarran was happiness. Did it matter if her relationship with Harper didn't ever quite get back to what it was as long as Yarran was okay?

'Are you running it?' she asked Jake.

'No. But I'm on the committee and each year there are several fundraising events. I suggested this one so I'm one of the contact people, but the actual running of the event is outsourced. The company responsible has run something similar in Townsville, although it wasn't a fundraiser, it was an attempt to break a world record.'

'For what?'

'The largest number of abseilers in a twelve-hour period.'

'How many people was that?'

'Over thirteen hundred.'

'Wow! How did they find that many abseilers?'

'The majority of those participants had never abseiled before, so prior to the event they weren't abseilers, just participants. I'm hoping we can break the record again as it makes for good publicity. We're aiming for fourteen hundred people.'

'And how does the fundraising work?'

'People pay to enter and then we also ask them to get sponsors.'

'Are you doing it?' Ali asked Yarran.

'I am. There are a heap of emergency service personnel taking part,' Yarran replied. 'Don't worry, I'll be coming to you for sponsorship.'

'Oh, the DJ is paying our song,' Harper said as she took Yarran's hand. 'Come and dance with me.'

'Good to meet you, Jake,' Yarran said as he let Harper pull him away.

Ali turned her attention to Jake, curious to hear more about this charity event that everyone but her seemed aware of. 'How did you get involved with this charity?'

'Come and sit outside with me and I'll tell you. We should make the most of this view if it's not too cold.'

They stepped out onto Lucas's balcony. The night was clear, the air was cool but there was no breeze. They gravitated towards a small outdoor sofa and some chairs that were grouped around an ethanol firepit. The sofa faced the Harbour Bridge and had the added benefit of seating two people. Ali chose the sofa.

'Are you okay out here? Will you be warm enough?' Jake asked as he sat beside her.

She could feel the warmth of the fire and the heat coming off Jake's body, but it was still cool. Her dress was a sleeveless sheath, there wasn't much of it, and it offered little protection against the evening air. 'I probably should have grabbed my coat,' she said.

'Here. Take mine.'

She started to protest but Jake had already shrugged out of his jacket and was draping it around her shoulders. It was warm from his body heat and she stopped objecting as the fabric wrapped around her. 'Thank you, that's much better. Now, tell me more about this charity and what you do.'

'I got involved with the charity because I wanted to give back. Not just financially, I wanted to make a difference with my time and experience. And not only my experience or skills in medicine. This is personal for me. I had cancer as a child—I know what it's like.'

'You did?' A thousand questions swarmed through her mind—when, what, how serious was it and how was he now? 'How old were you?' she asked first.

'Four. I was diagnosed with a Wilm's tumour. Stage two.' Ali frowned. She knew Wilm's tumours were rare. 'The doctors removed one of my kidneys,' Jake continued, 'and I had chemo for twelve months.'

Ali put one hand on her chest and took a deep breath. 'That sounds traumatic.' She could only imagine how she would feel if one of her nieces or nephews had received a similar diagnosis.

'Kids are tough. Resilient. And it wasn't all bad,' he said with a smile. 'I survived. And my experience led me to a career in medicine. This is my way of giving something back. This was a way for me to be involved in something that resonates with me. A chance to make a difference. I feel I have something to contribute to the charity, but I really enjoy getting involved with the events that involve the children. I know what the kids are going through.'

'Are there kids doing the abseiling?'

'Over sixteens can sign up. This is an activity that is fun and doesn't take a lot of energy. Just a bit of courage and the kids have plenty of that. My experience with cancer is kind of how I got into climbing in the first place. My parents were advised to steer me away from contact sports as a child—things like rugby, soccer and football were deemed too risky with one kidney—so instead I swam, played tennis and was eventually introduced to climbing.'

'You're okay now?'

'For the time being. The survival rate is good but there may be related health issues later in life.' He shrugged. 'Life is short. I want to experience it all. I've been given a second chance. I intend to make the most of it.'

'So, your cancer experience introduced you to climbing *and* led you to medicine?'

He nodded.

'You weren't sick of hospitals?'

'No. Doctors and hospitals saved my life. I was good at science, so I thought I'd like to do the same—save lives.'

'So that's why you chose anaesthesiology?'

'I figured what better way to save someone's life than to be responsible for it? To literally hold someone's life in my hands, to anaesthetise them and be the one to make sure they come through the other side. I didn't realise until I was older that doctors do a lot more than save lives. They can help to create it, can mend lives and sometimes as an anaesthetist I've even had to take it away, but I like to think I make a difference. It's a big responsibility and I love it but there might have been a little bit of a selfish element to the speciality I chose.'

'What's that?'

'I don't have to sacrifice my whole life. It leaves time for other pursuits. It leaves time for me to live my life. It's important to me to make the most of my second chance at life. But now, I want to hear about you. You and Ivy are good friends?'

'Yes, Ivy and I met at uni. We studied with Harper and Phoebe.'

'All four of you? Together?' Ali nodded. 'Did you introduce Yarran and Harper?'

'Yes.'

'Has that caused some issues between you and Harper?'

'Why do you say that?'

'You seemed a little tense with her. Different from how you are around Ivy and from how you seemed tonight when you arrived with Phoebe.'

'You noticed that?' Ali frowned.

'I've noticed a lot of things about you.'

He was watching her intently and she felt a warmth flow through her veins. She was sitting close enough to him to see the gold flecks in his eyes, shimmering in the glow of the fire. She felt herself leaning towards him, ever so slightly, almost unconsciously. She was aware of others on the balcony, but they were hazy, blurred. Jake was the only person who seemed to be in sharp focus. She could feel him drawing her energy. Drawing her towards him.

But before she embarrassed herself, before she ended up glued to his side, she remembered her experience with Adam.

Her experience with her ex had taught her she needed to practise caution. Adam had been smart, successful and attractive and he'd pursued her. She'd succumbed to him, fallen for his flattery. He'd made her feel validated—as a young, Indigenous woman it was something she'd craved at the time—but she should have been more cautious. She could be hot-headed and impetuous, but she needed to learn from her past mistakes.

She straightened up, putting some distance between them before she did something she might regret. Maybe their chemistry would prove too powerful to resist but now wasn't the time to find out.

'Yarran and Harper's story is a long one, but the abbreviated version is that I introduced Harper to Yarran and then she broke his heart.'

'They seem pretty happy though.'

'They are now. They've resolved their problems and are back together, but I felt like an idiot.'

'Why was that?'

'Harper was like a sister to me and when she broke Yarran's heart and ran off, she never said a word to me. Didn't say goodbye, just left, and I felt as if she'd dumped me too. As if our friendship meant nothing.'

'I take it that when you told me you had trust issues you weren't joking?'

'No, I wasn't. Not only because of Harper—my ex also did a number on me. I've forgiven Harper because I can see how happy Yarran is, but forgetting is proving to be a little harder and Harper and I are not as close as we used to be.'

She shivered as a chill ran down her spine. Despite Jake's jacket she was beginning to feel the cold as the temperature dropped.

'Would you like to go back inside?'

'Not really. I'm enjoying it out here.' She glanced at Jake's watch. It was later than she thought. They'd been sitting on the balcony for quite a while, ignoring everyone else at the party, she'd been lost in his company. 'But it's getting late. I should go home. I've had a hectic week.'

'Would you like a lift?'

'You drove?'

He nodded. 'I'm not a big drinker. I've got to take care of the one kidney I have. I don't want to make it work too hard.'

She wasn't a big drinker either. Years of being called out at any time of night to deliver babies meant she'd got into the habit of being careful. 'I'd love a lift,' she said as she gave him back his jacket. 'I'll get my coat and say goodbye to Ivy. I'll meet you at the lift?' She wasn't ready for anyone to see them leaving together. The hospital gossip mill would be running rife and she could do without that.

Jake was waiting for her with a smile on his face and she felt a thrill of anticipation as the lift chimed, announcing its arrival. He stretched his arm out, making sure the lift doors stayed open, letting Ali step in first. She draped her coat over one arm and pressed the button for the ground floor as he stepped in beside her. She brushed an errant strand of hair out of her eyes as she turned to face him and felt a tug on her ear as she tried to lower her hand.

'Hold on. Let me help you. You've got your bracelet tangled up with your earring,' Jake said. He stepped in closer, closing the distance between them. It hadn't been huge to begin with and she was pressed between Jake and the mirrored wall of the lift. He gently worked the charm bracelet free of her earring but didn't step back as the lift continued its descent. He was watching her with his dark eyes. Unblinking. Asking her a silent question.

Ali reached for him. Holding onto his jacket, she pulled him closer. She forgot about being cautious as she answered his question with her body.

He lifted her hand from his chest and kissed her fingers, slowly, deliberately, one by one, drawing out the moment of intimacy. Their faces were inches apart. He was watching her, studying her and then he moved another fraction closer, his head tipped slightly to one side. She tilted her face up to him and watched as he dipped his head, closing the gap between them. Only then did she close her eyes, waiting for the caress she was sure was coming.

Jake's lips brushed over hers, the gentlest of touches, so soft she wondered if it was nothing more than her imagination.

His mouth met hers again. His touch was firmer this time, more definite. Her lips parted and she tasted him. He tasted of champagne, bubbles and sunshine. She heard herself moan as his tongue explored her mouth. The outside world receded; it was condensed into this one spot, this one man.

Her heart raced in her chest and she could feel every

beat as Jake's lips covered hers. She closed her eyes, succumbing to his touch. His hand was on her bare arm, setting her skin on fire. She melted against him as her body responded to him. She was aware of nothing else except the sensation of being fully alive. She wanted for nothing except Jake.

She felt his hand move to her back. Her skin was bare between the straps of her dress, her shoulder blades exposed, and her flesh ached under his fingers. She felt her nipples harden as all of her senses came to life and a line of fire spread from her stomach to her groin. She deepened the kiss, losing herself in Jake before she remembered where they were.

Kissing in a public lift. Anyone could step in at any moment.

She pushed her hand against his chest, forcing him back, breaking the kiss.

'I shouldn't have done that,' Jake apologised.

Her heart was racing in her chest and her breaths were shallow. She could hear herself panting. 'It's okay. I wanted you to. I've wanted to know how that felt for a week. But not here.'

He took her hand as they exited the lift, holding it until they reached his car. He opened her door and she directed him to her apartment block and then to a visitor's park outside her building. 'Would you like to come up?' she asked.

'Are you sure?' he replied. They both knew where this was headed if he came inside with her.

Ali nodded. 'I'm forty years old. Divorced. No kids. I'm old enough to know what I'm doing.'

'I'm almost forty, divorced, no kids.' He grinned. 'I have no objections as long as you're sure.'

Alarm bells should have been ringing. He was not the demographic she'd told herself she wanted but the other voice in her head said—did it matter how old he was if it was just sex?

She decided to ignore the warnings. She was a grown-up. It didn't need to become a relationship.

Somehow they made it to her apartment without tearing each other's clothes off. She swiped her card and unlocked her door. He was right behind her, so close she could feel the heat radiating from him. She turned to face him and he claimed her lips with his mouth, kissing her swiftly and soundly.

His lips were soft but they weren't gentle. The kiss was hungry, intense and passionate. Ali had no time to think and Jake wasn't asking for permission. Not this time. He wasn't asking for anything. He was demanding a response. And Ali gave him one.

She kissed him back, unreservedly. Her hormones took control as blood rushed to her abdomen, flooding her groin and turning her legs to jelly. She knew she would have collapsed to the ground if she hadn't been in his embrace.

His hands were on her hips, holding her to him. Her hands were behind his head, keeping him with her. She walked backwards and he followed. His lips were on hers, his hands on her body, as she led him to her room. She didn't bother offering him something to drink or a tour of the apartment. Neither of them was pretending this was about anything more than desire, lust and longing.

She slid his jacket from his shoulders and then ran her hands under his shirt, trailing her fingernails lightly over his skin, and heard him moan. She grabbed the bottom of his shirt and pulled it over his head, exposing his flat, toned stomach. She dropped his shirt on the floor inside her bedroom door but as he started to undo his belt Ali stopped him.

'Let me,' she said. She undid his belt and snapped open the button on his jeans before sliding the zip down. She could feel the hard bulge of his erection pressing into her, straining to get free.

Jake stepped out of his shoes, not bothering to untie the laces, as she pushed his trousers to the floor. His jeans joined his shoes and shirt in an untidy heap. He was naked except for his underwear. Ali looked him over.

He was glorious. And he knew it.

He grinned at her and raised one eyebrow. In reply she put one hand on his smooth, broad chest and pushed him backwards until the bed bumped the backs of his knees and made him sit.

She stepped back from the bed. Out of his reach. He could watch but he couldn't touch. She wanted to tease him. She reached for the zip at the side of her dress and undid it slowly. She slipped one strap from her shoulder and then the other and let the dress fall to the floor. Jake's eyes were dark now, all traces of the gold flecks had vanished as he watched and waited for her.

She wasn't wearing a bra and she heard his short, sharp intake of breath as her dress dropped to the floor and she stood before him. She lifted her hands to remove her earrings but Jake held up a hand.

'Leave them in,' he said. 'You look sensational.'

CHAPTER SIX

JAKE'S VOICE WAS husky with desire. Lust coated his words, making them so heavy they barely made it past his lips.

Ali dropped her hands, leaving her earrings hanging from her lobes. She slid her underwear from her hips and went to him. She was completely naked but she didn't feel exposed. She felt powerful.

She stood before him and he reached for her, pulling her towards him, spinning her around and laying her on the bed. His thumb rested on her jaw. It was warm and soft, his pressure gentle. He ran his thumb along the line of her jaw and then his thumb was replaced by his lips. He kissed her neck, her collarbone and the hollow at the base of her throat where her collarbones met.

His fingers blazed a trail across her body that his mouth followed. Down from her throat to her sternum, over her breast to her nipple. His fingers flicked over the nipple, already peaked and hard. His mouth followed, covering it, sucking, licking and tasting. She reached for his underwear and pulled it from his body. His erection sprang free, pressing against her stomach.

His fingers were stroking the inside of her thigh. She parted her legs as his fingers slid inside her. His thumb rolled over her most sensitive spot, making her gasp. He kissed her breast, sucking at her nipple as his thumb teased her. She arched her back, pushing her hips and breasts towards him, wanting more, letting him take her to a peak of desire.

Still she wanted more. She needed more.

She rolled towards him and pushed him flat onto his back. She sat up and straddled his hips. His erection rose between them, trapped between their groins. Ali stretched across him, reaching for her bedside drawer, searching for a condom. Jake sat up and took her breast into his mouth once more. She closed her eyes as she gave herself up to the sensations shooting through her as his tongue flicked over her nipple. Every part of her responded to his touch. Her body came alive under his fingers and his lips and her skin burned where their bodies met.

She felt for the condom, finding it with her fingers. She picked it up and lifted herself clear of Jake, pulling her breast from his lips. Air flowed over her nipple, the cool temperature contrasting with the heat of his mouth. She opened the condom and rolled it onto him. Her fingers encircled his shaft as she smoothed out the sheath.

She put her hands either side of his head and kept her eyes on his face as she lifted herself up and took him inside her. His eyelids closed and she watched him breathe in deeply as they joined together.

She filled herself with his length before lifting her weight from him and letting him take control. His thumbs were on the front of her hips, his fingers behind her pelvis as he guided her up and down, matching her rhythm to his thrusts, each movement bringing her closer to climax.

She liked this position. She liked being able to watch him, she liked being able to see him getting closer and closer to release. His eyes were closed but his lips were parted, his breathing was rapid and shallow, his thrusts getting faster.

She spread her knees, letting him deeper inside her until she had taken all of him. Her body was flooded with heat. Every nerve ending was crying out for his touch. 'Now, Jake. Now.'

He opened his eyes and his gaze locked with hers as he took her to the top of the peak.

Her body started to quiver and she watched him as he too shuddered. He closed his eyes, threw his head back and thrust into her, claiming her as they climaxed together.

She collapsed onto him, their bodies slick with sweat, their skin warm and flushed from their effort. They were both panting as he wrapped his arms around her back, holding her to him. Content at last, she fell asleep to the sound of his heartbeat under her ear. To the feel of his lips pressed against her forehead.

'Good morning.'

Ali opened her eyes to find Jake watching her. They hadn't stopped to close the blinds last night and the sun was streaming through her windows. The light fell across Jake's naked shoulder, painting him with a golden glow. She smiled. 'Morning.'

'Did you sleep well?'

'Very,' she said as she arched her back, stretching out her spine. The sheet fell from her chest and Jake leant towards her, kissing her first on the mouth and then her shoulder.

'I'd love to stay and pick up where we left off last night, but I need to get moving. But can I take you out to lunch later?'

'I wish I could, but I promised my sister I'd babysit for her. Marli is pregnant with number three and she's due in a couple of weeks so this is their last chance to have some childfree time before that one arrives. Can we go for brunch instead?'

Jake shook his head. 'I can't. Will and I are going to an open inspection this morning and I need to go home and shower first.'

'Will is house-hunting?'

'No, I am. I've been staying at Will's since I moved back from Melbourne three months ago and I think I'm about to officially outstay my welcome. It's time I found a place of my own.'

'You haven't looked to rent something?'

'I'm moving back permanently so I always intended to buy something.'

'You didn't like Melbourne?'

'I needed a change after my divorce. This job gave me a reason to come back.'

'Is your ex still in Melbourne?'

'No. She's American. She's gone back to the States.'

'Were you married for long?' Ali asked, amazed to find she knew so little about the man she'd just spent the night with. The man she'd just had amazing sex with. Should she know more? What did his history matter if it was just a sexual relationship? Would it be better to avoid learning too much about him? But, again, her curiosity had got the better of her.

'Ten years.'

'That's a long time.'

'It was. We were married much longer than we should have been, given the circumstances.'

'What do you mean?'

'We got married for all the wrong reasons. Chrissie's visa was expiring, we weren't ready to break up and I couldn't move to the US because I was still studying so we decided to get married. At the time I thought it was a solution to two problems—Chrissie could stay in Australia and I could escape from under the eyes of my watchful, nervous parents. My mother in particular was always risk averse because of my cancer and the ramifications of my surgery and I needed to get away. In hindsight, they weren't good reasons. It wasn't fair to Chrissie. What's that saying—act in haste, repent at leisure? We grew apart, or perhaps didn't have enough in common to begin with, and eventually I let her down. When she needed me, I wasn't there. But after the divorce I wanted a fresh start and my parents are getting older. I'm an only child. It's time to be a dutiful son, or at least to try to be one. But,' he concluded, obviously deciding that potted history was sufficient, 'back to my house-hunting. I need to get myself organised. Buying a house is another step on my new path. Why don't you come with me to see the house and, if we've got time, we can grab a coffee before you go to your sister's?'

Ali was tempted, keen to spend some time with him today, but before she could reply both their phones start beeping rapidly as multiple messages came through. She picked up her phone as Jake rummaged through his discarded clothes, looking for his.

Check your email.

Have you seen today's headlines?

Bosses aren't happy.

She showed Jake her messages.

'I've got similar,' he said, holding up his phone.

Ali opened the local news app to be greeted with the headline *CELEBRITY BABY CRISIS!*

The story was about Jasmine and Poppy, quoting a source that said the babies were critically ill and needed lifesaving surgery. There was no quote from Aaron or Emma and as far as Ali was aware they hadn't even issued a statement to say the twins had been born yet. But someone had announced the news, along with several inaccuracies.

Hospital staff were under strict instructions not to speak to the press and Ali knew most would never dream of breaking patient-doctor confidentiality. But someone had.

'That's not good,' she said as an email pinged into her inbox. She opened it to find a reminder to all staff to maintain privacy. And announcing that the leak would be investigated. 'I think I'll go into the hospital just to check on Emma. See how she's feeling,' she said, as she swung her legs over the edge of the bed and sat up. 'If you want to text me the details of the house inspection I'll see if I can meet you there.'

* * *

Ali turned up the music in her car and sang along as she drove down Glebe Point Road on her way to meet Jake. She flicked her indicator on and took a side street, turning down a familiar road. When Jake had texted the address to her, she'd looked twice. She couldn't believe the house he was interested in had been her granny's! She didn't believe in coincidences, she always thought things happened for a reason, but she wasn't able to work out what this turn of events meant. Not yet.

She drove past the house. There was an advertising board on the front fence with a flag saying 'open' sticking out of it. She found a parking space and walked back up the hill. From the outside it looked the same as it had when she'd last seen it ten years ago when her gran had moved out after her grandad had died.

It was a terraced house. A narrow, two-storey building with a wrought-iron front fence and a decorative veranda. She walked up the path and stepped through the front door, curious to see if the inside had been updated. There was a room to her right that had been styled as a sitting room with a small study nook in the corner. She ignored the stairs leading up to the bedrooms and bathroom that were on the first level and headed for the back of the house. The inside of the house had been painted, carpets had been pulled up and floorboards polished, but when the passage opened out into a kitchen and family room she could see that hadn't been touched since her grandparents had done a renovation thirty-odd years ago. The house was full of people as terrace houses in inner Sydney always attracted lots of interest and there was certainly scope for a buyer to put their own stamp on the place.

Through the kitchen window she could see Jake and Will at the back of the garden underneath the loquat tree. She was pleased to see the old tree; she would have been devastated if it had been removed.

She made her way through the garden, suddenly feeling a little awkward now that Will was there with Jake. Should she greet Jake with a kiss or not?

Before she could decide Jake took her hand and kissed her cheek and she noted that Will didn't seem surprised by either the kiss or her presence.

'How was Emma?' Jake asked.

'She's okay. The media were being kept at bay and Aaron is going to make a statement later. Poppy's condition is stable, she's no better but no worse, and Emma was feeling more positive about the mooted surgery,' she told him before asking, 'What do you think of the house?' She was curious to hear his opinion. She wondered if he was looking for a renovation project or if the dated fixtures would put him off.

'I really like it. It has a good energy. This is the third time I've looked at it. I think this house has a lot of potential,' he whispered, 'but I won't say that too loudly. Don't want to increase the competition.'

She smiled, pleased he liked it even though she was surprised he had his sights set on a three-bedroom house. This was why he was in the wrong demographic for her.

'Did you know you used to be able to see the water from up in the tree? And from the little balcony off the upstairs bedroom at the back. I wonder if you still can?'

'You can see the harbour from the bedroom, but I

haven't climbed the tree. Yet.' He laughed. 'But how do you know that?

'This used to be my grandparents' house. My dad's parents,' she explained.

'Did you know it was on the market?'

'No.' She shook her head as she reached out a hand and stroked the trunk of the loquat tree.

'You wouldn't want to buy it?'

'I'm not really in a position to buy it. I've just bought an apartment.'

'You could sell that.'

'No. My apartment is all I need. It's safe, low maintenance, close to the hospital with good facilities. This house is far too big for me.'

'You could rent out a room.'

She shook her head. 'I'm too old for flatmates and I would rattle around in here by myself. The house needs a family. It needs conversation, laughter and love.'

Those alarm bells were ringing again. She'd have to make sure last night's activities were a one-off. She couldn't get involved with Jake. He had a lot of positive attributes, he was smart, considerate, handsome and good in bed, but he wasn't relationship material.

Ali had tried, and failed, not to check her phone constantly since the weekend. It was Tuesday and she hadn't seen Jake since she'd said goodbye at the open inspection and gone to Marli's. She hadn't bumped into him at work, hadn't heard from him aside from one brief text message. He seemed to have disappeared.

She pulled out her phone and reread his message from yesterday even though she knew it by heart now.

Thanks for a great weekend—catch up soon??

She'd replied.

Sure. Let me know what suits you.

But there had been no further contact.

She knew she shouldn't be bothered about that. It was probably for the best. He wasn't right for her anyway. He was looking at a family house. She should just let him go.

But her head and her heart were at odds. Or was it her head and her hormones?

Maybe all she needed was to find a replacement. Go on some dates and see what happened. Would she forget about him then? She wasn't sure it was going to be that easy to forget Jake Ryan.

Her phone beeped with a notification as she slid it back into her pocket.

Her pulse raced in anticipation as she pulled it out before disappointment sent her heart plummeting towards her stomach. It was a message from the girls' group chat.

Anyone free for lunch at Perc Up?

'Did you all have a good night?' Ivy asked as they sat down in their usual spot and waited for Harper.

'It was a fun party. Lucas's apartment is stunning,' Phoebe gushed.

'I can't believe you both left early.'

'I was tired,' Phoebe said.

Ali thought Phoebe still looked tired and was about to ask if she was okay, but Ivy hadn't paused for a breath.

'Ali, on the other hand, looked like she meant business. So spill, what happened with Jake? I noticed he left around the same time as you.'

'He offered to drop me home,' she replied, as there was no reason to pretend otherwise.

'You left with Jake?' Phoebe said, coming to life, just as Harper sat down.

Ali nodded as the spotlight was turned on her but made a mental note to check on Phoebe later.

'And...did you invite him in?'

'I did.'

'And?'

She could feel a smile spreading across her face, she was powerless to stop it. Despite not having a follow-up planned, and the fact she'd been telling herself she was better off steering clear of him, that didn't erase the fact that Saturday night had been one very good night. 'He spent the night.'

'OMG, that was fast work. '

'I figured we're both consenting adults.'

'No judgement from me,' Ivy said, holding her hands up in mock surrender. 'Sex on the first date isn't taboo.'

'Well, I'm not sure it was technically a first date.'

'Okay, he didn't ask you out, but I did invite him to the party for your benefit.'

'That's not what I meant. I meant we'd seen each other before.'

'What? How come we didn't know that? When?' Ivy was full of questions.

'Technically that wasn't a date either, but we had spent time together before Saturday.'

'Doing what?'

'Rock climbing.'

'What?'

'It's a long story but I promised to accept a challenge, remember? That was it.'

'So are you a thing?'

'I have no idea.'

'And he's a rock climber?' Ivy asked. 'I didn't know that.'

'The charity fundraiser for childhood cancer that Aaron mentioned in his interview last night was all Jake's idea,' Harper said.

'What interview?'

'Aaron was on the news and current affair programme on his network last night, talking about the twins in response to the story in the media over the weekend, and he mentioned the fundraiser,' Harper said. 'You haven't seen it?'

'No.' All three girls shook their heads.

Harper pulled out her phone and searched Aaron's social media. She played the interview for the others when she found it.

'Some of you watching might know that my wife, Emma, was seriously injured in a fire a few months ago. She is recovering, but remains in hospital, and last week she gave birth to our twin daughters. They were born prematurely, and unfortunately Poppy needs heart surgery. We are lucky in Australia to have access to exceptional, mostly free medical care and, believe me, every day I thank the staff at Sydney Central for the care they've taken of my family.

'Poppy is not well, but her condition is stable. The doctors assure me that both my daughters will be okay, but

there are a lot of children in hospital with more serious medical conditions than my girls, including cancer. In two weeks' time there will be a fundraising event for a childhood cancer charity, with proceeds going towards programmes like Clown doctors, respite accommodation for country families and camps for children in remission.

'The event is an abseil at Circular Quay and the organisers are hoping to break the world record for the most people abseiling in a twelve-hour period. The record of 1372 people is currently held by Queensland and I think New South Wales can eclipse that. I'm taking part, and I'd like to invite any of you watching to take part too, if you feel brave enough. Or, if you can't physically participate, to make a donation to the campaign if you can afford to.

'The website details are running on the bottom of the screen and will be in my social media feeds too.'

'Wow! Well done, Aaron.'

'It was clever to mention that Queensland holds the record. There's always healthy interstate rivalry between us and Queensland.'

'Should we sign up?' Ivy asked.

'Yarran and I have signed up,' Harper said.

'I think we should do it,' Ivy said.

'I will if you will,' Ali said. She didn't feel as though she had a choice. Not after Aaron's plea and if her friends were getting involved.

'Has there been any more news on Poppy's surgery?' Harper asked Phoebe as Ali wondered if any of the others had noticed that Phoebe hadn't pledged to take part in the fundraiser.

'I've asked Zac Archer, the cardiac neonatal surgeon

I met at the conference, if he would consult on Poppy's case. I'm waiting for him to get back to me but I'm hopeful he will agree to operate and then I'll be guided by him as to when it happens. I don't think she's strong enough yet to undergo surgery but he might think differently.'

Phoebe was having trouble maintaining eye contact with them while she outlined the plan and Ali's sixth sense was twitching. She knew there was something Phoebe was keeping from them.

Ali was lying on the couch in her apartment with her head in Jake's lap.

He'd gone looking for her today at the hospital, wanting to see her. He hadn't been able to stop thinking about her but work had been frantic for the past two days and he hadn't had a chance. She'd seemed a little reserved when he'd tracked her down and he was concerned she was having second thoughts about last Saturday night but when he'd invited her out for dinner she'd suggested a takeaway at her place. He was yet to determine if that was because she didn't want to be out in public with him or because she preferred the privacy of her own house.

He had stuff to sort out in his personal life—he definitely needed his own place to live and he still needed to settle into his role and mend his relationship with his parents—and he wasn't looking for a new relationship, but he hadn't been able to stop thinking about Ali. He didn't usually mix business with pleasure either. He'd met Chrissie through work...well, kind of. She was a sales representative with a medical supply firm so they hadn't actually worked together. But he didn't expect to do much work on the O & G ward. He could separate professional and private.

He looked around her apartment as he ran his fingers through her hair, massaging her scalp.

'What are you looking at?'

He looked down at her and smiled. 'Just getting a feel for you in your space. Will always says a home should reflect the person you are.'

'And what do you see?'

'Someone who values family.' Photos of her nieces and nephews were displayed around the room and drawings they'd done were stuck on her fridge. Her apartment was quite feminine to look at, decorated in soft colours, with plenty of plants and Indigenous artworks.

'How long have you lived here?'

'Almost four years.'

'You like living in an apartment?'

'I like some aspects of it. It suited me after my divorce. I wanted something close to the hospital, easy to look after but I'm starting to miss being able to feel the ground beneath my feet. House plants aren't really a good substitute for the earth. I feel a little disconnected, but I don't have time to garden. I don't need a house.'

'Four years is a long time to be single.' He was surprised that she was still alone. He knew family was important to her and she was gorgeous. He would have thought she would want a relationship. He thought someone would have swept her off her feet. He was certain many must have tried.

'Yeah. My marriage break-up was kind of rough. My ex did a number on me. He was another person in my life who betrayed my trust.'

He remembered her mentioning that at Ivy's party. He waited to see if she was going to elaborate.

'Adam was a lawyer, *is* a lawyer—I've got into the habit of talking about him in the past tense even though he's not dead, but he did kill our marriage,' she continued. 'We were both career-driven. I thought we had that in common. Obstetricians' hours are erratic, as you can imagine, especially before I became Head of Obstetrics and Gynaecology and still had a full patient list. He worked long hours too. When he said he was sleeping at the office because he was working on a difficult case, I didn't think anything of it. He'd done that before. But I came home one day and found him packing his bags. Turns out he'd been having an affair with one of his colleagues. He hadn't been staying at work—he'd been staying with her.

'I was blindsided and it's taken me a long time to get over. Not to get over him but over the way he treated me. The way he lied. But that's in the past now. I'm just glad the divorce was easy. There's no baggage. There's no reason to see him again. And no reason to talk about him either. So tell me, how many people have signed up now for your fundraiser? Aaron's interview must have helped your numbers?'

He noted her change of subject but he let it go.

'You saw that?'

'Harper showed me.'

'We had an additional two hundred people sign up today. I reckon Aaron's interview had a lot to do with that.'

'Do you know why he mentioned the fundraiser?'

'We spoke about it last week. I was talking to him

about the event and he offered to promote it. As a favour. He wanted to give something back to the hospital. He was going to post something on social media, I wasn't expecting anything on the news channels, but he thought if he was giving an interview to set the record straight after that news report about Poppy's health then he'd add that in. All for a good cause is what he said. The fundraiser isn't really related to Poppy's condition but, as Aaron said, it's still for kids, many of whom are in more need of help than Poppy is.'

'Ivy and Harper have signed up for the fundraiser.'

'Not you?'

'I know I was keen to try abseiling, it looked like fun when we were indoors and when we were talking about a distance of ten metres, but I'm not so sure about doing it off a building that's over fifty metres high. The idea makes me nervous.'

'The hotel has been picked because of its location on Circular Quay. With the Harbour Bridge in the background, it makes for good publicity shots.'

'I'm not worried about the location. I'm worried about the height and the fixings.'

'There are secure bolts. There are permanent fixtures on the roof that are used for the window-washing platforms. Would you think about taking part if you had a chance to try abseiling beforehand?'

'Where? At the gym?'

'No. There's a come-and-try event this weekend in the Blue Mountains, near Katoomba. If you wanted to go, we could stay overnight.'

'You're suggesting we go away for the weekend?'

'Why not? I know we can do a day trip but it might be

nice to spend the weekend together. Or Saturday night at least. Or have you already got plans?'

She shook her head.

'All right. I'll make the arrangements,' he said, noting to himself that, for the first time in over a year, he was excited about something.

CHAPTER SEVEN

'ALI, HAVE YOU got a minute? Ali?'

Ali looked up from her desk. She'd been lost in a world of daydreams. About Jake. For something that was supposed to be casual she spent a *lot* of time thinking about him. Today she'd been thinking about their upcoming overnight trip to the Blue Mountains, west of Sydney. This part of the world held a special place in her heart. It was her mother's country and, while she and her siblings had been born and raised on Gadigal land on Sydney's northern beaches, she still had an affinity with the Gundungurra people and their land. She loved spending time there, loved feeling connected to that country and she hoped she wasn't making a mistake by travelling there with Jake. She didn't want to make any memories that might be painful in the future. She didn't want to do anything that could possibly tarnish the love she felt for that country.

No. That was a ridiculous thought. An impossible outcome. She was attracted to Jake, that was certainly true, they had amazing chemistry, but no man was powerful enough to ruin her connection to country. The weekend would be fabulous.

Phoebe was hovering in her doorway and Ali turned

her attention to her friend. 'Phoebe, hi! Sorry, what did you say?'

'I just wondered if you have a minute? I need to pick your brains about something.'

'Sure. Is it about Poppy? Is she okay?' Ali couldn't imagine why Phoebe would need her opinion on Poppy. After all, Phoebe was the neonatal surgeon and she'd already told Ali she was calling in an expert neonatal cardiologist.

'No. It's an O & G question.'

That made more sense. Phoebe was still hovering. She looked uncomfortable, which was confusing. 'Come in, sit down,' Ali said, trying to put her at ease. 'What's the problem?'

Phoebe sat but she didn't sit still. She slid her hands under her thighs and jiggled her legs up and down as she talked. 'I have a friend. She's just found out she's pregnant and she's got some concerns.'

'What sort of concerns?'

'It's a geriatric pregnancy and she's worried about all the things that could go wrong.'

'Do I know this friend?'

'I can't tell you.'

'Okay. How old is she?'

'Forty.' Anything over thirty-five was classed as a geriatric pregnancy. It seemed harsh but the statistics indicated an increase in problems after that age. Not for all mothers but certainly in enough that extra care was needed. Extra monitoring.

'Is it her first pregnancy?'

Phoebe nodded.

'And how many weeks is she?'

'About six, I think.'

'Do you know if the pregnancy was planned or not. Did she have IVF?'

'What difference does that make?' Phoebe asked.

A lot, in Ali's opinion. 'If she had IVF then she would have had more tests and more screening as part of the process. If the pregnancy was a surprise, then she might not have been taking folic acid or extra vitamins—' both of which could be important in older mothers '—and she might have been drinking alcohol, smoking... The incidence of pregnancy complications doubles in women in the thirty-five-to-forty age bracket when compared to those in their twenties. It's something to be aware of. Has her GP referred her to an obstetrician?'

'I don't think she's been to the GP yet.'

'Well, that should be her first priority. And then she should make sure she gets a referral to an obstetrician who is experienced in geriatric pregnancies. She should have more regular reviews and possibly some additional tests.'

'What sort of tests?'

'Some women want genetic counselling. Are there any issues on her side? On the father's side?'

'I don't know about the father's side. She hasn't told him yet.'

Phoebe looked worried and Ali got the impression she wasn't hearing the whole story. Then her mind started putting together the things Phoebe had and hadn't said. Phoebe's pale complexion, the fact she looked as if she'd lost weight, her recent behaviour—no coffee, not signing up for the fundraiser, and Ali couldn't recall her drinking any alcohol at Ivy's party.

Was Ali putting two and two together and getting five?
She wasn't sure but unless Phoebe confided in her it was
all supposition on Ali's part. She'd have to take her word
for it that she was asking for a friend. But her sixth sense
was telling her something different.

'She knows who the father is though?'

Phoebe nodded. 'What would you do?'

'What are you asking? If you're asking if I'd go through
with the pregnancy, you're asking the wrong person. You
know I don't plan on having kids. Is your friend happy
about the pregnancy? Does she want to go ahead with it?'

'She wants the baby.'

'In that case, I'd advise her to definitely tell the father
asap. She needs to arm herself with the facts and get as
much information as she can—about her family history
and his. Then she can make decisions about what tests
to have. If there's no reason to be concerned, then regular consults with an O & G will be fine.'

There were any number of things that could go wrong,
especially in older mothers who were pregnant for the
first time compared to younger mothers or older women
who'd had previous pregnancies. Anything from gestational hypertension, gestational diabetes to abnormal
placental positioning, increased incidence of C-section,
miscarriages, premature births and babies with chromo-
somal disorders. Ali knew Phoebe would be well aware of
this and could pass the information on to her 'friend', but
she'd give her some reading in hard copy to look through
later. Stress, rampaging hormones and fatigue did interfere with a woman's memory and sometimes her ability
to absorb and retain information.

'I'll give you some information to pass on,' Ali said as

she hit 'print' on her computer. 'Tell her there's no rea-son to be overly concerned. While there are things that can go wrong, older mothers often have been taking bet-ter care of themselves in their thirties than they were in their twenties. She'll probably have more resources than a younger mum, as statistics show older mums are also likely to be better educated and have a higher income, which will help the baby. Geriatric pregnancies, despite the unflattering term, are not uncommon. In fact, in the past twenty years the number of women giving birth in their forties has almost doubled.'

She handed Phoebe the info she had printed out. 'There you go. Give her this to read, then she can have the dis-cussion about any further testing she might want. But re-member, she doesn't *have* to do any of these. The choice is hers. Do you know if she's planning on going private or public for her doctor? I can give you a couple of names of obstetricians to pass on.'

'Um, public, I think. I'll have to find out.'

'Okay. Is there anything else I should know?'

Phoebe shook her head. But she didn't look any more at ease than she had when she'd walked into Ali's office.

'My advice for now would be, tell her to book in for an ultrasound in the next couple of weeks, certainly by eight weeks, just to check the development.' The first step was making sure it was a viable pregnancy.

'Okay.'

Were those tears in Phoebe's eyes? Ali knew some-thing was definitely wrong and she could hazard a guess what it was but unless Phoebe was willing to confide in her there was little she could do.

Phoebe stood up; Ali stood too and wrapped her arms

around her friend. Trying to convey in the gesture that she was there for her and would support her.

'And if you have any other questions, I'm here, okay? If your...friend needs a confidential ear or some non-judgemental advice, I'm right here.'

'You won't tell anyone about this conversation, will you?'

'Of course not,' she replied as Phoebe turned to leave.

For the first time in days, when Ali found herself alone with a quiet moment her thoughts were not focused on Jake.

She made a note to pay attention. To be there if Phoebe needed her.

Jake indicated and turned off the highway in Katoomba and then into the driveway of their hotel in the Blue Mountains. Sydney weather was mild, even winter could be sunny and pleasant, but today was not one of those days and it had been raining since they'd left the city and, while it had eased to a drizzle, the weather was still inclement. Wind blew the rain sideways and the abseiling had been cancelled, the weather conditions making it too hazardous. Ali had expected Jake to cancel their plans, but he'd insisted that the accommodation and dinner were still booked so there was no need to change all of their arrangements. She'd happily gone along with the new plan but she hadn't been expecting this level of luxury.

'Are we staying here?' she asked as Jake pulled up in front of a five-star hotel that she'd seen in passing but never visited.

'Yes. Is it okay?'

She laughed, delighted. 'It's gorgeous. I've always wanted to stay here.'

'Me too.'

She was pleased he hadn't been there before. Pleased it would be a new experience for them both with no memories of ex-husbands or wives.

'This is much fancier than what I'm used to up here,' she said after they had checked in. 'This is my mum's country. We used to come here a lot when we were younger but we'd always stay with family.'

'I didn't realise that. I thought you grew up on the North Shore.'

'I did. But Mum grew up here. It's my second home. My spiritual home in a way,' she said as Jake set their bags down to swipe the card that opened their room.

A canopied bed took up a large section of the room but large picture windows framed a view of the trees and the Jamison Valley and lent a feeling of spaciousness to the accommodation. In the en suite, the bath was positioned in front of a window to take in the same majestic view.

'This is incredible,' Ali said as she spun around to face Jake.

'I'm glad you like it.'

She walked over to the window and Jake joined her. Standing behind her, he wrapped his arms around her waist.

'What would you like to do first?' she asked, tipping her head to one side to look back at him. 'The bed looks comfortable.'

'It does. But the rain has stopped. Why don't we go for a walk while the weather is okay? Then we get to look forward to coming back here later.'

The rain had eased but low cloud still hung over the valley and Ali knew the break in the weather was likely to be short-lived. 'All right. Do you want to go to see the Three Sisters?'

The Three Sisters, massive sandstone rocks jutting out of the cliff, were one of the area's most popular sights but Ali hoped the rain might keep some of the crowds at bay.

They walked hand in hand from the hotel to the lookout. The air smelt strongly of eucalyptus and Ali knew it was the oil from the leaves that bathed the mountains in a blue haze and gave them their name.

Ali led Jake down to the Honeymoon Bridge, which connected the cliff face to the Sisters.

'Do you know the story of the Three Sisters?' Ali asked as they stood underneath the first rock.

'No. Will you tell it to me?'

Information signs telling the dreamtime story were on display but because there were two versions of the ancient tale Ali was happy to give Jake her family's version.

'The Three Sisters are Meehni, Wimlah and Gunnedo and there are two stories about how they came to be here but because they are from the Gundungurra people— that's my mum's mob—that's the story we tell.

'The sisters lived in the Jamison Valley and when they were young they fell in love with three brothers from a neighbouring mob. The brothers wanted to marry them but marriage between the tribes was forbidden by law. The brothers refused to let that stop them and they kidnapped the three sisters. The brothers were warriors so they thought their plan was foolproof, but the kidnapping caused a tribal war. Now, Kuradjuri, a Gundungurra witch doctor, was worried about the three sisters so, in order to keep them safe, he cast a spell that turned them into stone.'

'Seems a bit harsh.'

Ali smiled. 'It would have been fine but, unfortunately, Kuradjuri was killed in the battle and no one else has ever been able to break the spell. So, here the Three Sisters sit, keeping watch for eternity over the Jamison Valley.'

'That story doesn't have a very happy ending.'

'Not yet. But there's still hope.' Ali laughed. 'It was one of our favourite stories growing up. We used to call the three sisters Alinta, Kirra and Marli, after ourselves, and we used to make our brothers and cousins fight pretend battles until we got tired of being stones and we'd join in.'

'There's five of you, right? And you all live in Sydney?'

Ali nodded. 'Yes. My parents, siblings, their partners, ten nieces and nephews, not counting the one Marli is expecting, grandmother and various aunties and uncles.'

'I can't imagine having such a big family. I'm lucky to have Will and his sister. They are like siblings to me but it's not quite the same thing.'

'We're lucky we all get along. Mostly.' Ali smiled. 'It's not always easy but even in our worst moments I never would have wanted to be an only child. I can't imagine it. Especially being a twin.'

'I'm not sure how I would have survived without Will. Because of my cancer diagnosis and treatment my parents were overprotective—which I get—but I often felt smothered and I think Will kept me sane. Spending time with him gave me the opportunity to live a normal life but it did drive a bit of a wedge between me and my parents.'

'How so?'

'Wrapping me in cotton wool just made me rebellious. As soon as I was old enough, I started pushing the boundaries, testing my physical limits, which in turn terrified my mother and led to lots of arguments. To escape all that I got married, moved to Melbourne then got divorced. In hindsight I probably shouldn't have used marriage as my escape route, but you live and learn. Other than my career I seem to be constantly disappointing my parents, which has strained our relationship. And my divorce certainly didn't help to repair the cracks in my relationship with them.'

'They didn't support you in that?'

'Not a hundred per cent. They're religious and, in their opinion, marriage is for life. They told me I should have tried harder to work things out but sometimes it's better to admit you've made a mistake and learn from it. Chrissie wasn't happy and I was making things worse. I'm hoping it's not too late to make amends with my parents at least. I've only got one family.'

He took her hand as they walked back across the bridge. The clouds had darkened and drizzle was falling again, making the walkway slippery underfoot. Jake looked up at the sky. 'I think the weather is about to put an end to our sightseeing. Can I interest you in high tea?'

'Is that what you call it?' Ali laughed and together they hurried back to the hotel, eager to get under cover before the heavens opened again.

The restaurant where high tea was served was beautiful. Large windows overlooked the valley, the tables were covered with crisp white tablecloths and sparkling chandeliers hung overhead. The table was set with bone china plates and teacups, polished silver cutlery and a vase of fresh flowers. Wait staff glided through the room delivering tiered silver cake stands to the diners.

Ali was glad she'd brushed her hair and applied some lipstick. After the walk they'd discarded their damp clothes, tried out the bed—it was as comfortable as it had looked—and then changed into fresh clothes for tea.

A menu listing dozens of different selections of tea, mineral waters and champagne was on the table and after the waitress took their order Ali looked around at the other guests and tried to guess what they were all doing there. What they were celebrating. There were a lot of couples, from honeymooners to retirees, and a larger group of women who she suspected were on a hen's weekend. She noticed a pregnant woman excuse herself from her partner and head for the bathroom. She had the gait of a woman in the very late stages of pregnancy and she looked quite uncomfortable.

The waitress brought their tea as a second waitress delivered their cake stand laden with Instagram-worthy afternoon-tea delicacies. Ali really wanted to start with a tiny lemon tart but she resisted the temptation—there'd be time for that later—and picked up a dainty cucumber sandwich instead. She'd finished the sandwich and a scone when she realised she hadn't seen the pregnant woman come back. Her seat at her table was empty and Ali's sixth sense started to buzz.

She picked up her handbag and stood up from the table. 'Can you excuse me?' she said to Jake. 'I'm just going to the bathroom.' She assumed the woman had gone to the loo. She'd quickly check on her.

Ali pushed open the bathroom door. The pregnant woman was leaning over the basin and gripping the edge so hard with both hands that her knuckles were white, and Ali could smell vomit.

She hurried across the room. 'Are you okay?'

The woman shook her head and started to cry. 'My water just broke and I can't move.' She stopped and gasped, her voice catching, and Ali suspected she was being gripped by a contraction. A strong one by all appearances. 'The pain is terrible.'

'Let me help you. I'm a doctor, an obstetrician actually.'

'Really?'

'Yes. I'm the Head of Obstetrics and Gynaecology at Sydney Central Hospital. Are you happy for me to help you?'

The woman nodded.

'Good. My name is Dr Edwards. But call me Ali.'

'I'm Olivia.'

'When is your due date?'

Olivia's baby bump was considerable. Ali wasn't worried about a premature birth, unless it was a multiple pregnancy.

'Ten days.' She broke off mid-sentence as another contraction took hold. They were less than a minute apart. This baby wasn't waiting for anyone. 'We're on our babymoon. My back has been achy all day, but I thought it was because of the different bed. I didn't think I was in labour.'

'This is your first baby?' Ali asked, thinking at the same time that Olivia had left the babymoon a bit late. With ten days to go anything could happen and, at the very least, by this stage in a pregnancy most women were getting fairly uncomfortable and the thing they needed most was a good night's sleep. But the excitement of a first pregnancy was real and the prospect of one last holiday was enticing.

'Yes.'

'It's just the one baby? You're not expecting twins?'

'Just…one,' she said as her breath caught again with another contraction.

'Let's get you into a different position,' Ali said. 'You might find kneeling on all fours more comfortable.'

There were only three cubicles in this bathroom and none of them were occupied. Ali checked the entry door into the bathroom and was pleased to see it had a lock on it. 'I need to have a look at you to see what the situation is,' she said as she helped Olivia down to the floor. 'But first I'm going to lock the door so no one can come in unexpectedly.' Ali knelt beside Olivia. 'I'm just going to lift your skirt and remove your underwear, is that okay? I need to see what the baby is up to.'

Olivia nodded.

'Do you know if you're having a boy or a girl?' Ali asked in an attempt to distract her from the unusual situation they found themselves in. She didn't have a lot of time to build rapport or establish trust, she just had to hope Olivia was okay with this.

'A girl.'

'And where are you booked in for the delivery?'

'North Sydney.'

Ali had pulled Olivia's underwear down and she could see the baby's head crowning. That wasn't ideal.

'Okay, Olivia, I need you to focus on your breathing,' Ali instructed as yet another contraction gripped the expectant mother. 'Little pants, blow out through your mouth, you're doing well. Now, I've got good news and slightly less good news. I can see the baby's head, which means she's in the right position. But she's in a hurry. You're not going to make it to a hospital.'

'I'm going to have the baby here? In a hotel bathroom?'

'It looks like it,' she replied. 'So, this is what we're going to do.' Ali had heard the distress in Olivia's voice. That was to be expected but she needed to keep her as calm as possible. 'I have a friend in the restaurant, he's also a doctor. I'm going to call him and he'll fetch your partner. I saw you with him in the restaurant earlier. What's his name?'

'Jeremy.'

'Okay.'

Ali dug her phone out of her bag and called Jake. 'Hi, I've got a bit of a situation in the ladies' toilet. I'm with a lady by the name of Olivia, she's in labour and I can't move her. I need you to find her husband. They were having high tea. He's sitting by himself at a table behind you. His name is Jeremy. I need you to explain what's happened to him and bring him to the bathroom while I call an ambulance.'

Ali spoke slowly, giving Jake time to follow her instructions, waiting for any questions before she hung up and turned her attention back to Olivia.

'Olivia, Jeremy will be here in a moment. I'll call an ambulance now, but I will be here with you until they arrive. Have you had any complications during your pregnancy? High blood pressure? Gestational diabetes? Any issues?' She wanted to know if anything out of the ordinary had occurred, partly so she was prepared and also so she could forewarn the paramedics.

'No. Nothing.'

Ali dialled 000 and explained the situation, leaving her number with the dispatcher in case they needed her. Jake knocked on the door as Ali ended the call and she got up to let him in.

Jeremy rushed straight to Olivia's side while Ali spoke to Jake.

'I've called an ambulance, they're on the way. Can you notify the hotel about what's going on? They'll need to organise another bathroom for guests to use and direct the paramedics here when they arrive. Can you also see if the hotel has a first-aid kit and some towels or, better still, some large tarps or plastic sheeting as well?'

Ali introduced herself to Jeremy before directing him to sit in front of Olivia to help support her in kneeling. Fortunately, Jeremy seemed fairly level-headed even if he was obviously overwhelmed.

Ali washed her hands and willed Jake to hurry. The moment he returned, laden with towels and a first-aid kit, she resumed her position on the floor beside Olivia.

She was just in time. Olivia was fully dilated.

'Olivia,' she said, keeping her tone low and calm, 'you need to get ready to push.'

'I can't do it.'

'I know it hurts but you're almost there.'

'Hurts!' Olivia snapped. 'I've never had pain this bad. It's excruciating. Are you sure it's supposed to feel like this? I don't want to do this!'

'You're doing an amazing job. Stay strong. You can do this. Not much longer and you'll be holding your daughter.'

'It hurts so much,' she wailed.

'I know. But you can do this. Try to relax.'

'Relax! You're kidding me, aren't you? Have you had kids?'

Ali could feel her shoulders tense. She should be used to this question. Her patients regularly asked her this, but it usually came up during antenatal visits, never in the middle of a delivery. And she'd always had time to build rapport with her patients. Had time for them to realise that it didn't matter if she had children of her own. That not being a mother didn't impact her skills as an obstetrician.

She forced herself not to take Olivia's question personally. Olivia was in stage two of her labour—women always got cranky then. 'No,' she replied.

'Well, how do you know how I feel?'

Ali bit back the retort on her lips that wanted to ask if Olivia would expect a male obstetrician to know how labour felt, instead saying, 'I've delivered hundreds of babies, Olivia. I've seen all there is to see, and I've heard all the complaints, but trust me when I say it will all be worth it in the end.'

'Olivia, Dr Edwards is trying to help you,' Jeremy commented before Ali could tell him not to bother.

'Don't you start.' Olivia turned on Jeremy, lashing out in pain. 'It's your fault I'm in pain. I just want to go home. I should never have come on this babymoon.'

'It's okay, Jeremy.' Jake tried to appease the poor man. 'This is all normal behaviour. You'll both have forgotten it by tomorrow. Did they warn you about this in antenatal classes?'

Jake was right. It was quite normal behaviour but Ali wondered how he knew what was discussed in an antenatal class. But she filed that thought away for later—she had more important matters to deal with.

'All right, Olivia, squeeze Jeremy's hands and get ready to push with the next contraction. Ready…now!' she instructed.

The baby's head crowned and Ali guided it out, feeling for the cord, relived to find it all clear. She looked up at Jake to find him watching her closely. She nodded. *All good.*

'All right, Olivia,' she continued, 'have a rest for a moment. You're almost done. One more push with the next contraction.'

Ali rotated the baby's shoulders with the next contraction and caught her as she slid out. Jake handed her a clean towel and as she rubbed the baby's back the newborn began to cry. 'Good girl. That's the way. Congratulations, Mum and Dad, you have a perfect little girl.'

The baby's colour was good and she had a healthy set of lungs on her. Ali quickly checked the baby's reflexes and calculated her pulse rate before lying her on Olivia's chest and covering her with a towel to trap some heat.

'Do you have a name for her?' Ali asked as there was a knock on the bathroom door.

'Chloe,' Olivia said as the paramedics called out, announcing their arrival.

Jake let them in and Ali gave a brief handover before they assessed Olivia and transported her and the baby to hospital. Jeremy, who insisted he was okay to drive, followed the ambulance, leaving Jake and Ali alone in the bathroom.

There was a chair in the corner of the room and Ali collapsed onto it, surveying the mess.

'Did that really just happen?'

'It did. You were amazing.'

Jake was grinning and Ali found herself extraordinarily pleased with his compliment. 'Thank you. I'm just relieved it went well. I've never had to deliver a baby outside a hospital before.'

'That's even more impressive, then. She was lucky you were here. Jeremy should buy a lottery ticket on his way to the hospital.'

Ali laughed. 'Maybe he will. Did you get to finish afternoon tea?'

'No. I was waiting for you. Do you want to go back to our table?'

Ali shook her head. 'I think I need a shower.'

'Okay. Why don't I run you a bath and then I'll sort out what's left of the high tea?'

Ali was luxuriating in the bubble bath when Jake reappeared clutching a fresh bottle of champagne. 'Compliments of the hotel,' he said, 'and they've offered dinner on the house too, if you're up for it, but in the meantime they're going to bring the rest of our high tea to our room.'

He popped the champagne cork and poured her a glass. He handed it to her before answering a knock on the door. He returned pushing the room-service trolley laden with a three-tier cake stand, a fresh pot of tea and the vase of flowers.

Ali was starving and she lay in the bath drinking champagne while Jake passed her the tiny treats.

'Can I top up your champagne?' he asked as she finished her glass.

'No, I've had plenty. But I think I'll get out of the bath. I'm starting to go wrinkly. Would you pass me a towel, please?'

Jake plucked a towel from the rail and held out his hand to her. Ali reached up, putting her hand in his, and stepped out of the bath. Jake wrapped the towel around her and pulled her close.

'You smell so good.'

Ali slid the towel down from her shoulders, wrapping it around her chest and tucking one end into itself to hold it in place. She stood on tiptoes and kissed Jake's lips. 'Thank you.'

'Do you want to get dressed?' he asked.

She shook her head. 'Not at all. I want you to get *undressed*.'

'I like your idea better.' Jake grinned as Ali started to undo the buttons on his shirt.

CHAPTER EIGHT

JAKE PRESSED HIS lips to the side of her face, in front of her ear, before moving lower, dropping kisses along her jaw. With a flick of his fingers he undid the towel that Ali had just knotted around her chest, leaving her naked. His fingers grazed her breast and her nipple peaked. He bent his head and pressed his lips against the swell of her breast before running his tongue over her nipple and making Ali feel as if she could dissolve.

She put her index finger under his chin and lifted his head, bringing his lips back to hers. She slid her arms around his neck as she pressed herself against him. His tongue explored her mouth. Tasting. Teasing, deeper and harder this time. There was an urgency to their movements now.

She felt his hand trace over the curve of her hip. Her skin was on fire. A waterfall of heat and desire started in her belly, overflowed and ran through her like a river. She could feel the moisture pooling between her thighs and she tightened her arms around his neck, holding herself up as her legs threatened to give way.

Jake scooped her up and carried her into the bedroom, putting her down on the edge of the bed as he divested himself of all of his clothes.

Ali reached for him, admiring his naked form as she ran her hand along the length of his shaft. She felt him quiver as her fingers rolled across the tip, using the moisture she found there to decrease the friction and smooth her movements.

He leant forwards and ran his fingers up the inside of her right thigh. Ali closed her eyes and spread her legs for him. He slid his fingers inside her, making her gasp as he circled her most sensitive spot with his thumb. She moaned and arched her back.

He reached for the bedside table and handed her a condom. She tore the packet open and rolled it onto him. He was hard and hot under her palm; she was warm and wet to his touch. She arched her hips towards him She was ready now. She didn't want to wait. She couldn't wait.

She opened her legs and guided him into her, welcoming the full length of him. She lifted her hips and let him fill her. He pushed against her and she met his thrusts, timing them with her own. They moved together, matching their rhythms as if they'd been doing this for ever.

Jake gathered her hands and held them above her head, stretching her out and exposing her breasts, and he bent his head to her nipple as he continued his thrusts. The energy they created pierced through her, flowing from his mouth, through her breast and into her groin where it gathered in a peak of pleasure building with intensity until she thought she would explode.

'Oh, yes, Jake, don't stop,' she begged.

His pace increased a fraction more and as she felt him start to shudder she released her hold as well. Their timing was exquisite, controlled by the energy that bound them together, and they cried out in unison, climaxing simultaneously, leaving them spent and sated.

'Do you mind if I check my phone?' Ali asked. 'It could be Marli.' She hated people answering their phones at dinner, but the notification sound alerted her to the fact that the message was on her family chat. 'After the day we've had, I don't want to find out she's gone into labour,' she said as she retrieved her phone after waiting for Jake's nod.

'Is everything okay?' Jake wanted to know. 'You're not going to disappear on me two meals in a row?'

Ali smiled. 'Everything's fine. It was just Kirra checking that I'm still calling in tomorrow.'

'Your regular family Sunday get-together?'

She nodded.

'Kirra's the middle sister? With four kids?'

'You've got a good memory.'

'Yarran has one child, Kirra has four, Luka, three and Marli is about to have her third.' Jake checked off Ali's siblings and their offspring on his fingers. 'But, other than Yarran and Harper, I haven't got my head around their partners' or their kids' names yet. You've got a big family. You didn't want to add to the number?'

'No.' Ali had been waiting for this question. She'd learned it was always only a matter of time before she was quizzed on her desire—or lack thereof—for children. She looked Jake directly in the eye and said, 'Does that matter?' knowing his response would make or break their time together.

'Not to me. To be honest, I hadn't thought about it until today when Olivia asked if you had kids. Given your choice of career, I imagine most people assume you have kids and it made me wonder.'

'Do you think people ask that question of male obstetricians? Males in general?' She heard the abruptness in her tone but frustration made it difficult to soften it.

'I didn't mean to upset you,' Jake said.

Ali knew he was trying to placate her, but she wasn't about to be soothed. 'Are you constantly asked if you have kids? Or why not? Or when you're going to start a family?'

'Okay, I get your point. I don't get asked those questions often at all.' He reached across the table for her hand and Ali forced herself not to pull away in irritation. She knew that if she wanted to have more than a casual relationship with Jake, then they needed to have this conversation at some point. It might as well be now.

Ali sighed and slowly withdrew her hand. 'You haven't upset me. Not really. I know I get defensive when this topic is raised but I'm constantly being asked if I have kids. Or when I'm going to have a family. If I say I'm not going to have kids, they assume it's because I can't. It seems inconceivable to most people that a woman might be childless by choice.'

'You don't want kids?'

'No. I never have. I've chosen not to and that's hard for lots of people to understand. I get judged a lot.'

Jake was nodding but Ali wasn't sure he really understood her meaning. Which was—was he going to judge her?

'Is it a problem for you?' she asked.

'It's your choice. Why would it be a problem for me?' He sounded puzzled.

'Because I like you,' she said. She needed to be direct, she needed to make sure Jake understood her message. 'And I'd like to spend time with you but in case our relationship develops into something more then I need to be clear about the fact that I don't want children.'

Did she want it to be a problem? Maybe she did. She liked him but she'd only intended on having a fling.

'Ali, it's fine. I haven't got plans to have kids. And I like you too. I enjoy your company as well and I'm happy just to see what happens.'

'I get that. But it's easy for you to say you don't want kids now. It's all fine until the moment you decide that, actually, you do want a family.'

Was she trying to create drama? Was she wanting to drive a wedge between them? Ali knew it was different for men. There was no time limit for them on starting a family. And most didn't have a biological clock ticking away. They didn't need one when they could sire children at any age. She knew Jake could have fun with her and then move on and start a family later. It had happened to her before. 'I don't want to mislead you about where I stand and I don't want you to mislead me either.'

'I'm not misleading you.'

'You're looking to buy a family house.'

'It's just a house.'

'For a family.'

'That's what you see because it was a family house for you. That's your association with it. I see a good investment. It's in a good location and I can afford it because it needs updating. That's where the appeal is for me. I need somewhere to live. Look at me.' He spread his arms out wide. 'I'm thirty-eight years old and sleeping in my cousin's spare room. Even if I wanted kids, I'm hardly the type of responsible male a sensible woman would think makes good father material.'

Ali disagreed. He was gorgeous, kind and had a secure job. He would be at the top of many a woman's list. 'But what about when you have all those things? If we want this relationship to go any further, I need you to say you don't want kids full stop. Not tonight,' she hastened to add. 'I want you to think about it properly. I don't want a rushed decision. Words are easy to say. I need them to have consideration behind them.'

'What do you want me to do?'

'Think about it, seriously think about it. Do you have friends with kids? Have you ever looked at them and imagined what it would be like to raise a child of your own? How that would feel? How did you feel when you were in Theatre for Emma's delivery? When Jasmine and Poppy were born?'

'How do *you* feel when you deliver babies?' he replied, turning the tables on her. 'It doesn't make you second-guess yourself?'

Ali shook her head. 'It's a privilege to be part of that moment in people's lives but there's certainly no hole in my life waiting to be filled by my own offspring. I get my fix from my nieces and nephews. That's enough for me. I love them and they love me, but I couldn't give myself over one hundred per cent to a child. I'm not cut out for that. And that's really what they need. At least initially.'

'All I can tell you is that I've never felt compelled to have a family,' he said. 'It's hard enough making a re-lationship work between two people. Throw kids into the mix and, from what I've seen, it just makes things even harder. If you ever want to see a reason why people shouldn't have kids, I'll introduce you to my father. I've been a continual source of disappointment for him.'

'I'm sure that's not true.'

'You can ask him yourself, if you like. My parents are celebrating their fortieth wedding anniversary next weekend with a big party. Come with me.'

'To the party?'

'Yes. You'd be doing me a huge favour.'

Ali shook her head. 'I don't want to meet your parents if this thing between us is only going to be short-lived. If you and I are not on the same page, if you want children, then this can't go any further. I really need you to think about my choice to not have children, to see if that's something you're prepared to sign up for. If not, there's no point continuing to see each other, let alone meet your parents.'

'You'd call it quits now?' he asked.

'I would. We have amazing sex, but I want more. I want a relationship. I'd like to see where you and I could go but I'm not prepared to invest my time and energy in something that can't last. I already lost my marriage over my decision not to have children.'

Jake frowned. 'I thought your ex had an affair?'

'He did. But he also got her pregnant. I don't know whether that was planned or not. He says it wasn't but, in the end, he chose her over me. The mother of his child.' Ali sighed. 'I didn't want kids, *we* didn't want kids, but all of a sudden he was leaving me for a woman who was having his baby. All of a sudden he'd decided he *did* want a family. He'd always said he was happy not to have children, that it didn't bother him, but, at the end of the day, he left me for a woman who gave him a child. But my biggest issue with all of this was the lies, the betrayal. I just wish he'd been honest with me. Not about having a family—I accept that he hadn't thought he wanted one until it was presented to him—but he could have been honest about not wanting to be with me. Why pretend? I was more upset about the affair, really. But the whole experience made me question a lot of things. My judgement mostly.'

'Would you have changed your mind if you'd known what he wanted?'

Ali shook her head. 'No. And that's what I'm trying to explain to you. I don't want a child and, given my age, even if I changed my mind, it's unlikely to happen. If you want children, a family, then I'm not the right person for you. I'd rather get that out in the open now, I'd rather not be discarded again because I don't want children. I'd rather leave now.'

Ali knew in her soul there was a real possibility that she could fall in love with Jake. There was a connection between them that she couldn't explain but it went deeper than amazing sex, much deeper, and she didn't want to end up with a broken heart.

Jake stopped outside the NICU on his way to see Emma and Aaron. He scanned the room through the glass window looking for Aaron. He couldn't see him, but Emma was sitting beside Poppy's crib holding Jasmine in her arms.

He knew the twins were making progress, gaining weight and getting stronger every day. Jasmine in particular was doing well, but they were still so tiny. He could empathise with Emma and Aaron. He realised how scared they must be, how worried they would be about their daughters, and he was glad he didn't have to go through that. Watching Emma with her babies gave him a little insight into how his parents must have felt when he was diagnosed with the Wilm's tumour. Watching Emma, he could understand his mother's protectiveness a little better.

He watched for a moment, thinking about Ali's question.

Did he want children?

He'd been giving it a lot of consideration over the past couple of days.

Chrissie had wanted children. He'd imagined that one day he'd be a father because that was what his wife wanted but he could still remember how he'd felt when Chrissie had fallen pregnant unexpectedly. How nervous he'd been. Scared. Worried about his own health. He only had one kidney—what if he had a young family and something went wrong with him? Where would that leave them?

He'd been terrified that they were doing the wrong thing. And he knew he hadn't supported Chrissie properly.

Why hadn't he told Ali everything that had gone wrong in his marriage?

He knew he'd kept quiet because he hadn't wanted to look like a failure.

When they'd lost the baby he hadn't known what to do. He'd never found the right words to say to Chrissie. And that frightened him. That someone had relied on him, and he'd let them down so badly. His guilt had consumed him, and he was disappointed in his behaviour. Disappointed in himself.

Ali had asked how he'd felt when Jasmine and Poppy were born. He couldn't recall feeling anything but relieved for Ali that the delivery hadn't had tragic consequences. It certainly hadn't raised any burning desire in him to have children of his own though. It was a terrifying prospect in some ways, to be solely responsible for another human life. He did that every day at work, but he knew what he was doing then. He'd studied for years to become an anaesthetist, no one taught parenting skills. He didn't want someone to be a hundred per cent reliant on him.

He could think of a lot of reasons not to have kids but couldn't think of many reasons why he should.

He scrubbed his hands and pushed open the door to enter the NICU. If Aaron wasn't there, he'd leave a message with Emma.

'Emma, hi, how are you doing?'

'Good. Starting to go a little stir crazy but I escaped over the weekend. Aaron took me out for dinner. Just a quick one—I found even after getting sick of these four walls, I couldn't bear to be away from the girls for more than an hour.' She smiled.

This was what Ali was talking about, Jake thought. This all-consuming love and devotion parents had for their children. Obviously with the recent traumatic events in Emma's life she was even more emotionally tied to her children than usual and would find it hard to be apart from them, but could he imagine being like that? He didn't know the answer to that.

'And Aaron, how's he managing?' he asked.

'I think he feels a little useless. And I'm worried about what he's up to at home—he's been tinkering. He's not good with downtime.' She laughed. 'Would you mind holding Jasmine for a moment? I just want to check Poppy's chart.'

'Sure. You haven't popped home to see what Aaron's been doing?' he asked as Emma passed him the baby.

'No. Ignorance is bliss. I've got enough to worry about without adding his projects to my list. But luckily he's now back in pre-production for the next season of his show. That should keep him occupied until Poppy's surgery and until we can bring the girls home.'

'Has Poppy's surgery been scheduled?'

'Not yet. But she's gaining weight so that's good news. I'm hoping that she'll be strong enough for it some time in the next few weeks.'

'I'm sure you can't wait to get them home.'

'Sometimes yes. And sometimes no. It's a little bit frightening thinking of how I'm going to manage. I get lots of help in here. Everyone has been wonderful.'

'The place won't seem the same without you,' he said. 'Could you pass on a message to Aaron for me? Let him know we've got fourteen hundred participants registered for the charity event. His celebrity status has really helped the project and I really appreciate his time and effort.'

'That's fantastic,' Emma said as she held out her arms, ready to take Jasmine back. 'He's really looking forward to taking part.'

Jake heard the NICU door open as he turned to hand Jasmine back to her mum.

'Jake!'

He heard Ali's voice and spun around. He could see

she was surprised to see him and realised she'd probably assumed he was Aaron as parents needed to don hospital scrubs to enter the NICU. Her gaze dropped to the baby in his arms and her expression clouded.

Her voice was tight as she said, 'I can see you're busy, Emma. I'll come back.'

'What's all that about?' Emma asked as Ali turned and fled.

'Not sure,' Jake replied, even though he knew exactly what was wrong. Ali was picturing him with a child of his own. Him holding a baby was the last thing he needed her to see. 'But I'm going to find out,' he said as he handed Jasmine back to Emma and hurried after Ali.

'Ali. Wait.'

She kept walking.

He knew she would have heard him. Was she going to pretend otherwise? She took two more steps before stopping and turning to face him.

She looked stricken and he could imagine what she was thinking. He reached for her, gently holding her forearm, wanting to make sure she didn't run away before listening to what he had to say.

'Emma asked me to hold Jasmine while she checked Poppy's chart. It's not something I'm in the habit of doing. It's not something I asked for. But I have been thinking about your question. A lot. And can I imagine teaching a child to surf, ride a bike, abseil? Yes, I can, but I don't imagine it has to be *my* child. And could I live without that? Definitely. I'm sure there are lots of rewarding moments being a parent but that doesn't mean life is unrewarding if you're not a parent. Through the charity I am already involved with other people's children—often—

and that's really satisfying. I don't need children of my own to feel complete. I want to find love again, but the first step is finding the person I want to spend my life with. It doesn't start with children. Not for me.

'I enjoy your company,' he continued. 'You've told me you enjoy mine. Let's see where this takes us. We might be enough but if you're going to let your assumptions derail us there's not much I can do. I'm just asking for you to give me a chance to prove to you that I mean what I say. Don't give up on us yet. On me. Come with me to my parents' party on Saturday night. Please.'

CHAPTER NINE

'JAKE, PLEASE CAN you try to relax? You're making me wonder what I'm getting myself into.'

Jake had been on edge since he'd arrived to pick her up for his parents' party and, as the Uber dropped them off at his family home, she worried that things were only going to get worse. He'd become more and more tense the closer they got to Double Bay.

'Sorry, you're right. It's just I always expect things to end in an argument.'

'Come on,' she said as she reached up to straighten his collar before kissing him soundly in an effort to distract him. 'I'm sure everything will be fine.' She didn't know what the future held for them, but she had chosen to give Jake a chance and if she could support him tonight she would. She didn't want him to feel alone. She wanted him to know he had someone in his corner.

They were greeted at the door by a hostess who took their coats and directed them to the rear of the house.

The house was large, too big for three people and definitely too big for a couple in Ali's opinion. The floors were parquetry, the furnishings antique and everywhere, on almost every horizontal surface, was a large floral arrangement in shades of red. Ali knew Jake's parents were celebrating their fortieth wedding anniversary and she could see they'd obviously gone with a ruby theme.

'Jake, darling, hello.' A glamorous dark-haired woman, dressed in red, was headed their way.

'Mother.' Jake bent down to kiss her and then she immediately turned her attention to Ali. Ali felt exposed under her striking blue gaze.

'You must be Alinta.' She held out her hand. 'Lovely to meet you. I'm Lara.'

'And I'm Howard, Jake's father,' said a man who, despite his height, had been two steps behind Lara. 'Welcome to our home.'

'Thank you,' Ali replied, a little flustered. From Jake's description of his relationship with his parents she'd expected them to be cool, emotionally distant, but they were warm and welcoming. 'Congratulations on your anniversary, such a big milestone. And the house looks spectacular, the decorations are amazing.'

'Chris organised it all for us. Have you met Jake's cousin, Will, and his partner?'

'I have.'

'Chris has a wonderful eye for setting a scene,' Lara said. 'They should be here soon.'

'Alinta, you work with Jake?' Howard asked.

'Yes, I'm an obstetrician at Sydney Central.' For some reason she felt it was important to make her job title clear.

'Ali is actually the head of Obstetrics and Gynaecology.'

'Really? That's impressive.' Howard sounded impressed but Ali didn't miss the sideways glance he gave his son. Had she heard something else underneath his compliment? Was it something in his tone that suggested he wondered what Jake had been doing with his time? Why *he* wasn't the head of a department. Was this what Jake had been talking about?

'Well, please, enjoy the evening,' Lara said as she put her hand on Howard's forearm and prepared to direct him elsewhere. 'Jake, you will make sure to say hello to our old friends, won't you?'

'Of course.'

Ali was grateful that Will and Chris were at the party too. Jake was expected to greet all of his parents' friends but Chris had rescued her from the introductions and whisked her onto the dance floor. But after several songs her feet were starting to complain about her high heels and she begged a break to get a drink.

Lara came over to them at the bar. She greeted Chris warmly and Ali recalled Jake's comment about how his parents reserved their judgement for him. 'Are you two enjoying yourselves?' she asked.

'It's a lovely party,' Ali said sincerely. She'd like to spend more time with Jake, but the food was delicious, the drinks plentiful and the music from the sixties and seventies ensured the dance floor was full.

'Chris, if you don't mind, I know Jake's godmother would love a dance with you,' Lara said.

'I think I'll have to start charging—do you think your friends will make a donation to Jake's charity every time I dance with them?'

'I'm sure they already have. They're always good supporters of a cause. I should know,' she said as she shooed him away. 'Jake gives so much of his time to that charity,' Lara said as Chris departed for the dance floor.

'Is that a good thing?' Ali asked.

'Yes. It's kept him busy after his marriage break-up. That was such a dreadful time; we were all so upset. But it's good to see him happy again. Making a fresh start,' she said as she looked appraisingly at Ali.

Ali didn't want her to jump to any conclusions about her relationship with Lara's son. 'He seems to be enjoying his job.'

'Yes, yes, that's wonderful but it's his personal life that he needs to work on. We'd really love to see him settled down again.' She was still looking closely at Ali, who began to feel more and more as if she was under inspection. 'Jake said you're the head of Obstetrics and Gynaecology? You seem young to have such a high level of responsibility.'

Was she fishing for information? Ali wished people would just ask direct questions. She was used to preconceived ideas based on her gender, looks and ethnicity. She hated trying to guess people's agendas.

'I'm forty years old,' she replied. There was no point pretending. She was older than Jake and she had a more senior role in the hospital and she couldn't change either of those facts. Not right now.

'And single?'

'Divorced.'

'Do you have children?'

'No.'

She knew the assumption now would be that she couldn't have them. That something was wrong with her. Or that she'd missed her window of opportunity.

'That's a shame.'

'Is it?' She wondered what Lara would say if Ali announced she and Jake were just having sex and not interested in a long-term relationship.

'Yes. I was hoping Jake would find a partner who would give him children and you of all people would know how fertility declines with age.'

Lara certainly wasn't keeping her opinions to herself. It was clear she thought if Ali wasn't going to provide her with grandchildren, then what was the point?

Be careful what you wish for, Ali thought to herself. She'd wanted direct questions but Lara's comment had taken her by surprise and she stood, speechless, while Lara continued. 'Jake would be a good father. He should have kids. It was such a shame about Jake and Chrissie. They should have tried harder to make their marriage work. They should have tried for another baby.'

'Another baby?' Ali wasn't sure if she'd heard Lara correctly.

'Yes. He hasn't been the same since Chrissie's miscarriage. We were all devastated. He'd been so happy about the pregnancy, and I really thought another baby would bring them back together but instead, they got divorced.'

Ali could taste the champagne in the back of her throat and thought she might be about to be sick.

She stood still, dumbstruck, as her insides turned to ice. She had absolutely no idea what to say and was still standing, silent and chilled to the bone, when Howard came and escorted Lara onto the dance floor.

Ali wished the ground would swallow her up.

She put her glass down on the table, unable to take another sip, and headed for the terrace. It would be cold outside, but she needed some fresh air.

But before she could make it through the door, Jake intercepted her. 'Is everything okay? You look pale.'

She stopped in her tracks and turned to him. 'I'm not sure,' she said, her voice steely and cool. 'Why didn't you tell me that you and your ex had a miscarriage?'

Jake shrugged. 'Why would I? It's not important.'

'Not important! How can you say that?'

'I meant, I didn't think it was important to tell you about it. Plenty of couples suffer miscarriages.'

'Your mum said you were devastated. You told me you didn't want children. I thought you might have mentioned that you lost a baby.'

'It didn't seem like a baby. Chrissie didn't look pregnant. I hadn't felt the baby move. Neither of us had. I didn't feel like a father.'

'Were you excited?'

'No. I was terrified. I felt trapped. The pregnancy wasn't planned. That was when I realised that our marriage was crumbling, but how could I leave now? How could I walk away when she was pregnant? Then when Chrissie miscarried, I was worried that the miscarriage was my fault. Was there something wrong with me? Had the chemo done some damage that was unexpected?'

'You should have told me,'she said.

'I let Chrissie down. I didn't want you to think I was a failure as well.'

'I don't think you're a failure. I think you're a liar. And that's much worse,' she said as she stepped around him.

'Where are you going?'

'Home.'

'I'll take you.'

'No.' She shook her head. 'I need some time on my own. Time to think about what this all means.'

'It doesn't mean anything.'

'I disagree. This isn't like finding out you lied about which football team you support, or that you're a cat person not a dog person. You and your ex-wife were expecting a baby! You only just told me you don't want children. How do I believe anything you've told me?'

'You're blowing this out of proportion. I didn't lie to you.'

'Don't tell me what I should be thinking.' Ali was angry. Really angry.

'It doesn't change anything. It doesn't change the way I feel about you, and it shouldn't change the way you feel. *That's* what's important.'

'No. What's important is that we're honest with each other. And what I'm feeling right now is that I need some time on my own. I think it's better if we don't see each other any more,' she said as she walked past him and headed for the front door.

She collected her jacket and bag and kept on walking. Jake's parents would probably think her rude for not saying goodbye, for not thanking them for the party, but she didn't care. She couldn't face them. She couldn't face Chris and Will. She couldn't face anyone.

She was holding back tears as she fled. She was a foolish, foolish woman.

She should have listened to her head when she first met him. She knew Jake couldn't be the right person for her but her sixth sense had told her otherwise.

She'd been fooled. But not by him.

She'd fooled herself.

She'd rushed things, forgotten that he was supposed to just be good sex. She'd let herself get carried away. Let her heart carry her away. Let her think they could have a future. She'd let her hormones rule her head. She'd gone all in way too quickly and now she was paying the price.

'You've got to be fricking kidding me.' Jake clenched his fists and stared after Ali as she walked out of the door before turning on his heel and heading in his mother's direction. He was furious—with Lara, not with Ali—but before he reached his mother he was intercepted by his cousin.

'What's going on?' Will asked. 'Did Ali have an emergency? I've just seen her leave.'

'My bloody mother.' Jake could feel the steam coming out of his ears.

Will put a hand out and held Jake's arm. 'Don't make a scene,' he told him. 'You'll regret it later. Come outside and tell me what's going on.'

'Mum told Ali about Chrissie's miscarriage.'

'What do you mean, your mum told her? You hadn't?'

'No.'

'Why not?'

Jake shrugged. 'It wasn't relevant.'

'Except it would seem that it was. She looked upset.'

'Ali doesn't want kids. I told her that didn't matter to me, that I was happy not having kids. I want Ali in my life. I'd rather have her and I didn't think that the fact that I *could* have been a father, but wasn't, was at all relevant. But now she knows, and she thinks I was trying to hide something from her.'

'You were.'

'But not for the reasons she thinks. She accused me of lying to her. She thinks that because Chrissie had an unplanned pregnancy it means that I want children. That doesn't even make sense, but she wouldn't let me explain. She wouldn't let me take her home.'

'Having a go at your mum over it won't help. It won't make any difference now the truth is out there. You should have been honest with Ali in the first place. Then it wouldn't matter what your mum said.'

Jake knew Will was right. It wasn't his mum's fault.

He ran his fingers through his hair and groaned. He wanted to punch something, throw something... Both reactions were completely out of character for him, but he was so angry. Except now he realised he was angry with himself. 'How do I fix this?'

'I don't know. But you'll need to talk to her.'

'She doesn't want to see me.'

'She'll calm down.'

Jake shook his head. 'I'm not sure that she will.'

'You're not fifteen. If you're meant to be together, you'll find a way. Give her some time, and use that time to build a compelling argument—or, if you can't do that, a compelling apology.'

Ali peered through the peephole in her door on Sunday evening before she opened it. If it was Jake she was going to pretend she wasn't home. But it wasn't Jake.

'Harper, what are you doing here?'

'Your mum said you weren't feeling well. She made you some soup and I offered to drop it off.'

'I'm not sick. I don't need soup.' Ali looked past Harper. 'Where's Yarran?'

'He's on a night shift. It's just me.'

Ali waited for Harper to pass her the container of soup. She didn't want to grab it from her, but she did want her to leave. She wasn't in the mood for small talk.

But Harper apparently had other ideas. 'Can I come in?'

'I don't really feel like company.'

'If Yarran was here, you'd ask us in.'

'That's different.'

'Why?'

'He's my brother. He's family.'

'You used to say I was like a sister to you.'

'That was before.'

'We were best friends once and I'm going to be family. You can't avoid me for ever. I'm not leaving until I know you're okay.'

'I'm not okay. I'm upset but I will be fine.'

'Do you want to tell me what's going on? Maybe I can help.'

'This isn't something you can help with. This is about something I've done. I've been an idiot.'

'Is it Jake?'

'Why do you say that?'

'I recognise the signs of heartbreak.'

'My heart isn't broken,' Ali lied. But wasn't that exactly how she felt? She'd been telling herself all day that she was going to be fine. That she couldn't possibly be this upset over a man she'd known for only a few weeks. 'It's my pride that's hurt. I've been a fool. I trusted Jake and he let me down.'

'What has he done?'

Ali had stepped back and Harper had followed her

into the apartment. Harper closed the door behind her and put the soup on the bench and flicked the kettle on. Ali didn't object. What was the point? She didn't have the energy to argue with Harper. They'd have a cup of tea and then Harper could leave.

'You'd think I'd know better by now. I trusted him and he let me down. He lied to me.'

'Lied? About what?'

'He told me he didn't want children. That he didn't need children in his life. Yet his mother told me he was planning a family with his ex-wife, but she had a miscarriage.'

'What did he say about that?'

'That doesn't matter. Don't you see? He was going to have a family. His mother said he was happy about it. Maybe he doesn't want children right now but what if he changes his mind like Adam did? I don't want to find out in a year or two that he does want children. I don't want him to leave me too. It's better to end it now. I'm not going to see him again. We'd barely started a relationship. I just need a few days to move on.' But her heart was heavy. 'I'm obviously not a good judge of character. Adam let me down. You betrayed me. Now Jake has done the same thing.'

'Don't you think you're being a bit melodramatic?'

'No.'

'At the risk of destroying our fragile truce, I think there's something you need to hear. You've always been very quick to make decisions. And to judge others for their decisions. Not everyone is like you. Not everyone sees the world in black and white, wrong or right, like you do. There's no middle ground with you.'

'What do you mean?'

'Maybe Jake didn't want children but when his wife fell pregnant what was he supposed to do? Maybe he changed his mind. Maybe he didn't. Theory and reality are two different things. Maybe when he was confronted with the reality of being a parent, he decided it was something he wanted. But that doesn't mean he's not allowed to change his mind back again. Maybe he's decided he'd rather have you. I've seen the way he looks at you.'

'But what if he changes it again? Where will that leave me?'

'I think you need to ask him that. You can't decide for him. You did that for me.'

'When?'

'When you decided I was in the wrong when I left Yarran and moved to London.'

'Well, you—'

'No. I wasn't,' Harper cut in. 'I did what I had to do at the time. There are two sides to every story, but you heard Yarran's and judged me accordingly.'

'You never gave me your side,' Ali argued. 'You never said goodbye.'

'Because I knew you would take Yarran's side so what was the point? In your mind, he would be right, and I would be wrong. It was all I could do to tell Yarran. I didn't have the energy to tell you as well.'

'It wasn't just Yarran that you hurt. You were my best friend and you left without a word.'

'I know. I'm sorry, I panicked. He's your twin, I didn't expect you to take my side, but I couldn't speak to you about how I was feeling. I knew I was breaking Yarran's heart and I couldn't stand to have you hate me as well.

Your family is so close. I never knew anything like that when I was growing up and after the childhood I had I was terrified that I wouldn't be able to live up to your family's expectations. I had no idea how normal families functioned. I didn't think I'd be able to do it. I couldn't bear the thought of letting Yarran down. I thought I was making the right decision. But I never got over him. I never forgot him. I never stopped loving him. He's forgiven me—don't you think you should too?'

'I have forgiven you for that. I see how happy he is now. He's had more than his fair share of sadness, of love gone wrong with you and then Marnie, he deserves to be happy and I can see that he is happy with you. I've forgiven you for that but I can't forget how betrayed I felt when you left without saying goodbye.'

'I promise you this is it. I'm not going anywhere. When I came back for this job, I never thought I'd have another chance with Yarran, but I did. He's my other half. My one. My everything. He completes me. When you meet the one you're supposed to be with you'll know what I'm talking about. Learn from my experience. I've wasted years running away because I didn't think I deserved love. You have a chance at something beautiful with Jake. I've seen how he looks at you. Why are you prepared to believe his mother over him? Surely he knows himself best. Don't throw it away over a misunderstanding. What is your heart telling you? It's the only thing that can be trusted.'

Ali didn't want to trust her heart. Her heart could break. Her head wouldn't.

'Take it from me,' Harper said, 'you need to learn to compromise.'

'But that's the problem,' Ali said. 'There's no middle ground with kids. You either have them or you don't.'

Jake was glad to be on the night shift for the week. He'd spent a couple of days hoping Ali would realise she was throwing away something special, but wishing for something wasn't going to make her see reason. He knew he needed to apologise if he was going to have any chance of salvaging the situation. But, as Will had said, his apology needed to be compelling. He'd listened to Ali when she'd told him about her issues with Harper and her ex-husband and he knew he'd only get one shot to make things right.

He'd come up with a plan but he needed time to put it into place. His days had been spent fine-tuning the abseiling event and hounding Will, who he'd coerced into helping him with his apology. He'd been pleased he'd had something to occupy his time and his mind during the day, but the nights were dragging.

He headed for the lift, relieved to finally have something to do. He'd been called to the fourth floor, to Obstetrics, and habit made him scan the corridor, looking for Ali. But it was almost midnight and she was nowhere to be seen.

His patient was a pregnant woman who had reportedly been in labour for fifteen hours and needed pain relief. The attending obstetrician, Melissa Merrigan, wanted her patient to rest—in her opinion it would be a while before she was ready to deliver.

Jake stopped at the nurses' station and picked up the patient file.

Marli Bowden; husband, Simon.

Marli was an unusual name. Ali's sister, Marli, was due any day and his gut told him this patient would be one and the same.

He knocked on the door and stepped into the room.

Ali was the first person he saw and his heart did a funny little flip before he remembered that she wasn't speaking to him. Before he registered that she did *not* look happy to see him.

Her saw her stiffen as he walked into the room and knew that getting her to forgive him wasn't going to be easy.

What was she doing there? She wasn't the attending obstetrician. She must be there for moral support. That was just his luck.

'Hello, Ali,' he said. He couldn't pretend she wasn't in the room.

'What are you doing here?' she asked, her expression steely.

'Melissa ordered an epidural. I'm the anaesthetist on call.'

'Right,' she said as she turned to her sister, 'I'll wait outside.'

Jake waited to see if she had anything more to say, if she had anything at all to say to him, but she simply walked past him and out of the door.

'Hi, Marli, Simon, I'm Dr Ryan,' he introduced himself to the two people who had stayed in the room.

'Ah, you're Jake.' It was clear from Marli's tone that she knew Jake had upset Ali. He wondered if everyone knew. 'She's really annoyed with you, isn't she?'

'Yep.'

'Would you like me to speak to her?' Marli offered.

'No, it's my mistake. I need to fix it.'

'Can I give you one word of advice, then? Ali has trust issues—unless you can regain her trust you've got your work cut out for you.'

'I know about her trust issues,' he replied.

But that was only one part of the problem. It had been his behaviour that had made the problem worse. He should have had full disclosure. Will was right about that. But Ali had jumped to conclusions. She'd put two and two together and got five. She'd assumed that because he hadn't mentioned Chrissie's miscarriage it meant that he ultimately wanted children. Which wasn't true.

Ultimately, he wanted Ali.

'I have a plan to fix things,' he told Marli, 'but if she can't bear to be in the same room as me then I'm not sure how I'm going to implement my plan. But you've got other things to focus on. Melissa said you're after an epidural. She wants to see if you can get a little rest before this baby arrives.'

'Yes. I thought baby number three would come quickly. It seems to have a different opinion from me.'

'It must be a girl,' Simon said. 'There are plenty of stubborn genes in the females in your family.'

'It'll definitely be a girl,' Marli said with a smile before she turned to Jake. 'We've got two already.' She turned back to Simon and said, 'I hope you weren't expecting a boy?'

'Not at all. I figured it would be another girl. The more the merrier, I say. I love my girls.'

Jake could see Simon's pride and love and for a split second he wondered if he would be as effusive if he were a father. He figured, of course he would. You'd have to love your kids, right?

But he could live without them. He was certain of that.

Ali was waiting in the corridor but she had her back to Marli's door and Jake knew she was planning on avoiding him.

'Ali, you can't avoid me for ever. You have to talk to me.'

'No, I don't.'

'We work together. You will need to talk to me.'

'When I need to talk to you in a professional capacity I will, but I don't need to otherwise. I want to believe you but I don't know if I can. I don't think I should trust you. I don't know if I should trust myself.'

'But you'd trust my mother over me? You're choosing to accept her version of my story.'

'She told me how happy you were to be having a baby. Why would she lie about that?'

'What was I supposed to tell her? That I was terrified? That I didn't love Chrissie enough? That when she miscarried I felt relief—then I felt guilty for feeling that way? I was a complete roller coaster of emotions and so was Chrissie for different reasons. I couldn't support her and that was the final nail in the coffin of our marriage.

'I learned at an early age to lock my feelings away. I saw how upset my mother got if I ever talked about being scared. I know she was frightened of losing me so I learned to shield her from my feelings. I haven't shared my feelings with my mother since I was four years old so I couldn't tell my parents how I felt. I couldn't tell them I was relieved. I couldn't tell them I didn't love Chrissie.

I knew what they would think and I was tired of disappointing them. I can't help it if my mother projected her thoughts onto my feelings after the miscarriage. I can't help it if she got it all wrong. Ali, you have to believe me. I haven't lied to you.'

Jake held his breath, hoping Ali would hear him. Hoping she would listen. But she was shaking her head.

'I can't do this now,' she said. 'Marli needs me.'

She walked away, taking Jake's hopes with her.

'Uncle Yarran,' Ali said as her twin entered Marli's hospital room. 'Meet Willa,' she said as she handed Marli's sleeping daughter to her brother.

Yarran cradled his niece in his arms and smiled at her. 'Hello, gorgeous girl, you finally made it.'

Ali watched Yarran and Willa. Holding babies suited him. He was a brilliant dad to Jarrah and Ali hoped he would have more children with Harper.

'Congratulations, Marli.' Yarran bent over to give Marli a kiss, making sure he protected Willa. 'Did you want to grab a drink tonight, Simon, to wet your daughter's head?' he asked his brother-in-law.

'I can babysit the girls for you,' Ali offered, knowing Simon was responsible for looking after his older daughters, Tallulah and Jazz, while Marli was in hospital. 'I haven't got any plans.'

'You should have plans,' Marli admonished. 'Why haven't you sorted things out with Jake?'

'There's nothing to sort out.'

'You could have fooled me. If there's nothing to sort out why were you on edge last night? You could have cut the tension with a knife,' she replied.

'What do you mean?' Ali asked.

'You disappeared as soon as Jake arrived and you only came back after he'd left.'

'You didn't need me in here while he gave you an epidural,' Ali said as she felt Yarran watching her closely.

'You need to talk to him. Cool your hot head and sort things out between you before the abseiling event on Saturday.'

'I'm not going abseiling,' Ali replied. She'd made the decision to pull out of the event last night. There was no way she could face Jake.

'Why not?'

'I'm too busy with work.' She gave the excuse she'd concocted.

'Rubbish,' Yarran said. 'Work hasn't changed in the past four days and Harper and Ivy aren't too busy. They've committed to it.'

'The cause will get my fundraising dollars even if I don't participate.'

'This isn't about time or fundraising,' Yarran said. 'This is about Jake.'

Ali looked at him, certain Harper must have told him what was going on. She hadn't specifically asked Harper to keep what happened between Ali and Jake confidential and so she should have expected her to tell Yarran. And she knew Yarran wasn't going to let this go.

'Don't be a coward,' he said.

'Kirra, Jack, Mum and Dad are taking all the older kids down to Circular Quay to watch. They're expecting to see you, Yarran and Harper all abseiling. Are you going to let them down too?' Marli added.

Ali thought she'd rather let them down than see Jake. That would be too painful.

'Our family are not quitters,' Yarran said, and Ali knew he was certain he'd had the last word. He was right. The Edwardses didn't give up.

CHAPTER TEN

SYDNEY HAD PUT on a perfect winter's day, calm and sunny with a forecast of twenty degrees Celsius, but Ali's mood didn't match the weather. Normally such a fine day would lift her spirits, but she couldn't shake her lethargy. She was not enthused about anything.

She found herself on tenterhooks whenever she was walking the corridors. Half hoping to bump into Jake, half terrified of seeing him. She didn't know how she would react if she saw him. She missed his company. Missed him. But she'd have to get over that. There was no going back.

She'd woken up this morning dreading the day, knowing it was almost inevitable that she'd see Jake, even if she might not have to speak to him. She'd given in to her family's pressure. Yarran was right. She wasn't a quitter. She was a mature, successful woman, she could behave like one and get through the day.

Ali had half hoped for bad weather, perhaps enough to cancel the abseiling event but she knew that wasn't in the spirit of the charity. With fourteen hundred people signed up for the event surely there would be enough participants to keep her separated from Jake, she thought as she, Yarran, Harper and Ivy made their way to the hotel at Circular Quay. Phoebe hadn't changed her mind, she wasn't participating, but she had donated to the charity and had promised to come down to support them.

An area in front of the hotel had been barricaded to separate the participants from members of the public—both those watching and others who were just passing by on their way to and from the ferry terminal and along the waterfront of the quay. Spectators had gathered at one end of the viewing area and Ali looked for her parents and the rest of her family, who were coming down to watch, even though she knew that they wouldn't be there yet. Check-in was almost an hour before their descent time—far too long for young children to stand and wait. They were most likely still on the other side of the harbour, waiting for the ferry.

Members of the media were positioned inside the barriers. Cameras were trained on the face of the hotel. Ali looked up to see a dozen figures, of varying shapes and sizes, abseiling down the hotel. As a couple reached the ground, journalists, trailed by their camera crew, approached requesting interviews. Ali wondered how long the media were planning on staying. The event was scheduled to go on for twelve hours—that would make for a long day.

Other participants, easily recognised by the bright yellow T-shirts they had been given with the charity name in large letters on the backs, were being directed to marshalling areas by the event organisers, who wore black versions of the same shirts.

Ali recognised one who was at the end of a rope, belaying a participant. She watched as a man made his final descent, both feet touching the ground, as Will high-fived him. She saw Will give some slack to the line before he said, 'Off belay,' and unclipped the man's harness. Ali leant over the barrier as the man headed back into the hotel and called out.

Will turned and jogged over to her, kissing her on the cheek. 'Hi, Ali, good to see you haven't changed your mind.'

Ali glanced up at the hotel. 'I have to admit I'm a little nervous looking at the height of the hotel.'

'You'll be fine. I promised to belay you—you'll be coming down in groups of ten, grab the eighth spot, that'll be me.'

Ali nodded and then hurried to catch up to Yarran, Harper and Ivy who were checking in before heading to the marshalling areas. They were assembled outside and then ushered into the hotel for a video and safety briefing. They stowed their belongings, got organised into groups of ten and were then escorted to the top floor of the hotel and up the stairs to the rooftop.

They emerged into the bright morning sunshine. People in yellow and black T-shirts were everywhere, dozens of them, but her gaze was drawn instantly to Jake. He had his back to her, but she picked him out immediately even though he was on the far side of the building.

She might not want to see him but the connection she felt was still there. It was going to take some time before she managed to put him out of her mind. To move on.

That was okay. She knew she'd get there. She didn't think she'd ever forget him, but she'd learn to live without him. It had only been a month—it was ridiculous to think she wouldn't be able to get over him. Wouldn't meet someone else.

So why did it feel as if this was it? As if she'd never find someone like him? As if she'd never find what Yarran had found with Harper, what her siblings, her parents, Ivy and Lucas had found? Life was unfair. Why did the person she'd fallen in love with have to be the one that she couldn't have—?

Oh, my God.

She was in love with him.

She stopped walking as the realisation hit her, and Ivy, who had followed her up to the roof, bumped into her back.

'Are you okay?' Ivy asked.

'No.' Ali was frozen in place.

'I'm sure it's perfectly safe. We'll be fine.'

But Ivy misunderstood Ali's hesitation. It wasn't a fear of heights that had stopped her in her tracks. It was her fear of being in love with Jake. Her fear of having to live her life without him.

She was in love with Jake.

She rolled the idea around in her head, wondering how she was going to deal with that, when Jake turned to look at her. He smiled and she almost burst into tears. He was everything she wanted. He was enough for her. More than enough. Even after such a short time she knew he was the one. And if she was truly honest with herself, she'd known in half that time. Why couldn't she be enough for him?

Why did she have to fall in love with someone whose dreams weren't compatible with hers? Why was she constantly drawn to the wrong men?

'Come on,' Ivy said, 'it's our turn.' She took Ali's hand and pulled her forward. The group in front of them had their harnesses on and were in the launch area, ready to go. Ali's group was next.

An event organiser positioned a harness on the ground and Ali stepped into it, relieved that Jake wasn't the one responsible for strapping her in. She didn't think she could stand to be so close to him, to have him touch her. Not now. She was feeling vulnerable, exposed and emotional. She needed to get herself under control.

She focused on recalling the video briefing, running through in her head the process of abseiling. But that didn't help. Jake had been the one who'd shown her how to do this. The whole experience was connected to Jake and her memories of him. She'd just have to get through the morning and then, somehow, find a way to deal with her feelings. With him.

She held her arms out as a second harness was slid around her shoulders, half listening as the straps were clipped together and the fastenings checked. The group in front of them were now stepping off the building, disappearing over the edge.

'All right, you can make your way to the launching area for a final check.'

Ali took a deep breath. It was her turn now.

Large, numbered squares had been painted along the edge of the roof, extending back several metres. A thick cable, hung with signs warning 'keep out', ran along the outer edge of the building, a couple of metres in from the drop-off to prevent anyone from getting too close until they were ready to abseil.

She could see metal frames bolted to the fixing points. The fixing points were permanent, strong enough to hold a platform and two men as the window cleaners' equipment was normally attached to these bolts. Jake had told her as much and it had also been in the safety briefing, a way to reassure the participants that everything was strong, secure and safe. Ali wasn't worried about the bolts but there were any number of other things that could fail—the rope, the harness...her courage.

She and Ivy followed Yarran and Harper to the far end of the roof, stepping carefully along a painted yellow line as directed by the instructors to make sure they didn't stray off course. Yarran and Harper took squares nine and ten, staying on the inside of a red rope that ran around the perimeter. Ali stepped ahead of Ivy to make sure she would get square number eight so Will could belay her as promised.

The event leaders were double-clipped onto safety wires, enabling them to move back and forward along the roof, unclipping one fastening at a time. There was one leader per participant and as Ali glanced to her left, she saw Jake unclip his tethering before reclipping himself opposite her. She knew he was about to check her harness and attach her to the abseiling ropes. This was the scenario she had been dreading but there was nothing she could do about it now. She had nowhere to go. She was trapped between him and the edge of the building.

His black T-shirt moulded itself to his frame, sitting flat over his abdominals and hugging his deltoid and shoulder muscles. He wore sunglasses so she couldn't see his eyes. But he could see hers. There was nothing for her to hide behind and she was afraid her emotions were on full display. Afraid her panic and longing, loneliness and regret were written all over her face.

'Hello, Ali.'

He stood directly in front of her as he checked her harness. His hands were at her waist, then at her shoulders, as he tugged on the straps and checked the carabiners.

Ali held her breath as her heart rate went crazy.

His touch felt intimate, a completely different sensation from how it had felt when the other instructor helped her.

Jake connected her ropes. She still hadn't said a word and if he noticed he didn't comment. 'You've got two harnesses, shoulders and hips, and two attachment points,' he said as his hands moved around her body. 'The shoulder harness is a back-up, you're nice and secure.' He was clipping her to the fixing point now, securing her to the roof before he unclipped one end of the red rope that had separated her from the edge of the building. 'All right, you can step through and stand with your feet on the marks,' he said.

Ali could see two feet stencilled at the edge of the building. She stepped into square number eight, positioned between Ivy at number seven and Yarran at nine. The painted feet faced the centre of the roof, so now she was standing with her back to the edge of the building. She looked over her shoulder—it was a long way down.

Her nervousness kicked in again. She hadn't really been worried about the activity, she'd been more nervous about coming face to face with Jake, but now she could see the drop she could feel her heart pounding, sending adrenaline coursing through her system. It was not helped by the fact that Jake remained in her square. If she put out her hand, she'd be able to touch him.

Jake and the other organisers had two-way radios enabling them to communicate with the team on the ground. One by one they called out, 'On belay!'

'Belay on!' came the response from each belayer down below.

'All right. Take a step over the edge.'

Ali looked at Ivy on her left and then Yarran on her right, waiting to see which one of them was going to go first.

Yarran had a grin stretching across his face as he gave everyone a thumbs up and stepped over the edge. He was fearless but Ali knew he'd done this manoeuvre plenty of times in his role with the fire department. His departure left Ali looking at Harper.

'Are we really doing this?' Harper asked. She looked nervous too, which cheered Ali up.

'I think so.'

'Ready?' Jake asked.

Ali nodded and took a step back, a few seconds after Ivy but slightly before Harper. She imagined she was in the climbing gym. If she didn't look down, she could pretend it was only ten metres to the ground and that there was a soft mat waiting at the bottom.

Yarran was already a few metres below them. He had his feet planted on the wall of the building and he was sitting back in his harness, relaxed, waiting for them all to step over.

Ali breathed out, exhaling audibly with relief as her harness held her weight.

They all began to walk down the wall, tentatively at first, one foot at a time, keeping their feet lined up with their hips. The ropes were holding and Ali let herself look down again.

Yarran was getting into the swing of the exercise—literally. She watched as he pushed off, swinging out into thin air, before coming back in, his feet wide, his knees flexed to absorb the impact as he landed back on the building back with a massive grin on his face. 'Come on, try it!' he encouraged.

Ivy gave a little push off the wall, not as powerful as Yarran's but enough to get her to swing out a little way before coming back to the wall. She repeated the move with a little more force and dropped several metres.

On her right Harper followed Ivy's lead. Not wanting to look tentative, Ali did the same, attempting a slight spring off the wall and back in. She breathed out—no disasters.

To her left she could see the Harbour Bridge, the sun on the water, ferries criss-crossing the bay leaving white water in their wake. She could hear the toot of the ferry horns, the sound of the traffic on the road to her right and the noise of the pedestrians and buskers milling around on Circular Quay below her. She was suspended above it all, but it didn't look too scary.

She did a second jump, no bigger than the first. She wasn't going to push hard. She didn't want to move too far from the wall—feeling as though she was within touching distance of the wall was somehow reassuring even though she knew the vertical surface was not going to offer any protection. She looked up to see she'd descended half a dozen floors but still had more than half the building to go.

Her gaze caught on Jake's gorgeous face peering over the edge, monitoring their progress. It was reassuring knowing he was there. It was a silly feeling—it wasn't as if he could do anything if something went awry and Will was the one controlling her descent.

Ali did a third jump and then a fourth. A little more forceful this time, a slightly bigger arc, a little longer spent curving out from the building, suspended in mid-air, her confidence growing. As her feet hit the building, she felt a jolt and her right hip dropped slightly. She looked at her right leg, wondering if she hadn't landed squarely but her feet were firmly on the building. She felt Will tighten the rope, taking the slack and holding her in position but she wasn't square on the building.

Her hips weren't level.

Her harness looked crooked and then she saw it. One of the carabiners had snapped.

She wasn't falling, she could feel that Will was holding her weight, but what happened next? What would happen if she kept descending?

She could feel panic rising in her chest. Her breathing was rapid, her heart was racing. She wanted to yell, wanted to tell someone that there was a problem, but she was frozen. Her throat felt tight, constricted. She couldn't force any words out and she wasn't sure who would hear her. Yarran, Ivy and Harper were all below her now and what could they do anyway? Yarran was the only one with any experience and he couldn't climb back up the building.

What was she supposed to do if there was a problem? She tried to recall the instructions from the safety briefing. She knew there was a signal. An arm signal. But she was holding tight to the rope with both hands and she was afraid to let go. She squeezed her eyes closed and pictured the briefing instructions. Arm out with elbow bent at ninety degrees indicated 'stop'. A straight arm, held out to the side, must mean 'there's a problem'.

She opened her eyes. Her chest was tight, her breathing shallow, she was feeling dizzy from a lack of oxygen. She forced herself to breathe, in and out, in and out, knowing she'd have to try a hand signal.

She tightened her grip on the rope with her left hand, just in case, and counted down from three in her head.

She loosened her grip on her right hand but couldn't make herself let go of the rope. She thought she might be sick. She started to shake.

'Ali, is everything okay?'

She heard Jake's voice. She looked up and saw him give the 'OK' signal—the tips of his thumb and forefinger pressed together to form an 'O' shape.

She shook her head.

'What is it?'

She was too far away from him for him to see the problem and knew that her body would be blocking Will's view as well.

'A carabiner has snapped.' She finally found her voice but it sounded weak and she wasn't sure if it would have carried up to Jake.

'I'm coming down.'

She saw him press his earpiece firmly against his ear before he disappeared from view and Ali fought back a rising wave of panic. He'd said he was coming.

She saw his back at the edge of the roof. Saw him glance over his shoulder, heard him call, 'On belay.' She saw the rope that Yarran had used tighten as the belayer took up the slack. Yarran must have made it to the bottom of the building, but Ali was too frightened to look down. She didn't want to see how far she was. She was terrified of falling. Of plummeting to the ground.

She didn't want to die. Not on camera. Not in front of her family. And not without telling Jake how she felt.

Jake stepped over the edge.

He was by her side in two large jumps. His belayer holding him in position.

'Don't let me fall.' Her voice wobbled and tears sprang in her eyes.

He reached for her harness, grabbing onto it with one hand while he wrapped his other arm around her back, holding her to his side. 'You're not going to fall. I've got you.'

He let go of her harness and checked her equipment. 'We gave everyone more carabiners and ropes than they needed for safety. You're okay.'

'I'm afraid.'

'Ali, look at me. I won't ever let anything happen to you. I promise.'

He let go of her in order to take a spare carabiner off his own harness. He fastened it to hers, feeding the second rope through the loops, securing her again.

'All right,' he said. 'We've got to get to the bottom. Are you ready?'

'No.'

'You can do this,' he said. 'We'll walk down the building, one step at a time. I'll be with you the whole way. Do you trust me?'

She did.

She nodded.

'Okay. Right foot first. Remember what I taught you. Step off, move your foot down, keep your steps small.'

He walked her down the wall, one foot at a time, until

they reached the bottom. When her feet were on solid ground, he wrapped her in his arms.

'Are you okay?'

She was shaking but she was okay.

She nodded and fought back more tears only this time they were tears of relief. She wanted to bury her head into his chest. To never let him go.

'I need to talk to you,' she told him.

'I'm in the middle of the event. I can't leave now.'

'I know that, but I've got some things I want to say. Can you come to my house when you finish?'

He nodded and started to unclip her harness as reporters and cameramen approached them.

'I don't want to speak to the media,' she said. The only person she wanted to talk to was Jake.

'You don't have to. I'll make a statement. Aaron is in the next group, so they'll be distracted by his descent soon enough. I'll tell them it was a minor mishap, but the safety measures held up. I don't want anyone to panic,' he said as Yarran, Harper and Ivy rushed over.

'Oh, my God, Ali, are you okay?' Ivy exclaimed.

'She's had a shock but she's fine. Can you look after her? I can't leave.'

'Of course.'

'I'll see you at your place, but it could be late,' Jake told her.

She didn't care. All she wanted now was to be with him. It didn't matter when or where.

Jake's nerves were stretched tight. He'd had to force himself to focus on the rest of the event—it had been difficult to keep his mind from wandering to Ali—and the adrenaline surge had left him feeling wrung out. He was relieved she was okay, that there hadn't been a tragic turn of events, and was also relieved that their safety protocols had been robust, but he was concerned about how she was coping. Was she replaying the incident in her mind? Was she freaking out? Were Yarran and Harper taking care of her? In hindsight, would she blame him for the scare? After all, he'd been the one to check her equipment before the event.

Will had assured him it wasn't his fault. The equipment had been checked before use and then double-checked once each participant had been fitted out. It was an unfortunate accident but it hadn't been his mistake.

But that didn't stop the guilt.

For a moment today he'd briefly imagined a world without Ali in it. The consequences could have been far worse and he knew, without a doubt, that he wanted a life with her. Now he just needed to convince her that they were meant to be together.

He wanted to go to her the minute the event finished but a post-event gathering had been organised in the hotel bar and he knew he needed to stay for one drink with the charity committee, event organisers and volunteers, but his feet were itching to get to Ali.

On the television screen behind the bar the news was showing a clip of the day's events. There was an interview with Aaron and then a shot of Jake with Ali. They were standing together just after they'd reached the ground, she was wrapped in his arms and they were looking at each other as if there were no one else in the world. Anyone watching would see how they felt about each other and the picture gave him hope.

He needed to see her.

As the news story concluded he went to find Will and asked, 'Have you heard from Chris?'

He and Will had been working on a project that he hoped would win Ali over. After the incident he'd decided that he needed to implement the plan today. Will had done his part and then roped Chris in to set the final scene.

Will made a phone call. 'Everything is ready,' he said as he hung up.

'Thank you.' Jake hugged his cousin. He was grateful for his help and support and just hoped that their efforts weren't going to be in vain.

'Don't mention it. Just go and get your girl.'

CHAPTER ELEVEN

ALI OPENED HER door and stepped into Jake's embrace. He kissed the top of her head and then kissed her as she tipped her chin up and tilted her face to his.

His lips were soft and warm and her world settled around her again.

'How are you?' he asked as she took his hand and led him into her apartment.

'I'm fine. I feel embarrassed about overreacting.'

'You didn't overreact.'

'I did a bit, but I was terrified. I'm okay now.'

'You're not furious with me?'

'With you? No. Why?'

'I checked your equipment.'

'It wasn't only you and, as you said, there was no way I could fall. Not unless all of the equipment failed. I freaked out but I really am okay now.' It was strange to find herself reassuring him, but it made her feel better to focus on his feelings. 'But the whole episode did make me realise a couple of things.'

'Like?'

She wrapped her arms around his shoulders and kissed him firmly. 'One, I don't think I'll ever put my hand up for abseiling again.'

'Fair enough,' he said with a smile.

'And two, there are some things I need to tell you.'

'I have some things to tell you too but there's something I want to show you first,' he replied. 'Will you come with me? We can talk once we get there.'

Ali frowned. She'd prepared herself to tell him how she felt the minute he arrived at her place and she didn't want to wait—worried that her courage might desert her—but she was curious to find out where he was taking her.

'Where are we going?' she asked as he unlocked his car.

'I have a surprise for you. A good one, I hope.'

He was quiet on the drive and his silence made her nervous. By the time he parked the car her stomach felt as if it were tied in a bundle of knots and it took her a minute to realise where they were.

He'd parked in front of her granny's old house and there was a 'Sold' sticker stuck to the advertising board.

'It's been sold,' she said. She could hear the disappointment in her voice, but she wasn't sure why she felt like that. It wasn't as if she'd been planning to buy it.

'Yes.' Jake opened the glove box and took out a key. 'It's been sold to me.'

'You bought it?' Her heart plummeted. She didn't want to hear that. Now she was glad she hadn't told him how she felt. This was a house for a family and she was convinced he only had bad news for her. She was convinced there would be no future for them. 'Why?'

'I needed somewhere to live.'

'But why this house?'

'What's wrong with this house?' he said as he got out of the car. 'I thought you'd be pleased it's gone to someone who appreciates it,' he continued as he opened the passenger door for her.

'It's a house for a family.' She looked at him, trying to read what was going on in his head but any sixth sense she had seemed to have deserted her. 'Is that what you want to tell me? That you want a family?' Thank God she hadn't embarrassed herself. Thank God she hadn't told him she loved him only to have it thrown back in her face.

'No, that's not why I brought you here. I told you I think this house is a good investment and it was also in my price range—those are the things that initially appealed to me. Will you come inside?' Jake held out his hand. 'I'll explain everything.'

Ali hesitated before placing her hand in his. She wasn't convinced it was a smart move to go with him. Was this a prelude to heartbreak?

But, once again, curiosity got the better of her and she got out of the car.

His hand was warm but it did little to dispel the icy chill that encased her heart. She let him lead her through the front gate. The porch light was on and Jake slipped the key into the lock, pushing the door open and bringing her across the threshold.

The house was empty. It had been staged for sale when she'd visited before, but the furniture had since been removed. Their footsteps bounced off the bare floorboards and echoed down the long hallway. Jake flicked on the lights and led her past the front room and the staircase into the kitchen and back living area.

The kitchen was stripped bare but there was a large roll of paper on the kitchen bench. Ali assumed it was paperwork from the sale and paid little attention to it until

Jake let go of her hand and began to unroll the paper to reveal architectural drawings.

'This is what I wanted to show you. My ideas for the house. Will and I have been working on plans for restoration and updating—being mindful of its heritage. I'd like your opinion.'

'Why?'

'Because what you think matters to me,' he said as he put some weights on the corners of the plans. 'I want to open up the kitchen and living room and put bifold doors out into the garden. The front lounge will become a study and I'll put a powder room under the stairs and upgrade the bathroom on the first floor. I'll turn the smaller of the three bedrooms into a walk-in wardrobe for the primary bedroom and the other bedroom will be a study-cum-guest room. And out here,' he said as he picked up a remote, 'I'll put a new deck.' He hit a switch and the back garden lit up. Festoon lights hung in the loquat tree and hundreds of fairy lights flickered around the garden.

Ali gasped in delight. 'Were those lights always there?'

'No. Chris put them up for me.'

'When?'

'This afternoon while Will and I were wrapping things up at Circular Quay. He loves to set a scene.'

'It looks magical.' Ali walked over to the back window and gazed out.

Jake followed her and wrapped his arms around her waist. 'I thought I could hang a swing in the tree for you.'

'What do you mean, for me?' She spun around to face him, her brow furrowed in a frown.

'I needed to find somewhere to live and this house was a good option—it's in a great location and it has lots of potential, but the best thing about it is its connection to you. I felt it was meant to be,' he said. 'I bought this house for us.'

'For us?'

Jake nodded. 'I want you to move in with me.'

Ali was confused. 'But this house needs a family.'

'It will be a family house. We will fill it with the family we already have. Your big one and my smaller one. That's enough.'

'You don't want children?'

'No.' He smiled. 'I don't want children. That's what I've been trying to tell you for days. I bought this house for you. For us. I want us to make a life together. Here. Just the two of us but sharing it with the people we love.'

'Is this going to be enough for you? Am *I* enough for you?'

Could she believe what she was hearing? She wanted to—her heart wanted to—but she was cautious.

'You are everything I need,' Jake told her. 'We have plenty of people in our lives. Your family, Will, Chris, our friends. There are plenty of people to share our love with, but I only want to give my heart to you. You are enough. You are all I need.'

'Are you sure?'

'I've never been more certain of anything in my life.'

'Just me? No children? Not now? Not ever?'

'If I'm going to be completely honest, I guess I always assumed I'd have children one day, but it wasn't a burning need in me. It wasn't something I had to do and, if I have to choose between having children or having you, I would choose you. Today, tomorrow, for ever. You are

my future. You are all I need. All I want. We can make a
life together and I know we can be happy. I love you, Ali.'

'You do?'

He nodded. 'I do. I've never felt like this before.'

'Not even when you got married the first time?'

'No.' He picked up her hand and kissed her fingers as
they curled around his. 'Nothing like this. I felt guilty
for so many things that happened in my marriage, but
I don't regret that it ended. It taught me many lessons.
Mainly that my relationship with Chrissie wasn't strong
enough to begin with and definitely wasn't strong enough
to withstand the challenges we'd faced.

'I could have had another baby with Chrissie if I
wanted to keep her happy, but I realised I didn't. Having a baby wasn't the solution. I'd always thought people
who imagined a baby would save a marriage were mad.
When I realised that was how I was thinking—that our
marriage needed saving—I took a step back and looked
at my life. And I wasn't happy. We'd grown apart. So I
chose not to have another baby and asked for a divorce
instead. But I have no regrets. Everything I went through
with Chrissie led me to you. We've both had failed mar-
riages but that doesn't mean we don't try again. It just
means we hadn't found the right person yet. And now I
have. I've found you.'

'And what if we grow apart?'

'We're almost middle-aged,' he joked. 'We've had all
our major growth spurts. I think we should now be pretty
fully formed humans. Any growing I do from now on I
want to do with you. I want to grow old with you. You
are all I need. I have thought a lot about this, about you,
about us, about what family means. I don't need children,

I never have, but I do need you. We will be a family, you and me. I bought this house for the future, our future, the one I'm hoping to build with you. And, one day, if you do want to get married again, I'll propose to you under that tree. I need you in my life, Ali. I don't want to live without you. I love you.'

Ali wrapped her arms around Jake and rose up on her toes to kiss him. 'I love you too.'

'Thank God. I was beginning to worry.'

'I think I've loved you for weeks but, hanging from the side of the building today, I knew I had to tell you how I felt. I just hoped I wasn't going to die before I got the chance.'

'I was never going to let anything happen to you. I never will.'

Ali smiled. 'I figured, as long as I lived, what happened next didn't matter. If I survived it didn't matter if we ended up together or not. It only mattered that you knew how I felt. That I was honest with you. And honest with myself. Sometimes I feel like I loved you before I even met you, that you are part of me and I know you are supposed to be part of my life.'

'Is that a yes? You'll move in with me?'

Ali nodded. 'Yes.'

'Hold that thought,' he said as he let go of her and reached for a bottle of champagne that had been chilling, unnoticed by Ali, in the kitchen sink in a bed of ice.

'Let me guess—something else Chris prepared?' Ali said with a smile.

Jake nodded. 'Seems there are plenty of people who want us to live happily ever after,' he said as he popped the champagne cork and poured it into two glasses. He handed one to Ali. 'Here's to us and our future together.'

'To us,' she said as she touched her glass to his. 'I love you. Always.'

EPILOGUE

'HAPPY?' JAKE ASKED as he kissed Ali's forehead.

Ali nodded. 'Perfectly.' She smiled as she stood in the shade of the loquat tree and looked over the garden at their house. 'This is better than I could have ever imagined,' she said.

'You're pleased with the house?'

Ali turned to Jake and wrapped her arm around his waist. 'Not just the house.' She had a fabulous life with Jake. She was completely content. The renovations on the house were complete and Ali and Jake were hosting their first Edwards family Sunday barbecue. The house—*their* house—and backyard were filled with family and friends. 'I hadn't realised until today how much I wanted to be able to accommodate everyone in a home of my own,' she said as she rested her head on Jake's shoulder. After years of going to her parents' and siblings' houses on Sundays it was lovely to be able to reciprocate.

'I promised you we'd fill the house with our family and lots of love.'

'You did. It's wonderful. I love it. And I love you.' She lifted her head as Jake bent his head towards her, their lips meeting in a perfectly synchronised kiss.

'Hold that thought,' Jake said as Yarran called to him from the barbecue.

Ali let go of Jake and watched as he walked across the garden. Sometimes she still couldn't believe how well things had turned out. She felt as if she'd been waiting all of her life for Jake and now she had everything she'd ever wanted.

As Jake stepped up onto the deck Ali's attention was diverted by the arrival of Jake's mother, Lara. She was carrying Ali's niece, Willa, Marli's youngest daughter, who was now eight months old.

'Hello, Lara,' Ali greeted her, 'and hello, gorgeous girl,' she said to Willa, who was beaming at her aunt and holding her arms out to Ali.

Lara passed her over. 'She looks good with you,' Lara said as Ali took her niece and settled her on her hip.

Ali steeled herself, hoping Lara wouldn't bring up the topic of grandchildren. She'd gone quiet on the subject recently—Ali suspected it was on Jake's instruction— and she hoped she wouldn't reignite the debate now that the house renovations were finished. 'Holding babies, delivering babies, is very different from raising babies,' Ali reminded her.

'I know. Don't worry,' Lara reassured her, 'I understand your position and I understand Jake's decision. It may have taken me a while to get my head around it but that was because of my own experiences and my own dreams.'

'What do you mean?'

'Howard and I tried for more children after Jake was born but it never happened. I put all my energy into Jake and when he was diagnosed with a Wilm's tumour I was so scared that I would lose him and that would be the end of my journey as a parent. The desire to have more children was something that never left me, and I felt guilty that I couldn't give Jake siblings. I wanted him to have more family and if he couldn't have siblings, I thought he should have children. I was putting my dreams onto Jake and that wasn't fair. All I really want is for Jake to be happy and I can see that he is. He has a family now, your family, and I wanted to thank you for letting me and Howard be a part of it too. I'm enjoying being a surrogate grandmother to your nieces and nephews.'

'That's enough for you?'

'It is. Jake's happiness and having a relationship with my son is more important to me than having grandchildren. The fact that we are re-establishing a relationship makes me happy and I think I have you to thank for that too.'

'You and I both want the same thing,' Ali said as Jake approached them. 'We both want Jake to be happy.'

Jake stopped at Ali's side and took her free hand. 'I need you to myself for a moment,' he said.

Lara took Willa off Ali's hip and carried her over to Marli, leaving Ali and Jake under the shade of the tree, giving them some space.

'If I could have everyone's attention for a few minutes.' Jake raised his voice, addressing their guests. 'Thank you all for coming here today to help celebrate the end result of our blood, sweat and tears. We want this house to welcome as many of you as often as you'd like to visit. It's a home for the generations. A home for love. Speaking of which, I think you all know how I feel about this gorgeous woman and I feel so lucky that she has chosen to make a life with me. Moving into this house is a big deal for us but I would like to acknowledge our commitment to each other in a different way.' He turned to face Ali. 'Ali, we have made a home together, but I'd like to commit to a life together. I love you and I promise to love you for the rest of my life. And now, with our family and friends as witnesses,' he said as he dropped to one knee, 'I'd like to ask you to be my wife. Will you marry me?'

Jake's proposal took Ali by surprise but in the best possible way. She looked at him, at his gorgeous face and beaming smile as he knelt before her, holding both of her hands. She heard the collective gasp of their guests and turned to them, looking at her parents, her siblings, Jake's parents, Harper, Ivy and Phoebe. Everyone was smiling but no one was smiling as much as Ali.

She looked back to Jake, who was still on one knee, waiting for her answer.

'I thought my life was complete since I met you. I thought I had everything I needed,' she told him. 'I didn't think I could want for anything more, but it turns out I want this. I love you, Jake Ryan, and yes, I will marry you.'

She didn't hear the cheers of their guests, she forgot that her entire family and her friends were watching on, she only had eyes for Jake as he got to his feet and took her in his arms and sealed their promise with a kiss. For the moment, nothing existed except their love.

* * * * *

PHOEBE'S BABY BOMBSHELL

JC HARROWAY

MILLS & BOON

To female friendships and the laughter,
tears and joy they inspire.

PROLOGUE

DR PHOEBE MASON maintained her composed smile as her colleague, world-renowned neonatal surgeon Zachary Archer, respectfully contradicted her opinion, flashing her the mildly apologetic version of his confident smile before giving his answer to the member of the audience.

Phoebe shivered, gripping the microphone tighter, both flattered by his flirty look and niggled that he'd failed to agree with her suggested management of patent ductus arteriosus, or PDA.

Of course she could handle his professional challenge. As Head of Neonatal Surgery at Sydney Central Hospital, she was usually considered the expert at the Advances in Neonatal Surgery conference, which this year was being held in Brisbane. But with the presence of Dr Archer, a man known for his unfailing self-belief, ambition and that intuitive edge that some people deemed arrogance, the questions posed to the panel of experts on the stage had never been more vigorously debated.

'...and while the recommended intervention for pre-term neonates of this age and weight is open heart surgery,' Zachary Archer said, glancing pointedly at Phoebe once more so a titter of nervous laughter passed around the auditorium, 'I have had success with cardiac catheterisation in patients weighing as little as seven hundred grams.'

Catching the spark of rivalry in his gunmetal-grey eyes,

Phoebe looked away, fighting the urge to say something... provocative. While they had attended conferences together before, they'd never actually met. But there had always been something about Zach Archer that called to the woman in her, a woman who had little time and even less inclination for the demands of a personal life. Except something about the way he'd looked at her with amusement twitching his lips and interest in his eyes made her raise the microphone to address the audience once more.

'Of course,' she said, 'while a trans-catheter closure of PDA is minimally invasive and therefore preferable in terms of operative risk reduction and shortened recovery time for the patient, I think we can all agree that, with the exception of my esteemed colleague Dr Archer, for the more...cautious surgeon, open heart surgery is considered standard for very low birth weight patients.'

'Next question,' the panel facilitator stated, carrying the microphone to another audience member with their hand raised.

Aware of her heart thundering with excitement, Phoebe kept her gaze averted from Zachary and stifled her smile. Even so, she sensed his observation, felt it slither over her skin like a wisp of silk. If they were alone and not seated on a stage watched by three hundred delegates, they would definitely be flirting.

What was wrong with her? She hardly ever flirted.

Perhaps it was because today was her fortieth birthday. Perhaps because it was the final day of the conference. Tomorrow she'd return to Sydney, to her jam-packed week at work. Her friends were determined to organise a celebratory night on the town for the milestone, but coordinating everyone's schedules was an impossible task. But it seemed her neglected femininity, not happy to be short-changed, had had enough of work and had staged a revolt, raised an army of hormones targeted at the most single man in the room. Zach Archer was also a notorious commitment-shy bachelor, married to his job, which included high-profile charity work for global neonatal charity Nurture, for which he was often in the media.

Phoebe took some long, slow breaths, dismissing the unexpectedly fierce flare of attraction. The arrival of the big four zero had never bothered her before. She was happy with her career, had all the social contact she required with her mum and her wonderful friends Ali, Harper and Ivy, fellow doctors at Sydney Central Hospital. She'd even recently taken up yoga.

Life was good.

The discussion topic switched to the treatment of Tetralogy of Fallot, and Phoebe passed the microphone to the woman seated to her left, smoothing her palm down her thigh, straightening the wrinkle in her charcoal skirt.

As the conversation once more highlighted the contrast between her surgical approach and that of Dr Archer, she couldn't help but wonder if the sparks demonstrated in their professional differences of opinion would transfer to the bedroom...

Later that evening, at the close of conference social event in the hotel bar, Phoebe sipped her boozy cocktail, the Hanky Panky, for which the cocktail lounge was renowned. Set on the ground floor of the hotel, the dimly lit and luxuriously decorated bar was chic and sophisticated. Floor-to-ceiling sliding doors opened onto the street outside allowing in the warm sultry air and sounds of the vibrant city.

As her conversation with a professor at Sydney's University Hospital—a man with the bushiest grey eyebrows Phoebe had ever seen—came to an end, she found her gaze wandering the gathering, seeking out Zachary Archer. A little light flirtation with someone her own age, someone unmarried and, like her,

uninterested in a relationship, might be just the birthday celebration she needed.

She took another gulp of the cocktail, the sinking feeling
in her stomach telling her that her sexy colleague had probably already left Brisbane. He grew up in Sydney, but rarely
spent any time there. Instead, he travelled the world, consult-
ing on complex cases and performing surgeries that would
make other specialists quake in their theatre shoes.

Her degree of dejection forced her to recall the last time
she'd been on a date. Was it that guy Ali had set her up with?
Some cousin of Ali's cousin whose divorce had just been fi-
nalised...? Struggling to picture the man who had been so dull
that, by the end of the evening, Phoebe had resented that she
had shaved her legs and dressed up, she resigned herself to
finishing her Hanky-Panky and heading upstairs to her hotel
room to pack her weekend bag.

'Dr Mason.' Over her shoulder a deep voice drawled, sending thrilling little shivers down Phoebe's spine.

She knew that voice, had struggled to erase it from her head
since they'd clashed on the discussion panel that afternoon.
Spinning, she faced Zachary, matching his confident smile
with one of her own.

'Dr Archer,' she said, her voice emerging calm and unruf-
fled while her stomach took a pleasurable tumble. He wore
dark jeans and a claret-coloured slim-fit shirt that made the
gold flecks in his eyes pop and outlined his broad chest and
ripped physique.

'You can call me Zach.' He held out his hand and Phoebe
took it, steeling herself against the physical contact.

'Phoebe,' she said, sliding her hand from his warm and
firm grip.

Why was his brand of confidence, intuition and work dis-
cipline so attractive? Or was it just that as a single, self-con-

fessed workaholic he represented the ultimate in unattainable men and therefore was a perfectly suited partner for some harmless flirtatious banter?

You don't need a man, darling.

Her mother's often recited mantra played in her head as she willed her pulse to calm down after that handshake. It was true, she didn't, but she could want one every now and then, especially when they were as tempting as Zach.

'So you disagree with my methods?' he said in his direct way, diving straight back into their earlier debate on their surgical interventions of choice. The intense stare was back too, a hint of playfulness and a whole lot of interest.

'Only the risky ones.' One of the reasons Phoebe loved her job taking care of tiny, vulnerable babies was because it tapped into the protective aspects of her personality, ones that developed from a childhood of being close to her single-parent mother after being abandoned by her father.

'Are you offended? Is your ego horribly bruised?' Phoebe smiled up at him—even with her wearing heels, he was still taller—her eyes batting as if of their own accord, no doubt fuelled by the gin in her cocktail.

Zach's smile widened, the white of his teeth flashing in the dim lighting. 'It takes a lot more than a little friendly professional debate to damage my ego, I assure you.'

'That's good.' Laughing, Phoebe sipped her lethally strong drink. 'We couldn't have your reputation tarnished by a little healthy competition, now, could we?' Aware she'd slipped seamlessly into full-on flirting mode, Phoebe resolved to sound less breathless the next time she spoke. If he wanted her, she wasn't going to do the grunt work for him.

'I'm not sure which of my reputations you're referring to,' he said conspiratorially, dipping his head closer and dropping his deep voice, 'but I am always open to friendly rivalry, although you should know that I always win. Ask my three siblings.'

His broad smile and cool grey eyes were full of playfulness.

Phoebe laughed again, enjoying herself. 'Where's the fun in that?' As if of their own accord, her feet inched her into his personal space until she was bathed in the heat radiating from his body. She rarely let her hair down, and while her professional success was ultimately fulfilling, she was still a red-blooded woman who deserved to celebrate her birthday. Sparring with him certainly beat packing her bag and an early night.

'The fun is in being the best.' He stepped closer, raised his glass—a high-ball full of ice and amber liquid—to hers and they clinked them together, his stare dipping to her mouth when she took another hasty swallow to conceal her body's eager reaction.

Phoebe rolled her eyes at his arrogance. He didn't need any encouragement. His drive and determination reigned supreme. He knew what he wanted and made it happen.

Did he want her?

'Don't get ahead of yourself, Zach,' she said, her breathing tight. 'You might convince me that you're overcompensating.'

As if answering her unvoiced question, he shot her a look of pure, unadulterated heat, bending forward to breathe his reply close to her ear. 'Trust me, I'm the best in all areas of my life.'

The tickle of his breath down her neck made Phoebe's head spin with longing.

He straightened, held her gaze, stared through the suspenseful few seconds that passed and then took a lazy sip from his glass.

Left in no doubt of his interest, Phoebe swallowed hard. 'Well, cheers to that,' she said, her voice a little croaky.

'Can I get you another drink?' he asked, seeing that she was almost done with her cocktail.

'Perhaps.' Although she was tipsy after one. 'It *is* my birthday today, the big four zero.'

He raised his eyebrows in surprise. 'Well, then, happy birthday, Phoebe.' He spoke her name in his low and seductive voice, his stare tracing her features and landing back on her mouth.

It was highly distracting. All she could think about was what it would feel like to kiss him. Was she seriously contemplating taking this to the next level?

As they gazed at each other, non-verbal communication passing between them, the rest of the bar's patrons seemed to disappear. 'So, are you leaving Brisbane tomorrow?'

That wasn't too obvious a question. And unless she sensed that, like her, Zach was only interested in commitment-free sex—a one-off, no strings—she would back off.

He nodded. 'I'm off to the UK tomorrow. I have a three-month visiting-surgeon post at London Children's Hospital.' To stop her being jostled by a man carrying four drinks through the throng, Zach took her elbow and guided her closer.

He smelled divine, his expensive-smelling aftershave tickling her nose. Trying not to swoon, Phoebe widened her eyes at his news, impressed. The fact that he was leaving Australia tomorrow solidified her thoughts. Their respective departures in the morning provided a neat end to what could be a perfect night. A gift to herself.

'Well,' she said, draining the last of her drink, her stare drawn to the open neck of his shirt and the tantalising peek of his chest, 'I'll decline that offer of a drink, thanks. These cocktails are lethal and you should probably get some sleep before your early flight. That long haul to London is punishing.'

Reading her subtext, he dipped his excited gaze to her

mouth, where she licked the last of the sweet cocktail from her lips. 'I probably should.'

She held out her hand, holding his eye contact as her pulse tripped wildly. 'I'm glad we finally had the opportunity to meet. The debate was…stimulating.'

'I'm glad I could oblige and look forward to our next discussion.' Zach took her hand, this time lingering, his warm grip electrifying the nerves of her arm.

To an observer, they would appear as professional colleagues, shaking hands, the delicious tendrils of sexual chemistry ensnaring them invisible.

'Although, sometimes,' she said, practically whispering now, so turned on by the white-hot smoulder in his stare, she needed to get away from him before the entire bar noticed, 'actions speak louder than words.' Reluctantly releasing his hand, she took one of her hotel-room key cards from her pocket and discreetly pressed it into his hand, her intention loud and clear.

His pupils dilated, his jaw muscles bunching as if he was as desperate to conceal his desires as Phoebe as their fingers brushed. He gripped the card, gripped her hand, holding her captive for a few suspended seconds.

'You're sure?' he asked, his voice low in the crowded and noisy bar.

She nodded, excitement bubbling up in her chest. This thing between them had been brewing all day. They clearly wanted the same thing. 'Absolutely. Room six-three-nine. One night.'

'I can work with that,' he agreed.

They might differ in their professional approaches, her independence and his competitive streak meant they would likely disagree on most things, but when it came to pleasure, they obviously spoke the same language.

Slipping her hand from his, Phoebe left the bar on shaky

legs and headed towards the hotel lifts, certain that, after a discreet amount of time, he would follow.

She entered the lift and smiled at her reflection in the mirrored interior whispering *'Happy birthday...'* under her breath.

CHAPTER ONE

Three months later

REACHING THE FRONT of the queue at Perc Up, the café closest to Sydney Central Hospital, and therefore responsible for caffeinating most of the hospital staff, Phoebe swallowed the swell of nausea turning her stomach.

'Can you get me a peppermint tea, please?' she said to a startled Ali at her side, shoving some money at her friend and leaving the line, hurrying away from the normally soothing smell of roasted arabica beans.

Trying to hold onto the half of her breakfast that she'd managed to eat, Phoebe joined Ivy and Harper at a table they'd snagged in the sunny window, which was lush with overhanging plants in pots suspended from industrial-style exposed beams overhead.

As Phoebe took a seat, neither woman paid her much attention. Fortunately they were too caught up in the fact that they were both recently engaged to notice that Phoebe was a little green around the gills.

Zoning out of their chat about wedding guest lists, Phoebe contemplated her situation for what felt like the millionth time. When she'd hooked up with Zach in Brisbane three months ago, she'd hoped for a no-strings night of passion, a gift to herself in celebration of a milestone birthday. What she hadn't anticipated was a condom malfunction and that, at the ripe old age of forty, she'd end up pregnant. The shock of her discovery a few weeks ago was still fresh, compounded by the humiliation that, medically, she would be considered a geriatric mother and the relentless morning sickness she was still trying to hide from her friends and work colleagues.

As Ali joined them at their table, Phoebe plastered a smile on her face and tuned into Ivy and Harper's conversation, which, as it had since Ivy had announced her engagement to her sexy surgeon fiancé, Lucas Matthews, centred on her impending nuptials in seven weeks' time.

'The bridal bouquet is a very serious matter, ladies,' Ivy said, her green eyes bright with excitement and a hint of reprimand that her three maids of honour might indeed take flower choice a little more seriously. 'I need your advice—gardenias or lilies?'

'Definitely lilies—gloriosa are my favourite,' Phoebe said, throwing herself into the debate to stave off another wave of nausea. She should have declined the invitation to meet this morning before their respective days began, but she hadn't wanted to draw suspicion by her absence and they often gathered at Perc Up for an early pre-work coffee.

A server appeared with Phoebe's tea, attracting curious stares from Ivy and Harper, who were fully aware of Phoebe's usual coffee addiction.

'I have a bit of a headache and a big day in Theatre today,' Phoebe explained, sheepishly glancing down at her pretty teacup and saucer with an internal wince. She hated keeping secrets from her friends.

As if to distract the others from Phoebe's unusual choice of beverage, Ali chipped in, 'Gardenias, definitely gardenias.'

The debate raged on with Harper suggesting lily of the valley.

Phoebe met Ali's sympathetic look with one she hoped

conveyed her gratitude. As Head of Obstetrics and Gynaecology at the Central, Ali was the only other person who knew about the pregnancy. Phoebe had never had a regular cycle, so she didn't connect the dots that her one passionate night with Zach had resulted in an unexpected pregnancy until she began to feel nauseous and had developed sore breasts. Then, aware of the risks being an older mother posed, but not ready to confide in anyone, she'd initially consulted Ali for advice on the pretext of 'asking for a friend'. Of course she hadn't been able to fool Ali for ever, eventually coming clean a few days ago.

The coffees arrived and Phoebe shamelessly distracted her friends with more wedding talk. 'What are your favourite flowers, Ivy?'

As her friend gushed excitedly about the amazing florist she'd found to make her bridal bouquet, guilt crept over Phoebe's skin like heat rash.

She wanted to tell Harper and Ivy her news, but she hadn't even told her mother yet. She'd vowed not to tell anyone else until she'd informed Zach.

Her poor, overactive stomach pinched with nerves now that she'd invited thoughts of Zach into her head. While the other three women sipped reviving coffee and chatted animatedly about ceremonies and caterers and honeymoons, Phoebe toyed with her tea, idly swirling the teaspoon around and around for no reason, the pale golden liquid now as unappealing as the idea of coffee.

She would see Zach later that afternoon for the first time since that incredible, but fateful night.

Just over three months ago, she had awoken in her Brisbane hotel room the morning after to find Zach gone. He'd left a brief note, the perfect goodbye, written on a sheet of hotel stationery in his neat, confident handwriting:

I enjoyed helping you to celebrate your birthday.
Take care, Z

And she'd successfully put the wonderful memories behind her, focused on work, which, as for Ali, Harper and Ivy, had included the high-profile case of Emma Wilson, wife of a local celebrity and host of the TV show *If You Build It*, Aaron Wilson, and their twin daughters. Emma was injured in a house fire while still pregnant and was first seen by Harper in the ER before being transferred to Ivy and her fiancé, Lucas, for surgical care. Then, a month ago, Ali delivered Emma's twin girls, Jasmine and Poppy, when she went into premature labour. Now Poppy, who'd been diagnosed with a congenital heart defect, was under Phoebe's care on the neonatal intensive care unit.

But she couldn't put off seeing Zach any longer.

'—and I saw the perfect dresses for you all to wear as my maids of honour,' Ivy said, snagging Phoebe's attention away from her well-versed speech.

Hi, Zach, remember that amazing night in Brisbane? Well... surprise—I'm having your baby!

Latching onto the subject of maid-of-honour dresses instead of indulging her panic, Phoebe tried to smile. Her face felt rubbery, fake. At fourteen weeks pregnant, her favourite trouser suit had been a little tight around the waist that morning. She'd definitely be showing a baby bump by the time Ivy walked down the aisle. There'd be no hiding it in the type of gown Ivy would likely choose for them to wear.

Her time for keeping her secret to herself was running out.

'So, today's the day, huh?' Ivy asked Phoebe, changing the subject so abruptly, Phoebe realised that she must have appeared distracted.

Phoebe stared blankly. All she could think of was that today was the day she would have to tell Zach he was going to be a father.

Frowning, Ivy clarified. 'That guy is arriving, isn't he? The one you've invited to corroborate on, you know, the case we're all involved with.'

Naming no names as they were in a public place, Ivy was referring to Poppy Wilson.

Phoebe nodded, feeling light-headed with doubt and confusion and guilt. 'Yes. Zachary Archer,' she mumbled. 'He arrives this afternoon.'

And she'd have to drop her bombshell before he'd even had time to acclimatise.

Looking impressed, her friends stared as if waiting for her to elaborate. Only her mind blanked, stuck on how great a lover Zach had been and how she'd never once imagined when she'd invited him into her bed that she'd end up pregnant. Phoebe had long ago abandoned any dreams of motherhood, choosing instead to focus on her career, to devote her maternal impulses to her tiny patients.

'Have you two worked together before?' Harper prompted when Phoebe sat like a rabbit trapped in the headlights.

A question she could answer without being cagey!

'No. But his reputation in the field made him the first person I thought of to assist.' Poppy had been diagnosed with a large ventricular septal defect that had so far failed to close spontaneously, as often occurred. They wouldn't normally operate on a baby of her weight, but the hole in her heart was causing side effects that had so far proved resistant to medical intervention. Surgery was now the only option.

Oblivious to the sense of impending doom pounding Phoebe's heart at Zach's possible reactions, Ali asked, 'He's from Sydney, isn't he? He went to medical school with Jake,' she said about her new man.

'Yes, I believe so,' Phoebe said weakly. When she'd confided in Ali, she had refused to discuss the baby's father. It was only fair that she told Zach first. 'But he's rarely here. He travels a lot, gets invited to centres all over the world to lend his expertise.'

Mentally calculating how many hours she might have before she saw him again, before she would have to impart her news, Phoebe wished she'd taken the coward's way out and informed him over the phone, or by email. But by the time she'd realised what her amenorrhoea and other symptoms meant, she'd already invited him to consult on the high-risk and highly publicised surgery. Then, when she'd confirmed her pregnancy with a test, it had made sense to wait for him to arrive in Sydney and tell him in person. Only now that the moment was almost upon her, she wanted to run away and hide from the inevitable conversation.

Swallowing, she pulled herself together. It wasn't as if she'd become pregnant on purpose, nor did she require anything of him beyond her obligation that he be informed.

'You look pale, Phoebs. Are you ill?' Harper said, eyeing Phoebe's untouched tea.

'I'm just tired,' she fudged, taking her first sip and trying not to wince at the unappealing taste. 'It's been a busy week.'

'Well at least my wedding gives us all something to look forward to,' Ivy said, turning the talk back to the main topic. 'It will be a chance for us all to get out of scrubs and get glammed up. Perhaps there'll be a dishy single guest we can hook you up with, Phoebs. That will put some colour back in your cheeks.'

Harper chuckled with Ivy, and Ali hid behind her coffee cup, avoiding comment. That was the trouble with loved-up friends, they turned into raging matchmakers, keen to spread the joy they'd found to anyone left single.

'You know me,' Phoebe said, reminding her friends of her fierce independence. 'I don't need a man.'

Because they'd heard Phoebe's mantra so many times, Ivy and Harper rolled their eyes, appeased for now. Only Ali, the woman in the know, still observed Phoebe with a small frown of concern that tightened the knot of nerves in Phoebe's stomach.

Was Ali imagining some sort of happy ending for sad spinster Phoebe? Did she think the baby's mystery father might sweep in to save the day and marry her poor, knocked-up friend?

Glancing away, Phoebe shuddered at the very idea. She had no intention of allowing her new life as a mother to be any different from her current self-sufficient existence. She was confident that she could handle one little baby without too much disruption to her schedule. She just needed to align all of her ducks, starting with informing Zach later today.

As if the universe had decided she'd already suffered enough probing questions for one day, Phoebe's phone pinged. She read the screen, relief flooding her system as she abandoned her tea and stood.

'Sorry, lovely ladies, I have to go. My first patient is being prepped. Hope you all have a good day.'

Rushing across the street to the hospital, she breathed a little easier. No matter what Ali thought, what Ivy and Harper might think once they knew of her pregnancy, Phoebe was happy to go it alone. She was a competent, capable medical professional, a mature, independent woman who didn't believe that happy endings necessitated falling in love. She would simply tell Zach her news, explain that she needed nothing from him, remind him that they'd both known that night in Brisbane was a no-strings, one-off arrangement and that nothing had changed.

Once they'd operated together on Poppy Wilson, Zach could go his merry way and her normality could resume.

She had things all neatly figured out.

CHAPTER TWO

ZACH HELD HIS scrubbed clean and still dripping arms in front of him and placed his back against the scrub-room door, anticipation and excitement playing tug-of-war with his gut.

It had been three months but the memories of that night with Phoebe Mason had stayed fresh in his mind. When he'd received her email asking him to come to Sydney and consult on a high-profile and risky surgery, he'd been captivated at the idea of seeing her again, this time in her work environment.

Even before her request had come in some part of him had subconsciously hoped their paths would cross in the future. No matter how much he'd coached his thoughts after they'd slept together, adamant that their one night had been perfect, that Phoebe with her self-sufficiency and pragmatism and clear expectations was exactly the sort of woman he was drawn to, he couldn't scrub her from his mind.

And now he was about to see her again.

Pushing through the door into Theatre Three, Zach eagerly scanned the room. Despite the fact that she was scrubbed up, concealed from head to toe by forest-green surgical garments, he'd have known her anywhere. He recalled the sexy curves of her body, the elegant slope of her neck, the way she held her head as if she were a strict headmistress on the lookout for misbehaving children.

For a second she didn't notice his appearance, giving him

a few moments to compose himself, breathe through the rush of adrenaline the sight of her caused. The last time he'd seen her, she'd been asleep on her stomach, her dark blonde hair splayed over the pillow, her back and shoulders bare, the white sheet bunched around her waist. He'd paused, marvelling at her beauty, desperate to trace the golden freckles that dotted her shoulders and follow the dip of her spine with his fingers, to lean forward and inhale the scent of her hair.

Now, dragging his gaze from her curves, he forced himself to shut down the reel of erotic memories from that unforgettable night.

He cleared his throat, alerting Phoebe and the scrub nurse to his presence.

Phoebe's bright blue eyes widened above her surgical mask, evidence of a blush visible on her high cheekbones. 'Dr Archer. What are you doing here? I wasn't expecting you until this afternoon.'

Her clipped, businesslike voice told him she intended to play their reunion cool.

He'd expected that. Each of them had made it clear that their one night in Brisbane wouldn't be repeated, but he couldn't help the sinking feeling in his stomach.

'Good morning, Dr Mason, good to see you again,' he said, taking a sterile towel from the theatre nurse to dry his hands and then donning sterile gloves and surgical apron.

'My apologies for surprising you,' he added, adjusting his gloves while the nurse tied the strings of the apron. Phoebe hadn't moved a muscle since she'd spied him, as if she was in shock. 'My flight arrived this morning, so rather than twiddle my thumbs, something I'm not very good at, I'm afraid, I thought I'd come in, acquaint myself with the set-up here at Sydney Central before our meeting.'

Phoebe stared, seeming more discombobulated than he'd

anticipated. He hadn't meant to disrupt her day by showing up early and gatecrashing her surgery, he just struggled with idleness. The need to strive that he'd been raised with in his highly competitive family was a hard habit to break.

'I did clear it with the theatre manager. Didn't he tell you?' he said.

Still silent, Phoebe shook her head.

Zach clasped his gloved hands together in front of him, a habit he'd developed as a medical student in order to remind himself not to touch anything once he was sterile. 'I can leave if it's a problem...'

Still looking at him as if he'd walked into this disinfected environment carrying an open vial of some deadly virus, she raised her chin a fraction. 'Well, I had planned for us to meet in my office later, but, as you're here, I'd be happy for you to stay and observe.'

She didn't sound at all happy.

Zach chuckled to himself, glad to see that the sparks they'd generated in Brisbane were still dangerously flammable.

'Good. Excellent.' Zach stood beside her to await the patient. He felt her stiffen as if he'd moved into her personal space, but they were most definitely a respectable distance apart. Interesting. Either she wanted to make it absolutely obvious that their physical relationship was over, or she was still reacting to him the way she had when they'd flirted in Brisbane, when her passion had matched his that night, kiss for kiss, touch for touch.

'So how have you been?' he asked, his voice low so they wouldn't be overheard by the theatre staff, who were bustling around preparing the OR for the first patient on Phoebe's operating list.

She needn't worry that he'd take her invitation to jointly operate on Poppy Wilson as an invitation back into her bed.

He wasn't about to cast aside his casual attitude to dating and swear her his undying love. He wasn't sure he even believed in the fickle emotion after the example he'd witnessed growing up, when, after having four children together, his parents decided that they could no longer tolerate the sight of each other.

'Well, thank you.' She kept her stare averted, the slightly strangled sound of her voice reminding him of her sexy moans and cries of passion as they'd surrendered to what had been insanely strong chemistry.

Now she was acting as if he had some sort of communicable disease, as if she regretted inviting him to corroborate on a ventricular septal defect surgery on the newborn daughter of local celebrity Aaron Wilson and his wife Emma.

Maybe joining her in Theatre had been a mistake. Only the minute he'd emerged from the shower after his long haul from London, impatience to see her again had gnawed at him, like hunger. He'd anticipated his ongoing attraction, expected some lively debates on their differing surgical approaches, looked forward to getting to know Phoebe a little better as a surgeon and woman he admired.

'Are you sure you have no objections to me observing your surgery?' he asked, pretending to ignore her cool-as-a-cucumber act.

'None at all,' she said, glancing his way so he saw the glimmer of challenge in her eyes. 'Given that we're going to be corroborating on the Wilson case, it makes sense for us to get to know each other's surgical style, although, from the panel discussion in Brisbane, I'm certain that they will be wildly different.'

Zach chuckled. At least she'd brought up Brisbane so he didn't have to.

'Exactly my thought,' he said, enjoying the way she seemed flustered by his presence, but it seemed, would never admit it. 'Of course, we also proved in Brisbane that when it counts, we were able to find some…common ground.'

At the veiled innuendo he couldn't resist, Phoebe flushed. Zach smiled beneath his mask and, reading his expression, she shot him a look full of venom. He was irking her, but his trusted intuition told him that the woman she'd portrayed that night three months ago—the playful and passionate woman—was still there, underneath the distant and professional guard she had slammed up the minute he'd walked through the door.

And his gut feelings had never steered him wrong.

For reasons only known to Phoebe, she wanted to pretend that they hadn't spent the night pleasuring each other's bodies, that he didn't know every detail of how she looked naked, that their chemistry was a thing of the past. Like him, Phoebe liked to be in control and to call the shots, and, despite how those similarities led to the inevitable friction currently on display, he liked that aspect of her personality. He'd backed her into a corner by showing up early, but he had no doubt that if she wanted him to leave her OR, she would most definitely say.

Just then, Phoebe's tiny patient was wheeled into the OR by the anaesthetist.

Zach caught Phoebe's sigh of relief.

'So, tell me about your case?' he asked as he and Phoebe stood back to allow their colleagues to ready the patient for the impending surgery.

'It's a pretty standard, uncomplicated oesophageal atresia,' she said, looking up at him so he was bombarded anew by the way she had stood on tiptoes to kiss him. 'The patient is a three-day-old boy born at full term by normal vaginal delivery. Nothing to challenge your legendary skills, I'm sure.'

Zach shrugged, unperturbed by her attempts to chase him off. 'On the contrary,' he said, smiling. 'No case is too mundane to pique my interest. That's what makes me the best: attention to detail.'

She wasn't going to get rid of him that easily. Despite having no interest in dating, what with his workaholic tendencies, and not to mention his general cynicism towards commitment, he hadn't been able to get Phoebe off his mind since they slept together. As she was the first woman in years to provoke his fascination, he was more drawn to her than ever, even when her body language was practically shoving him out of the door.

'In that case,' she said as they took their positions opposite each other across the operating table, as if they'd worked together for years, 'I hope you feel my routine surgery makes your enthusiastic early appearance worthwhile.'

She looked up. Their eyes locked in challenge.

'I'm looking forward to it,' he said, his heart galloping because the sexual tension he'd assumed was one-sided seemed to have returned with a vengeance, mutual and stronger than before.

As Phoebe and the theatre nurse prepared the operative field with sterile surgical sheets, Zach's gaze stubbornly noticed the wisps of escaped hair caressing her neck below her hat and the way that her eyelashes seemed longer and lusher than he remembered. He couldn't help but tune into her every movement, to the soft sigh of her breathing and the scent of her subtle but highly distracting perfume.

Whatever happened between them during his short time in Sydney, it certainly wasn't going to be dull.

The emotion of facing Zach over a tiny baby she was about to operate on while, unbeknown to him, their own baby grew inside her rose up inside Phoebe, pressing on her lungs. She hadn't considered that Zach breezing into her OR early and unannounced would completely flummox and derail her. But

his confident swagger, the heat and challenge in his stare—
challenge she'd had no choice but to accept, given her stubborn
streak—had brought a violent collision of her expectations
and her stark reality.

Phoebe willed her breathing to slow. She couldn't have him
thinking that his mere presence was enough to unsettle her
equilibrium, to shock her system with delicious memories of
the things they'd done together that night in Brisbane, to rouse
her into another tit-for-tat verbal sparring match she could tell
he'd enjoyed.

So he was even more attractive than her memory recalled,
his shoulders impossibly broader, his height more impressive,
his confidence hovering on the arrogant side of charismatic.
It didn't matter that the minute he'd appeared in the OR her
brain had shut down, instinct and hormones holding her body
ransom so all she could think of was how it had felt the first
time they'd kissed.

Because she was her mother's daughter, raised to live on
her terms, Phoebe didn't do weakness. She wasn't about to
start just because Zach liked to play by his own rules, appear-
ing when it suited him rather than when he'd been invited.
No doubt he'd leave in accordance with his own agenda, too.

Fine. That suited her down to the ground.

She'd tell him he was going to be a father, tolerate his ir-
ritating presence until they'd operated on Poppy, and then
watch the trail of dust he would no doubt leave behind when he
scarpered back overseas, never to be seen again. Just like her
own father, who'd not only deserted Phoebe and her mother,
but had blamed Rosa Mason for *trapping him into marriage*.

Ducking her head to avoid Zach's perceptive eye contact,
she glanced at the anaesthetist, seeking the all-clear to proceed.

'We're good here,' said her colleague with a nod.

Shoving all thoughts of Zach and how effortlessly he'd rattled her from her mind, Phoebe reached for the scalpel from the tray of sterilised instruments. Instead of her fingers closing around the metal handle as she'd expected, she found herself gripping Zach's gloved hand.

She slammed her gaze to his, snatched her hand away. But it was too late. The warmth of his touch took her back to that night, to the way he'd worshipped her body all night long, telling her how beautiful she was and murmuring sexy things.

'Sorry.' He smiled, withdrawing his hand. 'Force of habit. I'm usually in the driving seat.'

Phoebe dragged in a steadying breath, desperately trying to ignore his imposing presence and the way he was looking at her as if their night together was at the foreground of his thoughts.

But of course he was used to running the show. She'd learned how he liked to take control in the bedroom when he'd commanded every kiss and touch, driving her body to the point of exhaustion with pleasure.

Trying to forget his prowess as a lover, she picked up the scalpel and cast him a withering look. 'Well, today I'm afraid you'll have to take the passenger seat.'

'I'm all yours, Dr Mason,' he said.

As she focused on her job and not the man opposite, the flustered gallop of her heart settled. She made an incision in the fourth right intercostal space and then prepared to enter the mediastinum, the surgical approach one she'd done a thousand times. Only never before watched by a man who'd not only seen her naked, but also kissed every inch of her body.

To her surprise, Zach stayed silent while she worked slowly and methodically to reach the unformed oesophagus. If she hadn't been so attuned to his proximity, as if her body's muscle memory sensed the source of all that pleasure was once more nearby, she might have forgotten he was there.

But she could tell that Zach was practically itching to get his hands on the instruments. Taking pity on him, she inserted a retractor into the incision she'd made into the chest cavity and passed it to him to hold. 'I can see that you're not very good at merely observing, Dr Archer.'

'You're right. I do like to have purpose, to know my role, whatever the situation, so thanks for putting me to use.'

Recalling how he'd put those hands to use, that mouth, when he'd driven her wild, she swallowed hard, her throat dry.

'Not good at being superfluous, then?' she asked, already certain of his response. Men like Zach—ambitious, over-achieving perfectionists—measured their worth by their success. He was married to his work for a reason.

His emotional unavailability had been a major point in his favour when she had invited him into her bed. She had known exactly where she stood with him. Now that she was carrying their child, her expectations of him as a father were realistically negligible.

But Phoebe didn't need him for anything. She just needed to tie up the loose ends and tell him her secret.

'No, I'm afraid I was raised in a competitive household and have three high-achieving siblings. Fortunately for me that's translated into a world-leading career in a field that I love.'

Fascinated by his casual comment and the insight it gave her into his personality, Phoebe automatically adjusted the position of the retractor he held, a move that necessitated touching his warm and strong hand once more.

Impressed that a surgeon with Zach's pedigree was content to hold a retractor, a job traditionally undertaken by the most junior member of the surgical team, Phoebe smiled to herself, forced to re-examine his reputation for arrogance.

While the surgery progressed, she was constantly aware of Zach's scrutiny in the same way she'd been in Brisbane. She located the proximal blind end of the oesophagus, the normally patent tube that connected the mouth to the stomach, which in this case hadn't formed correctly so the baby couldn't feed. She created an opening in the tube so she could join the two ends of the oesophagus together. She was about to comment on how impressed she was that he'd managed to keep his criticisms of her surgical technique to himself, when he piped up.

'You have a bleeder,' he said, passing her the diathermy probe before she had a chance to reach for it.

'I see it,' she said, both grateful for a second pair of eyes, and irritated by his intrusion. She cauterised the tiny blood vessel, carefully moving aside the baby's lung to allow room for the suction tube.

That was when the cardiac monitor alarm blared its warning, and everyone froze.

The anaesthetist, who had been sitting at the head of the table, jerked to his feet and examined the heart trace spewed out by the cardiac monitor, which monitored the rate and rhythm of the heart.

Phoebe held her breath, her own heart rate through the roof. Peri-operative emergencies were a surgeon's worst nightmare, but never more so than when the patients were tiny, vulnerable, newborn babies.

As the alarm continued to sound, all eyes were glued to the digital reading of the heart trace on the monitor. The baby's heart was beating abnormally high.

Fighting off the instinctual panic the emergency warning created, Phoebe tried to set her emotions aside and think. There were many possible causes for the alarm, the most life-threatening a cardiac arrhythmia, which could be the result of the anaesthetic, the surgery or an undiagnosed issue with the heart's electrical conductive system. But whatever the cause, the surgery couldn't proceed until the episode was treated, or resolved spontaneously.

Adrenaline rushed through her blood. She glanced at Zach, saw the same concern and confusion in his eyes. Losing a patient on the table, while rare, was a heartbreaking reality of her job. She'd never grown used it and now that she was carrying her own child, it was as if the stakes were amplified tenfold.

Aware that she was senselessly projecting and that Zach was still ignorant of the existence of his child, a situation she vowed to rectify as soon as they'd finished this surgery, she looked away from him.

'Is it an arrhythmia?' she asked the anaesthetist, the seconds passing at the rate of what felt like hours while the alarm continued to blare out its warning.

Preoccupied, the anaesthetist shook his head. 'Looks like sinus tachycardia.'

'Why don't we check for pneumothorax?' Zach said, his stare transmitting his support.

Phoebe nodded, inspecting the operative field, while Zach adjusted the position of the retractor to aid her view.

Every surgery carried risk. All surgeons worked with that knowledge. But this should have been a routine procedure.

As quickly as it had begun, the heart rate settled to normal, the alarm falling silent. Phoebe battled hand tremors as her adrenaline dissipated, leaving only the alien sense of gratitude for Zach's calming and supportive presence.

Refusing to be complacent, Phoebe said, 'Let's double-check that there's no pneumothorax and that I didn't miss another bleeder.'

Nodding, Zach assisted, inspecting the chest cavity for signs of surgical complications, while the anaesthetist monitored the baby's blood pressure, respiratory rate and other vital signs, which to everyone's collective relief remained stable.

'It looks good to me, Dr Mason,' Zach said when Phoebe had checked every nook and cranny of the operative field, twice.

Phoebe nodded. 'Are you happy for us to proceed?' she asked the anaesthetist, who gave her the all-clear once more.

The rest of the surgery passed uneventfully, but the minute Phoebe sneaked away to the female changing rooms, she braced her hands on her thighs and bent double, releasing the tension caused by the emergency that had taken place with every deep inhale and exhale.

With her panic subsided, another realisation struck.

Despite the fact that he'd joined her surgery, uninvited, despite the fact that she was glad he'd been there, the time to confess her bombshell had arrived. When it mattered, it seemed she and Zach might be able to set aside their personal life and work together, successfully. It not only benefited their last patient, but boded well for Poppy Wilson, too.

Unless, when she told him her news, everything changed.

CHAPTER THREE

STRAIGHTENING HIS TIE and rolling back his shoulders, Zach tapped on the already ajar door bearing Phoebe's name and poked his head through the opening.

'Come in.' Phoebe beckoned him, smoothing her hand over her neatly pulled-back hair in a nervous gesture.

She looked pale. Zach wondered if she'd been spooked by the emergency in the OR or if she was still regretting inviting him to the Central.

'Hi.' Zach smiled, hoping that, as mature professional adults, they could fully dispense with the awkwardness of earlier. After all, sex was just sex, even when it had been the best sex of his life, and they'd proved that, despite being former lovers, they had worked well together on the oesophageal atresia surgery.

Phoebe was a meticulous surgeon, handling the unforeseen emergency with impressive calm that only inflamed Zach's attraction to her further. All surgeons dreaded the sound of those alarms, although sometimes, like in that case, the cause for a raised heart rate or drop in blood pressure never became apparent. Even so, he'd admired the way Phoebe had checked twice before proceeding with the operation. It showed a humility that he couldn't help but respect.

Still eyeing him warily, Phoebe stood as Zach left the door ajar and stepped further into her office. She'd replaced the hospital's green scrubs with an immaculate charcoal trouser suit that cinched in at the waist and accentuated her figure. The sage-green blouse made her blue eyes a shade brighter, but her expression was distant. Physically, she took his breath away. But despite the time they'd spent together in Brisbane, she seemed determined to demarcate boundaries, her body language making it clear that they would be staying on opposite sides of her clutter-free, blond oak desk.

His heart sank.

Clearly the easy-going reunion he'd imagined wasn't going to become a reality.

'Have a seat.' She indicated the lone chair facing hers, no hint of the warmth he'd hoped to coax out now that they were alone.

Zach hesitated, irked that their first private interaction since he'd forced himself to leave her warm hotel room bed while she slept naked would feel like a job interview.

'How are you feeling now?' he asked, instead of sitting. 'That turned out to be far from the run-of-the-mill surgery you promised.' He flashed his cheeky smile, the one his mother claimed had saved him from trouble on more than one occasion as a kid, trying to lighten the atmosphere in the hope that she'd drop her guard a little.

'I'm fine, thank you.' Looking away, she took a seat, straightened the pen on her desk, once more stroked her hair. 'Yes, things did get rather fraught there for a minute, just to keep us on our toes.'

When she looked up, the briefest hint of vulnerability flared in her eyes. It gave him hope that, as he'd predicted, the Phoebe he'd spent the night with in Brisbane was hiding somewhere behind this buttoned-up, untouchable and aloof version.

The question was, why?

Making one last attempt to break the ice, Zach gestured at

the open door. 'I hoped we could catch up over coffee. I noticed a popular café across the road,' he said, hoping to chip away at her frosty resistance.

Away from her work environment, perhaps they could have a genuine conversation, two mature adults who knew the intimacies of each other's bodies, respected each other professionally, and still had to work together.

Her teeth snagged at her full bottom lip, reminding him of her kisses, her sighs, the sexy things she'd said when they'd been intimate. 'I'm…um…off coffee at the moment. It's a detox-challenge thing going around the hospital.'

She flushed, glancing away, and Zach decided enough was enough. They didn't know each other well, but neither were they strangers. She'd invited him here and now she was acting as if she couldn't wait for him to leave.

Time to clear the air.

'Look—' Zach stifled a sigh and took the proffered seat. 'Am I making you uncomfortable or something? Did I upset you by inserting myself into your OR? Because I apologise for that.'

She shook her head. 'I'm not upset. I'm glad you were there.' Her clear gaze meeting his, for the first time open. 'I'm also grateful that you're able to consult on the Poppy Wilson case. I know you're in high demand and, given what happened in Brisbane, I wondered if you might decline for personal reasons. But, like me, you've put all of that behind us.' She waved her hand dismissively. 'Which is great.'

Yeah…really great…

Zach frowned at her prepared-sounding speech, torn because he respected her for raising the subject of Brisbane. But who was she trying to convince that all that messy physical attraction was in the past—him or herself? For Zach, chemistry as strong as theirs was almost impossible to ignore.

'By "all of that", I assume you mean the four times we had sex?' It was a low blow, but the part of him that had been desperate to see her again couldn't resist reminding her how good they'd been together.

'Yes.' She swallowed hard, nodded absently, the exposed skin in the vee neck of her blouse turning pink.

Relieved to know that she wasn't as unaffected as she'd have him believe, but feeling uncharacteristically irritated, as if he was being somehow managed—a situation for which he had no tolerance—he leaned back in the chair and rested his ankle on the opposite knee.

'I'm a professional, Phoebe. I'd never allow sexual chemistry to interfere with work.' Even when, for him, that chemistry was as rampant as ever, maybe even more so than before because of the three months of anticipation.

'Exactly,' she said in a tone that implied that part of the conversation was over. Composing herself, she donned her glasses and logged into the computer. 'So, let's get you up to speed on Poppy Wilson, shall we?'

She angled the monitor his way so they could both see the screen, clearly still keen to keep him physically separated, when he would have preferred to share the same side of the desk.

Feeling mildly dismissed by work Phoebe, Zach clenched his jaw and nodded for her to proceed. Where was the woman he'd struggled to forget, the woman who'd flirted, seduced him and passionately shattered in his arms?

While she outlined Poppy's medical history following her birth at thirty-two weeks gestation by uncomplicated caesarean section, Zach tried to ignore the sensual way her mouth moved. The trouble was, the urge to kiss her again beat at him relentlessly, like a wasp flying at an unopened window.

And the attraction was most definitely mutual. He hadn't

missed the way her stare had checked him out when he'd entered her office, the way she touched her neck every time their eyes met. Why had she locked herself away behind this fortress of polite professionalism, especially now that they were alone? And more disturbingly, why was he allowing it to get to him?

He should feel relieved that she knew what she wanted and had stated it so honestly that night in Brisbane. Working together with all of that chemistry flying around had the potential for them to be tempted into another liaison. At least this way, with Phoebe making it abundantly clear that, beyond needing his assistance on this high-profile surgery, their association was over, kept things simple, something he normally sought out.

'So unless you have any objections,' she said, bringing him back to the surgical plan for Poppy, 'I propose that we use a traditional open surgical procedure via the right atrium approach and a synthetic patch. Would you like to see the echocardiogram?'

'I would,' Zach said, standing and coming around to her side of the desk, uninvited, so he could gain a closer look at the images on the screen. If their attraction was now one-sided—if, for her, he was just any other colleague—she wouldn't be at all bothered by his proximity.

'I can turn the monitor around,' she flustered, opening a new screen to show him the Doppler scan, which would likely illustrate the abnormal flow of blood through the defect in the inter-ventricular wall of Poppy's heart.

'It's no problem,' Zach said, bending over her shoulder, his determination to prove his point backfiring as a cloud of her floral scent engulfed him, making it hard for him to think about anything but the fact that when he'd left her bed after that night, her scent had clung to his skin. 'I do my best thinking on my feet,' he added, 'and this way, we can both see without craning our necks.'

She stiffened as he rested his hand on the back of her chair and peered at the screen. While he watched the images, Phoebe touched her throat nervously, toyed with the thin gold chain she wore around her neck.

As much as he wanted to give her a little nudge out of her comfort zone and have her admit that she too still felt this thing bubbling away between them, Zach backed off. He'd had his fun with Phoebe and he'd seen what he needed to see from the scan pictures.

Now he'd just have to focus on the job, try to ignore his ongoing attraction and console himself that whatever dreams he might have subconsciously harboured about them hooking up once more were never going to happen.

Before he could retake his seat on the other side of the desk, Phoebe's face drained of colour. She placed a hand on her forehead, her other hand gripping the arm of her leather chair.

Alarmed by her pallor, Zach rushed back to her side. 'Phoebe, are you okay?'

The doctor in him couldn't help but reach for her radial pulse at her wrist, which was steady but a little fast.

'Just a bit a dizzy,' she muttered. 'I didn't eat much breakfast.'

She pushed her chair away from the desk and dropped her head between her knees. 'I'll be fine.' Her voice was muffled. 'I'll see you later.'

Even dizzy she was still trying to get rid of him. Clearly she was feeling unwell. He couldn't just leave her like this.

'I'm not leaving until I know you're okay,' he said, restless with concern and frustration that her independent streak seemed to be a mile wide. 'Tell me what I can do for you. Do you want a glass of water? Some food from the canteen?'

He curled his fingers into useless fists, his protective urges, the need to act, to fix whatever had crept up on her leaving him rigid with impotence.

Why wouldn't she accept his help?

'Can you please page Dr Ali Edwards?' she said eventually. 'She's a friend of mine who works here.'

Reaching for the desk phone, Zach made the call to the hospital switchboard to summon Phoebe's friend. When he hung up, he persuaded her that it might help if she lay on the sofa. He scooped one arm around her waist, guiding her unsteadily to lie down. Then he removed her shoes and propped her feet up on the arm of the sofa in order to redirect blood back to her head.

She was still pale, her dark lashes stark on her cheeks where she kept her eyes closed. Zach paced, his heart frantic behind his ribs. Perhaps she'd been more upset by the emergency in Theatre this morning than she'd let on.

'I'm okay now,' she said, cracking open one eye to look up at him. 'Thank you.'

Her colour had returning slightly, so he collected a glass of water from the sink in the corner of the room and helped her back into a sitting position. 'You should always eat a decent breakfast,' he said, handing her the glass, 'especially before a surgical list.'

He didn't mean to sound patronising, but she'd scared him. The way she'd clung to his hand, rested her weight against his side while he'd walked her to the sofa, the biggest shock of all. Phoebe was the most self-sufficient woman he'd ever known. Certainly the Phoebe he'd encountered this morning would only have leaned on him if absolutely necessary.

Phoebe had barely taken two sips of water when a tall woman with black curly hair and big brown eyes, which were etched with concern, entered the room, slightly out of breath.

'Are you okay?' She rushed to Phoebe with only a cursory glance Zach's way, automatically taking her friend's pulse, as Zach had done.

'Fine,' Phoebe mumbled. 'I just felt a little bit faint. I'm okay.' She looked up at Zach as if she wanted to say more but needed him to leave first.

Zach shoved his hands in his pockets, helplessness a tight knot in his stomach. Perhaps he should give the friends some privacy. He would leave, but not before ensuring that Phoebe was truly okay and not simply putting on a show of independence for his benefit.

As if remembering social etiquette, Phoebe made introductions. 'Ali, this is Zachary Archer. He'll be operating with me on Poppy Wilson. Zach, this is my friend Ali Edwards, Head of Obstetrics and Gynaecology here at Sydney Central.'

Relief drained through his body. At least Phoebe was speaking, feeling well enough to ensure everyone understood that they were just colleagues.

Ali briefly nodded at Zach and then turned her attention back to Phoebe. 'I'd like to take your blood pressure. There's a sphyg in the examination room next door.'

Zach liked Ali Edwards already. She seemed to be taking no nonsense from her friend.

To his surprise, Phoebe nodded compliantly, shooting Zach another wary glance, this one tinged with what looked like fear.

Was she scared of him?

She stood, her shoulders slumped as if weighed down with a sense of inevitability.

Zach held his breath, held his ground, trepidation building inside him like a head of steam. What on earth was going on here? He wasn't leaving until he understood.

Phoebe squeezed Ali's arm. 'I'll meet you next door in a second.'

Ali hesitated, glancing his way with a frown Zach was certain must be mirrored in his own expression.

Seeing that her friend was reluctant to leave her alone with him, Phoebe urged, 'I'm fine, Ali. I just need to talk to Zach, alone.'

Her voice was strong once more and full of determination, her cryptic statement making Zach's skin prickle with a sense of foreboding.

CHAPTER FOUR

WHILE HER HEART pounded away behind her ribs, Phoebe held Zach's quizzical and intense stare, feeling utterly exposed.

Her dizzy spell had arrived with impeccable timing, her moment of weakness in front of him even now making her desperate to be alone, to have him leave, to stop looking at her with worry and confusion that somehow only added to the weight of her secret.

Because she was swamped by guilt.

The moment had come, snatched out of her control by the events of the morning—being caught off guard by his unscheduled appearance, the emergency in Theatre, which only added to her sense of vulnerability and the effects of the pregnancy hormones hijacking her body.

Ali closed the door and Phoebe looked down at her twisted hands, away from Zach's searching expression. 'Sorry about that.' She cleared her throat, needing to sound as in control as she'd planned. 'I um…need to tell you something.'

She couldn't have him finding out that he was going to be a father in front of Ali. She owed him some prior warning, some privacy in the moment. It was bound to be as much a shock for Zach as it had been for her.

Taking in his worry-etched face, she winced. She should have ripped off the plaster, told him the minute he'd walked into her office, the minute he'd walked into Theatre even. But he'd looked so handsome in his midnight-blue suit, looking at her as if he wanted to be back in that hotel room in Brisbane, as if he wanted to slide his fingers into her hair and tilt her face up to his kiss, that she'd been overcome by a wave of lust and gratitude that he'd helped her finish the oesophageal atresia surgery and she'd bungled her well-prepared speech.

Zach's frown deepened. He shoved his hands in his trouser pockets, defensively. 'Okay, I'm listening.'

Perching on the edge of her desk, she wiped her sweaty palms down the legs of her trousers. She was making such a mess of this, when in her head her confession had been succinct, unemotional, a done deal whereby she would have been in control.

Only now, she was all over the place.

'Um...about Brisbane,' she said, gnawing at her lip. If she'd done this over the phone, or via email, she'd have avoided having to look at him while she imparted her life-altering news. She didn't know Zach well enough to know how he'd react. But she wasn't a coward and the minute she told him he'd likely want as little to do with her as possible, so it really didn't matter.

'I thought we'd put Brisbane behind us,' he said, throwing her words from earlier back in her face.

He seemed miffed, as if he'd expected something more from their reunion. But surely he hadn't imagined they would pick up where they left off? He'd been as adamant as her that it was a one-night deal.

'I did say that.' Phoebe nodded, gripping the edge of her desk. Hysterical, inappropriate laughter clogged her throat. Was he under the impression that she wanted to talk about the best sex of her life, when she'd worked hard since the next day to forget it?

There was no way to soften the blow, and the longer she

dithered, the harder it was to say the words. She dragged in a breath and simply blurted it out. 'I have put it behind me, but the thing is I'm pregnant.'

Now that she'd dropped her bombshell, relief forced her to exhale a long sigh.

She waited, sympathetic to his confused reaction.

Zach's frown intensified, deep grooves etched between his brows as his eyes darted over her face. He was trying to judge if she was joking, no doubt. 'We used condoms.'

Expecting his disbelief, she nodded, trying to dim the recollections from that incredible night where once they'd touched each other, they hadn't been able to stop.

She'd never been so insatiable for anyone before, and Zach had seemed equally ardent.

'I know,' she said. 'One of them didn't work.' Compassion for him swelled in her chest. Of course he'd experience the same shock she had when she'd seen that telltale pink line on the pregnancy test. She'd had over a month to get used to the idea.

He stood stock-still, his arms now hanging by his sides, his eyelids blinking occasionally the only part of him to move.

Phoebe winced, taking pity on him, rushing ahead to the reassurance part of her speech. 'The thing is, I thought you should know, but I don't need anything from you.'

His eyes darkened, bewilderment and anger warring for control of his expression. 'But it took you, what, two months to tell me?'

Caught red-handed, Phoebe fidgeted with her necklace. 'I didn't realise myself for the first two months. I've never had a regular cycle. Then, when it was confirmed, I... I thought it was best to tell you in person,'

As if deaf to her reasonable explanation, he gripped the back of his neck and paced towards the door, spinning once he ran out of carpet. 'Hold on, did you lure me here, invite me to Sydney on the pretext of needing my help with a surgery just to drop this in my lap?'

Phoebe bristled, appalled. 'No! The timing of my discovery around the same time I invited you here to consult on Poppy Wilson's surgery was coincidental, not manufactured, I assure you. I didn't want to tell you by email or even on the phone, and I figured as you'd agreed to come anyway, I could wait and tell you face to face.'

Zach held up one hand, cutting off her explanation. 'So in summary, just so I understand: you wanted me to know that in six months' time I'm going to be a father, but you don't need me to be involved, in fact, it probably suits you best if I'm not. Do I have that right? Have I missed anything?'

Queasy with nerves and guilt, drained from the emotions of the morning and a little embarrassed that she'd not only almost fainted in front of him, but also messed up her grand declaration, Phoebe blustered, 'I mean, I want the baby to know its father—'

'Well, that's something, I guess,' he interrupted, his lips thinned with annoyance.

How had she managed to offend him so deeply? This had gone much better in her head, where they'd had endless mature, respectful versions of this conversation. But perhaps that was the point. She'd had time to prepare, and he was understandably shell-shocked.

'What I mean is,' she rushed on, hoping that they could get the matter cleared up before her clinic began in thirty minutes, 'we both knew in Brisbane that neither of us was looking for any kind of relationship or commitment, and this pregnancy...' she placed her hand over her still-flat stomach '...changes nothing.'

Zach looked as if he was about to argue the point, his gaze

resting where her hand was for a second. In a moment of insanity, Phoebe imagined him dropping to his knee, producing a ring and frogmarching her down the aisle.

She shuddered at the ridiculous and implausible thought. Zach looked as if he regretted ever meeting her, and she had no intention of confusing lust for love, if that even existed. Having a child together certainly wasn't enough to keep her own parents together. In fact, her father had used Phoebe as his argument for leaving, saying he'd felt trapped, as if he hadn't been an active participant in his own wedding and Phoebe's conception.

Proposals! Huh—she'd spent too much time surrounded by her loved-up friends.

As if on cue, Ali popped her head around the door, her curious gaze darting between Phoebe and Zach. 'Um… Ready when you are, Phoebs.'

Phoebe nodded and sighed, a tension headache forming. Ali had no idea that Zach was the father—no one knew. But her astute friend must be dying with curiosity given recent events.

This was turning into an uncontrollable nightmare.

Taking in their expressions, Zach's stony and Phoebe's no doubt defensive, and clearly cognisant of the tension in the room, Ali glanced at Zach uncertainly. 'I'll um… just wait then, shall I?'

Phoebe dithered, uncertain what to do next. She wanted to check that all was well with the baby after her near faint and she knew Ali always carried a portable foetal Doppler heart ultrasound in her pocket. But should she invite Zach into the examination? She'd assumed that he would have heard her news and have stomped away by now.

Instead, he turned to Ali, taking control of the conversation. 'I'd like to be present. If it's okay with you,' he said, turning back to Phoebe.

Completely thrown by the determination of his request, and with two pairs of eyes awaiting her approval, all Phoebe could do was nod and follow Ali into the examination room next door, a silent and brooding Zach bringing up the rear.

As he closed the door to the examination room behind them, Phoebe's friend Ali glanced over at Zach, her eyes practically on stalks with curiosity. Still reeling from Phoebe's shock announcement, still processing the flutter of bemused excitement making it hard to draw a deep breath, Zach looked to Phoebe for his cue. He had no idea how much Phoebe had confided to her friend. Perhaps no one knew that she was pregnant. Perhaps Phoebe didn't want anyone to know that *he* was the father. But he had rights too, and being out of control, being uncertain of his role, was not a situation that suited Zach's personality.

Then he spied a portable ultrasound machine in the corner and clenched his jaw. Confused and annoyed that he might have been the last to know about the pregnancy, he breathed through the impulse to set the record straight to Phoebe's friend.

I've just found out I'm the father of this baby.

We hooked up once and I'd been hoping we might again, but she's been keeping this from me.

No, we're not together and Phoebe can't wait to get rid of me because she can do all of this alone.

Deciding to leave the explanations up to Phoebe, Zach focused on his breathing. His hands were trembling. He was going to be a father. Was the baby okay? Did Phoebe's dizziness mean something was wrong?

'Ali…' Phoebe said as she climbed onto the examination couch and waved her hand vaguely in his direction, 'Zach is… um…the father.'

Ali quickly contained her surprise, schooling her expression into a serene smile he assumed was her consultation face.

'Yes,' Zach said, sticking out his hand for a handshake as if they were any other excited expectant couple here for their first check-up. Except they weren't a couple. And from Phoebe's actions this morning, which in light of her news now made perfect sense, from what she'd said about needing nothing from him, it was barn-door obvious that they never would be.

'So you already know that Phoebe is pregnant?' he asked, swallowing the renewed pang of disappointment he'd experienced when faced with Phoebe's distant attitude. It wasn't as if he'd been about to propose to her, but the fact that she not only considered him superfluous, but had also kept him in the dark about his baby while confiding in her friends made his hackles rise. For a high achiever who took charge of every aspect of his life, the lack of control, the insignificance, was as intolerable as it was alien.

Ali had the good grace to flash him an apologetic look. 'Um...yes. I learned the wonderful news recently. Congratulations.' She beamed while she fastened the blood-pressure cuff around Phoebe's arm.

Zach deflated. This woman was an obstetrician, qualified to advise and care for Phoebe and their unborn baby. Part of him was grateful that she'd known about his baby before him.

Phoebe sagged back against the pillows, eyeing Zach warily. 'Now that we've done the introductions, can we please do this? I have clinic soon.'

'So you two met in Brisbane,' Ali fished as she removed the blood-pressure cuff and added to Phoebe, 'Your blood pressure is normal, by the way.'

The word *met* could clearly be substituted for *hooked up*.

'Yes.' Phoebe flushed, telling Zach what he'd already guessed at: that Phoebe had most likely told her friends nothing after Brisbane. That she obviously considered Zach a footnote in the story, someone she'd have never thought about again without this unforeseen consequence of their night together. To independent Phoebe he was irrelevant, just a man who'd inadvertently provided sperm.

This was why he didn't trust relationships. People were all about their own agenda, he'd seen that when his parents' marriage had crumbled and they'd gone from a loving couple with four children to two individuals who suddenly couldn't stand each other.

'Wonderful,' Ali said, smiling at Zach as if he might be the man of Phoebe's dreams.

Zach bit his tongue. There was no such man. Phoebe had made it clear just now, and by her reluctance to tell him straight away, that she needed Zach as much as she needed a six-month supply of alcohol.

'Neither of us wants a relationship.' Phoebe rushed to clarify, as good as telling her friend to forget whatever romantic ideas were putting that fascinated excitement in her eyes. 'It was a one-night thing.'

'In fact, you knew about my baby before I did,' Zach added, pointedly, 'as I've literally just been informed.' Zach clenched his jaw, because Phoebe was right. He'd always enjoyed his life the way it was, his relationships casual. Anything more required feelings, and Zach knew from the disaster his parents had made of their marriage that feelings, love, never lasted, even when you'd been committed for years and had a family.

But that was before.

Having taken years of flak from his parents and siblings for his single, childless status, he'd never once imagined that he'd have a baby of his own. Except it was happening.

Phoebe stared daggers his way, likely because she'd already explained that she'd intended to tell him in person, hence the delay. But he wasn't feeling reasonable. He'd been manipulated and dismissed, given no time to come to terms with the fact that his life was changed for ever.

Aware of the drop in temperature in the room, Ali busied herself with the scan, changing the subject with true professionalism. 'My registrar wheeled over the ultrasound machine, so let's see if we can see the little one, shall we?'

Phoebe exposed her abdomen and Ali squirted on some ultrasound gel. Ali positioned the scan wand over Phoebe's lower abdomen and moved it around, pressing buttons to alter the image resolution as she peered closely for signs of a foetal sac.

Zach stared at the grainy image on the screen, his heart thudding in his throat with anticipation. He'd just been told the news and now he was about to see his baby for the first time. Trying to grapple with it all made his head spin.

With another click, the screen froze on an image of his and Phoebe's baby.

Zach stilled, time slowing. He stared in utter wonder at the baby's head, the heart, the arms and legs. It was a miracle, one he'd always respected, given his occupation, but now he was looking at his own baby.

He was going to be a father.

A hot lump of emotion lodged in his throat and he instantly knew he would walk over burning coals to meet any need their baby might have, now or in the future. Stunned, he glanced at Phoebe, who was staring too. She might not have even been aware of it, but her hand was gripping his arm so tight, he wondered how he'd missed her touching him.

Ali pressed another button and the image switched back to real time, only now there was sound, the rapid flutter of the heartbeat they could clearly see on the screen.

A surge of protective love eclipsed every other thought in Zach's head.

'Is everything all right?' Phoebe asked, releasing Zach as Ali handed them each a printed photo of their tiny baby.

Dazed, Zach scoured the photo and perched on the foot of the examination couch before he fell to his knees.

'Everything seems perfectly normal,' Ali said, replacing the wand and handing Phoebe a box of tissues so she could clean up.

'As a doctor,' Ali said, 'I'm recommending that you try to eat regularly. I know it's hard with the morning sickness, but we don't want any more fainting spells, do we?'

Phoebe nodded her agreement, zipping up her trousers. 'I'll grab something before my clinic begins.'

Ali glanced Zach's way once more, her smile now full of sympathy that made him feel somehow insignificant, as if she too suspected he wouldn't be in the picture for long.

'I'll leave you two to talk,' she said and quietly left the room.

Silence bellowed in his head as he placed the precious scan photo in his inside jacket pocket.

Phoebe was carrying his baby. Phoebe wanted nothing from him.

He looked at her, desperate for a cue on what he was supposed to say, how he was supposed to act, for the first time in his life—a life of constantly striving, of focusing solely on his work and trusting his instincts, the strength of his convictions unwavering—totally and utterly lost.

CHAPTER FIVE

PHOEBE STARED AT ZACH, her heart skipping a beat with compassion at his bewildered expression. She'd only ever seen him supremely confident, decisive, certain in his ability to command his own universe. Now his stunned expression brought her hot shameful guilt for not telling him sooner bubbling to the surface. She'd had weeks to come to terms with the life-changing news she'd literally just dropped in his lap. She herself was still reeling from seeing their baby for the first time.

As she glanced down at the scan picture once more, Phoebe's jaw dropped in wonder. She was mesmerised by the image. Until the moment she'd seen their baby's tiny heart beat on the screen, she'd half believed that the multiple tests she'd performed, the amenorrhoea and the pregnancy symptoms were all imagined somehow. But now that she'd seen the proof with her own eyes, held photographic evidence in her hand, a wave of love washed over her as reality dawned.

This was truly happening. She was going to be a mother.

Wanting to reassure Zach, she swung her legs over the edge of the examination couch so they sat side by side. 'Look, Zach, it's okay. However you're feeling is fine, honestly. I'm still a little overwhelmed by all of this myself, so I understand.'

She'd watched his earlier confusion morph to disbelief and then annoyance and return full circle back to confusion. She'd cycled through the same raft of emotions when she'd first found out.

Zach scrubbed a hand over his face as if he could snap himself out of the shock. 'I don't know how I'm feeling, to be honest.'

Phoebe nodded, caught off guard by his vulnerability and his honest admission. She wanted to touch him, to take his hand and comfort him, but she wasn't certain her gesture would be welcome. She didn't know this version of Zach and the man who'd swanned into her OR, into her office earlier, flashing his sexy smile and playing havoc with her hormones was understandably nowhere to be seen.

'That's okay too,' she said, her voice soft and patient. 'It's a lot to take in.' Realising that the joy of the moment was ever so slightly dampened for her too, because she couldn't share it with him the way she would if they were a couple—laughter through tears, a hug, a kiss, staring at the grainy image together while they held hands—Phoebe supressed the urge to reach out to him, physically.

They'd made this baby together during a night of incredible passion. And while she'd waited for the scan confirmation that all was well from Ali, her first instinct had been to reach for Zach. She'd acted on autopilot, needing some contact in case he'd been feeling as nervous as her, but also needing the connection for her own comfort. Somewhere in the deep recesses of her mind, she'd known that they were in this together.

Now that the moment had passed, she drew on her self-sufficiency once more.

'Look,' she continued, hoping to set his mind at ease, 'I have absolutely zero expectations of you. Having this baby was *my* decision. I know how much you travel with your work, so of course I don't expect you to be around. I'm perfectly happy doing this on my own. My mother was a single parent, raised me alone, so I've had a great role model. I'm confident that I'll do as good a job of raising our baby.'

At Zach's continued silence, which in itself was fairly worrying for a man so self-assured, she rambled on. 'Honestly, I have everything figured out.'

She was a busy professional career woman. She could slot one little baby into her life, no problem.

'Ask my friends,' she continued. 'I am the queen of lists, super-organised. This isn't going to change me in the slightest.'

Still quiet, Zach shifted beside her. Growing aware of his closeness, of the way her body naturally leaned in his direction, of his delicious manly scent and the way her gaze more often than not landed on his mouth when she looked at him, Phoebe was forced to admit that she was still helplessly drawn to his charisma, intelligence, not to mention astounding physicality.

But she'd get over her attraction, which was likely a product of her pregnancy hormones. Once he left Sydney, she'd no longer have that confusing distraction.

'And of course,' she continued, 'whenever you're back in Sydney you're welcome to visit the baby. If you give me a picture of yourself, I'll keep it in the nursery, talk about you all the time so the baby grows up knowing who you are.'

Her concern that he remained mute was becoming quite alarming. If he'd only say something, anything, she'd know that he was okay.

As if the universe had heard her request, Zach pulled his vibrating phone from his pocket and glanced down at the screen. 'I have to go,' he said, tucking his phone into his jacket and standing.

'Oh, of course.' Phoebe shrugged on her professional demeanour to match Zach's businesslike tone. She exhaled, glad that the worst was over. Duty done, she'd informed Zach that

their night in Brisbane had produced consequences and, aside
from his understandable shock, everything seemed to be going
to plan.

Phoebe stood, buttoning up her jacket and straightening her
hair. 'Me too, actually. My clinic is about to start.'

Despite the way she'd bungled her announcement, this was
now going exactly the way she'd planned. So why, as she
faced him, did a trickle of silly disappointment sneak under
her guard?

Zach stared back, his expression inscrutable. Phoebe tried
not to squirm, chewing her lip. She blinked away the silly
burning sensation behind her eyes. Surely she wasn't hoping
that he'd want to be a part of their lives, hers and the baby's?
She had first-hand experience of how wrong things could go
when one person in a relationship felt trapped. Her father had
readily moved to the town where Phoebe's mother had grown
up and then later resented his choice.

'Is there a canteen in the hospital?' he asked, the abrupt
change of topic taking her by surprise.

'Um, yes. It's on the fourth floor, directly above us.'

He nodded, looking more like his old self. 'Are you free
tonight?'

Another subject switch. Phoebe's head was beginning to
spin.

'Um...'

'I think we should talk,' he said, his voice persuasive bor-
dering on inflexible, as if he was back in control. 'We need to
have an adult conversation about this, away from the hospital
when neither of us is rushed.'

She nodded, unable to argue with his calm logic, or the determination in the set of his jaw. 'Yes, of course. I'll be finished here by six thirty.'

This was good. Once they'd settled all of the details like

adults, once Zach had had a chance to come to terms with the news and ask any questions he might have, they could move on and life would get back to normal, exactly what she wanted.

'Perfect—I'll meet you back here at six-thirty.' He straightened his tie, which somewhere along the way during the past forty minutes had become ever so slightly askew.

'But first,' he added, his voice clipped, decisive in a way that reminded Phoebe of their difference of opinion on the panel discussion at the Brisbane conference, 'I'm going upstairs to buy you some lunch, which I'll leave with your clinic receptionist. No arguments.'

He moved to the door, glanced over his shoulder one last time, his stare sweeping over her from head to toe so that, when he left the room, she collapsed back onto the couch and dragged in a few calming breaths, both annoyed at his high-handedness and horribly turned on.

Running a shaky hand over her hair, she had time for only one thought as she rushed to her clinic: *That went as well as could be expected.*

CHAPTER SIX

ZACH DISLIKED NOTHING more than being caught in the fork of an impossible choice. It reminded him of his parents' messy divorce and the way they'd appointed him go-between. Sitting opposite Phoebe at Tutto Bene, the small casual Italian restaurant close to the hospital, later that evening, with her news and her subsequent dismissal still spinning in his head as if his brain were buffering, Zach feared that whatever happened tonight would trigger his most deeply ingrained insecurity: failing.

Glancing away from Phoebe, who was perusing the menu, he forced himself to stop staring. He'd thought she was beautiful before he'd known about the pregnancy, but now she seemed to glow from within, her skin softer looking, her hair more luxurious than he remembered. Even her voice seemed to carry a hint of new contentment.

But his continuing attraction and renewed fascination with the woman who had occupied his thoughts since Brisbane was completely irrelevant.

All that mattered now was the well-being of her and their baby.

Swallowing down the foreign taste of doubt, Zach reasoned his current position, where Phoebe had dropped her bombshell and then deemed him superfluous, was precisely the reason he'd always avoided the commitment of a serious relationship all these years. Zach didn't do failure. In avoiding emotional entanglement, he'd been able to focus solely on his career, his work ethic a result of being raised in a family encouraged to aim for the stars.

And while, now he was an adult, the constant rivalry between him, his two older brothers and his older sister drove him mad, something he avoided engaging in if at all possible, his life choices had also become a point of one-upmanship. He was the only unmarried sibling, the only one without children.

Until now. Now he was going to be a father...

'I'm starving,' Phoebe said, snatching him from the memory of how, needing to clear his head and come to terms with the shock news, Zach had cancelled his meeting at Nurture, the neonatal charity he often worked for, thrown on his running gear and pounded out twenty-five kilometres along the shoreline before he was able to rationalise his turbulent thoughts. As he'd bent double to catch his breath, sweat pouring from his skin, two certainties had arisen: one, the surprisingly strong surge of both excitement and protectiveness that he'd experienced for the tiny baby whose picture he now carried in his wallet, and two, the determination that he and Phoebe had much to work out.

She closed the menu, clearly decided on what she wanted to eat and smiled up at him. 'The gnocchi here is really good. It's my favourite.'

Shutting down the image of Phoebe coming to this restaurant with a date before jealousy stole what was left of his own appetite, Zach focused on using this opportunity to play catch-up, piecing together the facts he'd learned from Phoebe's conversation with Ali earlier. 'Have you had very bad morning sickness, then?'

He was glad to see that Phoebe's appetite had returned, but now that she was already into the second trimester of this pregnancy, he wanted to know what else he'd missed. Not only had he rushed out this afternoon and bought up every child-development and parenting book he could find, for some bizarre reason, he couldn't shake the feeling that he should have been there for Phoebe during those early weeks, not, from the way she'd resolutely maintained her stance on going it alone, that she'd have allowed it, no doubt.

Eyeing him warily again, as if she was suspicious of his motives, Phoebe sipped her water and shrugged. 'It's not too bad now. I usually make up for it by eating more for the rest of the day.'

'I'm glad that it's settling,' he said. Now that he'd raised the hot topic, Zach had many more questions, so she'd better get used to the idea. 'Are you taking pregnancy vitamins?'

'Of course.' She sat straighter as if offended. 'I'm doing everything I'm supposed to do. I've even given up my favourite: coffee. I just can't stomach it any more, even the smell.' She shuddered.

'I didn't mean to accuse you,' he said, as if he were traversing a path of eggshells. 'I just feel as if I've missed so much already. You should know by now that I like to stay informed.' He hadn't planned to become a father, but, now that it had happened, his head was full of dreams and fantasies of the future.

Phoebe's eyes widened. She looked startled by his admission.

'So there's no detox challenge at the hospital?' he asked, calling her out on her earlier excuse.

'No.' She glanced down, sheepishly. 'I panicked when you suggested coffee. I'm sorry about that.'

Zach clenched his jaw, trying to cling to his indignation given that she'd lied and then dismissed him, as if he had no investment in becoming a father. Except knowing that she was carrying his child, seeing her vulnerable after her dizzy spell, witnessing the unguarded moments of her interaction with her close friend and the way she'd been as awed as Zach by the ultrasound scan images had shown him new sides to Phoebe's personality that he couldn't help but find appealing.

More fool him.

Frustrated at his weakness for a woman who'd clearly stated that she was done with him more than once, he looked away from her profile as she placed her order with the server.

She was certainly testing the resolve he'd made to set his attraction aside so he could verbalise his feelings about the pregnancy and a way forward clearly. Every time she shifted in her seat or rested an elbow on the table, the neck of her blouse gaped, revealing a vee of creamy chest. But he had much bigger issues to raise than his ongoing fascination with her. Like how, when it came to the child they'd made together, she'd already written him out of the story.

Determined to clear the air now that he'd had a chance to come to terms with the news, Zach waited until they were alone once more and said, 'I handled things badly earlier. I think I was in shock, if I'm honest.'

Shocked was an understatement; more like poleaxed. The idea of becoming a father in six months' time when he wasn't even in a relationship with the baby's mother had sent his brain spinning. He was always careful with his sexual partners, always used protection, but no method of contraception was one hundred per cent reliable. Then, as the seconds passed, the shock had been replaced by wonder, awe, joy.

'I handled it badly too,' she said, looking genuinely regretful, catching him off guard. 'I was a bit shaken myself in the beginning, as you can imagine.' She swallowed and a fresh wave of empathy took hold of his usually analytical mind.

'When I knew you were coming to Sydney, I'd planned a whole speech for when you arrived,' she said, toying with her water glass. 'But then you showed up early and I bungled it. I'm really sorry about the way you found out, Zach.'

Because he wanted to reach across the table and take her hand, show her that he'd forgiven her almost immediately back in her office, Zach instead took a sip of mineral water, avoiding alcohol in solidarity with a teetotal Phoebe.

He watched her over the rim of his glass, saw her uncertainty and doubt. It wasn't every day she had to confront a man she barely knew with life-changing news, especially when they hadn't planned to see each other again and when they'd been careful. He could understand the awkwardness and amplified emotions of the situation, particularly on the back of an emergency in the OR and when she'd been feeling unwell.

'Well, I've had some time to think since this afternoon,' he said, trying to ignore the fact that every time she looked at him, he recalled the way she'd automatically reached for his arm while they'd waited for the scan to locate their baby's rapid heartbeat.

In that tense split second, despite her assertions of going it alone, she *had* needed his presence for comfort.

Why had that felt so good? Was it just the ingrained caring that was a part of his job? Or was it evidence that, despite how she'd assured him that he had no role in the pregnancy, he'd seen a way that he could be of use beyond his relationship with his baby?

Of course he had a role. A vital one, although she might not like the idea.

'I know you said that you don't need me,' he said, trying and failing to hold onto the brief flicker of anger he'd felt when she'd dismissed him earlier, 'which is totally your prerogative. But I think it's important that I be around, for both you and the baby.'

His baby.

She might not need him, but their baby needed its father as much as he needed to be a part of his child's life.

Phoebe gaped, disbelief written all over her heart-shaped face. 'You want to be involved?'

Zach nodded. 'Of course.' Just because he was no more interested in a relationship than she was, didn't mean that he couldn't support her through the rest of the pregnancy now that they were to be parents.

'But…your lifestyle,' she said, frowning, 'the way you travel. It's hardly suited to changing nappies and sleepless nights.'

Faced with her patronising comment, Zach bit back his first retort. He didn't want to upset her or even argue the point. She was right. He was forty-one and single. He'd certainly been around the block, had a healthy sex life, but he'd always avoided commitment. He couldn't see the point in investing all of that time and energy into a relationship when it was most likely doomed to failure, the way his parents' twenty-six-year marriage had ended.

Being trapped in the middle of his parents' bitter divorce as a teenager had given him a deep and lasting insight into the fickle transiency of love.

But this wasn't just about him and Phoebe any longer. There was their baby to consider.

'And your lifestyle *is* suited to a baby?' he said, pointing out how similar they were and taking no satisfaction from the flush that pinkened her cheeks.

She raised her chin, challenge shining from her stare. 'You're right—neither of us planned this. But as we saw from the scan, it's happening. And I'll figure out the logistics, rest assured.'

'Alone?' he asked, while she straightened her cutlery on the white linen tablecloth, avoiding his gaze.

'Yes, alone. Lots of people do,' she said, meeting his gaze with defiance, as if reiterating her independence. 'Just because I'm pregnant, doesn't mean that I've changed who I am as a person.'

'Of course not,' he said, wondering where her fierce self-reliance originated. 'But this is going to be a major adjustment for both of us. I'm an uncle, so I've witnessed how a child changes *everything*.'

Their lives would never be the same again. How could they? He'd seen his siblings' lives both exponentially enriched and, in some ways, turned inside out by parenthood, not that any of them would admit to the latter, given the competitive streak that ran through all of the Archer siblings.

'And although I don't exactly have all of the details worked out right now,' he continued, pointedly holding her gaze, 'I want you to know that I intend to have a role in my child's life.'

A full and active role.

She could be as independent as she pleased, but Zach wouldn't tolerate being superfluous as a father, better that she understood that from the start. He had as much right as she did to parent their child. 'You're right, Phoebe,' he continued, 'we didn't plan this, but we made this baby together. That means we need to find a way to parent our child together too.'

Even if they weren't a romantic couple.

She looked away, a ghost of a smirk around her mouth. 'Of course.'

'What does that look mean?' he asked, sensing her unspoken cynicism. 'Don't you believe that my intentions are sincere?'

Was she suggesting he'd lie, go back on his word, shirk his responsibility once the baby was born? That showed how little she knew him. Just because they weren't in a relationship didn't mean that he would abandon his child or Phoebe. They were doctors, acutely aware that pregnancy sometimes carried risks and complications, especially a geriatric pregnancy. Zach wanted to be around, not only for their baby's welfare, but also in case a complication arose.

For now, he'd keep that to himself. Clearly Phoebe had a pretty low opinion of him if she thought him capable of simply walking away from both her and the baby he already felt fiercely protective of.

'It's not that I disbelieve you,' she said, looking uncomfortable, as if cornered. 'I'm sure that you mean what you're saying right now.'

'But?' he asked, because he knew it was coming. 'You think I'll change my mind?'

'But a child is for life,' she said, condescendingly, as if this thought hadn't yet occurred to him, as if their baby were a puppy he wouldn't have time to walk or a brightly painted fridge that seemed like a good idea at first, but then grew tiresome. 'That's a long-term commitment.'

Zach offered her a tight smile. 'Are you suggesting that the novelty of being a father will wear off? Because you know from my reputation as a surgeon that I'm not a quitter.' Once set on a course of action he deemed best, Zach committed one hundred per cent. Being a father that his child could depend upon, loving his child unconditionally so their baby grew up emotionally secure was the only satisfactory course of action.

She met his stare, her eyes full of resolve and something else, maybe hurt, vulnerability. 'It happens.' She shrugged, obviously expecting him to fail.

But the more Phoebe pushed him away, doubted his abilities, set him up for failure, the more determined her insinuations made him to also prove her wrong in the process. Not only would they be finding a way to co-parent their child, but they'd also be getting to know one another personally, starting right now, so that he could challenge whatever prejudices she held and make sure she understood the real Zach Archer.

In the same way that he strived to be the best surgeon he could be, he'd also aim to be the best father any kid could have. Not that he knew the first thing about raising a child, but he'd make it work in the same way he tackled any new challenge: with drive, determination and gallons of self-belief.

She took a sip of water and added, 'I haven't seen my own father since I was four years old, when he walked out on me and my mother.'

Zach's jaw started to ache where his muscles were clenched hard. So this casual admission was the root of her pretty low opinion of him, her own father the yardstick she measured all fathers against.

'I'm sorry that happened to you,' he said, his voice softening with empathy. 'But just because some men walk away from their responsibilities, doesn't mean that *all* men will. This is my baby too.'

Rolling her shoulders back, she clasped her hands together in front of her as if, having shown him one tiny glimpse of vulnerability, she was once more blocking him out. 'I know that, and I think it's better for all three of us, you, me and the baby, if we keep things real, keep our promises and expectations pragmatic. You and I need to be honest with each other for the baby's sake.'

Nodding his agreement, Zach considered his next words carefully. She didn't trust him, that much was clear. A part of him couldn't blame her. This so-called father of hers had abandoned her and never returned. It stood to reason that she'd be cynical about the intentions of her own baby's father. But Zach wasn't that sort of man. He constantly held himself to the highest standards in everything he did. He would give his all to parenting this baby, a baby he'd never imagined but already loved with shocking ferocity.

Did every parent experience this overwhelming swell of emotion?

'I agree,' he said, leaning back in his chair to give Phoebe some emotional space. 'So I'll start right now. If I'm honest, it feels as if you'd rather that I wasn't part of the picture.' He kept his voice even, despite that itch of impotence flaring anew, galvanising him to fight his corner. She might not realise that she was doing it, but she'd begun pushing him away, even before she'd told him about the baby. Her expectations of him couldn't be any lower.

Watching her reaction, her expression turning from one of shock to one of defensiveness, he tried to relax his shoulders, aware that this situation, the lack of control, was pushing him so far out of his comfort zone he'd need a GPS to find his composure once this meal was over. Perhaps he could be a little more objective about her point of view if he weren't still enslaved by their chemistry.

'That's not true.' She shook her head, rejecting his claim, although she couldn't meet his stare. 'I'm just highly aware of the circumstances, that's all. We're not in a relationship. We have demanding jobs and yours takes you all over the world.' She looked at him then, her eyes hardening. 'Realistically, I'll be doing this alone, and I'm absolutely fine with that.'

Zach bit his tongue. He *did* travel a lot. But she was setting him up to fail at fatherhood even before the baby was born. Just because they'd only planned on a one-night stand, didn't mean he had no interest in the unforeseen consequences. Just because he was male didn't mean he should be measured against another man's shortcomings. Just because he wasn't the one carrying the baby, didn't mean that his feelings were any less relevant.

He *would* be a good father.

Failure wasn't in his vocabulary. That was why he avoided his large family's gatherings whenever possible, having, up until now, no interest in the competition to produce grandchildren for his parents, a race in which he'd always been automatically disqualified by default.

But things changed. People changed. Priorities changed.

For a second, he imagined telling his parents that their youngest son had finally produced their next grandchild. They were going to be overjoyed.

'I'm sorry that you have so little faith in me,' he said, taking the gauntlet that she'd so casually thrown down. 'But you and I are both similarly dedicated people. We like to do things to the best of our ability. I saw that today in the operating theatre. I plan on applying that same dedication to raising our child, as, I suspect, will you.'

Still suspicious, she eyed him non-committally.

'So, I have a proposition,' he added with a smile, embracing the challenge to show her how wrong she was about him, confident as always in his own abilities. 'I'm due in Perth in three weeks for a month-long visiting-surgeon post. How about we use the time I'm in Sydney to not only figure out a plan for when the baby arrives and for the future, but also get to know each other better? As you said—honesty is the best policy.'

That hadn't been the point of her speech, which had been to demonstrate her surety that he would behave just like her own father. But he and Phoebe understanding each other, learning the other's priorities, goals and values, could only be a good thing in the long run, especially for their baby.

'What do you say?' he asked, raising his glass. 'To getting to know each other and to co-parenting.'

Phoebe touched her water glass to his almost reluctantly, doubt lingering in her eyes. 'To getting to know each other.'

Determined to show her not only that he was a man of his word, but that he could also be trusted, he resolved to be patient.

But one thing was certain—if Phoebe thought she had everything neatly sorted, excluding him from his baby's life in the process, she'd grossly underestimated his single-mindedness.

CHAPTER SEVEN

LATER THAT WEEK, Phoebe walked into the neonatal intensive care unit, or NICU for short, where tiny newborn twins Poppy and Jasmine Wilson were inpatients, her stomach tight with nerves. She should be getting used to seeing Zach around Sydney Central by now, but the impending sight of him, after everything that had transpired that first day, was something she both looked forward to and dreaded.

She'd been utterly thrown by his assertions at dinner that first day. She'd never in a million years have imagined that he'd want to hang around, to be involved with the pregnancy and participate in raising the baby. She'd almost spluttered out her water when he'd proposed that they would not only be co-parenting, but also getting to know each other better and making plans for the future.

But he was still leaving in under three weeks, a fact that helped her to put his promises into perspective. Maybe, once he'd left Sydney, she and the baby would be a little easier to forget.

Phoebe turned the corner, her emotions all over the place once more. She spied Zach waiting at the desk, and her heart galloped. He was so handsome, so imposing and yet calmly confident. The way he'd steered the conversation at Tutto Bene, so self-assured that he'd figure out exactly how to be everything he needed to be—doctor, parent, platonic partner to the woman carrying his child—it was seriously impressive.

Of course, there were many hurdles ahead. Plenty of time for him to change his mind or mess up.

As she approached, she saw that Zach was chatting to one of the ward nurses, a pretty, bubbly redhead in her early thirties. Out of nowhere, white-hot jealousy pierced Phoebe's side like a stitch.

Of course Zach's charisma and self-possession naturally put people at ease, making him approachable and engaging. Not to mention the fact that he was the sexiest man Phoebe had ever known, something she just couldn't ignore, no matter how hard she tried. She'd already heard the whisperings around the hospital, tales of the new hottie neonatal surgeon with the sexy deep voice, dreamy eyes and yummy backside.

Resisting the urge to fan her flushed face, Phoebe interrupted. 'Dr Archer.'

She paused at his side and flashed both him and Nurse Maynard a smile. It meant nothing to her if Zach wanted to move on to his next casual conquest. Despite his reassurances that he intended to be there for her and the baby, she'd meant what she said. She didn't need him, nor did she have any intention of acting on her inescapable attraction to the man. They might be about to become parents, but that didn't mean that Phoebe needed a romantic relationship in order to be happy. Rosa Mason had seen to it that her only daughter would be raised to know her own worth and never rely on a man.

Rather than shaping his own destiny and taking care of his responsibilities, Phoebe's father had blamed Rosa for his disappointments in life. Phoebe only had one memory of the man, a vague blurry image of him pushing her on a merry-go-round, his smiling face looming in and out of focus with each revolution, distorted by her dizziness.

But there was more to being a father than donating sperm. As Phoebe had grown older, she'd stopped watching the door waiting for him to come back and take her to the park once more. Instead, she'd channelled all of her disappointment into being helpful to Rosa, who'd worked long, hard hours to be all the parent Phoebe had needed.

Thinking about her mum, she realised that now that she'd told Zach about the baby, she would no longer need to keep it a secret from her mum. They spoke most evenings on the phone, were very close. Or perhaps she'd wait until she had time to visit, tell her mum in person.

'Shall we?' she said to Zach, gesturing that he follow her to the side ward where the twins and Emma, their mother, were inpatients. Baby Jasmine, Poppy's twin, was growing stronger by the day, so Emma had once more been admitted in order to try and establish Jasmine on breast feeds alone prior to her discharge.

Pausing at the sinks outside the side ward, which afforded the high-profile family some privacy, Phoebe donned a surgical mask and washed her hands. Becoming aware of Zach's eyes on her as he mirrored her actions, she looked up.

'How are you feeling this morning?' he asked, his grey eyes soft and probing, as if she were made of glass.

'I'm fine,' she said, tugging some paper towels from the dispenser with unnecessary force, unused to anyone other than her friends asking after her well-being.

As if he doubted her automatic response, his gaze slowly and thoroughly roamed her features in that highly distracting way she recalled from that night in Brisbane when he'd made her feel like the only woman in the world.

'You still look a little pale,' he said, his voice low and intimate as he dried his own hands, stepping closer as if they were the only two people on the ward.

Phoebe stepped back, away from the tall, impressive wall of his body, from the heat he emanated and the memories of being clutched to his naked chest, clasped in those strong arms of his.

'I didn't sleep very well,' she said, defensive and aroused, a confusing mix that left her irritable. Did he intend to check in with her every morning in his quest to show her that he'd meant what he'd said about wanting to be involved? Did he disbelieve that she was taking all possible steps to ensure a healthy pregnancy? Surely delivering food and asking after her health was taking his paternal duties too far. They weren't a couple, so there was no need to shower Phoebe with such devoted consideration.

'I managed to finish my breakfast, so that's progress,' she said, because he was still staring, his attentiveness unsettling. She wasn't used to it and had no intention of growing dependent on his concern. It made her feel somehow incapable or beholden.

'Good.' He smiled, looking inordinately pleased, as if she'd won a gold medal for muesli consumption. 'I'm glad.'

To her horror, Phoebe's hormone-ridden body actually preened, as if craving his praise. Well, that was enough of that.

'Emma Wilson,' she said, deciding to bring him up to speed on the ordeal the Wilson family had already been through these past three months since Emma was first admitted, 'is the mother of twins, Poppy and Jasmine, who were born by uncomplicated caesarean section performed by Ali Edwards, who you met.'

Zach nodded at her summary. 'Yes. I arrived early and read Poppy's and Jasmine's notes. I told you—I like to be prepared.'

Taken aback by his diligence and commitment, Phoebe blinked up at him. So far, everything she thought she'd known about Zach Archer was being systematically challenged. Despite his reputation for taking charge, he'd willingly acted as her assistant in Theatre these past few days. Rather than freak him out, as she might have guessed, her news that they were going to be parents hadn't sent him running. Instead, he'd declared they should get to know each other so they could act as an effective co-parenting team. And now, when he could easily have slept in to recover from his jet lag, he'd come in before eight in the morning to bring himself up to speed on Poppy Wilson's history.

'Okay, then,' Phoebe muttered, a little breathless, 'let's go meet the Wilsons.'

They entered the room to find the tall, dark and handsome Aaron Wilson alone with his daughters. The well-built man was sitting in an armchair holding a sleeping Jasmine in the crook of his muscular arm.

Aaron looked up from staring lovingly at his tiny daughter, who wore a pale yellow hand-knitted hat, one of hundreds a year that were donated to the unit by the volunteer knitters of Sydney. Smiling in welcome, Aaron explained that Emma was just dressing after a shower.

'Aaron, this is Dr Archer, the specialist I told you about,' Phoebe said, a flush of silly pride warming her chest, as if she had some sort of ownership of Zach.

But of course she didn't. Just because she still fancied the pants off him, didn't mean she'd changed her stance on relationships. And Zach hadn't said anything about them rekindling what they'd shared in Brisbane, so her hormones could forget it.

'Call me Zach,' Zach said, shaking Aaron's free hand. 'It's good to meet you. And this must be Jasmine.'

The two men talked for a few minutes about Jasmine's progress, her weight gain and attempts at breastfeeding, Zach taking the lead on the consultation and leaving Phoebe free to simply watch him in action.

Zach had indeed thoroughly read the extensive notes on both twins, and even, it seemed, on Emma, the questions he asked relevant and insightful. This was what made him so good at his work. His meticulous attention to detail, his inexhaustible self-belief and his ability not only to take the initiative, but also to humbly relate to people in a way that instantly put them at ease.

A little awed by Zach, Phoebe listened while he explained that because both twins were so small and tired so rapidly, they were still being fed Emma's expressed breast milk by nasogastric tube. That Jasmine had been latching on for short periods of time overnight was a good sign that she might soon be ready for discharge.

Poppy, however, was a different matter.

Before they could move on to discuss Poppy's progress, Emma called for her husband from the adjoining bathroom. Aaron stood and moved to place Jasmine back in her crib, but Zach intervened.

'Here, allow me.' Without hesitation, Zach relieved Aaron of his tiny bundle, scooping an undisturbed Jasmine into his arms.

While Aaron left the room to help his wife, Phoebe gaped, her heart pelting away with excitement behind her ribs. Rather than place Jasmine back in her crib, Zach held her with the same reverence that Aaron had displayed, glancing down at her as if she were the most fascinating thing he'd ever seen.

Phoebe froze, spellbound by the sight of Zach holding Jasmine's head in the palm of his capable surgeon's hand. He didn't coo or rock the baby, merely stared, his gaze taking in her sleeping form from head to toe.

Phoebe's stomach flipped over and over as reality rushed in, almost swiping her feet from under her. In the messy confusion and bungled announcement that their one passionate night had led to consequences—their own baby, in her rush to control her hormones and switch off her still rampant attraction to the man, in her insistence to show that she didn't need his help in parenting their child, she'd completely overlooked the fact that, as a world-leading neonatal surgeon, Zachary Archer had some serious baby-handling skills.

She swallowed, her throat dry. Just watching him in action with Jasmine, all six-foot-plus of him, unselfconsciously holding a baby, almost made her body spontaneously combust with lust.

His words that night in the restaurant hit her in the centre of her chest, more potent than the first time she'd heard them, when she'd managed to easily dismiss them as mere lip-service.

I intend to have a role in my child's life.

What if he truly meant it? What would that mean for Phoebe? Would she have to see him all the time, be constantly bombarded by lust?

No, even if he did plan to accompany her for blood tests and scans and deliver her lunch if she was too busy, he was leaving Sydney soon, although perhaps not soon enough…

She'd arrogantly misjudged Zach, assumed that he'd react in ways she'd imagined her father might have reacted from the tales her mother told. That didn't mean anything had changed. They still weren't a couple. And just because he didn't resent her for his altered circumstances at this moment, the way her father had blamed her mother before he'd walked out on them, didn't mean that he'd always feel that way. Maybe one day, when reality dawned, when fatigue set in, when perhaps the burden of parenthood became too heavy, he might blame Phoebe for disrupting his old life.

Who knew how those strains of worry and responsibility might affect the fragile, co-parenting relationship he seemed to think would be easy? No matter what assertions he'd made, the novelty of Sydney, of three a.m. feeds and sick-up stains on his expensive shirts would surely fade.

Getting to know each other beyond their well-established chemistry was one thing. Agreement, compromise and expectation were entirely different beasts. Neither of them had any experience of those things as far as long-term relationships were concerned.

As Phoebe tried to get her breathing under control, tried to put everything back into perspective, Zach carefully transferred a still-sleeping Jasmine to her crib. She looked away, because Zach holding a baby was ten times hotter than the Zach already stirring up her libido and confusing her with thoughtful gestures and enquiries, as if he cared about her as well as their baby.

Because her legs felt unsteady, she gripped the edge of Poppy's crib. She and Zach were going to be parents, just like Aaron and Emma.

Only unlike the Wilsons—a loving and committed couple—they'd be separate, alone.

Co-parenting. It had sounded progressive and neat when Zach had said it over dinner, but now she couldn't shake the feeling that it also sounded lonely. Seeing his gentle and nurturing side was bound to bring her doubts and fears to the surface. It gave her an insight into how he might parent their own child, a tantalising glimpse of how their child's life might differ from what her own had been.

Just then, Emma and Aaron emerged from the bathroom, Emma still walking gingerly to protect her sutured abdominal incision, while Aaron lent her his arm for support.

Zach introduced himself to the twins' mother, offering a handshake and his signature charismatic smile that shunted Phoebe's body temperature a few degrees higher.

How dared he be so good at everything? No wonder she was all over the place again. Just when she thought she'd figured Zach out, he surprised her anew, like those impossible puzzle cubes, where one move undid each previous solution.

'So, I know it's been explained to you before,' Zach said, 'but I just wanted to go over the plan for Poppy's surgery one more time.' He clarified every detail of ventricular septal defect, an abnormal connection between the two main chambers of Poppy's heart, in a non-patronising way, drawing diagrams to illustrate the surgical procedure they would undertake to close the defect so that the direction of blood flow was corrected.

By the end of his explanation, Aaron and Emma seemed a little starstruck, just like Phoebe.

'So,' he continued, glancing Phoebe's way to include her in the conversation, 'while Poppy has the most common form of congenital heart defect, and while Dr Mason and I have done this type of surgery many times before, Poppy's prematurity, her low weight and the fact that she has been so resistant to our attempts to delay the operation, to treat her symptoms medically until she gains some more weight, make this surgery just a little more challenging.'

'That's why I brought in Dr Archer,' Phoebe said, conscious of the Wilsons' understandably concerned expressions. 'He's the best there is, so even though the defect in Poppy's heart is large, Zach and I have been over the scans and both feel happy with the surgical approach he's just outlined.'

'Why don't we examine Poppy, while you jot down any questions you might have?' Zach said, modestly breezing over Phoebe's compliment.

As Zach listened to Poppy's heart, Emma and Aaron held onto each other's hand tightly while they discussed the information and came up with their most immediate questions.

Phoebe's respect for Zach had gone through the roof. He possessed just the right balance of optimism versus caution, outlining the potential risks of surgery in as compassionate and informative a way as possible. As Phoebe had met the family many times before, she could see that Aaron and Emma felt empowered by their good understanding of the surgery and of the complications of both proceeding with the operation, and waiting, as was the usual case in patients with VSD.

Removing his stethoscope from his ears, Zach held the bell in place over the front of Poppy's chest.

'Have a listen,' he said, handing the earpieces to Phoebe, who fitted them in place. With his hand, he gently positioned her hand and the bell of the stethoscope.

For a few seconds they stayed like that, Phoebe listening to the whoosh of Poppy's heart murmur, Zach holding her hand in place, his eyes locked with hers, silent communication passing between them.

He could have just been asking for her corroboration on the quality of the heart murmur so they could confer later. But the intimacy of the moment, the gravity of examining the unwell neonate together while their own baby grew safe and sound inside her, made Phoebe take a closer look at the type of man Zach was.

A complex man of integrity and professional dedication. A man of strong convictions.

Phoebe nodded to show him that she understood his unspoken message, doctor to doctor, parent to parent: their tiny patient, unlike her sister, was seriously unwell.

Phoebe repositioned the stethoscope over the base of Poppy's lungs, finding the faint crackle that indicated fluid build-up.

As he'd done, she passed the stethoscope earpieces back to him and replaced his hand with hers, this time guiding him to listen to the lung fields. The abnormal functioning of Poppy's heart was causing congestion in the lungs and other organs. The longer that went on, the greater the risk of irreversible organ damage. That was why the surgery couldn't be delayed any longer.

Wrapping up the examination, Zach covered Poppy with a blanket. They answered Aaron and Emma's questions honestly and with compassion they clearly shared. This family had been through so much, their inspiring strength arising from their loving relationship. Now that she and Zach were having a child of their own, Phoebe understood a fraction of the Wilsons' anguish and concern.

They left the room together, headed downstairs to Phoebe's office, Zach the first one to break the loaded and pensive silence.

'So Poppy is on the list for surgery early next week?' he asked.

Phoebe nodded, pushing through a set of double doors. 'Yes. I'll speak to the intensive care team, ask them to increase the inotropes and diuretics, see if we can optimise her lung function for surgery.'

Zach paused, touched her arm, bringing her to a halt, halfway down the stairs. 'I want you to know that, regardless of what's going on with us, personally, I'm glad you called me in on this case.'

Phoebe nodded, her burning eyes locked to his and her throat tight. 'I'm glad that you're here.'

She didn't need him, but she was grateful that he could assist on the surgery, his experience and intuition easing some of her concerns for Poppy and their shared secret bonding them in a way she couldn't have imagined when she invited him to Sydney.

She smiled and they set off once more. A strange empty

feeling hollowed out her chest. They might be willing to tackle Poppy's case as a team, but could they tackle any future hurdles involving their own child as such? Would Zach even be around, as promised, to share the load? Or would she have to muddle through alone, the way her own mother had?

Just because he'd made some pretty ambitious declarations about being involved, didn't mean that she could rely on him to keep his word. People changed their minds, tended to their own needs, behaved selfishly. For as long as Zach was around, she'd need to take extra care to maintain her independence. No matter how much she struggled with their ongoing chemistry, no matter how good it felt to have him work temporarily at her side, emotionally, Phoebe could only truly rely on herself.

That Friday evening, a rare bout of nerves gripped Zach as he knocked on the closed door to Phoebe's office, the strength of which he probably hadn't experienced since his very first kiss.

Although he had spent day after day harmoniously working alongside her, Phoebe seemed to be the only woman alive who could tie him into convoluted knots. At work, they gelled, their complementary styles building on their mutual respect. But beyond professionally, there was a wall around Dr Mason that Zach just couldn't seem to scale.

They were going to be parents. He wanted the respect and cooperation they enjoyed at work to extend to their personal relationship, so, by the time the baby arrived, he and Phoebe operated as a team.

The door to her office swung open. 'Oh, hi.' Phoebe's face registered shock, but quickly turned to a hesitant smile. 'Did you need something?' she asked, adjusting the strap of her bag on her shoulder as if she was on her way home.

Perfect timing.

'I was hoping I could make you dinner.' Zach slung his

hands casually into his trouser pockets while his heart pounded away nineteen to the dozen with those nerves, which made a mockery of his reputation for calm, unemotional decision-making. Now that she'd as good as written him off as a father, the pressure to prove himself trustworthy, to show her that he was a man she could rely on, was almost as overwhelming as the urge to seek out her company over and over again.

'I figured you might be tired after the busy week.' He stepped closer, relieved to see the flicker of interest in her unguarded stare, her rapid blinking matching the tempo of his pulse. 'It will give us a chance to talk, to get to know each other as we agreed.'

There was little time to talk about their personal lives at the hospital, what with surgery lists, clinics and ward rounds. On top of Phoebe's workload, Zach had also spent part of the week at the local clinic run by Nurture, seeing his own referrals.

Observing him with a fascination that left his body temperature a few degrees higher, Phoebe tilted her head. 'You cook?'

It shouldn't give him a kick of satisfaction to surprise her, but it did. And it also proved his point. They'd learned how to pleasure each other's bodies that night in Brisbane, they knew they could work together, but they still had so much to learn about the other's personality, passions and dreams.

'I do.' Zach nodded, his smile widening. 'Very well, in fact.'

Rolling her eyes, Phoebe teased, 'Of course you do—I'd expect nothing less. But aren't you staying at a hotel?'

Zach shook his head, confident now that he could win her over. 'I have an apartment here in Pacific Point.' The coastal suburb was a thirty-minute drive south of the city, his base whenever he was back in the country.

Phoebe raised her eyebrows, surprised and obviously impressed by his postcode. 'Um... I'd like nothing better than a home-cooked meal, but...'

'I'll take you home later,' he cajoled, part of him expecting another of Phoebe's quick and efficient brush-offs.

'It's not that. It's just that I was on my way home for a soak in the bath.' She gnawed at her lip, her cheeks flushing.

Trying not to think of Phoebe's naked, wet body, Zach kept the disappointment from his voice with effort. 'Perhaps another night, then.'

He stepped back to allow her room to pass, but had barely moved when she touched his arm. 'Unless… You could cook at my place, you know, while I take a bath.'

'I can cook anywhere there's a kitchen,' he said with a grin, willing to do anything to spend another hour in her company.

She smiled, a vision that warmed his insides like a dram of whisky. 'Good. I live a ten-minute walk from the hospital. Although I have no idea what's in my fridge, but there's a mini-mart right next to my apartment if you need anything specific.'

Zach shrugged, relieved that she wanted both his company and his culinary skills. 'Good. Then it's all sorted.'

Zach held open the door and followed her along the corridor towards the exit. It was a small thing, but his steps were lighter now that she'd accepted his offer to cook. It felt like a tiny breakthrough in winning her trust.

Zach kept his satisfied smile to himself as they left the hospital and set off past the neighbouring office blocks, street-level shops and abundant cafés. The pavements were thick with commuters all heading for underground car parks, the train or the ferry, the atmosphere hindering intimate and meaningful conversation.

'So what can you cook?' Phoebe asked, amusement tugging at her mouth.

'I told you, I'm good. You name it and I can cook it.'

She laughed at his boast. 'So who taught you? An ex-girlfriend?'

Did he detect a hint of jealousy in her voice?

'I told you in Brisbane—there haven't really been many of those, especially not the serious kind.'

They paused at the intersection to wait for the lights to change. Phoebe looked up at him with curiosity.

'My parents taught me and my brothers and sister to cook,' he said, breaking the suspense. 'They worked long hours, sometimes shift work, so meal preparation was a team effort in the Archer household. I'm the youngest of four siblings, so after my siblings left home, I had plenty of time to hone my skills. I like food.' He tapped his flat stomach, rewarded by the way Phoebe's gaze swept over the body he kept in shape, appreciatively.

'What do you normally cook after work?' he asked, to gauge her likes and dislikes in order to come up with something quick, tasty and nutritious.

She offered him a sheepish smile. 'I live in central Sydney. I'm surrounded by cafés and restaurants. There's even an award-winning delicatessen on my street. I'm usually too busy to do more than a little reheating, maybe throw a salad together. There's no real point spending hours cooking for one person.' She shrugged and Zach nodded, wondering if she ever grew lonely.

Still haunted by the look of defeat on her face when she'd confessed to being deserted by her father, Zach resolved to understand what made her tick. On the surface she was self-possessed, competent, ambitious. But, like him, she'd never married. Had her father's abandonment given her a fear of commitment? It certainly explained her rather cynical opinion of Zach, one he hoped to change.

'I know what you mean,' he said, returning to the convenience of city living.

Their lives were similar: work, sleep, repeat. Busy lives that were only going to become busier once the baby arrived.

But he had no doubt that he and Phoebe would make co-parenting work.

Of course he'd need to spend more time in Sydney if his baby was in Sydney.

'So any food dislikes, allergies or pregnancy aversions I should know about?' he asked as they crossed the road.

She shook her head, smiled. 'No. I like food too, and now that the morning sickness has pretty much stopped, I seem to be always hungry.'

'That's understandable,' he said. 'Your body is growing a whole new human being.' Now that it was happening to him, the miracle of pregnancy struck him in a way he'd previously taken for granted. Did Phoebe feel the same wonder?

Zach had watched Aaron Wilson hold Poppy's sister, Jasmine, with envious fascination when they'd met earlier that week. Zach's own love for their child had hit him like a sledgehammer. The baby hadn't even arrived yet, but he already knew he'd do anything to defend and safeguard his child. But the real shock had come when the same feelings emerged whenever he thought about Phoebe.

Perhaps they could become friends, share the joys and trials of parenthood, be there for their child and each other.

Swallowing at how his fantasy sounded suspiciously like a relationship, Zach glanced at Phoebe.

'This is my building,' she said, pointing up at a mid-rise across the street as the lights changed.

They were about to step into the road when some idiot on an electric scooter whizzed past them from behind.

Phoebe yelped, ducking aside, colliding with Zach. His arm went around her waist automatically, his heart thumping as he glared after the inconsiderate commuter. Aware that he was clutching her in his arms for safekeeping, Zach glanced down.

'Are you okay? What an idiot,' he muttered. 'You could have been knocked to the ground.'

Protective urges flared along with the desire ransacking his anatomy. His arm flexed, bringing her closer as if of its own accord, bathing his senses in pure Phoebe—her subtle scent, the soft gust of her breath, her heart thudding against his chest.

'I'm okay,' she said, looking up at him with wide eyes. Only instead of seeing alarm or annoyance Zach detected reciprocal arousal.

So much for the fantasy of friendship. Friends didn't look at each other this way. Because he couldn't help himself, his gaze dipped to her parted lips, the urge to kiss her strong and instantaneous, like a primitive reflex.

But just because he'd kissed every inch of her body and made her cry out his name that night three months ago, just because she was looking up at him as if she wanted another night in his arms, didn't mean it was a good idea. In fact it could ruin his plan for a mature and considerate co-parenting team.

Flushing, Phoebe disentangled herself from his grip. Zach dragged in a breath, part of him wishing he *had* kissed her. But the moment was gone. They stepped back into the flow of pedestrians once more and made it to the entrance of Phoebe's apartment building in strained silence.

She keyed in a code and Zach followed her inside. Like a needle stuck in a scratch on a vinyl album, he kept returning to his physical attraction to the woman carrying their baby. His resolve to move past their sexual compatibility had been badly shaken by that thirty seconds of contact on the street, making the sensible and logical path he'd decided upon blurry and insubstantial like a wisp of smoke. He was right back where he'd started, craving Phoebe as much as he had that very first night they met, even though indulging those cravings could be disastrous.

* * *

Phoebe emerged from her bedroom, freshly bathed and dressed in her most comfortable track pants and sweater. The relaxing bubble bath had done nothing to calm the frantic, bone-melting excitement of stumbling into Zach's arms. But she couldn't hide in her own home, no matter how much she wished she could hide from the memory of his embrace, his searching expression as he'd gazed down at her, looking as if he might kiss her while their hearts thudded against each other. Drawn to the wonderful aromas coming from the kitchen, she padded hesitantly down the hall on bare feet, her insides a tangle of nervous anticipation.

Inviting him here had been a mistake. He was too tempting. At least at the hospital her inhibitions were contained by the fact that they were rarely alone.

Her stomach growled, but it was the sight of Zach in her small but well-equipped kitchen, his shirt sleeves rolled up, that made her mouth water. The strong, defined arms that had held her so tightly on the street, that had crushed her with such passion when they'd conceived their baby, were now gently whisking eggs in a bowl with the same skill he wielded a scalpel. Why was a man competent in the kitchen such a turn-on?

Or perhaps everything Zach did appealed to her.

'Whatever you're cooking smells amazing,' she said to cover the fact that her whole body shuddered as if desperate for more of his touch.

He looked up from the stove, his gaze meeting hers before taking an appreciative tour of her overheated body. 'I've made two of my quick and easy meal staples: Spanish omelette and three-ingredient chocolate mousse. Does that sound good?'

Phoebe nodded, swallowing hard at how easily she could grow used to having him in her home. 'Impressive. Is there no end to your talents?'

Silly question. Zach did everything to the best of his ability, be it the most intricate surgery or the simplest thoughtful gesture.

'Nope.' He winked and her breath caught. 'You should definitely share that opinion with my siblings when you meet them.
We're a competitive bunch.'

Refusing to kill the mood by asking why and when she was
likely to meet Zach's family, Phoebe peered over his shoulder
at a pan of simmering potatoes and another softening diced
onion on the stove, noting how he'd not only skilfully manoeu-
vred his way around her kitchen, but also managed to connect
his phone to her speaker and stream some chilled atmospheric
music so this felt like a date.

'Can I do anything?' She watched him remove the cubes
of potato from the water with a slotted spoon and add them
to the onion.

His every move seemed to brush her sensitised skin, his
relaxed stare making her feel exposed and...needy, as if getting to know his personal side made their chemistry harder
and harder to fight.

'You could lay the table. I wasn't sure where to find place
mats.'

To save herself from answering why she was fighting her
attraction so hard, Phoebe laid the table in the adjoining dining area, setting two places side by side rather than the usual
lonely one so they could both enjoy the distant harbour view
overlooking her small balcony.

'Want a drink?' she said, opening the fridge and taking out
a bottle of sparkling mineral water.

'Sounds good.'

She stood on tiptoes, reached overhead to retrieve two
glasses from the cabinet above the stove. She must have imagined the small, strangled sound he made, because when she

glanced his way he was adding the whisked eggs to the sizzling-hot pan.

Their chemistry was obviously mutual, but unlike in Brisbane, when their flirtation had been fun and finite, things were now more complicated. They had to work together. They were supposed to be building their relationship as parents.

If only her hormones weren't so persistent, reminding her how good they'd been together and how Zach would be leaving again in a couple of weeks anyway.

'So what do these highly competitive siblings do?' she asked, perching on the bench next to him, so she could indulge her curiosity and at the same time watch him cook.

'Jacob is a lawyer,' he said, dividing dark, glossy chocolate mousse between the small glass bowls she'd never once used. Normally she'd be trying to inhale the rich chocolate aroma, but all she wanted to do was nuzzle Zach's neck and inhale the delicious scent of his aftershave.

'Will runs his own successful export business,' he continued, placing the bowls of mousse in the fridge. 'And Janet, my sister, is head of Fly Media. They own Channel Ten and Matinee, the streaming service.'

Phoebe raised her eyebrows. 'Wow—what an inspiring family. Hopefully you've passed on some pretty smart genes to our baby.'

The thought of their child taking after Zach warmed her chest. Would she think of him every time she looked at their child, every time he or she said something smart or acted with kindness?

'I think our baby will also get those from you,' he said, licking a smear of chocolate from his thumb in a way that made Phoebe wish she could do the same.

Fortunately the distracting sight prevented her from wondering if she would miss him and their easy connection once he'd gone.

'My family is over-the-top competitive,' he said, with a wince. 'I hope *that* doesn't get passed on.'

Still hot and flustered from the remembered taste of his skin, Phoebe looked away from his sensual mouth, which had kissed her in every way possible: a soft tease, demanding and passionate, slow and seductive...

Stop thinking about kissing.

'So it's not healthy competition, then?' she said, taking a sip of ice-cold water, hoping to extinguish some of the heat coursing through her veins.

Zach shook his head, focused on finishing the omelette. 'Not if you call constant one-upmanship healthy, but it's kind of how we were raised. My parents are the children of Nigerian immigrants to Britain. They themselves emigrated to Australia from London when I was young. They weren't particularly well off, but they inherited a strong work ethic and encouraged all four of us to strive, to aim as high as we could in our chosen careers.'

'I'd say you've all made them proud by the sounds of it.' She didn't know his siblings, but Zach was a great guy, the whole package—caring, hard-working, talented.

'Oh, they are proud,' Zach said, turning off the heat and serving the omelette onto two plates. 'But family gatherings are pretty unbearable, with everyone trying to outshine each other. Who owns the biggest house or the best car? Whose wedding was the most extravagant and who has the most adorable children?' He shot her a quick glance. 'Not that I've entered myself into that particular competition, until now, but I think our baby will win, hands down, don't you?'

Phoebe froze, a lump stuck in her throat that Zach had already thought about their baby being cute. His intense eye contact was both playful and vulnerable in a way that made her want to reach out and cup his face, stroke her thumb over his cheekbone, tug him forward for the kiss she just couldn't scrub from her mind. What else had he imagined about the baby? Was he excited to meet their child, like her? Did she really want to know or was it better to hold back from sharing their dreams and hopes, given that he'd soon be leaving with no plan that she was aware of to return?

'Definitely,' she murmured, sliding from the bench and backing away from the moment of emotional intimacy.

'Dinner's ready,' he said, carrying the plates to the dining table, where she joined him with their glasses of water.

'So all your family lives in Sydney?' she asked as Zach placed her omelette in front of her. As he took a seat at her side her appetite for food disappeared.

How was she supposed to eat with him this close?

Zach nodded. 'They do, but my parents are divorced and deliberately live on opposite sides of the city, as far away from each other as possible.'

'So how many nieces and nephews do you have?' He probably knew more about kids than Phoebe did.

His fork hovered over his plate, his gaze dipping to her stomach, his eyes softening. 'Our baby already has seven cousins on my side.'

Our baby...

'Seven cousins...' She gasped, a little overwhelmed by the size of the extended Archer family, now their child's family too. While she'd been daydreaming about which of Zach's looks and personality attributes the baby would inherit, she'd overlooked the fact that he or she would also inherit a crowd of relatives on the Archer side.

She stared at Zach, unable to look away from his expression, which displayed the same hope and excitement she experienced every time she imagined finally meeting the tiny person growing inside her.

Compassion welled up in her chest. Of course Zach would feel the same connection to his unborn child. He'd love it as fiercely as Phoebe, was perhaps already falling in love with their growing baby.

Why was she only now considering the full implications of Zach wanting to be involved in their child's life?

'What about your family?' he asked, as if he hadn't noticed her sudden flare of panic at the enormity and complexity of their unorthodox situation. 'You mentioned your father...'

Phoebe shook her head. 'Talking about him is only going to take ten seconds. He married Mum, they had me and then he claimed he felt trapped.' She made finger quotes to highlight her poor excuse for a father's justification for doing a runner. 'For as far back as I can remember, it's always been just me and Mum,' she said, pushing the delicious-smelling eggs around her plate. 'I'm an only child, so we're very close.'

'What does your mother do?' he asked, his gaze searching as if he could see Phoebe's doubts and insecurities rising to the surface. But she'd long ago stopped wondering about the selfish man who'd donated half her genes.

Her worth was in no way reflected by the actions of a man like that.

'She's a community midwife in rural Queensland,' she said, smiling because, unlike her father, her mum was a force of nature.

He smiled. 'That's handy.'

Phoebe laughed. 'I'm hoping to persuade her to move to Sydney when she retires next year.' She took a bite of omelette, groaning when the sublime, perfectly balanced flavours hit her taste buds, although now that she'd realised the full implications of Zach being a part of her and the baby's life, now that she was more confused than ever about her attraction to him, she doubted that she'd be able to finish half of what was on her plate.

'I'm sure the lure of her grandchild will help. Is she excited about the baby?' Zach asked, watching her eat with a satisfied smile on his face.

Phoebe looked down, unsettled. 'I um…haven't told her yet. I'm visiting home soon, thought I'd keep it a surprise, tell her in person.'

She couldn't confess that there was a tiny part of her that feared her mum's disappointment. Rosa knew exactly how hard it was to raise a child alone without any emotional or financial support from its father. She wouldn't want the same for Phoebe.

A small frown tugged Zach's mouth. 'So you don't have any other family here in Sydney? No one to help you with the baby?'

His question left her irrationally defensive. 'I have my amazing girlfriends, who I'm sure will help out if I need it. You met Ali. Harper heads up Sydney Central ER and Ivy is Head of General Surgery.'

'Are they happy for you?' Zach asked, inadvertently poking at another of Phoebe's soft spots.

'I haven't told Harper and Ivy my news yet, although I won't be able to hide it for much longer.' She automatically rested her hand on her belly. 'What about you? Have you told anyone?'

As soon as Phoebe told her friends, her mother, they would naturally ask who the father was. Until she'd told Zach, she hadn't been prepared for that question, but now she realised that she'd need to have an answer at the ready.

Catching Phoebe off guard, Zach slid his wallet from his pocket and took out the scan photo Ali had given him. 'I'm going to tell my parents soon, separately of course, break the news that they're going to be grandparents again.' He smiled, sliding the grainy photo onto the table between them. 'I was wondering if you'd mind me showing them this.'

Phoebe stared at the photo, aware of Zach doing the same at her side. The urge to reach for his hand, to rest her head on his shoulder and whisper *Look what we made* was almost too strong to fight.

'Of course I don't mind,' Phoebe whispered, looking into his eyes. 'What happened with them?'

Was his parents' divorce the reason he avoided commitment?

Zach sighed, leaning back in his chair. 'They grew apart, finally divorcing when I was seventeen.' He shrugged, but nothing was ever that simple.

'After four children?' she asked, trying to understand the family dynamics. To understand Zach, who must have been more affected than he wanted to admit.

He scoffed. 'I know, right? They loved each other once, but now they can't be in the same room.'

'That must make things hard for you and your siblings.'

He nodded. 'It's exhausting, like crossing a minefield. We don't mention one parent in front of the other. At celebration times we're tugged in two different directions. Although, as the youngest, I copped the worst of being trapped in the middle after my siblings had all left home.'

Phoebe's heart thudded behind her ribs. No wonder he stayed single, preferring to focus on something with guaranteed success—his work.

'That must have been hard, Zach. I'm sorry.' Empathy squeezed her lungs, making it hard to breathe.

He cleared his throat and straightened in his chair. 'My time as piggy in the middle certainly gave me a unique insight. I would never inflict the heartache and uncertainty of a messy divorce on my child.'

As they finished their dinner, Phoebe marvelled at how much they had in common when it came to their views on relationships, their pasts, their families. The more she learned about the father of her baby, the harder it was becoming to resist their chemistry. Until Zach left Sydney she would need to take extra care to keep her distance, because what she absolutely couldn't do was allow feelings to cloud their already complex situation.

CHAPTER EIGHT

'THIS IS LITERALLY the best thing I've ever tasted,' Phoebe gushed, licking the spoon and then her lips after the first spoonful of chocolate mousse.

Zach looked away, pretending to find the view of the city from her small balcony fascinating, a long groan of frustration sounding in his head. If he'd thought her sexy little moan of delight at her first bite of the tortilla earlier had been bad enough to make him sweat, watching her lick the dark chocolate mousse from the spoon, her eyes closed in bliss, was enough to put him in a premature grave. She was literally killing him, the two-seater outdoor sofa that they shared making any sort of distance from temptation impossible.

'Glad you like it,' he croaked to stop himself from asking if he could taste it from her lips. The suggestion that they abandon the chocolate mousse for a different, more satisfying type of dessert lingered on the tip of his tongue.

What was he thinking? And why was he torturing himself this way?

Because aside from how much he still wanted her physically, he couldn't help but be drawn to her as a person, the future mother of his child, a kind and intelligent woman who, despite the example set by her absent father, had learned strength from her strong mother. Afflicted anew by the protective urges he just couldn't seem to switch off where Phoebe was concerned, he pondered why it gave him such satisfaction to cook for her. Yes, he applied his perfectionist tendencies to cooking, another thing at which he could excel. But it was more than just bragging rights. That she'd invited him to her home and given him the use of her kitchen, that she'd talked about her father and probed him about his family, made him feel as if slowly but surely, piece by piece, he could eventually win her trust. A prize worth striving for.

'So, have you thought about baby names?' he asked, hoping that her guard was sufficiently lowered to talk about the future.

She turned to face him, surprised by his question. 'Um, no. I guess I should give that some thought and you should too. We can swap notes and come up with a shortlist.'

Zach nodded, enjoying Phoebe's relaxed company and the excitement in her eyes whenever they discussed the baby. 'Just to warn you, as soon as I tell my mother about the baby, she'll start knitting a mountain of baby clothes, as she has done for her other grandchildren.'

Phoebe's eyes lit up as she licked another spoonful of mousse from the spoon.

'You don't have to use them if you don't like them,' he reassured her. Perhaps he should introduce Phoebe to his parents before he left Sydney. They were no longer a couple, but they would embrace and love this grandchild and Phoebe the way they had his siblings' children and partners. Perhaps it would be good for Phoebe to have a local family contact for those times when he was away? It would certainly ease his mind to know that she had some family close by.

'Oh, that's wonderful,' she said, genuinely delighted. 'My mother can't knit, so it will be all gratefully received.'

As he thought about his work commitments, being away from Sydney, from Phoebe and the baby, Zach's stomach churned. How would he make his job and fatherhood work?

He certainly wouldn't tolerate doing the two things in a half-hearted fashion. But could he just move permanently back to Sydney? Phoebe had made it quite clear on multiple occasions that she was happy to go it alone.

But what did *he* want?

Taking another spoonful of mousse, she eyed him thoughtfully. 'Do you want to know the sex of the baby?' She glanced away, her voice growing quieter. 'I'll be happy to email you a copy of my next scan.'

Zach hesitated, his chest tight. Until he heard where Nurture might need him next, he wasn't sure where he'd be by the time of Phoebe's next scan, but it wouldn't be Sydney.

Could he truly tolerate being anywhere else while Phoebe was here alone, working full-time, struggling with fatigue with no one to help out, giving birth to his baby, alone? From her breezy, unemotional enquiry it was clear that Phoebe expected him to be absent, whereas he knew from the hollowness inside how much he would hate missing out on that next scan, or any other development in the pregnancy.

No one could be in two places at once. He'd have to make a choice, something that, until he'd met Phoebe, he had always found straightforward.

'Do *you* want to know the baby's sex?' Zach asked, his pulse thrumming in his throat at the intimacy of the turn in this conversation and how much closer he felt towards Phoebe.

'I'm not sure,' she whispered, as if caught up in the same spellbinding emotions and dawning realisations as Zach.

They were going to be parents, he and this woman he constantly wanted to be around. When he'd agreed to come back to Sydney for Poppy's surgery at Phoebe's request, he hadn't anticipated their growing emotional intimacy, nor had he imagined that he would want her so badly he could barely breathe.

'Well,' he said in a quiet voice, brushing a strand of hair

away from her cheek, mesmerised by the way her stare clung to his, 'I think, as you're the one doing all the work at the moment, and you're the one who'll have to go through the birth, knowing the sex or not should be your choice. All I really want is a healthy baby, safely delivered and that you're okay.'

Of course he wanted the best for her, the best for their baby. But the idea of Phoebe in pain gave him chills. What if she needed him and he was overseas? What if he planned to be back in Sydney for the birth but the baby came early? It happened all the time. And why was he suddenly desperate to move whatever mountain necessary to be there for Phoebe for all of it?

Zach dropped his hand onto the back of the sofa to stop himself from touching her face. Until he figured everything out, it was best not to make promises he wasn't certain he could keep. He'd already done a complete mental flip tonight, initially convinced they needed to be a platonic team and then certain the best thing was to get all this sexual chemistry out of their systems.

'I think your brothers and sister should be worried,' she said, her voice low, her stare flicking between his eyes. 'You might give them a run for their money with the fatherhood thing.'

Zach swallowed. 'You think so?'

Phoebe nodded, her eyes shining.

He was too choked by her faith to gloat. Until a week ago, he'd never given much thought to being a father, but from the minute he'd seen that scan, heard the rapidly fluttering heartbeat of their baby, he'd wanted the best of everything for his and Phoebe's child.

'If I do decide to find out if it's a boy or a girl,' she said, her gaze dipping to his mouth in a distracting way that made him recall that moment on the street, when he'd almost kissed her, 'I'll let you know.'

'Okay,' he said, the urge to lean over and kiss her now almost overwhelming. Perhaps he should. Perhaps if they slept together again they could move on, focus on the plan to make co-parenting a success for the future.

Or it could ruin their chance at amicably raising their child together apart and make an already delicate connection much more complicated.

With the last hint of chocolate dying on her tongue, Phoebe placed her empty bowl next to Zach's on the table, her pulse flying. 'That was delicious. Thanks, Zach.'

He was still staring at her as if he was poised to pounce. But maybe it was her imagination fuelled by hormones.

Except Zach had barely touched his own dessert while they'd talked about the baby. But he'd watched her eat hers, his eyes following the spoon to her mouth as if he wanted a taste from the same spoon, or from her lips.

Because he was still silent, because the chocolate, the hormones, Zach's proximity and their growing closeness had all conspired to make her unbelievingly aroused, she filled the conversational gap with nervous chatter.

'The pregnancy hormones have given me terrible chocolate cravings,' she explained, brushing a speck of lint from her trouser leg, thinking of the violent mood swings and mental gymnastics she'd experienced since he'd arrived in Sydney. 'Perhaps because chocolate helps with the random bouts of inexplicable tears.'

She chuckled but Zach just stared, his head tilting as if in empathy.

She'd almost cried at least twice during the meal, once when she'd tried to visualise seventeen-year-old Zach trapped in the middle of his parents' divorce and again when he'd carefully tucked their baby's scan photo back into his wallet with as much care and tenderness as he'd used when he held newborn babies.

Why wasn't he saying anything?

'—although sadly, chocolate doesn't seem to help with the hormonal fluctuations,' she blabbered on. 'No one talks about that particular pregnancy side effect. I am constantly horn— Oh!'

She stopped talking, her face flaming as she realised that she was over-sharing, confessing intimate details of her overactive libido to the sexiest man alive, a man she knew could cure all of her pent-up frustration.

'Sorry, I forgot that you're not one of my girlfriends.' She fanned her face, embarrassed.

'Don't apologise,' he said, his voice gruff and his pupils dilated. 'We said we'd be honest. You can tell me anything, Phoebe.'

'Can I?' She stared, lost in his stare, a victim of the undeniable sexual tension that had ensnared her since the minute Zach had walked into the OR that first day.

He nodded, watching her lips as if waiting for a confession. But was it wise to raise the subject of the chemistry they were clearly both trying to ignore, to admit that she still wanted him as badly as the night of her birthday, perhaps even more, to suggest that they resume their fling for what time he had left in Sydney?

Exhaling a shaky breath, she stopped fighting. 'Because I'd have to tell you that I can't stop thinking about that incredible night in Brisbane.'

She might have imagined his groan; it was so low. 'Only if I can tell you I can't either.'

Light-headed, she held his stare, knowing that they were playing with fire, that she might open a door that might be difficult to close when the time came for Zach to leave. 'I still want you,' she whispered, 'but I'm scared to complicate things. We have to think about what's best for the baby.'

One night with Zach hadn't been enough to quench their chemistry, which was dangerous, intoxicating, nuclear-reactor hot.

As if he'd been waiting for permission, Zach reached for her hand where it rested in her lap. His strong, warm fingers gripped hers, his thumb stroking her knuckles in a soothing way.

'Thank you for your honesty. I agree, we'd need to be careful. To put the baby first.' His gaze flicked over her face, ending on her mouth. He wanted to kiss her.

She nodded, licking her lips, tasting the remnants of his dessert. Her head swam from the rush of his words and the heady possibilities.

'What do you want?' Her voice was husky with need. She trusted him with her body, but there was no room for feelings, which could only get in the way.

He leaned closer, cupped her face. 'I want you. But I don't want to hurt you.'

As if a fuse had been lit, the tingling sensation of his touch detonated in her chest, flooding her already needy body with heat. With a sigh of release, liberated by their honesty, she tilted her face up to his, their lips now only a whisper apart.

'I won't let you,' she said, transfixed by his lips, which were saying all the right things, which could deliver on their promise of pleasure. 'Think of it as a temporary fling to help me with my hormonal cravings, the way you've satisfied my chocolate cravings tonight.'

She smiled, tired of hiding how he made her feel.

He was leaving in a couple of weeks. Neither of them would risk feelings creeping in. They were too alike in their desire to avoid romantic complications. They could embrace a physical fling and then part amicably.

Once the baby arrived, she'd have no time for anything beyond juggling the demands of work and parenthood.

With a groan, his face grim with an almost pained expression, Zach's fingers flexed at the nape of her neck drawing her closer. His lips covered hers, hard, desperate. She clung to him, kissing him back, parting her lips to welcome the touch of his tongue to hers. He tasted like chocolate, rich and decadent. She moaned, gripping his shoulders, curling her nails into his flesh.

He pressed her back against the sofa, his powerful body surrounding her, holding her, matching her passion. She spread her legs, bucked her hips, seeking out the friction she craved before she actually combusted.

He pulled back, stared down at her, his eyes smoky with desire and his breath gusting. 'I've wanted to do that since that first day in Theatre.'

'Me too.' She nodded, her hands fisting his shirt, sliding underneath to caress the smooth skin of his muscular back as he swooped in and kissed a path along her neck.

His hand stroked her thigh, raised it over his hip so he could pin her back against the sofa with his hips, rocking into her, driving her wild.

'Zach... I want you,' she moaned, her body awash with tingles of desire. He was hard between her legs. She dropped her head back, exposed her neck to his kisses, granting him access to all of the places that made her toes curl with delight now that she'd finally surrendered to her desires.

Zach cupped her breast through her T-shirt, drawing out a whimper from her throat. If they didn't move to the bedroom soon, she'd have to start begging.

But no sooner had his palm cupped her sensitive flesh,

coaxed the nipple erect, than he stopped, pulled back, dropped his hands to her waist and rested his forehead against hers, breathing hard.

'What's wrong?' she whispered, dazed, her hand resting over his galloping heart.

He knelt back so she could see his expression in the dark. 'We need to stop. I got carried away.'

'Why do we need to stop?' she asked, confusion making her voice whiny. 'Have you changed your mind?' She held her breath, praying he was still on board with the fling idea.

He stared, his gaze intense while indecision flitted over his expression 'No, absolutely not.' He dragged in a ragged breath, gripped the back of his neck, composing himself. 'It's just that you were tired when we left work and we have an early start tomorrow. You need your rest.'

'Oh… Of course. You're right.' Disappointment was rock in her stomach. Wishing that he weren't so noble, Phoebe nodded, tugging her sweater down and sitting on the edge of the sofa while she toyed with the idea of luring him to the dark side.

'We'll take a rain check, okay?' As if his mind was made up, Zach sat beside her, a determined set to his mouth. He put his arm around her shoulders and pressed a chaste kiss to the top of her head while their rapid breathing normalised.

'Absolutely.' She rested her head against his shoulder so she could sniff his neck in consolation.

How dared he be so honourable? But now that he'd mentioned it, she was tired.

After a few minutes, Zach stood, held out his hand and pulled her to her feet. Tilting up her chin, he pressed a kiss to her lips, his eyes still harbouring a hint of lingering arousal.

Inside the dark apartment, he grabbed his coat. 'There are leftovers in the fridge in case you can't be bothered to cook tomorrow.'

They moved to the hallway and opened the front door, the look he shot her full of regret. 'I hope you manage to get a good night's sleep.'

'Thanks for cooking dinner,' she said, scared she might actually drag him back inside and hold him hostage for the night.

He crossed over the threshold, almost reluctantly.

Phoebe gripped his arm, stood on tiptoes and kissed him once more, a proper goodbye that she could tell almost turned the tide on Zach's highly impressive resolve.

'That's for the chocolate mousse,' she said, desire turning her voice husky. She wasn't playing fair, but she wanted to leave him with an appetiser for next time.

Who knew when *next time* would be with their busy schedules?

Looking gratifyingly torn, Zach kissed the tip of his finger and pressed it to her lips. 'I have plenty more chocolate recipes to help with those cravings.'

'I look forward to it,' she said, aware that she might come across as a lust-struck teenager if she didn't release him soon.

He dragged in a deep ragged breath that told her he was struggling to leave as much as she was struggling to let him go.

She stepped back inside the apartment. 'Goodnight, Zach.'

'Goodnight, Phoebe.' His gaze swept down her body one last time, lingering for a second on her stomach. 'Goodnight, baby,' he whispered, meeting her stare once more.

His eyes were full of promises. The ones that left her wishing away the unknown length of time until they could be together again were welcome. The ones that accompanied his words to their unborn child she didn't dare believe.

This time, the third time that evening, she surrendered to the bout of hormonal and fatigue-induced tears, but only once she'd closed the door and was alone.

CHAPTER NINE

A FEW DAYS later there was a collective breath-hold in Theatre Three as the cardiopulmonary bypass machine was weaned off in preparation for leaving Poppy's newly repaired heart and tiny lungs unsupported.

Zach locked eyes with Phoebe across the operating table. Her emotions were easily identified in her eyes, the only part of her face visible over the top of her surgical mask. Hope that they'd done their job, that when Poppy's heart was restarted, the repair would hold. Comfort from the way they'd supported each other during the surgery, effectively working as a team. And the hardest thing to witness: a hint of fear.

Zach normally left his feelings at the door when he was operating but working together intuitively with Phoebe to repair Poppy's heart had amplified every emotion he'd been experiencing since that night at her apartment, when they'd opened up about their pasts, talked about their baby and then kissed.

Zach gave Phoebe a small nod of encouragement, showing her that he too felt all of her concerns. The fear for Poppy was real. The surgery to fix the large defect in the heart wall had been technically difficult and long. But where every surgery was important, the stakes on this one seemed greater, perhaps because Zach and Phoebe carried the secret knowledge of their own child. They could empathise with the Wilson family in a deeply personal way.

'Normothermia achieved,' the anaesthetist said as Poppy's core body temperature reached thirty-six degrees.

Phoebe blinked, her gaze not wavering from Zach's as they silently communicated.

This was the moment of truth.

The time had come to restart Poppy's heart and hope that the surgical repair was sound. Like Phoebe, he'd performed this surgery many times before. But Poppy's fragile condition, her low weight and prematurity added to the risks and therefore to the degree of clinical concern.

'Blood gasses look good,' the anaesthetist said. 'Adding inotropic support now.'

Phoebe's mask moved. Zach wondered if she was chewing her lip in a nervous gesture. Their growing emotional connection, the way she'd started opening up to him, showing him glimpses of her vulnerable side, had him questioning everything he thought he knew about himself, about his work, about the kind of life that had previously given him contentment. If they weren't sterile and in the middle of a surgery, he'd reach out and take her hand for her comfort and for his own.

At the nod from the anaesthetist, Phoebe removed the clamps from the major vessels to and from Poppy's heart. For a few tense seconds as the organ filled with blood, she and Zach stared, willing the heart to beat of its own accord. Zach was about to reach for the defibrillator paddles, when there was a brief flickering of the cardiac muscle, and the heart began beating a regular rhythm, which was picked up by the monitor, the sound amplified throughout the OR like a triumphant fanfare.

An audible collective sigh of relief passed around the room.

Zach grinned under his mask, his stare hopefully conveying his admiration to Phoebe. 'Well done,' he said in a low voice, a sense of pride and togetherness warming his blood.

They'd done it, worked as a team, operated together on this tiny vulnerable baby girl, for whom the immediate signs were promising.

'We have sinus rhythm,' Phoebe said, slowly exhaling, like Zach, fighting for composure.

Zach wanted to hold her so badly, it almost killed him to stay professional. The surgery wasn't complete—Poppy needed them still.

Phoebe dragged in a long breath. 'Thanks for your assistance,' she said, her stare lingering on his as if she had so much more she wanted to say. 'Let's check for leaks and repeat the echo.'

Zach nodded, checking the integrity of the atrial sutures for signs of leakage. As if he'd been postponing thinking about it until Poppy was out of danger, reality rushed his mind.

He and Phoebe wouldn't be working as a team for ever. He'd soon be leaving Sydney, leaving her and the baby behind.

How could he justify his absence given the new and delicate closeness between him and Phoebe? Perhaps he could finish up his current commitments in Perth and relocate to Sydney permanently... He'd be on hand to help out with the baby when Phoebe needed him. His child would grow up spending equal amounts of time with both parents. He and Phoebe could continue to work on their relationship, which would be vital for everyone's happiness in making their complex situation work.

But what would Phoebe think of his idea?

Focusing once more on the job in hand, they repeated the transoesophageal echo scan to ensure the synthetic patch was working and the blood flow through Poppy's heart was normalised before proceeding with the final stage of the operation.

'Everything looks good,' he said to Phoebe, directing the suction to the small collection of fluid around Poppy's heart.

Phoebe nodded and began to suture closed the pericardium, the sac around the heart.

Zach assisted by stitching the drains into place. A growing sense of harmony gripped him, as if Phoebe's success was his success, and vice versa, where he'd previously considered himself a bit of a lone wolf. Self-sufficient. Complete.

As he watched Phoebe work, knowing that this beautiful, smart and dedicated woman would soon be the mother to his child, the alien yearning feeling in his chest that he'd awoken with for the past two mornings intensified. The closeness he felt towards her went beyond physical attraction.

For him, the baby gave them a shared bond that felt unshakable in a way he'd never before imagined he would experience. Now that he'd come to terms with the fact he was going to be a father, he wanted to explore the future with Phoebe, to discuss everything from baby names to pre-schools. To figure out their respective parenting styles and brainstorm the likely hurdles, the ups and downs so they could prepare for anything.

But that had always been Zach's way: identify an issue and work to find a solution, not that their baby was an issue, more like a wondrous gift.

Snapping him from his thoughts, Phoebe said, 'I'm happy to close up here, Dr Archer, if you want to finish for the day.'

She kept her head down, her stare focused on closing the chest, the operation almost complete.

'Um, of course.' He stepped away from the table, trying not to feel dismissed now that she no longer needed his assistance. 'Would you like me to speak to Poppy's parents, let them know that the surgery has been successfully completed?' He peeled off his gloves and tossed them into the bin.

'Yes, please,' she said, casting him a quick cursory glance.

He knew what it was like to be *in the zone* while operating. But for a few minutes, he'd felt so emotionally in tune with her, been so carried away with his daydreams for their child, that he'd almost forgotten that Phoebe cherished her independence. That Sydney Central was *her* turf. That she might not welcome him living and working on her doorstep.

'Tell them I'll be along shortly to speak to them also,' she added, 'once Poppy is back on NICU.'

'Sure.' Zach hesitated, struggling to separate the tangle of feelings today—a long and tense day—had unearthed.

But now he recalled how Phoebe preferred to keep her emotions in check. If she did need to talk, to decompress after such a personally meaningful surgery, she wouldn't necessarily choose to confide in him. Perhaps he was getting ahead of himself with his imagined emotional connection and his enthusiasm to dream about the future.

Stripping off his mask and apron, Zach left Theatre in search of Emma and Aaron. While he explained to them that the surgery had gone to plan, that, so far, there were no complications, that Poppy would need to spend the next few weeks on NICU, but now that the hole in her heart had been patched closed she would begin to thrive and gain weight, catch up to her twin sister, a part of him worried that he and Phoebe might not be on the same page, emotionally. Where he wanted to discuss the feelings raised by today's surgery and be there to support her the way he hoped they could support each other as parents in the future, the way Aaron and Emma supported each other, Phoebe was still pushing him out of the door. Just as she'd tried to do that first day.

And maybe she was right to keep her emotional guard up. What did he know about making a romantic relationship work? What if they tried to be more than friends and parents and failed, just as his own parents had? He wouldn't want to put their child in the middle of any hostilities. The last thing they needed was to bring all of their respective baggage to their fledgling co-parenting relationship before it had even had a chance to become established.

As he left the hospital, he resolved to moderate his flights of fancy. No matter how well he and Phoebe worked together, no matter how compatible they were physically, how close he imagined them to be, they both needed to tread carefully.

Now that they'd operated on Poppy, his role here at Sydney Central was almost over. Zach was in no position to make promises.

And his role in Phoebe's life? The other night they'd agreed to a temporary fling.

So why was it no longer so straightforward in his mind?

Later that night, Phoebe knocked at Zach's front door, restless energy winding her tight like a spring. It was late, dark. She wrapped her arms around her waist to ward off the chill in the air and tried not to overthink the reason she was standing on Zach's doorstep, spinning out of control.

Facing him in Theatre while they'd worked together on Poppy's long and tense surgery, Phoebe hadn't anticipated how much she would rely on Zach's reassuring presence. His extensive experience, his surgical intuition and encouragement—all a balm soothing her concerns for baby Poppy and her family.

It was only natural to project those fears, her doubts and questions for the future, onto their own situation given their shared secret—their own baby—and the nature of their work. Except every time she had looked up, Zach had silently communicated his understanding and emotional support in his eyes, as if they were already a parental team as well as a professional team.

That was what had rattled her to the core, because she had soaked up his compassion and comfort like a sponge.

But she couldn't rely on him for her emotional well-being. She couldn't need him at all.

Sucking in the cool night air, she tried to slow down her panicked breathing. It must be her hormones tricking her, exposing her vulnerabilities. Once Zach left Sydney, life would go on as it had been before they'd met. She would revert to operating alone, cooking for one, making her own plans for the baby.

All without Zach.

Before she could register the hollow pang of loneliness that rose up, the door swung open.

Phoebe's stomach swooped at the sight of him. He was so sexy—relaxed and casual in jeans and a shirt, his feet bare.

'Can I come in?' she said as his surprised expression quickly turned to delight.

'Of course.' He beckoned her inside and closed the door. 'Are you okay?'

Scared to witness his eagerness to see her, she nodded, looked away.

Was she okay? Part of her was spiralling, shaken that she already missed him, even though he was standing right there.

'Is Poppy okay?' Zach asked, his beautiful eyes framed by a frown of concern.

'Everything's fine. Poppy is doing really well.' It was only Phoebe disintegrating as she wrestled with the enormity of it all. In those few brief seconds in Theatre when they had watched Poppy's heart, willing it to restart, she'd wanted so badly to reach out and hold Zach's hand, knowing that he understood how she might have been feeling, because they were going to be parents.

Everything would change.

She would no longer just be Phoebe; she'd be Phoebe plus the baby. Even if Zach wasn't always around, he would be a part of their baby's life for ever, as would his family. She would need to build new relationships, welcome the Archers into her new life as a mother, into the baby's life.

Poppy's highly emotive surgery had made Phoebe realise that, as a mother, she would feel her own baby's pain and heartache and disappointment. Only unlike the Wilsons, she would be doing it alone.

No wonder that, overwhelmed, she'd as good as sent Zach away and finished up alone.

As if aware of her inner turmoil, Zach cupped her face and peered into her eyes. 'I'm glad you're here.' He kissed her forehead. 'I wanted to make sure you were feeling okay after the surgery.'

Phoebe's eyes stung at his consideration. He made her feel cared for, almost cherished.

'I don't want to talk about the surgery,' she said, shaking off his concern and embracing the feeling she'd known her whole life. That no one was coming to rescue her, so she had to be strong, self-sufficient. 'I just wanted to see you.'

Because his eyes were full of questions that she didn't want to answer, she leaned closer and placed her hand on his chest. 'Kiss me.'

Distract me from the way you make me feel.

As if he were slowly but surely building himself into the very foundations on which she stood, brick by brick. As if she might crumble when he left.

She must be confusing her fears for the baby's future with her own needs. Understandable after a gruelling day at work.

Zach's lips hovered close, his stare searching hers, as if he wanted to push her to discuss her feelings. Perhaps he needed to express his own, and she was being selfish.

But if they talked, if she voiced how derailed she was by her realisations that her life was about to change in ways she probably couldn't even contemplate, she might need more than another night in his bed. She might need his assurances for the future. A guarantee that in the same way that they'd made their baby together, they would shoulder the responsibilities and soothe their child's hurts and disappointments as a team. To know that he'd be there when it mattered and that she wouldn't have to face the hurdles and uncertainties of parenthood alone.

Determined to block out her thoughts, she gripped his waist and tugged him closer. 'I want you, Zach.'

Playing dirty, she pressed her lips to his neck, nuzzling kisses up to his jaw while her hand snaked under his shirt. She needed the distraction of pleasure. A reminder that this was just a fling, nothing to do with feelings. To guard her heart like never before.

Although their connection was deepening as they spent more time together, although she'd opened up to him about her personal life, their situation remained the same. He was a wonderful man—kind, caring, considerate. But relying on him emotionality in any capacity was simply too risky, went against every lesson on autonomy she had learned in her for-mative years, abandoned by her father and encouraged by her mother to be self-reliant.

No matter what she might want for her baby, there was no parallel life where she and Zach had met under different circumstances, fallen in love, raised their child together as a family.

There was only here and now. Two people who had sworn off relationships, determined to do the best by the child they had made.

With a groan of defeat, Zach tilted her face, covered her mouth with his, unleashed the passion—life-affirming and distracting—she craved. The minute their lips touched, his coaxing and hers greedy, her ruminations, the doubts and fears and unattainable fantasies that flickered into her mind's eye at her most vulnerable moments, ceased.

She relaxed, leaning her weight into his arms, which held her so tightly she could feel his heartbeat, his rapid breaths, the growing hardness of him against her stomach.

This was what she wanted. This physical temptation had been there since his return to Sydney. Right now, it was the only certainty she had. And when it was over, when Zach left, they could move on, two mature adults who respected one another and would always be connected by the life they'd created.

While their kisses deepened, each one more voracious than the last, Zach's hand cupped her backside, pressing them close below the waist, his other hand cupping her breast.

Her body melted, flooded with heat, her mind blissfully quiet. 'Where's your bedroom?' she said, when she'd dragged her mouth from his and shoved off her coat, letting it fall to the floor.

Bending, Zach scooped her up, one arm at her back and the other under her thighs. 'I'll show you the way.'

He strode down a darkened hallway and nudged open the bedroom door with his shoulder. The sumptuously made bed dominated the room, which was dimly lit with recessed lighting, warm and inviting despite its masculine décor.

Zach placed her on her feet and tunnelled his fingers into her hair, reverently kissing her face, her jaw, her neck as if she were precious, treasured. 'You are so beautiful. So talented. I was proud to work with you today.'

Although she didn't need his validation, Zach's compliments registered, powerful sentiments she tried to block out. Pretty words cost nothing. Phoebe's father must have once whispered quite a few to her mother. But how quickly had those endearments turned bitter, accusatory, justifications for him to leave?

'Don't talk,' she said, yanking at the hem of his T-shirt,

tugging it over his head and tossing it aside so she could run her hands over his warm, dark skin, his springy chest hair, the defined muscles that gave him his physical strength so that when he held her, she felt...protected.

But she was strong too. Emotionally. No matter how tough things became when the baby arrived, no matter what the future held, she would survive without Zach.

She would emulate Rosa Mason, raise their child to be independent, happy and confident.

Phoebe's urgency as they stripped off their remaining clothes spurred Zach on. Except once they were naked, side by side on the bed, he slowed things down, his hands thoroughly caressing every inch of her body. His lips exploring all of her sensitive spots. His kisses rendering her weak with need, until she was clawing at him, begging.

'Zach,' she whispered, when he finally covered her body with his, scraped her hair back from her face and stared into her eyes. She was so exposed by the way he looked at her, the way he relentlessly cherished her body, she almost couldn't breathe.

Their hearts thudded together. Phoebe found herself held captive by what she saw in his stare: desire, respect, understanding, as if he knew her deepest fears and wanted to walk at her side while she fought her own battles.

'I'm here,' he said, and slowly pushed inside her, skin to skin, so there was nowhere left to hide. Zach surrounded her, engulfed her, invaded her, his determined, all-consuming passion rendering her ridiculously close to those hormonal tears that were never far away.

'Don't make promises,' she whispered about the two words she distrusted the most. He was here for now, but he would go, indefinitely. All she could rely on, all she wanted from him, was this moment of pleasure.

But her demand had also exposed her fear, another valuable piece of her most vulnerable self. He frowned, stroking his fingers through her hair. Would he argue the point when he knew as well as her that their time as lovers was finite before they embarked on the more important and enduring relationship of parents?

As he moved inside her, claiming her body with his touch, watching her react to his lovemaking, speaking to her with his eyes, it seemed to Phoebe that they were talking the same language, that he too harboured concerns for the future and understood the potential for messing things up if they weren't both, oh, so careful.

But as the release she'd craved tore a cry from her throat, as she clung to Zach, buried her face against his neck while he crushed her in his arms as if he'd never let her go, Phoebe feared the time for careful had already passed them by.

CHAPTER TEN

STILL DAZED BY the force of their passion, Zach lay beside Phoebe, one hand resting on her stomach over their growing baby. Great surges of desire welled up inside him. Not physical desire, although that was pretty constant in Phoebe's presence, but other intangible desires for things he'd thought he would never want: a family, stability, roots.

Zach relaxed. An emotional day combined with phenomenal sex would release all kinds of happy hormones and endorphins.

'I want to take you shopping,' he said, stroking his fingertips along the bumps of her ribs. 'I thought we could buy some things for the baby.'

The minute he spoke the words, Phoebe stiffened in his arms.

Frustrated that he'd clearly made a mistake by voicing his growing excitement, he added, 'You know me—I like to plan and be prepared.'

And he would soon be heading to Perth for a month before his next overseas posting with Nurture, which had yet to be announced. He didn't want to miss out, didn't want Phoebe to kit out a nursery alone.

But perhaps she felt rushed.

'Unless you think it's too soon.' Propping his head on his hand, he looked down at her where she lay on the pillow next to his, her face flushed and her hair a wild tumble. Breathtaking.

When he'd opened the door earlier to see her standing on his doorstep, all of the warnings he'd told himself to stay emotionally detached had evaporated. He couldn't ignore their growing connection. A big part of him welcomed it. They were having a baby together. Whatever happened in the future, he would always care for and respect Phoebe. If only she'd let him.

'Hmm…' she mumbled non-committally.

Zach bit his tongue, sensing her withdrawal. Perhaps she was simply drained from the emotions of the day. That was why he'd wanted to talk, to share their fears and concerns for the future after Poppy's moving surgery. But the Phoebe who had stepped through his front door had been a woman on a mission to keep tonight about sex.

So why had his simple request to buy a crib together killed the mood?

'I know it's a little early,' he said when Phoebe stayed quiet, 'but I just thought we could shop for things before I leave for Perth.' He smiled, hoping his excitement would be contagious.

'Um… I'm busy this weekend,' she murmured, sounding far from enthusiastic.

Disappointment settled like a boulder in his chest. Was he pushing too hard? Crossing a line? Perhaps she'd prefer to go shopping with her friends or her mother.

'Okay,' he said, stroking her arm. 'I'm not trying to take over. I just want you to have the nursery of your dreams, that's all. Dad tried to foist the Archer family crib on me when I told him about the baby. But as it's been used for four of his children and a handful of grandchildren, it's seen better days.'

'I haven't given much thought to the nursery, to be honest.' Phoebe sat up, clutching the sheet to her chest. 'So I'm um…not sure what I want.' She swung her legs over the edge of the bed and turned her back on him while she searched for her discarded clothes.

Confused, Zach also sat up. He wanted to touch her again, to stroke her back in a soothing gesture, to kiss her and find the fun post-sex vibe they'd shared in Brisbane, but she was clearly in a hurry to get away.

'Phoebe, is everything okay?' After that night at her apartment, after she'd come to him tonight, he hoped her guard was a thing of the past. They'd said they'd be honest.

'Absolutely.' She donned her underwear and stood, scooping up her skirt from the floor without looking his way.

Was he missing something?

'Don't rush off,' he said, wincing at the pleading tone of his voice. 'Have you eaten dinner? I could make you something.'

'I should go.' She tugged her blouse free of the tangled sheets. 'I have an early start tomorrow. There's a press conference being held at the hospital for the Wilsons. Hospital management thought it would be a good idea to field questions on the family's progress, given the unprecedented interest in Poppy's surgery.'

Having slipped on her blouse, she focused on the buttons.

As he watched her don her professional layers as she dressed Zach battled her easy dismissal. The miles of distance she was inserting between them reminded him of that first day in her office. But they'd come so far since then, hadn't they?

'You should come, if you can.' She looked at him then and his stomach tightened at her businesslike tone. 'I'd value your input and it will be good public relations for both the hospital, and your charity work.'

'Sure. I'm happy to attend the press conference,' he said, rising from the bed and slipping on his boxers and T-shirt, while he battled the disconcerting feeling that somewhere along the way he had come to crave more of Phoebe than she was willing to share and the feeling obviously wasn't mutual.

Aware that this loss of control where relationships were

concerned was new territory for him, he tried to remind himself that he'd agreed to a fling without feelings. The fact that Phoebe was succeeding at the sex-only plan they'd stipulated better than him made irrational panic squash his lungs.

But he couldn't switch off who he was. He cared about this woman in a way he'd never before experienced. She was carrying his baby. Was he a fool to want to plan and prepare and dream about the near future when they'd become parents, when Phoebe seemed determined to rush out of the door?

Was this how his parents' marriage had soured? Poor communication, mismatched expectations, distance and hurt feelings?

Feeling vulnerable and somehow short-changed, as if his needs were irrelevant, Zach dropped the subject. It was getting late and Phoebe still had to travel back to the city.

He walked to the front door, pulling her into his arms one last time. He kissed her, pressing her back against the wall, cupping her face, sliding his thigh between her legs and swallowing up the mewling sounds she made, the relief that she clearly wanted him physically as much as he wanted her compensation for the niggling thought that she still didn't trust him.

'I'm glad you came over,' he said, when he'd eventually pulled back.

He didn't need Phoebe's permission to shop for their baby, he'd just hoped that he could be an integral part of this pregnancy, in the same way he intended to be in their child's life. But perhaps she still didn't trust that he'd be there for their child. Perhaps she still believed he would let her down.

She stared up at him, and he stroked her hair back from her face, his gaze searching the silvery depths of her passion-glazed eyes. 'I want to ask you to stay the night, but I'm sensing you'd rather not.'

He should be okay that she was leaving. She'd said no

promises and he hadn't made any. They'd agreed that keeping boundaries in place was the sensible thing to do for everyone. Except he wasn't feeling sensible. His burgeoning feelings for this woman had left him unsettled, helpless, aware of a looming sense of failure.

Three of his least favourite things.

'I'll see you in the morning,' she said, pressing a final kiss to his cheek before hurrying out into the night.

As he watched her drive away, he told himself that her emotional shielding benefited them both, helped him to focus on what mattered—the baby and the practicalities of their situation—rather than on his feelings for Phoebe. The trouble was, when it came to the latter, he feared he had little control.

And that scared him more than anything else.

CHAPTER ELEVEN

SITTING AT ZACH'S side in the hospital conference room the following morning, Phoebe struggled to concentrate on the question asked by a news reporter from Channel Six, which was fortunately directed at one of her hospital management colleagues.

She was a mess, perfect timing given she faced the assembled press invited to the Wilson family's live press conference. Public concern for the couple and their twins was high in part due to Aaron's celebrity status, but also the house fire that had brought the family into Sydney Central, followed by the dramatic premature birth of the twins and Poppy's congenital heart defect. Flowers, cards and gifts arrived at the hospital by the armload, well-wishes and messages dominating the hospital's social media sites.

Phoebe inclined her head, hopefully giving the appearance that she was fully focused on the discussion taking place, but all she could think about was the man sitting at her side.

Going to his house last night after such an emotionally fraught day had been a big mistake. She'd tried to keep her feelings in check, tried to keep her distance, but if was as if their bond was already so well established that she hadn't been able to hold off the tide of emotions when he'd held her in his arms while they'd made love.

Beside her, he shifted in his seat, softly cleared his throat.

She glanced his way, the lure of his stare as impossible to resist as the rest of him. As if they were the only two people in the room, Zach raised his eyebrows the merest fraction in question.

Are you okay?

Relieved to see none of the hurt he'd worn last night when she'd cagily avoided his suggestion to go nursery shopping, Phoebe gave a tiny nod, looking away before she made a fool of herself in front of all Australia by throwing herself into his arms.

After worshipping her body so thoroughly, after cracking open the shell around her heart with his consideration and tenderness, when he'd made the thoughtful invitation the excitement on his face had been the final straw for Phoebe. Too late, she'd realised that she was already in danger with Zach.

She'd failed to stay immune, his attentiveness and empathy combined with the frenzied passion that had followed proving that when it came to her feelings, she was, after all, only human.

But she needed to shove those feelings back inside, to pull herself together, and fast.

'So how long before baby Poppy is discharged?' one of the journalists asked, as if on cue, dragging her attention back into the room.

The hospital's communications manager, who was fielding questions, glanced her way, inviting her to answer.

'We are very happy with Poppy's progress so far,' Phoebe said, her pulse doing a little dance as Zach straightened his tie in her peripheral vision. He looked so sexy in his tailored suit. She wanted to bury her face against his neck and drag in the unique scent of him, which she'd blissfully worn all over her skin to bed last night.

'But she's been through a significant surgery,' she added, her powerless gaze shifting to Zach's as if for his corroboration. 'And while we're hopeful that her post-op recovery will continue without complication, it's still early days.'

Phoebe wouldn't commit to an estimated discharge date for Poppy. The Wilson family had already been through enough turmoil. She wouldn't get their hopes up. It was better to take one day at a time.

'Dr Archer, can you elaborate on the surgery?' the next question from the audience came. 'Was it technically challenging?'

Phoebe plastered a stoic expression on her face while she listened to Zach's confident voice fill the room through the microphone on the table in front of them, trying to ignore the memory of it throaty with desire and, worse, flat with disappointment at her lukewarm response.

'Any surgery on a neonate of Poppy's size is technically challenging,' he said, looking her way so she had to brush aside the weight of her guilt and nod. 'But fortunately, Poppy had Dr Mason's skill and diligence on her side. That meant the operation passed without a hitch.'

Seeing the pride in his eyes once more, Phoebe wanted to sink into her chair. It was the same expression he'd worn in Theatre yesterday when Poppy's heart restarted and their repair held, the same look he'd worn when he invited her to go shopping for the baby.

While Zach explained the intricacies of the surgery in his clear and concise way, Phoebe choked at the memory of his hand lovingly covering their child.

Of course, a part of her was desperate to nest, to fill her spare bedroom with baby paraphernalia, to plan the décor and build furniture. Now she'd had her first scan, seen the baby in real time, the building excitement was tangible. Were she and Zach a couple, she'd have jumped at the chance to shop together, to paint the nursery together and argue over which screw went where as they assembled the cot. But in reality, they weren't a couple. Zach was leaving Sydney in a matter of days, as he'd reminded her last night, and hadn't once mentioned when, or even if, he might return.

So she'd held back, scared to play happy families when she would soon be alone once more. Forced herself to as good as decline. Dashed out to her car before allowing the inevitable tears to fall. What other choice had she? It would be hard enough to avoid thinking of him every time she looked at their baby, even harder if she laid their baby in a crib they'd chosen and built together. She needed to protect herself, to run away from the feelings she was terrified to analyse in case they told her she was becoming dependent on Zach.

As he finished his explanation of the VSD repair surgery, Phoebe smiled his way. Their eyes locked for a split second, long enough for Phoebe's pulse to go crazy. He was wonderful. This was his baby too. He deserved to feel excited, to ponder names and plan a nursery. She owed Zach more than she was currently offering.

Her attempts at of self-preservation were denying Zach a relationship with their baby, exactly what she didn't want.

He was falling in love with their baby in the same way she was. It was natural, beautiful, a part of who he was. She'd been so focused on him leaving that she'd overlooked how the paternal bond between father and child could be as strong as the maternal one.

Underneath the table, she discreetly placed her hand over their child in the same way he'd done the night before. Their baby would be lucky to have the love and support of both parents. It would grow up knowing three grandparents, aunties and uncles and cousins in a way that Phoebe herself had never known.

No wonder she'd developed an emotional connection to

an amazing man she both respected and liked, who she was sleeping with while carrying his baby. That didn't mean she should put scary labels on those emotions, or that they could be trusted, or that she should freak out. She and Zach had a plan to enjoy this fling while it lasted, and then seamlessly transition into parenting together.

All she needed to do was stick to the plan.

'Now that the blood flow through Poppy's heart is moving in a normal direction,' Zach continued, looking to Phoebe before addressing the audience, 'her risk of complications—heart failure, pulmonary hypertension—has greatly reduced. Currently she is still on a ventilator, but she'll have another scan later today to determine her progress.'

Phoebe nodded, adding, 'Poppy is a fighter and she has an amazing team on her side.'

'That's all the questions we have time for,' the communications manager said.

'Before we conclude,' Phoebe spoke, 'on behalf of the Wilson family and the staff at Sydney Central, I'd just like to thank Dr Archer for making time in his busy schedule to return to Sydney. His surgical skills are in constant demand all over the world, so we appreciate that he was able to spare the time to consult on this case.'

Praying that only she'd heard the way her voice broke when she'd said his name, Phoebe averted her gaze from Zach. She didn't want to think about how much time they had left. She didn't want to imagine how bereft she would feel when he walked away. She didn't want to wonder if she'd ever see him again, to watch the door and wait for the phone to ring the way she had as a confused little girl missing her father.

As the press conference ended, she stood and quickly ducked out of the room. The past twenty-four hours with Zach had tugged her in all directions. She needed to unpack her feelings in private so she could face him without the urge to beg him to stay.

Zach chased after Phoebe, his longer strides catching up to her clipped pace along the corridor while his heart thundered. Why had her vote of thanks just now, on top of her leaving his place last night, sounded like a goodbye speech? And why, when they'd both always known that his time here in Sydney was temporary, when he had responsibilities in Perth, patients relying on him, was he chafing at the idea of ever being anywhere else?

'Phoebe, wait!' he said, touching her arm to snag her attention. She smiled, but not quickly enough for Zach to miss the hint of anguish in her eyes.

He knew her now. She could no longer hide from him the way she'd been doing since that first day. But despite everything they'd been through with the baby and working together, despite him feeling closer to her than ever last night, she was still pushing him away.

'Do you have a second?' he asked. 'Can we talk?'

Why was she already as good as shoving him on a plane? Why was she reluctant to talk about baby names and shop for the nursery? Why had she left his bed last night, while he'd lain awake for hours, covered in her scent and wishing she were back in his arms?

'Of course.' She put her hands into the pockets of her lab coat and glanced along the corridor.

Zach released an internal sigh at her closed-off body language. Perhaps the question he should be asking was why he kept presenting himself for rejection. Just because he never gave up, was he taking his self-belief too far? He'd never done this before. What if pushing her to open up destroyed what they had? Perhaps any relationship between them, because of his commitment issues and Phoebe's lack of trust, was doomed to failure.

What then? What would that mean for their child? He knew first hand from watching his parents' marriage implode how being caught in the middle felt.

'Why don't we um…talk in my office?' she said, looking nervous, as if she expected him to pounce on her at work. Part of him wanted to do that very much, to loosen her pulled-back hair, to kiss her until her eyes glazed over with passion the way they had last night, to hear her whisper his name with the same desperation.

But a bigger part of him wanted answers to the questions he just couldn't silence.

Zach followed her to her office, his lips pressed together, to stop himself from saying something that would push her further away, the way he had last night.

Inside, she closed the door behind them and turned to face him. 'Zach, I want to apologise for last night, for my lack of enthusiasm for shopping. I was tired. Poppy's surgery really took it out of me, but I want you to know that I'd love for us to go shopping for the baby together.'

Zach nodded, momentarily stunned by her turnaround. 'No need to apologise. I'm happy that you like the idea.' Deciding that there was no time like the present, he pushed on. 'I wish you hadn't rushed off last night. Poppy's surgery was emotional for me too. A first in fact. I couldn't stop projecting hypothetical concerns for our baby, and I wanted to ask if you'd felt the same way. Understandable given the nature of our work.'

She nodded, her eyes misting, so he stepped close and slid his hands around her waist. She gripped his biceps, looking up at him with so much uncertainty his heart felt bruised.

'I did feel the same,' she whispered. 'Which is why my apology is very much needed, Zach.' She rested her hand on her stomach. 'This is your baby too. You have just as much right to choose nursery furniture and names, to have concerns for the unknown and to be excited for the future.'

She looked down, snagging her bottom lip with her teeth as if ashamed. 'I might have lost sight of that for a second, and I'm sorry.'

Because he couldn't stand the vulnerability in her eyes, because it felt natural and he was done questioning why, he tilted up her chin and pressed a soft kiss of forgiveness to her lips. 'This is a complex situation for both of us. It's okay that we're making it up as we go along.'

She nodded, rested her head on his chest over his galloping heart. He held her close, sucked in the scent of her shampoo, closed his eyes, wishing this moment where she was leaning on him for emotional comfort could last for ever.

'I know you're scared to rely on me,' he said, gripping her tighter because she stilled in his arms. 'I know that your trust is a hard-won thing, and I know you said no promises. But—' he pulled back to stare into her eyes, needing to say it anyway '—I promise to always do my best to be there for you and the baby, whenever either of you need me.'

'Thank you,' she whispered.

He wanted to say more, to confess that he was convinced the only viable solution to this co-parenting thing was for him to reside permanently in Sydney. But if the idea of one shared trip to the baby store had freaked her out, she wasn't ready to hear his thoughts on relocating. Because every time he imagined himself living here, full-time, he also imagined him and Phoebe continuing to date.

Swallowing, he willed his heart to slow. She wasn't interested in a relationship. He didn't know how to make one work. There was no guarantee they could make it as a couple. If they tried, they might ruin what they were trying to build for the baby: stability, an amicable co-parenting situation. Romantic feelings only ruined relationships, led to disappointment and bitterness and affected everyone else in the firing line. Their child deserved better than that, and Zach would do everything in his power to ensure that he or she was happy.

'I've been thinking—' she looked up at him with wide eyes '—about your parents. Do you think they'd want to meet me? As they live in Sydney too, they'll want to spend time with our baby.' She shrugged. 'I might even need their help.'

Feeling as if he'd won a skirmish in an epic battle, Zach grinned. 'Of course they will want to meet you. You're the mother of their future grandchild.'

'Okay, good. I just wasn't sure because, you know, we're not a couple, but if you think it's a good idea...'

'I had hoped that once you get to know them, you might feel comfortable enough to ask them for support, if I'm not around.' A strange hollowness expanded inside him at the thought of Phoebe, the baby and his parents spending time together while he was elsewhere, as if he were being torn in two, limb from limb.

She nodded. 'I look forward to meeting them.'

'I'll ask them for some dates they're free that might work for you.' Zach smiled, a kick of primal emotion under his ribs. He admired her independence, respected her self-sufficiency, but these small gestures gave him hope. He knew how hard it was for her to lower her guard and rely on others.

She was so strong but was genuinely trying to embrace all of the changes to her life that the baby would bring. Because he couldn't stop himself, he cupped her face, kissed her lips, her cheeks, the tip of her nose and her closed eyelids.

She stood on tiptoes and curled her arms around his neck, pressing her mouth to his, parting her lips and touching her tongue to his, turning a sweet kiss passionate. As was the way of their chemistry, their embrace escalated, their hands roaming each other's bodies, each of them panting, as if they couldn't find enough contact for satisfaction.

Phoebe's sexy little whimper brought Zach to his senses. He dragged in air and slowed things down, pressed chaste kisses to her lips.

'Sorry about that,' she said, resting her forehead on his chest as she gripped his arms. 'These hormones are making me insatiable for you.'

Zach chuckled. 'Well, I'm here for that, whenever you need me.'

She laughed, joyful and unguarded. Zach's spirit soared. He wanted to put that look on her face every day, until she believed that he wouldn't let her or their baby down.

'What did you want to see me about?' she asked, bringing him back to one of the reasons he'd chased after her.

'Oh, yes. I wanted to invite you to a fundraiser next weekend. It's the Nurture Neonatal Trust annual ball. I was wondering if you'd like to go.'

'Aren't you leaving for Perth that weekend?'

'I leave on the Monday.' Zach shook his head, wishing he could cancel his commitments. This fragile new understanding between them felt important, a breakthrough. He should be here for the scans and the introductions to his family. But just because he was slowly earning Phoebe's trust, just because for a moment last night, when she'd lain in his arms, their heartbeats crashing together, he'd had the fleeting urge to hold onto her for ever, didn't mean he should risk spoiling this good thing they had going.

Better to excel at one thing than risk failing at two.

At his reminder, her eyes clouded over, increasing Zach's guilt. 'In that case I'd love to go, although I might have to wear a loose-fitting gown. My skirts are becoming tight in the waist.'

Zach slid his hands to her hips, tugging her close, fantasising that they could sneak home and spend the day in bed until everything slotted into place. 'So does this Saturday work for you? For the crib shopping?'

She winced. 'I'm sorry. I can't this weekend. I have plans. It's my friend Ivy's hen party.'

Zach braced himself against the wave of disappointment. 'Okay.' The days were disappearing fast. He wanted to spend as much time as he could with Phoebe before he left. But of course she had commitments too.

'Want to see some patients?' she said, tucking some escaped hair behind her ear.

'Let's do it,' he said, this chat leaving him hopeful that they would work everything out. Work was always a good distraction.

But as they headed to the NICU, their first stop on Phoebe's ward round to check on Poppy, Zach couldn't help but feel that, up to now, he'd used his work to find solace for the gaping hole in his personal life. Why else would a part of him be dreading leaving Sydney?

In the past, that had never bothered him all that much. So why had it changed? Reluctantly, he acknowledged the answer: Phoebe.

CHAPTER TWELVE

THAT WEEKEND PHOEBE closed her eyes and tried to relax back into the sumptuous leather chair while the masseuse massaged the instep of her foot with divine-smelling lavender and geranium oil. This day at Serenity Spa with the girls was just what she needed to settle the tumult of emotions she'd experienced since Zach had come back into her life. Sleeping with him again while grappling with some major realisations that, despite thinking she had everything all figured out, her life would never be the same, had unleashed all kinds of unsettling thoughts and amplified her already fragile emotional balance.

Hopefully this fun and relaxing weekend, after a week where she and Zach had worked together by day and made love every evening, neither of them acknowledging the loud countdown of his remaining time in Sydney, would set her back on a more emotionally stable path.

As if sensing Phoebe needed a distraction from her thoughts, bride-to-be Ivy, who was undergoing the same foot treatment in the next chair, said, 'I could get seriously used to this. Perhaps I should get married more than once, or marry someone who owns a beauty spa.'

'Except you're madly in love with Lucas,' Ali said as Phoebe and Harper chuckled.

'Oh, yes.' Ivy giggled. 'There is that small point to consider.'

Phoebe sighed with contentment at the love and camaraderie around her. 'You are all so revoltingly loved up.'

As she beamed down the row of pedicure chairs occupied by her friends, her heart fluttered. They all deserved the love they'd recently found, Harper seizing her second chance with dishy Yarran, Ivy finding Lucas after having her heart broken by her cheating ex, and divorced Ali blissfully happy with her adrenaline junkie, Jake.

Thinking about her friends' love lives only amplified her sad lack of one, because her temporary sex life didn't count. Except sometimes when Zach held her, or kissed her tenderly, it seemed as if he was about to say something...momentous. What would it be like to be loved by a man like Zach, a man who gave his all to his passions, a man who, if she could believe his promise, would never let down their child the way Phoebe had been abandoned and repeatedly let down by her own father, who should always have been there for her, even if his marriage to her mother had failed?

In those moments, she dared to imagine that he wanted more than the fling they'd agreed on, unleashing fantasies of her and Zach and their baby together as a family.

But just because they were going to be parents, just because he loved his child, wanted to be in his child's life, didn't mean he wanted to be romantically involved with Phoebe. Neither of them had any experience of making commitment work.

Her fantasy was flawed for heaps of reasons, not least of all that Phoebe knew better than to pin her hopes for happiness on another person.

'You looked sad, just then, Phoebs,' Ivy said, reaching across the space between their chairs to take Phoebe's hand. 'Don't worry, Lucas has four single male cousins who are coming to the wedding. We'll soon have you fixed up, loved up, shacked up—'

'Knocked up,' Harper added, and she and Ivy burst out laughing.

Phoebe smiled weakly, her stomach taking another swoop when a member of the spa staff appeared carrying a tray of champagne flutes. 'Champagne, ladies?'

The others murmured their delight, each taking a glass and leaning over to clink them together in celebration of Ivy's hen do. Phoebe fought the panic beating at her chest. She should have anticipated there'd be alcohol, that she'd need to make yet another excuse. But given she'd had to abandon her jeans this morning for a loose-fitting skirt, she reasoned there was no more hiding it from her friends. Any day now a pair of eagle eyes would notice her tiny baby bump, and she was tired of lying to them by omission. The jig, as they said, was most definitely up.

Time to come clean to Ivy and Harper.

'Could I please have something non-alcoholic?' she said to the staff member, avoiding the curious glances of her friends.

'We have sparkling elderflower cordial. Does that sound good?'

'Lovely, thanks.' Phoebe waited until the woman had left the room before turning to face her friends.

Three sets of eyes watched her, waiting. Ivy and Harper's brimmed full of curiosity, and Ali's were soft with sympathy and a hint of excitement.

Phoebe smiled at all three of them, dragging in a fortifying breath. 'I absolutely don't want to make a big deal of this. It's Ivy's day. She's the reason we're all here. But I'm not going to be able to hide it for much longer, and you've probably guessed anyway. I'm pregnant.'

She exhaled a breath shaky with nerves, reasoning that she would need to get used to saying it aloud, given that she'd have to apply for maternity leave soon, not to mention all of the hospital staff who'd be offering their congratulations. A tremor of apprehension rattled thorough her. Not only would she be telling her mother face to face later this week when she visited Rosa, she'd also agreed to meet Zach's parents.

Speechless, Ivy beamed at Phoebe, her green eyes dreamy.

Harper nudged Ivy's arm. 'I told you so.' Then added to Phoebe, 'Congratulations. I am so excited for you. I'm going to be an auntie.' She placed her champagne on the arm of her massage chair and clapped her hands with glee.

Phoebe laughed, covering her mouth and blinking away the silly burn of tears as she stared at her friends, women she couldn't imagine being without.

'I'm happy for you, too,' said Ivy, her hand flat on her chest as if she was struggling with her emotions.

'Thank you.' Phoebe sagged with relief. Now that her friends knew, she only had to worry about telling her mother. 'Now that you all know, there's no need to talk about it further. We can get back to Ivy's hen party.' She settled back in her chair, hoping the subject was closed.

'Whoa, hold on,' Harper said, turning to face a sheepish-looking Ali. 'You knew?'

Ali, shrugged, momentarily cornered. 'I was sworn to silence—doctor-patient confidentiality. But thank goodness I no longer need to keep a secret from you guys.' She collapsed back into her chair dramatically. 'That was torture.'

Ali and Harper laughed together, showing the depth of their healed bond after their past falling out.

Phoebe smiled, her heart swelling now that all four of them were close once more, the way they had been at med school. Really, life was good. With these wonderful friends on her team, once the baby arrived, she felt confident that everything, including her new platonic relationship with Zach, would fall into place.

It had to.

'Wait, who's the father?' Ivy asked, her eyes shining with so much excitement, Phoebe squirmed with discomfort. No doubt her friend wanted the same happily ever after for Phoebe that she and the others had found for themselves.

Only a relationship—love, marriage—wasn't for everyone. Life sometimes gave you lemons. Phoebe would just be the odd one out of the group.

Strangely deflated by the idea, she imagined facing Zach every time he came back to Sydney to visit the baby. Would she be over their fling? Or would she miss his arms? His kisses? The way he cared?

'It's that Zach guy, isn't it?' Harper said, a gleam of satisfaction lighting her hazel eyes. 'I knew there was something going on when I saw the way the two of you kept gawking at each other at the press conference. He's totally into you.'

He was into her for now. But he'd soon be gone, indefinitely, with no mention of returning. 'There's nothing going on,' Phoebe said, blinking rapidly, refusing to succumb to tears today. 'But yes, Zach Archer is the father. We had a one-night stand at the conference in Brisbane.'

Even saying the words gave Phoebe butterflies in the pit of her stomach. Rather than working the physical cravings from her system, their lovemaking only intensified with every night they spent together.

But those nights with Zach were numbered.

'So you're not an item?' Ivy asked, a small frown of confusion on her face. 'Is he with someone else?'

'Of course not,' Phoebe said, pierced by white-hot shafts of jealousy at the idea of Zach moving on. But of course he would at some stage. He was a virile single man. He would meet someone else.

How would she face him and a new date, perhaps arriving

to pick up the baby for an outing, and not want to stamp her ownership all over him in indelible ink?

Except he wasn't hers...

Slapping on the upbeat mask she wore when cornered, she turned to her friends. 'You know me, I'm not looking for a relationship, and neither is Zach.'

But maybe one day he'd change his mind, meet a woman he couldn't live without, look at her the way he looked at Phoebe but actually say the words that Phoebe sometimes heard in her fantasies.

'So what about the baby? Have you talked about how you're going to raise him or her?' Ali asked, using her compassionate doctor's voice, which left Phoebe wanting to pull the hood of her robe over her head and hide.

'We're going to co-parent. But Zach travels a lot, as you know, so we'll have to see how that works out.' Could her friends hear that tremble in her voice? Could they see the secret fear she had barely acknowledged herself, that, by going it alone, she was making a huge mistake?

I promise to always do my best to be there for you and the baby, whenever either of you need me.

The problem was, she didn't know how to rely on anyone, having spent her entire life being self-sufficient and sceptical of any vow made by a man. She'd had no choice but to rely on herself.

'So you're not sleeping together?' Harper asked with a degree of intuition that made Phoebe's skin crawl.

She blushed, a slave to her hormones once more. 'Um... well...yes, we are, but only until he leaves the week after next. It's purely practical.'

To distract her friends from their line of questioning, and herself from daydreaming of a future where she and Zach were an item, she offered them a mischievous smile. 'He's pretty good at that, and I'm a bit hormonal.' She shrugged, laughing when Ali fanned her face, impressed.

Ivy clapped her hands excitedly, and Harper just stared, gobsmacked.

Glad that she'd managed to shock her friends into silence, Phoebe accepted her glass of elderflower cordial from the staff member and took a long, bolstering sip. For now, she'd navigated a big hurdle by coming clean to Ivy and Harper, but if she knew anything about her friends, it was that her reprieve from their searching questions wouldn't last for ever.

The Serenity Spa had a wonderful outdoor swimming-pool complex, complete with sauna and hot tub. The entire area was set among shade-offering trees, a veritable jungle of shrubs and flowers adding to the tranquil oasis vibe. While Ivy and Harper relaxed in the hot tub, Phoebe and Ali sat in the shade of an enormous umbrella on comfy poolside loungers. Phoebe had taken a swim, but the sauna and hot tub were a no-no. She didn't want to come over all faint again and embarrass herself or ruin Ivy's day, and her *news* had already dominated enough of the hen do.

Wondering if she might find something in the spa boutique to wear to Zach's Nurture fundraising ball, Phoebe rested her hand over the slight swell of her stomach, giving way to the building excitement of impending motherhood, while she wondered if this was the last time she'd be able to wear a two-piece. Her mother had developed extensive stretch marks during her pregnancy, so Phoebe would probably do the same. Not that it mattered. No one would see them but Phoebe.

'I think he's good for you, Phoebs,' Ali said from behind her closed eyes. Like Phoebe, she wore one of the spa's fluffy white robes over her bikini as they dried off from their swim.

'Who?' Phoebe asked, playing dumb.

'Zach.' Ali opened her eyes, levelling a serious look Phoebe's way. 'I've never seen you so…radiant.'

Phoebe scoffed, uncomfortable with the idea that Zach was responsible for her glow, if indeed she had one. 'It's the hormones,' she bluffed. 'They're a blessing and curse, I assure you. One minute I'm euphoric, the next I'm crying because there's a cute kitten on my social media feed.'

But Ali was right. Zach had changed her life. Not only when they'd conceived the baby, but he'd also helped her to come to terms with the idea that her world was about to be turned upside down.

'It's not just that,' Ali pushed, sitting up to look Phoebe in the eye. 'You seem happy, light-hearted. It suits you.'

Her friend was fishing in her subtle way, giving Phoebe a chance to examine the vagaries of life. Ali had never wanted children, and Phoebe would never have imagined that she'd become a mother at forty. But thanks to Zach, with every passing day she became more and more excited to meet her baby. Of course, she'd have to make it through the birth first.

'I probably won't be so composed when I'm surviving on no sleep, have cracked nipples and baby blues.' Staring at her new pedicure, the coral-pink nail varnish on her toes, Phoebe wondered for the millionth time where Zach would be on the baby's due date. She deliberately hadn't questioned him on his schedule, assuming that he would be overseas, working for Nurture. Would he make a special trip back to Sydney for the birth of his baby? Or would the absence make him change his mind, go back on his word and decide that the demands of fatherhood were just too much trouble after all?

No, Zach was going to be a great father.

'You know that you don't have to do it all alone, right?' Ali said, her dark eyes searching.

That was the trouble with friends you'd had since childhood:

they knew you too well, had witnessed you at your best and worst, were privy to your darkest fears and sometimes your greatest hopes.

But Phoebe had barely allowed herself to imagine what those might be for herself, the sneaking suspicion that they involved Zach making her shy away from examining the fantasies too closely.

'I know.' Phoebe faked a broad smile, trying to keep the conversation light. 'By the look on Ivy's face earlier, I'm certain I'll have plenty of offers of help. Plus I want you all to be godmothers, so no shirking your baby-minding responsibilities.'

'We'll all be here for you, Phoebs.' Ali swung her legs over the edge of her lounger and faced Phoebe. 'But you know that's not what I meant. See, this is what you do.'

Uh-oh—now she was serious.

As she stared straight ahead to avoid Ali's no doubt sympathetic expression, her focus blurred. Ali intended to have her say, and a part of Phoebe welcomed her friend's viewpoint. Except she was used to being the captain of her own ship, those habits hard to change. And an even bigger part of her was terrified that her friends would think she was making a big mistake by giving up on Zach.

Being a parent was hard. Being a solo parent, twice the challenge. But a baby alone wasn't enough of a reason for two people to be together. She would never want him to resent her in the future because he felt...trapped.

'What do you mean?' she asked, her stomach hollow with trepidation.

'I mean, my darling, that sometimes you have this tendency to push other people away, even us, your friends.'

Phoebe gaped, appalled. Did she? If so, she didn't do it consciously...

'You know that I'm not used to asking for help,' Phoebe said, icy fear trickling through her veins at the thought that maybe Zach would think the same thing. Now, backed into a corner, forced to think about the vulnerabilities that stemmed from her childhood, her needs beyond her job, the fleeting dreams of a fantasy future that she usually dismissed, she felt that sickening feeling return, like the gnaw of hunger.

Except it was fear.

'I know that you're a strong and capable woman,' Ali said, 'who, quite rightly, doesn't need a man to feel whole. We all love that about you. But Zach seems like a really decent guy.' Her voice turned softly persuasive. 'Jake remembers him from med school, said he's ambitious and driven, but straight as a die.'

'I know,' Phoebe whispered, her brain awash with memories of the kind, considerate and passionate man who'd literally turned her world upside down, firstly back in Brisbane when one night of incendiary chemistry had created a life, a little piece of her and a sprinkling of him, and then again with his constant emotional support, his quiet acts of chivalry, his inexhaustible sense of humour. When he devoted his time and energy to something, be it her pleasure or making an omelette, he did so with the dogged persistence she had once thought was arrogance, but now recognised as one of his greatest strengths.

Zach committed.

'I like him too,' she confessed, just saying the words bringing her out in goosebumps of terror. Her throat burned with unshed tears. But just because he'd been there for her this past couple of weeks, just because he'd vowed to be there for their child, didn't mean that she could trust him with her heart, put it on the line and suggest they have a proper relationship. She'd never trusted anyone that way, always ensuring her own soft landing.

'But relationships take effort,' she said, glancing away from the empathy in Ali's stare. 'Even when there's a child involved, a strong reason to make it work, relationships fail. You know that, and I know it because of my parents. Zach too has divorced parents, and they have four children together!'

It wasn't just her feelings to consider; it was about the baby, too. She needed to be stronger than ever for their child. She and Zach couldn't afford to mess this up.

Taking her silence as permission to continue, Ali said, 'I know, and I'm in no way suggesting that you haven't already thought all of this through, but if you get on well enough to work together, to sleep together, to plan to raise a baby together, don't you think there's enough there on which to build a relationship? People get together on the grounds of much less.'

'Perhaps.' Phoebe nodded, watched Ivy and Harper climb from the hot tub and head for the outdoor showers.

She turned to her friend. 'But neither of us has risked a committed relationship before, and in all the time we've spent together, we haven't talked about the possibility. I think that's because we've both figured out that if we try to have more and fail, we'll ruin things for the baby. Zach's parents put him in the middle when they split. He wouldn't want to inflict the same on his child, and I respect him for that.'

'But it's not just about the baby, is it?' Ali urged. 'The two of you are also individuals who deserve happiness in your own right.' Scooting closer, Ali touched Phoebe's arm. 'What do you want? In here?' She pressed her balled fist to her chest, impassioned.

Phoebe shook her head, bewildered now that she'd been forced to think of the one thing that had thrown her into confusion this past week: the desires of her heart.

'I don't know,' she whispered, scared to admit that she'd spent years ignoring the emotional demands of that organ. 'I keep going around in circles. I can see the logic for both sides of the argument. Alone is what I know. But Zach and I have so much in common and we'll be raising the baby together anyway...' She sighed, deflated. Her world was more topsy-turvy than ever.

Ali tilted her head sympathetically. 'You know that I love you and I'll support you, always, whatever you do. But I'd hate to see you throw away a chance to be a family with Zach because you're scared, hung up on being...practical.'

Phoebe smiled, laughed through the tears stinging her eyes. 'I guess you make a good point.'

'Think about how you feel when you're with him,' Ali continued. 'And then figure out what you want, for yourself, not just for the baby's sake.'

Phoebe nodded, wiping her eyes. A flutter of excitement formed under her ribs, telling her that Ali's reasoning spoke to some long ago shut-down part of Phoebe. Her friend was right. She could open herself to the idea of a relationship with Zach and examine what she truly wanted. They were good together and she had nothing to lose by just considering the possibility of a relationship.

But would Zach even be interested? Would he be willing to change his lifestyle for her? Even if he wanted to try and have a relationship with Phoebe, he would struggle to find the time, given his current work schedule...

There was long distance and then there was simply impractical. She didn't want to become something holding him back, someone to blame when the pressures of family life, something Zach had never craved, took him away from the work he loved. Resentment and bitterness would kill any relationship stone dead. Wasn't it better to keep her guard up, keep things non-committal and focus on their plan to raise the baby?

Hearing her mother's deeply ingrained words—*'never rely*

on a man'—she swallowed the lump of fear in her throat and looked away.

Across the pool area, Ivy was headed their way, a big smile on her face, leaving Harper under the outdoor showers.

'Can we finish this discussion another time?' Phoebe said. 'I want today to be all about Ivy.'

'Of course,' Ali said, mollified.

Slapping a smile on her face, Phoebe waved at Ivy, glad for the distraction and reprieve from thinking about Zach.

'I've had the most brilliant idea,' Ivy said, sliding into her robe and wrapping her head in a towel turban. 'I'm going to message Lucas and ask him to invite Zach to the wedding. If he's going to be the father to my future godchild, I think we all need to get to know him a bit better.'

She smiled triumphantly and Phoebe's heart sank.

'It's your wedding.' Phoebe smiled weakly, her insides a mess of anticipation and dread. 'You're the bride.'

There was no way out, unless Zach declined the invitation. But would he fly back from Perth just to be Phoebe's plus one?

Without looking at Ali again, Phoebe lay back, closed her eyes, pretending to relax while inside she ticked like a time bomb. Having Zach as a guest at the wedding all but labelled them a couple, and part of her understood her friend's desire for a bit of harmless matchmaking.

The invite would prompt a conversation about him returning to Sydney. Maintaining the status quo, denying the need to think about her feelings and what she truly wanted, was the coward's way out. She'd never thought of herself that way, but the alternative, deciding that she wanted more with Zach and presenting the idea to him, seemed a sure-fire way not only to open herself up to his rejection, but also to ruin everything they were planning.

As Harper joined them and they headed to the changing

rooms to dress for lunch, all Phoebe could think about was how neither solution suited her, that she needed a plan C and couldn't for the life of her come up with one, and that was her biggest problem of all.

CHAPTER THIRTEEN

THE NURTURE NEONATAL TRUST was an international charity whose aim was to standardise best practices in global neonatal care. Zach had undertaken pro bono work for them for the past six years in far-flung places where access to cutting-edge neonatal surgery was limited by poverty or politics.

Zach had always found the work highly rewarding.

But as he took Phoebe's hand and led her to the dance floor in the ballroom of the Sydney Sails Hotel, he couldn't imagine anything would ever beat the feeling of having Phoebe on his arm.

She looked stunning in a full-length black beaded gown that hugged her figure, showing off her slight baby bump. And although he didn't normally bring a date to these functions, preferring to network, this evening, knowing that she was carrying their child, seemed way bigger than a date.

As he pulled her into his arms, their secret warmed his chest. He had the urge to announce to the entire room that this wonderful, caring, smart woman was not only with *him*, but would also be the mother of his child.

Phoebe laughed up at him as he spun her around. She fitted into his arms as if she were made for him, as if they were empty without her, as if, together, they were somehow...two halves of a complete whole.

'You look absolutely beautiful tonight,' he said, resting his cheek against hers, the crush of feelings in his chest all but choking him.

'You said that at my place and in the car.' She chuckled, her blue eyes alight with excitement and mischief.

Zach gripped her tighter. 'It's worth repeating.'

He locked eyes with her, the urge to kiss her so strong, he almost did. But public displays of affection might prompt questions Phoebe wasn't ready to answer. She lived and worked in Sydney. He didn't want her subjected to gossip or to make things awkward for her after he left for Perth Monday.

Her heart thumped against his. 'Well, I'm definitely showing now.' She glanced down at her stomach. 'Especially in this dress.'

Zach smiled weakly. They hadn't discussed breaking the news about the baby wider than close friends and immediate family. It was Phoebe's call who she wanted to know in her workplace. But the part of him more and more convinced that he wanted to ask her to give their relationship a chance was desperate to tell the world.

'How did your mum take the news?' she asked, looking up at him, her blue eyes emphasised by smoky eye make-up, so he feared that she might be able to see deep inside his soul.

And what would she see there? His desire, his excitement, but also his fear. Fear that she would reject him. He was a major risk for her, perhaps if tonight went well, he'd take her home, make love to her and pop the question.

He'd never done this before—built a romantic relationship. But just like when he'd operated solo for the first time, if he applied his intuition and drive, he'd surely get what he wanted.

He wanted Phoebe.

'Both of my parents are overjoyed for us,' he said in answer to her question as he recalled their delight and congratulations. 'And as I predicted, they can't wait to meet you.'

She smiled hesitantly at first. 'Really?'

Zach nodded. 'Of course. They even re-watched the press conference when I told them that you were sitting next to me. I also told them you were keen to meet them too, but they understood that you have a busy schedule.'

Of course, his mother had also bombarded him with the inevitable unanswerable questions he'd expected. Like, *'Why aren't you together?' 'Have you considered proposing?' 'Don't you want to be a family?'*

At the time, Zach had easily dismissed them. But after, in the quiet solitude of his apartment, missing Phoebe and wondering how the hen party was going, he'd forced himself to come up with answers.

Not to the impractical marriage question, at which he'd rolled his eyes, but as he'd mulled over the reasons they weren't an item, he'd grown more and more convinced that they should be one.

Now he just had to choose his moment and persuade Phoebe.

As if relieved, Phoebe exhaled with a small shudder. 'So it's really happening, then? No going back now.' She laughed it off, but there was a nervous edge to her voice.

'It's really happening.' He held her a little closer, his hand flat between her shoulder blades, because whenever he was with her, close just didn't feel close enough.

Looking up at him, she sobered, chewing her lip. 'I finally told my friends Harper and Ivy last weekend at the hen party.'

Zach kept his surprised reaction from his expression, knowing that for Phoebe, as for him, spreading the word might have invited other people's opinions on their co-parenting plan and how that might be...triggering for someone with her trust issues. 'How did they take it?'

'Good.' She sounded overly reassuring. He guessed that she'd probably faced similar questions about the baby's father.

'They asked about you, of course,' she confirmed. 'They're all very supportive. I'm lucky to have them in my life.'

'They're lucky to have you, too,' he said, staring deep into her eyes, spying her vulnerability there.

She paused, nibbled at her lip and stiffened slightly in his arms. 'Ivy said she planned to invite you to her wedding next month.'

'She has,' he said, sensing Phoebe's discomfort at the idea.

'You'll still be in Perth,' she stated, her voice carefully emotionless. 'Don't feel as if you have to come back for it. It's a major hassle for you. I think my friends just wanted to know you a bit better as we're going to be in each other's lives as parents.'

Parents, not lovers or a couple...

Seeing a return of the wariness he thought they'd put behind them, Zach hesitated. As maid of honour, she was an important part of her friend's wedding party. If his presence at the event was going to make her uncomfortable, to raise questions about them, perhaps he should stay away.

'I already accepted, with the proviso that my commitments might change,' he said, trying to keep his hurt and disappointment that she didn't seem to want him there from his voice. He'd been about to ask her what she thought of the idea, but she obviously hadn't invited him to be her plus one.

'I said I would let them know as soon as possible if I couldn't make it back,' he added, trying to salvage the wrong turn his dream evening had taken with Phoebe's clear apathy.

Composed, as if she had no preference either way, Phoebe nodded and glanced away. 'So tell me about your work for Nurture,' she said, changing the subject.

Zach bit back a groan of frustration as yet again she put a slice of emotional distance between them. Was he alone in his feelings for her, or perhaps he just needed to give her some more time?

Zach explained the international work the charity undertook and then added, 'The work is so rewarding it doesn't feel like work, you know. I see places that I wouldn't normally travel, see real people living very different lives in very different places from the life we take for granted.'

Staring up at him, she smiled as if seeing him for the first time. 'I can see that it means a lot to you.'

'I've been a part of it for many years.' He shrugged. 'They have fifty-six branches all over the world. If possible, they either fly the patient to the nearest tertiary centre or fly in the relevant specialists. The cases are varied, often rare, the presentations unusual.'

She smiled up at him, her expression impressed, and Zach realised he might have overdone his enthusiasm. 'That's amazing, Zach.'

It had been an amazing experience for a man without personal commitments. But of course all of that was about to change. Zach was looking forward to the next chapter of his life as a father, probably his greatest challenge, because, just as he'd promised Phoebe when he'd first found out about the baby, he wanted to give his all to fatherhood.

As the dance came to an end, Zach led Phoebe towards their table. At the edge of the dance floor they were stopped by a colleague of his, Debbie Ellis, a Sydney-based anaesthetist who had also volunteered for Nurture for many years.

'Zach, it's so good to see you on our home turf,' she said, standing on tiptoes to press her cheek to his in greeting.

'Debbie, this is Phoebe Mason from Sydney Central.' He smiled, placed his hand in the small of Phoebe's back in that possessive way that was now second nature.

Phoebe tensed.

Zach immediately dropped his hand. Clearly she wasn't interested in anyone thinking they were together. His stomach twisted with the fear that, despite the fact that they had spent most of the past two weeks constantly together, maybe he and Phoebe were on entirely different pages, emotionally.

'Debbie is an anaesthetist at Harbourside Hospital,' he explained, desperate now for the evening to end so they could have a meaningful conversation about their future.

The two women shook hands and the three of them chatted for a while, discussing the dire traffic situation in the city and the plans for a brand-new hospital in the eastern suburbs.

'So, have you heard? Nurture is sending you and me to South America for four months,' Debbie said, raising her glass to Zach.

'No, I hadn't heard.' Zach kept his composure while his heart banged. 'I thought Nurture were announcing their upcoming projects after dinner tonight.'

He glanced at Phoebe, who quickly adopted a serene smile that made his teeth grind. But he'd seen her flicker of dismay, the doubt and disappointment.

Did she honestly believe he'd go to South America for four months when their baby was due? Did she still think so little of him that her expectations of him as a father were still on the floor? And if she still believed him capable of running out on her and their child that way, she must also believe that he had no feelings for her at all, perhaps because she had none for him...

Trying to reassure Phoebe with his eyes, he changed the subject. Nothing was yet confirmed. Zach would wait for the official announcement by Nurture. But even if Debbie was privy to inside information, Zach had the option to decline the work offered him by the charity. And on this occasion, decline it he would.

With a tight smile, Phoebe excused herself and headed for the ladies' room. Zach watched her retreat, his stomach full of lead. He'd always planned to return to Sydney for the birth of his baby. He'd even been imagining some sort of happy family fantasy, where he announced he was staying in Sydney and Phoebe welcomed his news with open arms and declared that she wanted them to have a relationship. But from the look on her face as she'd turned away just now, his fantasy couldn't be any further from reality.

Phoebe entered the hotel room Zach had booked for the night, her feet hesitant, as if she were made of glass and one wrong step would see her shattering into tiny shards on the plush carpet.

She'd never felt so conflicted. Trying not to think about how their lovely evening had soured, she kicked off her heels and placed her bag on the table.

Zach's vague answer about attending Ivy's wedding had been the first warning siren. But the news that he'd be spending the last trimester of her pregnancy in South America had knocked the breath from her lungs. It had taken every scrap of her energy to choke down her heartache and jealousy and appear unaffected, to smile and laugh and clap her way through the rest of the evening, which had begun with such promise when she'd danced in his arms and allowed herself to dream that maybe they stood a chance.

But fairy-tale endings weren't for everyone. Hadn't she always known that? Except somewhere along the way, she'd forgotten.

As if aware of her fragility, Zach gently reached for her hand and tugged her into his arms in silence. Could he tell that she was one kiss away from begging him not to leave on Monday?

But she would never ask him to choose between embarking on a relationship with her and the work he so clearly loved.

Raising her lips to his, she kissed him, blocking out the searching look in his eyes and the clamour of feelings she'd only there, on that ballroom dance floor, finally acknowledged.

She wanted all of Zach. She wanted them to take what had begun as a physical fling and build on it through trust and honest communication, through everything they had in common, through love for their child. Her friends had been right. They had as good a shot as anyone else of making it.

But that had been before she realised exactly what was at stake if she confessed her dreams for the two of them and asked Zach to return to Sydney. He would have to choose—her or his charity work.

She just couldn't do it, in case he chose his career, in case he returned out of a sense of duty and later regretted it.

'Phoebe,' he groaned, pulling back from the heated passion of their kisses. 'We should talk.'

While she slid his tux jacket from his shoulders, she trailed her lips along his jaw and down his neck, knowing the distraction would make him shudder.

'After,' she said. 'I want you, Zach. Seeing your colleague kiss you made me jealous.' She admitted the truth, tugging his shirt from his waistband and sliding her palms against his skin, followed by the light scrape of her fingernails, because these past weeks as his lover had taught her that it drove him crazy.

'She's just a colleague,' he said, his eyes stormy with desire for her. 'I'm focused on you and the baby, only interested in *you*.' He slid open the zip of her gown and she stepped out of the garment. 'And before you ask, no, we've never slept together.'

'I had no intention of asking such a personal and intrusive

thing. Who you've slept with in the past is none of my business, Zach.' Nor was his future.

Because a personal conversation might break her, she undid the top buttons of his shirt and tugged it over his head, pressed kisses to his bare chest. If this was goodbye, she wanted to be with him one last time, to imprint every second of the night on her memory so the next time she saw him, whenever that might be, she might stand a chance of being over him.

'What if I want it to be your business?' he said, dropping his head back, exposing his neck to her kisses. 'What if I want more of you than sex? What if I want to fall asleep with you in my arms, to wake up with you there too, to make you breakfast and hold your hand?'

As if carried away by the fantasy, he groaned, banded his arm around her waist and hauled her flush against his chest. He pressed kisses along her collarbones and over the tops of her breasts, which were still encased in her strapless bra.

Phoebe closed her eyes and surrendered to his touch, blocking out his words, shoving aside the mental images he'd created. They formed a pretty picture, but, in reality, it wouldn't work out. There were too many obstacles to navigate. Their priority had to be the baby. Phoebe didn't want her child—*their* child—to grow up the way she had, not knowing its father.

Between the baby's happiness and her own, the choice was an easy one.

They moved to the bed, their passion burning out of control, as always. Phoebe pressed her lips all over Zach's body, tasting his skin, absorbing his sighs and groans, making him restless, driving him to desperation until he growled, scooped his arm around her waist and slid his body over hers.

'I won't go,' he whispered, breaking the rules, staring down at her while their hearts thundered together, chest to chest.

She had no idea if he meant to Perth or to South America,

but it didn't matter. He must have sensed her turmoil. Perhaps he too realised that this was their goodbye.

'Shh,' Phoebe said, shaking her head and silencing him with a kiss. The part of her that Ali had forced her to examine, the part of her that at the start of the night had been certain she wanted a relationship with Zach, was desperate for his promise to be true, for it to be what he wanted.

But tonight's words wouldn't be enough. At some point in the future, those heartfelt intentions, whispered in the throes of their passion, might turn to bitter resentment, especially when his time and his loyalties were torn between the career he loved and the sacrifices he'd made.

She couldn't ask it of him, not now, not ever.

'Make love to me, Zach.' Wrapping her legs around his hips, she clung to his shoulders. He trailed kisses down her neck, took one sensitive nipple into his mouth and then the other, driving her wild until she forgot all about holding something back from him in order to protect her heart.

She gave him everything, allowed her emotions to brim in her stare as he pushed inside her, his lips seeking hers once more, his hand roaming her thigh, her hip, her waist and her breast before cupping her face and drawing her closer to his kiss.

'Phoebe, I want us to talk,' he said between snatched breaths as their tempo built. 'I have things I want to say.'

Even now, near the height of desire, Zach showed the determination she admired.

Balanced on the precipice of her orgasm as they stared into each other's eyes and he moved inside her, she nodded her agreement. The time for the conversation she'd been putting off was almost there. If only she could avoid it for ever…stay in his arms for ever.

As they climaxed together, Phoebe buried her face against

his neck, blinking away the sting of tears in her eyes. As she clung to him, she feared that she was falling for Zach, in spite of everything. But she couldn't fall. Instead, she had not only to let him go, but also to push him away, one last time.

Her final act of self-preservation.

CHAPTER FOURTEEN

ZACH STROKED HIS fingers through the soft silk of Phoebe's hair, enjoying the feel of her sprawled naked over his chest. His heartbeat hadn't yet returned to normal. He doubted it ever would. How could it when he was strung too high, his feelings for the woman in his arms, the woman he'd decided earlier tonight in the ballroom downstairs that he couldn't live without, crushing his lungs like blocks of concrete?

How had he managed to hold them inside for so long? And how could he release those feelings slowly enough so he didn't scare Phoebe away? Because ever since the conversation with his Nurture colleague, he'd sensed her slipping from his grasp.

'I want us to date,' he said, laying it on the line without preamble. Why had he forgotten that as soon as he saw something he wanted, he went after it? He was Zach Archer. He aimed high and always achieved his goals.

And no goal had ever meant more than Phoebe.

'Zach...' she whispered, sounding resigned, as if she'd been expecting some kind of revelation from him and had a logical let-down speech already prepared. 'It's not going to work.'

'Why not?' He tensed, refusing to accept her pushing him away until he'd told her how he felt.

'For the same reasons that it was never going to work,' she said, sitting up and clutching the sheet to her nakedness. 'I live here, and you don't. Neither of us has any experience at making a committed relationship work, and, most importantly, we agreed when we started this fling that we'd put the baby first.'

Her arguments were sound, leaving little room for disagreement. Except his desires wouldn't be silenced by reason, by a pact made when his feelings for this woman were only one fraction of what they were now. 'We can still put the baby first and make time for each other. Couples do it all the time.'

Phoebe sighed and then faced him, gorgeously sexy, achingly beautiful and absolutely determined. 'And you don't think that trying to start a relationship when we live in different cities, different countries, when we have demanding jobs, when a newborn baby has to be our number one priority, is going to make it impossible?'

Zach stared, giving her arguments proper consideration. But all he came up with was how she'd written them off before they'd even had a chance to start. The same way she'd written him off as a father back in the beginning. But maybe that was the problem. Her fear of rejection was making her scared, that was all.

Zach gripped her hands, desperate for her to understand his point of view. 'I haven't agreed to go to South America. I can decline. I can move back here after my time in Perth and—'

Before he'd even finished speaking, she began shaking her head. 'No. I think you *should* go to South America. Your charity work is important to you, Zach. I saw that this evening. You know that I'm not going to stop you from seeing your child when you return, or ever, but the baby alone is no reason for us to be together.'

'Wait a second,' he spluttered. Where had that come from? Did she think that he only wanted to be with her so he had access to his child? After everything they'd been through, her opinion of him was still in the gutter, as if she didn't know him at all.

'I'll be fine taking care of the baby by myself until you return to Australia,' she ploughed on, 'and then we can discuss the arrangements, visitations, custody, all of that.'

'I want to discuss it now, Phoebe.' Pressure built in his head. This wasn't going how he'd planned. 'This isn't just about the baby; I want you too.'

He cupped her face and urged her stare back to his, so he could search for her true feelings beneath the fear. 'You're just scared. I am too. I know neither of us has done this before, but we can make it work. We can make anything work.'

Unless he was wrong. Unless he'd been the only one to risk his heart and Phoebe had kept hers safe. She'd been pushing him away from day one. But how many more knock-backs could he take? How many hints did he need before he admitted defeat? Maybe in the same way his parents' relationship had ended, he and Phoebe just weren't meant to be...

'And what if we can't, Zach?' Her eyes turned stormy, desolate. He wanted to hold her until she believed in him the way he believed in himself, the way he wanted to be there for her, always.

'What if our relationship goes the same way as my parents', or yours, or my friend Ali's?' she continued, pragmatically, slamming up barrier after barrier. 'What then? I don't want our baby to be fatherless. I don't want them to wonder if it's you every time the phone rings or when someone knocks on the door. To only half enjoy their birthdays because they have one eye watching and waiting for someone who is never going to turn up, because, just like your parents, we can't be in the same room any more.'

Zach winced, her throwing back that snippet of information he'd shared with her in a vulnerable moment a stinging slap in the face. 'I told you that I'm not that man,' he gritted out, his voice falling ominously calm. 'I'll always be there for my child. Always.' Although he didn't want his child to be exposed to the atmosphere of bitterness and resentment Phoebe suggested was inevitable.

In his head it was very clear. These were two separate issues. But she didn't want to hear his feelings. For her this was clearly still a physical relationship.

'I know you will,' she said, her expression sincere and passionate, as if he was missing some vital part of her argument. 'And I'm so grateful that our baby will have you in its life. That's exactly what I want, Zach. I want you to be the amazing father I know you're going to be. I want our baby to know he or she can rely on you, always, that you won't let them down. Ever.'

'But you're not willing to risk the same for yourself? To trust me when I say I'll figure things out and always be there for you too?'

Deflated, she sagged. 'Is it worth risking what we have now—a respectful relationship, two people committed to raising this child, giving it the best of everything we can give? Isn't it better to focus on making that work? Better for all of us. You, me and the baby.'

Zach opened his mouth to speak and closed it again. How could he argue with that? She made sense. If he could rewrite his own history, would he take two parents who could communicate without resentment, without putting their children in the middle, over two who'd loved each other but then watched that love burn out and turn to ash?

It was obvious that Phoebe had no feelings for him beyond the respect she talked about, otherwise she'd be willing to trust him, to give them a shot at a proper relationship.

Perhaps she was right, perhaps it was better her way...

'You know I'm right,' she said, her voice flat. 'Believe me, I wish it were as simple as giving us a try, making it up as we went along. But we're not a couple of teenagers. At least this way...' she reached for his hand, placed it over the swell of her stomach '...no one gets hurt, including our baby.'

Zach clenched his jaw, defeat a sour taste in his mouth that he'd never liked. Clearly for Phoebe it was black and white. They could parent together, but she just wasn't willing to take a risk on him when it came to her own heart.

He could fail at one thing or fail at both. The choice was his.

CHAPTER FIFTEEN

A SUMPTUOUS AFTERNOON tea at Betty's café was a ritual
Phoebe and her mum looked forward to whenever Phoebe
made the trip home, as she had two weeks after Zach's departure. But as their waitress deposited a three-tier cake stand
full of yummy goodies on the table and left, Phoebe doubted
that she'd be able to eat a single thing for the nerves robbing
her appetite.

'So I wanted to ask you a favour,' Phoebe said, diving right
in before Rosa Mason noticed that Phoebe wasn't attacking
the delicious delicacies with her usual gusto.

'Darling, you can ask me anything, you know that,' Rosa
said, pouring tea for them both into fine bone china floral
teacups.

Rosa was about to cut her scone in half, when Phoebe
dropped her bombshell, too nervous and distracted to sugar-
coat it.

'Can you recommend a good midwife in Sydney?' She
smiled weakly, fearing Rosa's reaction to the news she was
about to become a grandmother.

Her mum's knife clattered against the plate. 'Are you pregnant?'

Phoebe nodded, nerves fizzing in her veins. 'Yes. I'm
around nineteen weeks.'

While Phoebe sucked in air and waited for her mother's

response, Rosa covered her mouth with her hand. 'Oh, my goodness.' She rose from her seat opposite Phoebe and gave her daughter a hug. 'Oh, darling, that's wonderful news. I'm going to be a grandmother.' Rosa's eyes filled with a sheen of moisture.

Phoebe sagged, relieved at Rosa's elation. 'I wanted to tell you in person, not over the phone, but I've been so busy at work,' she said, explaining the delay.

'I can't believe it. I'm in shock. I didn't even know you were seeing someone.'

Phoebe's empty stomach took another dive. 'I'm not, Mum.'

Her personal life was a mess.

Rosa blinked in confusion. 'Oh… Well, how very modern of you, darling. Did you use a donor?'

Phoebe sighed, searching for the strength to explain the complexities of her situation with Zach and deciding the truth was best. 'No, it was nothing like that. I had a one-night stand. He's a neonatal surgeon. We met at that conference I attended in Brisbane.'

As if she'd set aside thinking about Zach after the Nurture ball, as if he'd merely been waiting in the wings of her mind to make a grand reappearance, Phoebe once more saw his hurt expression as clearly as if he were sitting across the table.

Rosa's eyes widened with excitement. 'He's not that lovely doctor who operated with you on that tiny Wilson baby is he? The one from the press conference?'

Phoebe had had no idea her mother had even seen the media coverage of her involvement with the Wilson family. 'Um… yes. Yes, that's him—Zachary Archer.'

They had parted maturely with a goodbye kiss and he'd left for Perth. And ever since, Phoebe couldn't shake the feeling that she'd done something terrible.

'But you're not seeing each other?' Rosa frowned, her expression just like those of Ivy and Harper when she'd explained it to them that day at the spa.

'Well...we have been seeing each other, but he's left Sydney now, so we won't be seeing each other again, aside from when we parent together. Separately, obviously.'

Spoken aloud, with her feelings all over the place, the situation that had seemed so complicated became ridiculously simple.

Why weren't she and Zach a couple? He wanted it, she wanted it. It made so much sense. Of course she'd made a huge mistake in rejecting Zach's suggestion that they date seriously. Why else was there a big gaping hole in her chest, as if she had misplaced something irreplaceable?

'I guessed there was something between the two of you when I saw the way he doted on your every word on the news.' Rosa nodded sagely, glancing at Phoebe in her Mum way.

Phoebe tried not to squirm. 'Mum, he did not dote on me.' It didn't matter if it made sense. She'd deliberately, consciously pushed Zach away without stopping to truly listen to what he had to say, and now it was too late. He was gone, already in Perth and unlikely to return any time soon. Why would he when Phoebe had given him nothing to return for?

'Oh, well, you know your own life best, darling. I'm just saying what I saw when you looked at each other. I know what love looks like. It was obvious to anyone with eyes that he's smitten with you.'

Love? Had she fallen in love with Zach? A buzzing noise sounded in Phoebe's head.

Oh, no... She loved Zach. That was why she was so completely terrified to give him an inch. She loved him and he could really hurt her.

'I take it he knows he's going to be a father?' Rosa said,

with that hint of accusation Phoebe had heard many times before whenever Rosa mentioned Phoebe's father.

'Of course he does.'

'But what, then?' Rosa said, her voice growing shriller. 'Has he done a runner?'

'No. It's not like that, Mum,' she hissed, leaning closer, the urge to defend Zach strong and instantaneous. 'He's going to be a great father. He's so excited. He wants to go shopping for a crib and baby clothes. He wants to choose names and to introduce me to his parents. And I—'

I ruined it.

'And you what?' Rosa waited, her scone untouched, her tea going cold.

'He wanted us to have a relationship and I pushed him away.'

'Ah,' Rosa said, her voice tinged with sympathy. 'I understand now.'

'What do you understand?' Phoebe swallowed, desperate for her mum to make it all better the way she had when Phoebe was a little girl.

Rosa's gaze softened as she tilted her head. 'That you're scared to trust this man with your heart.'

Phoebe nodded. *Terrified.*

'Can you blame me,' she whispered, 'when the only example I've ever known was my father, the man who broke yours?'

Rosa winced and reached for Phoebe's hand in understanding. 'Your feelings are your feelings, darling. And while your father wasn't a great role model, we were very young when we got together. We probably shouldn't have rushed into marriage. You are a strong, mature woman who knows her own mind. If this Zach fellow, who by the way sounds lovely, has earned your love, I have no doubt that he deserves it.'

'He is lovely,' Phoebe admitted, glancing down at the tea she was too grief-stricken to touch. Not only had she fallen deeply in love with him, if her mother was to be believed Zach might be as crazy about her, and she'd thrown him away.

What had she done? How could she win him back?

'Do you regret falling in love with a man who let you down so badly?' she asked, fighting the urge to catch the first flight to Perth.

Rosa considered the question Phoebe had never before asked. 'No, because if we hadn't met, hadn't rushed into our relationship, we wouldn't have made you. You were the best thing your father and I ever did together. My only regret was that he wasn't mature enough to be the father you needed.'

'I have everything I've ever needed in you, Mum.'

Rosa blinked away tears. 'You are going to be a wonderful mother. You and Zach sound well suited, but I'm certain that you will figure out a way to be wonderful parents, together or apart. And I'll be there to support you, whatever you choose to do.'

Phoebe nodded, torn in all directions. She couldn't rush to Perth to tell Zach she'd messed up, changed her mind, loved him. She had work—Poppy Wilson was off the ventilator and doing so well she was likely to be discharged this week—Ivy's wedding, her maid-of-honour duties.

'And I say this to all my first-time mums,' said Rosa with an encouraging smile. 'To be the best mother you can be, you have to tend to your own happiness, too.'

Phoebe hid the panic catching her breath. She had finally worked out what she needed to be happy: Zach. Except thanks to her fears holding her back, he was so far out of her reach, he might as well be working on the moon.

After a long day of surgeries at Perth Memorial Hospital, Zach shuffled into his barren hotel room without turning on the lights. Despite the lack of reminders in the anonymous room, he sensed Phoebe everywhere. He might as well be back in his Sydney apartment, where the rooms echoed with Phoebe's laughter, her scent lingering on his bed sheets, and the box of tea he'd bought because she could no longer tolerate coffee sat in the cupboard, mocking him for his foolish dreams.

It didn't matter that physically she was four thousand kilometres away. It was as if he'd carved out a Phoebe-shaped space in his chest and carried her with him when he'd left.

Except she didn't want him in return.

She'd chosen safety over him, kept her emotions locked away. Dismissed his suggestion that they try to make their relationship work as if it had already failed.

And scared of the failure she seemed to think was inevitable, he'd caved.

Why had he given up without a fight? When he wanted something, when he believed in a course of action, he chased it to the end, made it happen, succeeded.

And he'd never wanted anything more than he wanted Phoebe. Maybe that was the answer. The stakes were higher, the risk of failure more devastating because he was in love with her.

Stunned with disbelief, he stepped into the en suite bathroom and started the shower on autopilot, tossing his scrubs into the laundry bin and rubbing at the pain behind his sternum.

Was this love? The endless obsession with her in his thoughts, the constant desire to be close to her, this ache in the centre of his chest that had more than once these past two weeks made him worry he was having some sort of cardiac event?

Sick at the possibility that he'd fallen in love with a woman who'd consistently knocked him back, Zach gripped the edge of the sink and dropped his head. Maybe an icy cold shower would freeze the heartache and he would be able to rational-ise that Phoebe had been right. It was better to focus on their relationship as parents, one they just had to make work.

Just then his phone rang. His heart lurched, concern that it was Phoebe and something was wrong his first, terrifying thought.

Snatching it up from the bed where he'd dropped it, Zach saw it was his father. He took some deep breaths and picked up.

'Hi, Dad. Is everything okay?' Zach willed his pulse to set-tle, now convinced that this feeling of utter futility, of wanting to crawl out of his skin, must be love. He loved Phoebe and he'd walked away because he was scared to fail.

'Hi, son,' Henry Archer said. 'All good here. I'm just com-ing back to you with some dates that might work for meeting Phoebe. Sorry that it's taken me a few days. Work has been very busy.'

Zach's empty stomach turned to lead. He'd forgotten that he was supposed to be arranging a time for his parents and Phoebe to meet. Only now that things between them were more distant than ever—a few polite texts, the odd email—would she still want to meet his parents?

Trying to ignore the concern that by telling her he wanted a relationship before he'd left Sydney, he'd ruined what they'd already had, doomed their chance at an amicable co-parenting arrangement, Zach winced. 'That's great, Dad. Thanks,' he said, making a note of the weekends his father was free over the next couple of months.

Phoebe wanted the best for their child. Neither of them would allow anything to get in the way of that, but Zach also wanted her for himself, for his own happiness, for ever.

Zach scrunched his eyes closed as he listened to his dad ramble on about something inconsequential, his stomach turning for what felt like the millionth time since Phoebe and him had said goodbye.

Why hadn't he realised that he was in love with her sooner and told her that? Had some part of him, the competitive part that always needed to be the best, held back from complete honesty, fearing that deep down he lacked the skills to make a committed relationship work? Had he done exactly what he knew would trigger her own fears by letting her down, giving up when things became too hard?

'So when will you be back in Sydney?' Henry asked, dragging Zach back into the conversation.

'I'm um…not sure, probably another two weeks.' Zach glanced at his suitcase in the corner, indulging in his daily fantasy of packing up early and flying back to Phoebe. But his surgical schedule at Perth Memorial was booked out for at least the next two weeks with cases that had waited months for his visit, patients and their families relying on him to honour his commitments.

'That doesn't sound like you, son,' his father said. 'I've never known you to be uncertain of anything.'

Oh, Zach was certain of some things. He'd declined the trip to South America with Nurture, opting instead to undertake some Sydney-based work. Whatever happened with Phoebe, whether she wanted him or not, Zach would stay close by so he could be there for both her and the baby.

'Yeah, well, you know exactly how life sometimes trips you up.' Zach laughed bitterly.

What he really needed was to see Phoebe again, to tell her in person that he wasn't giving up on them, that he'd always be there for her, that the most important ingredient to any relationship's success was love. He loved her. He should have told her that.

Curling his hand into a fist with frustration, he waited out the loaded seconds of silence on the other end of the phone. 'Is this to do with Phoebe?' Henry Archer said with surprising insight. 'Are you having relationship problems?'

Zach gritted his teeth, wishing things were that simple. 'We're not together, Dad. I told you that.'

'Well, your mother and I talked, and—'

'Wait! You and Mum talk?' Zach gaped, mind blown. 'Since when?'

Zach sank onto the bed, the assumptions he'd made about his parents' marriage and divorce shaken as if the whole hotel were being rocked by seismic activity.

'Yes, we do, when it concerns the welfare of one of our children,' his father said. 'You'll understand that now that you're having a baby of your own.'

'What I don't understand,' Zach said, trying to get to grips with the fact that he'd built his whole relationship belief system around the example set by his parents, only for it to morph before his eyes, 'is you and Mum talking, when you can no longer stand each other.'

'Nothing is ever that simple, Zach. I respect your mother. She's a wonderful woman. She gave me four amazing children.'

'But...' Zach deflated. Stunned speechless. But what if all this time he'd focused on the wrong thing, the fear that a relationship might fail? What if, when it came to relationships, to love, he should trust his intuition the way he did in the operating theatre? Now that same intuition was screaming that he'd made the biggest mistake of his life in not fighting harder for Phoebe.

He wasn't a quitter. He always got the job done. If she had no feelings for him, he deserved to know, but he also owed it to himself to tell her how she'd changed his life.

'So what did you and Mum discuss about me?' he asked, his jaw aching from grinding his teeth.

'Well, we watched that press conference on the news, and your mother rang to say she thought you'd finally fallen in love and to ask if you'd confided in me.'

Zach opened his mouth to deny it, but closed it again. Had it been that obvious to others? But just because he loved her, didn't mean that she returned his feelings.

'I'm sorry if the breakdown of my relationship with your mother hurt you, Zach. I know things weren't easy for you during the divorce and, for that, I apologise. Your mum and I had many wonderful years of marriage before growing apart. And one thing we've always agreed upon is how proud we are of our family. All we've ever wanted is for all four of you to be happy. I guess we both feel that it's been hard watching you fill your time with work, but neglect your heart.'

Stunned, Zach said nothing. His father was right. He had neglected his personal life.

'I have absolute faith in you to make the best of any situation, son. You always do,' his dad said. 'If you say that you and Phoebe are better off co-parenting, then I know you'll make it work. Just always be true to yourself, that's all I ask.'

'Thanks, Dad,' Zach said, the hollowness inside him expanding as he acknowledged his truth. He wanted more than the practical co-parenting relationship he'd allowed Phoebe to convince him was as high as they could reach. He wanted it all. He wanted his family to be together: him, Phoebe and their baby. He wanted to take care of Phoebe, to cook for her and dance with her and make love to her until she realised that she would always be able to rely on his love.

Now he just had to wait until he could confront Phoebe face to face, to see into her eyes when he told her that he loved her, and hope that it wasn't too late.

CHAPTER SIXTEEN

Two weeks later

IVY'S BRIDAL GOWN was a close-fitting lace sheath that hugged her figure to the knee and then swished in an elegant fishtail as Lucas, tall and handsome in his tux, swirled his new bride around the dance floor. As the next song began, an upbeat cover version of an old sixties classic that had everyone joining the bride and groom for a boogie, Phoebe discreetly left her seat.

Fighting off the waterworks once more, she ducked out of the exquisitely decorated ballroom where the wedding reception was being hosted and headed to the bathroom. Locking herself in a cubicle, she collapsed back against the door in relief and sniffed into her last tissue.

Why were weddings so emotional, every *ahh* moment amplified by her hormones?

Ivy and Lucas's ceremony had been beautiful, their personal vows leaving not a single dry eye in the congregation. But now that they were officially man and wife, now that the cake had been cut and the speeches were over, Phoebe took a moment to indulge in a tear or two for her own shattered dreams.

She wasn't going to have her own happy ever after.

Pressing her hand to her chest, where the burn of grief was strongest, she relived the less celebratory parts of the day, how she'd watched the door, willing Zach to appear. It was a test she'd set herself, a bargain. If he came to the wedding, it meant that he might be open to giving her a second chance. She'd planned to take him aside, tell him that she'd changed her mind, that she wanted them to make their relationship work. Who knew, she might have even plucked up the courage to tell him that she loved him...

Only she'd woken up to that realisation too late. He was in Perth thinking that she had no feelings for him, because she hadn't been able to put them into words during their few shared texts. Now she'd never know what his response might have been, because he hadn't shown up, and she couldn't blame him for his absence.

She'd obviously pushed him away one time too many.

Swallowing convulsively, she looked up at the ceiling, blinking rapidly. She would be okay. Just as Rosa had for her, Phoebe would ensure that her and Zach's baby was happy and healthy, no matter what. And just because he wouldn't be a part of Phoebe's life in the way she wanted, she knew Zach would move mountains to always be there for their child.

Resting her hand over her baby bump in a silent promise to their little one that he or she was going to be the luckiest baby alive, Phoebe dried her eyes and tossed the tissue into the toilet.

For the first time that morning Phoebe had felt the baby move, a slight fluttering feeling, like bubbles popping. Her first instinct had been to call Zach, to share the wonderful, miraculous news and excitement with him, knowing that he'd be as awed as she had been. Her hand had even reached for her phone, and then reality had come crashing down on her once more. She'd thrown away the right to call him, to rely on him emotionally, to share her fears and dreams with him, when she'd thrown his gentle proposal that they date in his face.

By indulging her doubts that a relationship between them might not work out, she'd rejected Zach, and, in the process, ruined her chance for her own happy ending. Now she had to go it alone, just as she'd told Zach she could in the very beginning.

Because she couldn't hide in the toilets all night, licking her wounds, she left the cubicle and washed her hands, grateful that her waterproof mascara meant she'd avoided panda eyes with all the welling up. Facing her reflection, she thought of Rosa's ringing endorsement.

Phoebe *did* know her own mind. She wanted more for herself than her fear had allowed her to reach for. She wanted it all with Zach: a wonderful father for their child *and* a loving and committed relationship for herself. She deserved it all, just like her friends. Her deep-rooted belief that she was somehow unlovable because the man who'd donated half her genetic material had abandoned her had shaped her thinking for far too long. It was time to move out of her own way and use her independence to go after her own dreams.

But what if it was too late?

She couldn't leave Ivy and Lucas's wedding reception yet; this was Ivy's special day and she was a maid of honour.

Maybe she could book a flight to Perth for first thing in the morning...

Deciding to head outside for a breath of fresh air, for five minutes away from the party atmosphere to pull herself fully back together, she bypassed the ballroom and slipped outside through the nearest exist into the cool night.

The ballroom opened to wraparound terrace, which was strung with a million twinkling fairy lights, like stars. Phoebe selected the far corner, away from the few guests who'd wandered outside for a break from dancing. With her plan to track down Zach and confess her feelings taking shape, Phoebe breathed a little easier. Soon she would be able to face her friends, to enjoy the rest of the evening, to dance, and see Ivy, Harper and Ali happy without being crushed by the devastation that, through her own foolishness, Zach wasn't by her side.

'Phoebe, are you okay?'

Phoebe turned to see Ali approach, wearing a frown of concern on her beautifully made-up face.

Phoebe nodded, determined to stave off further tears. 'I'm fine, just standing here trying to figure out why I've allowed fear to dictate my life for so long. Why you could see it that weekend of Ivy's hen party and I couldn't.'

Ali wrapped an arm around Phoebe's shoulders. Their heads rested together, side by side, while they shared a moment of understanding. 'We're all slaves to our fears. Are you talking about Zach?'

Phoebe nodded. 'Yes. Before he left for Perth, he said he wanted us to have a relationship and I self-sabotaged, just because I don't know how to do that. Because I've always been on my own, cherished my independence like some sort of lonely badge of honour. But Zach was right. We had something special and I should have been brave, given us a chance.'

Instead, she'd dismissed a wonderful man, a man who, time and time again, had proved he could be relied upon. A man who not only shared her career, but also shared her dreams. A man who'd been willing to make himself vulnerable and explore what had started as a fling but had the potential to be so much more.

'It's not too late,' Ali said, her voice soothing, giving Phoebe's seed of hope wings.

'I don't know, Ali,' she whispered, terrified that hope wouldn't be enough. 'Perhaps it *is* too late. I thought he might come to the wedding, that I could tell him how I feel, but he didn't show up. I ruined it. What if he can't forgive me?'

There was a pause, a few beats of loaded silence that made Phoebe's skin crawl.

'I think you'll still have that chance to tell him how you feel,' Ali said, pulling away and glancing over Phoebe's shoulder.

Phoebe frowned, the hairs on the back of her neck prickling to attention. She shook her head. 'He's in Perth,' she said, confused by the expression on her friend's face.

'Is he?' Ali said, backing away, her nod of encouragement full of inside information.

Phoebe turned back to the ballroom, to where Ali had been looking, her heart in her throat.

Zach skidded to a halt at the entrance to the ballroom, pausing to catch his breath having just run from the underground parking garage as fast as he could. While his heart pounded, his lungs on fire, his gaze frantically sought Phoebe, darting left and right over the darkened room, which was in full-blown party mood.

There were at least twenty round tables, lavishly set for ten people, each bearing a large floral centrepiece, which obscured his view. Determining that Phoebe wasn't among those few people seated, he focused his search on the dance floor, where flashing lights obscured the faces of the people dancing.

Frustration coiled in Zach like dynamite about to blow. He wanted to raise the lights, stop the music and commandeer the microphone, demanding the location of Phoebe Mason, as if it were a matter of life or death.

In some ways it was. He loved her. His heart was dying without her. He'd tried to get through these past weeks in Perth without her and he was adamant that that kind of existence was definitely not living.

Making his way closer to the dance floor around the edge

of the tables, he scanned the moving crowd, trying to identify faces.

Panic gripped his throat.

What if she'd already gone home? What if she'd fallen ill?
What if she was here but refused to hear him out?

Why had he allowed that missed opportunity to pass him
by? He should have told her how he felt that day of the Nurture fundraiser when she'd lain in his arms. Instead of trusting the powerful emotions, trusting his gut instinct, he had
shied away from confessing how deeply he'd fallen in love.

But now he wasn't giving up without a fight. He'd go to her
apartment. He would find her one way or another. Beg for a
second chance.

He cast his gaze around frantically, his heart lurching, as
if it had always known Phoebe's location.

He spied her through the windows. She was outside, being
comforted by her friend Ali, each of them wearing matching
deep red gowns.

Ice rushed through his veins. He ran outside, stopping in
his tracks as Phoebe turned around.

Before he had a chance to register how stunning she looked,
her neck exposed by her hairdo, her strapless gown revealing
her pale shoulders and the small but noticeable swell of a baby
bump, he swept his doctor's eye over her from head to toe.

'Are you okay?' he asked, breathless from the run and the
panic that maybe something was seriously wrong.

'I'm fine,' Phoebe said, her reassurance restarting his heart.
'You're here. I thought you were in Perth.'

Ali seemed to have slinked away, leaving them alone.

'I was. I rushed back. For you.' He didn't want to talk about
the endless journey following his final surgery. He wanted to
hold her, to kiss her, to get down on his knees and beg her to
give him a chance to prove that his love could be relied upon.

'You look beautiful,' he said, awed by how stunning she was, inside and out. He stepped closer, because he just couldn't stay away.

'Thank you,' she said, blinking up at him as if she couldn't believe he was real, giving him hope.

'Phoebe.' He gently gripped her upper arms, his nervous system abuzz at the contact. 'I know that everything you said last time we saw each other made sense, that focusing on being parents is the safest course of action, that we should put the baby first, but the thing is, I don't care about safety. I don't care about being scared of the future. I care about you. I love you. I want to be with you. For ever.'

Swallowing hard, he searched for all of the flowery words he'd recited on the endless-seeming four-hour flight from Perth.

'For the first time in my life,' he blurted, urging her to hear him, 'I don't have everything all figured out, which in itself is pretty terrifying. But I promise you that I know how I feel.' He balled one fist and rested it over his heart. 'I love you. I want you. I want the three of us to be a family, a proper family. I can figure everything else out—a new job, where we'll live, which lightweight stroller you prefer from the shortlist I've made. None of that matters. I just can't be without you. Please say you'll give me a chance to keep my promise to love you for ever and always be there if you need me?'

Because her eyes filled with a sheen of tears and because she was too far away, he cupped her face, tilting her head so he could draw her close and still keep eye contact. 'Not that you do need me, or that you have to need me, but please say you'll let me be there for you, just in case.'

To his delight, she laughed, tears spilling free onto his thumbs. 'Of course I need you. I love you too. I want you too. And I want us to be a family, because we already are, Zach.'

'You love me?' he whispered, his heart trying to beat right out of his chest.

She nodded.

He swooped, pressing his lips to hers, kissing up the salty taste of her tears, pouring his all into showing her what she meant to him. 'I love you too.'

'I'm sorry I pushed you away,' she said. 'I'm sorry that I was scared to rely on you. But I know your heart, Zach. I know that you'll always do your utmost. I know that I can depend on you and I'm committed to us, too. You're right—we'll figure everything out, because being without you just doesn't work for me.'

Because her words touched his soul, because, with her love, he was the best, most complete version of himself, because he was dangerously close to begging her to marry him, right here on this balcony at someone else's wedding, he peppered her face with kisses—her jaw, her eyes, her nose and then her lips again.

Phoebe wrapped her arms around his neck, their embrace turning heated as she pressed her gorgeous body against his and parted her lips, deepening their kiss.

Zach spared a fleeting thought for the partygoers inside the ballroom, who if they happened to glance outside would see him and the woman he loved making out while their baby was nestled between them, safe and sound and loved. He just couldn't muster the energy to care, every piece of him committed to loving this wonderful woman.

'Zach,' Phoebe mumbled against his lips, pulling abruptly back from his kiss. 'The baby's moving. It happened for the first time this morning. Quick.'

She grabbed his hand and held it to her stomach, her eyes alive with excitement and love.

Zach held his breath, certain that nothing could make this

moment, their declarations of love, any more perfect. And then it happened, the faintest tap against his palm.

'Did you feel it?' she asked, her eyes wide with wonder.

Zach nodded, almost overcome with love, ready to fall to his knees and kiss the life their love had created. 'It's magical. You're magical. Everything I'll ever want.'

They kissed again, only breaking apart when the wolf whistles and cheering began from the open doors of the ballroom, where a small group of the wedding party had gathered, including the bride and groom and Phoebe's friend Ali.

Phoebe laughed, covering her mouth with her hand. 'Ignore them,' she said, tugging his waist and resting her head over his heart with a contented sigh.

'Come on, she said, looking up at him, 'I want to introduce my man to my crew.'

Zach smiled and slipped off his jacket, draping it over her bare shoulders in case she was cold.

'Lead the way,' he said, taking her hand and following her inside to where the party raged until dawn and the rest of their lives began.

EPILOGUE

Seven months later...

PRESSING A KISS to Zach's cheek, Phoebe swished the skirt of her bridal gown—an elegant ivory sheath with embroidery around the bust and following the edges of the low back—aside and left her new husband's side, already missing the way his hand rested between her bare shoulder blades every time they stood close.

Heading for the table where her three best friends were gathered, she waved over at the Wilson family—Emma, Aaron and the healthy nearly one-year-old twins, Poppy and Jasmine—and then cast one more glance over at her darling boy, Noah Henry Archer, who was being thoroughly spoiled by all three of his grandparents. Smiling as Noah reached for her mother's elegantly perched fascinator, causing Rosa, Henry and Veronica to laugh, Phoebe sighed contentedly.

'Your speech just now made me cry,' said Ivy as Phoebe joined them at their table, dabbing at her red eyes with a balled-up tissue. 'It's a beautiful wedding.'

Phoebe hugged each of her three maids of honour in turn, lingering to show them how much she valued both their friendship and their support. She would never have made it through the first three months of motherhood without her friends or without Zach. It turned out that everybody needed a crew, and together with her sexy husband, and Noah's incredible grandparents, these three amazing women were it for Phoebe.

'I told you the pregnancy hormones were a killer.' Phoebe laughed, winking at Ivy as she slid into a spare chair at the table. 'But at least you and Lucas get to enjoy the other...shall we say *side effects*?'

As a collective giggle erupted, a waiter appeared with a tray of fresh champagne glasses. Phoebe and Ali helped themselves to bubbles, both Harper and Ivy declining by raising their flutes full of water.

'She's not wrong.' Harper winked suggestively, one hand rested on her six-month baby bump. 'It's been four months since our wedding, but Yarran and I are still very much in the honeymoon phase, if you know what I mean.'

'We know what you mean,' Ali said, rolling her eyes. 'But please, for the love of your friend, do *not* elaborate on the details of my brother's sex life.'

All four women laughed as Harper slung an arm around Ali's shoulders and pressed a smooch to her cheek, leaving behind a perfect kiss of red lipstick.

'A toast to Phoebe and her gorgeous boys,' Ali said, raising her glass, her stare a little misty.

'Cheers!' The others joined in and they all took a drink.

'I too have a toast,' said Phoebe, once more holding her glass aloft. 'I didn't know when we were medical students that you three wonderful women would be the most important friendships of my life, but here we are.' Her throat closed up as she glanced at her friends, meeting their stares in turn.

'I won't be here for long,' heckled Ali playfully, rescuing Phoebe from ruining her mascara with tears.

'I meant metaphorically, but yes, Ali, we all know that you and Jake are off on another adventure overseas. Just remember to send us a postcard from your world travels.'

Phoebe smiled as Ali glanced over at Jake, who was out on the manicured lawn with Yarran and Lucas, all three of them tossing around a rugby ball with Yarran and Harper's son, Jarrah.

'But what I really wanted to say,' said Phoebe, sobering, 'is that you three have been there for me through my pregnancy and with the wedding and with Noah, in ways I could never have imagined when we were all younger. So thank you. To you, my darling friends. I am so happy that we have travelled together to this point in our lives, friends for ever. To Ali and Ivy and Harper.'

They clinked glasses, both Harper and Ivy welling up once more.

'I can't take any more hormonal tears,' Ali said, laughing as she stood. 'I'm going to cuddle Noah in case crying at the drop of a hat is contagious.'

Phoebe blew her a kiss. 'Don't try and steal him. I'm watching you,' she called after a retreating Ali.

Just then, Zach motioned her to join him once more.

'Excuse me, ladies, but my new husband needs me,' Phoebe said, ignoring Harper's lewd comments and Ivy's dreamy stare as she made her way back to Zach's side, her overriding thought how much she needed him in return.

'I missed you,' he said, pressing a kiss to her lips, his hand once more finding her bare back.

'I missed you, too,' she said, smoothing the lapels of his tux jacket. Her heart hurt at how gorgeous he looked. She couldn't wait for the wedding to be over so they could be alone.

'It's time for our first dance as husband and wife,' he said, taking her hand and leading her to the dance floor, signalling to the band to play their song.

'I'm so happy,' Phoebe said as she glided around in his arms, her feet barely touching the floor. 'Thank you for our beautiful boy.'

They looked over to where Zach's dad, Henry, was holding the baby up to watch his parents' first dance, his chubby little arms and legs jerking excitedly.

'Thank you for being mine,' Zach said, tilting up her chin so he could whisper a kiss full of promise over her lips, uncaring that all their friends and family were watching.

'Always,' she said, getting lost in his stare.

'I'll hold you to that promise, Mrs Archer,' he said, and swirled her around and around.

* * * * *

COMING SOON!

We really hope you enjoyed reading this
book. If you're looking for more romance
be sure to head to the shops when
new books are available on

Thursday 31st August

To see which titles are coming soon, please visit
millsandboon.co.uk/nextmonth

MILLS & BOON

MILLS & BOON®

Coming next month

THE VET'S CONVENIENT BRIDE
Luana DaRosa

Rafael released her hand and stepped forward when the judge turned the paper around for him to sign. He placed the pen on the paper with no hesitation, signing his name on the indicated line. Then he stepped back, holding his hand out to her.

Maria took the pen and focused on the paper in front of her. A small tremble shook her hand as she put the tip down on the line and she hesitated, the weight of what she was about to do coming down on her shoulders. This was the price she had to pay to keep her sanctuary from financial ruin.

She swallowed the lump in her throat and signed her name with a flutter in her stomach. The pen came down on the table with a clang of finality. Done.

Maria was now married to Rafael.

They turned to look at each other, an unbidden current springing to life in her chest and arcing through the air between them. She shivered, biting her lower lip to stop her heart from racing and keeping her mind in the present. Nothing they were doing was real. It was all a ruse. The heat in her veins, the quiver in her stomach—they were results of the circumstances they were in and not true feelings.

Loud clapping spooked her out of the moment passing between them, and her head whipped around. The other party in the room cheered at them, clapping and hooting for the union they thought was as real as their own.

Maria's spine stiffened when a person from the group called out, "Aren't you going to kiss your bride?"

Cheers erupted again, and Rafael glanced at her with a slight frown. The question in his eyes was easy to read. He wanted to know if he could kiss her.

Maria swallowed and gave the faintest of nods. His features softened at her consent and everything around her slowed down as his hands wrapped around hers, pulling her closer to him. His scent enveloped her, the smell of lavender and something primal which eluded words. A tremble clawed through her when she watched his hazel eyes narrow and his face come closer.

For a moment, Maria couldn't breathe as the anticipation thickened the air. Then, his lips brushed against hers, and the connection this touch created stoked the tiny flame she'd been carrying for Rafael into a roaring fire that pumped through her veins with every beat of her racing heart.

Continue reading
THE VET'S CONVENIENT BRIDE
Luana DaRosa

Available next month
www.millsandboon.co.uk

OUT NOW!

Available at
millsandboon.co.uk

MILLS & BOON

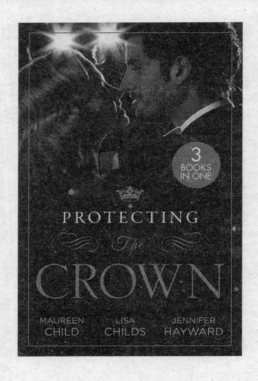

LET'S TALK
Romance

For exclusive extracts, competitions and special offers, find us online:

- MillsandBoon
- @MillsandBoon
- @MillsandBoonUK
- @MillsandBoonUK

Get in touch on 01413 063 232

MILLS & BOON

THE HEART OF ROMANCE

A ROMANCE FOR EVERY READER

MODERN

Prepare to be swept off your feet by sophisticated, sexy and seductive heroes, in some of the world's most glamourous and romantic locations, where power and passion collide.

HISTORICAL

Escape with historical heroes from time gone by. Whether your passion is for wicked Regency Rakes, muscled Vikings or rugged Highlanders, awaken the romance of the past.

MEDICAL

Set your pulse racing with dedicated, delectable doctors in the high-pressure world of medicine, where emotions run high and passion, comfort and love are the best medicine.

True Love

Celebrate true love with tender stories of heartfelt romance, from the rush of falling in love to the joy a new baby can bring, and a focus on the emotional heart of a relationship.

Desire

Indulge in secrets and scandal, intense drama and sizzling hot action with heroes who have it all: wealth, status, good looks…everything but the right woman.

HEROES

The excitement of a gripping thriller, with intense romance at its heart. Resourceful, true-to-life women and strong, fearless men face danger and desire - a killer combination!

To see which titles are coming soon, please visit

millsandboon.co.uk/nextmonth

JOIN US ON SOCIAL MEDIA!

Stay up to date with our latest releases, author news and gossip, special offers and discounts, and all the behind-the-scenes action from Mills & Boon...

 @millsandboon

 @millsandboonuk

 facebook.com/millsandboon

 @millsandboonuk

It might just be true love...